Powers of Two

is published on behalf of

Arisia 2004

for their
Guest of Honor
Tim Powers

Powers of Two

by

Tim Powers

The NESFA Press
Post Office Box 809
Framingham, MA 01701
2004

CONTENTS

The First Concrete Evidence

by Tim Powers

In February of 1975 I was twenty-two years old, just finishing up my Bachelor of Arts in English at California State University at Fullerton, and beginning to take classes that would apply to getting a Master's degree; my vague goal was to be a college literature professor. I had known Jim Blaylock for three years, and we had already invented our imaginary poet William Ashbless, who has occupied a fair amount of our time ever since. And Blaylock and I had known K. W. Jeter for a year or so, and the three of us frequently got together at a bar in Orange called O'Hara's, where we would discuss the stories we were writing.

We were college students, so we spent a lot of time in cheap bars and going to movies like Bergman's *Scenes From a Marriage,* Russell's *Mahler,* and Antonioni's *The Passenger* (none of which I'd see again now; though de Palma's *The Phantom of the Paradise,* which impressed me then, still impresses me). Among the books we were admiring were Thompson's *Fear and Loathing in Las Vegas,* Donleavy's *The Ginger Man,* and Cary's *The Horse's Mouth* (all of which still strike me as admirable). Bob Dylan's *Blood on the Tracks* was a new and splendid album (and now it's old and splendid). When friends got married, the people setting up the weddings often strove for "the *Godfather* look."

Blaylock and I were each working on a long, plotless novel—mine was called *Dinner at Deviant's Palace* (which had not much similarity to the book eventually published with that title—I just liked the sound of the phrase, which I had derived from Robert Downey's movie *Greaser's Palace* and E. R. Eddison's book *A Fish Dinner in Memison),* and Blaylock's was called *The Chinese Circus.* Jeter—a more accomplished writer—had already finished *Dr. Adder,* and also a novel called *Seeklight,* which he had, dazzlingly, sold to a publisher. It was to appear in July.

The publisher was Harlequin Books, famous for their sappy-looking romance paperbacks; but they were going to try out a science fiction line, edited by Roger Elwood, who had edited any number of respectable anthologies.

And Jeter told us that the new line was looking for several more authors to discover! Blaylock and I immediately shelved our interminable novels and began scribbling fresh things.

I wrote about 4,000 words of a novel, and an outline, and I showed it to Jeter—and he told me that it was no good, because nothing happened in it. This was true, actually—these Harlequin novels had to be precisely 55,000 words, which seemed like an awful lot to me—so I was starting slow, wary of using up my whole outline's-worth of events too quickly. I suppose I would have said I was "developing my characters" or something, but the result was that for three chapters my characters hardly did more than eat lunches and . . . well, all I can recall now is the lunches. Talk, too, I expect—"filling in background," I might have said by way of excuse. I can't go back and check, because I threw the chapters into the fireplace one day.

"Start where the action starts," Jeter told me. This seemed like a spendthrift way to write a book, but I tried it his way and in March I put the chapters-and-outline in the mail.

And on Tuesday the 22nd of April, 1975, I got a letter from Elwood. He said he liked what I sent him, but needed to see one more chapter, since I was an unknown, before he could send me a contract. Of course I agreed to write another chapter, and promised he'd have it in a week.

Like many young English majors, I was keeping a "journal" in those days—and I see I wrote on April 29, "this letter was the first concrete evidence I've ever had to believe that my writing is at all worthwhile. Even if Elwood should decide that subsequent chapters were terrible, I'd know I'm good enough to *interest* a big editor.

"So I wrote the fourth chapter, typed it last night, and mailed it early this morning. Air mail. If he doesn't take it, I'm in a bit of inconvenience. I've spent a week writing the chapter, and would have to write two term papers (20 and 10 pp.) and read four books and do a considerable bit of research, all in two weeks. If he takes it, which I think he will, I'll take an incomplete in those two classes and devote my time to writing. I'll keep my political science class because when it's finished I'll have my B.A.; and I'll keep fencing because it takes no time outside of class."

And on the 5th of May Elwood did accept it, with a deadline of August 15—and so I quit the classes I'd been taking toward a Master's degree. In my journal I noted, "I am, for the time being, at least, a writer. I'm enjoying writing the thing; working from a previously-worked-out outline eliminates the kind of snags I was running into in *Deviant's Palace*—I always know more-or-less what's going to happen next."

By the beginning of June I was half done with it, and by the beginning of July I was confident enough to take a long weekend off and drive up to San Francisco, with Jim Blaylock and his wife Viki, to attend the Westercon science fiction convention. Roger Elwood was there, and we learned that Harlequin's science fiction line was to be called "Laser Books." As I noted in my journal for the 5th of July, "Jim and I agreed that almost anything would sound better, but what the hell."

On August 7 I finished typing the handwritten manuscript—which now had a title, *The Skies Discrowned*—but somehow I still hadn't received a contract for the book. Elwood had been assuring me for months that the contract would be along very soon, any day, in fact—but in the meantime I didn't have it, and didn't want to send the completed manuscript to him until I did have it. What if, I thought, he doesn't like the book? Why would he issue a contract for a book he knows he doesn't like?

So I told him I needed to have the contract before I'd send the manuscript to him.

And on August 9th, I went to a party at Philip K. Dick's house. I hadn't seen him since about mid-'73, though we'd been good friends for a year or so before that; he had got married, and become a bit of a hermit. But his marriage was looking unsteady now—he was "scheming on" some girl at the party—and we were quickly back on the old footing.

I finally mailed the manuscript to Laser Books after getting a Western Union Mail Gram from Elwood dated the 25th of August, assuring me that a contract would definitely be along very shortly; and he accepted the book, and in fact before the end of the month the contract did arrive.

I showed it to Phil Dick, and he told me not to sign it. He said Harlequin was keeping the foreign rights, and this wasn't acceptable. I thanked him, but when I got home I signed the contract and put it in the mail.

What, after all, did I care about foreign rights? If it were to have no foreign editions, or if it had hundreds of foreign editions for which I would be paid nothing, didn't concern me at all. I could write other books, and deal sensibly with the foreign rights on *them*. All I wanted right now was to get the thing safely published.

And it duly appeared in May of the next year. On the cover, along with my name and the title, were the words "General Editor Roger Elwood," and Phil Dick was with me when I first found copies at a bookstore. I bought several, and Phil told the clerk, "This guy wrote this book!" The clerk smiled and looked at the cover and said, "Congratulations, Mr. Elwood!"—which Phil thought was pretty funny.

And I wrote a second book for Laser, *An Epitaph in Rust*. This one was published in so grossly rewritten a form that I resolved not to sell to Laser again, and in any case Harlequin folded the line soon after, having decided that science fiction couldn't measure up to romances.

For a few years after that I was back to sending manuscripts to publishers and getting them rejected, but the publication of these two books (the correct versions of which you have here, with no intrusive editing) had effectively deflected me from wanting to be a college literature professor; I didn't go back to graduate school. And eventually I sold a third book, to Lester del Rey, and then a fourth to Beth Meacham at Ace Books—but if it weren't for K. W. Jeter and Roger Elwood, and the heady experience of seeing these first two books in print, I'd today be teaching "Twain to Modern," and "Analysis of Literary Forms," and maybe—with a wistful air, I like to think!—"Creative Writing."

—Tim Powers
San Bernardino, California
October 2, 2003

To Roy A. Squires

THE SKIES DISCROWNED

BOOK ONE

The Painter

Though the many lights dwindle to one light,
There is help if the heavens have one;
Though the skies be discrowned of the sunlight
And the earth dispossessed of the sun,
They have moonlight and sleep for repayment,
When, refreshed as a bride and set free,
With stars and sea-winds in her raiment,
Night sinks on the sea.

— A. C. Swinburne

CHAPTER 1

The crowd in front of the Ducal Palace always fascinated Francisco Rovzar. The great stone arch of the barbican seemed to frame a picture of all human endeavor and misery. Here a curbside magician produced gouts of flame from his mouth, there a cowled priest shambled along, flicking passersby with holy water from a leather bag at his belt. A knot of moaning women waved rolled, ribbon-bound petitions at the procession of judges who hurried out of the cleric's gate to get some lunch before the afternoon sessions commenced. Grimy children in tattered clothes or none at all howled and chased each other through the gutters. Smoke from the fires of sausage vendors and jewelsmiths curled in gray ribbons up into the blue sky.

Francisco prodded his horse forward, through the gate. The guard recognized him and waved his slingshot amiably. Francisco waved back at him, then turned to make sure his father was following. The old man was rocking unsteadily in the saddle, muttering and frowning fiercely. His horse was stopped.

"Come on, Dad, we're going in," Francisco called. His father gave the horse a spasmodic kick, and it trotted up beside Francisco's mount. "Pull yourself together, Dad," said Francisco worriedly.

"I'm all right," the elder Rovzar said with an exaggerated nod. "Hell, when I did that portrait of Bishop Sipstand, I was so drunk I couldn't see him. I painted him from memory, and he said it was the . . . the best painting he'd ever seen. Don't worry about me, Frank."

Frank smiled and shook his head, but he was still uneasy. Only two hours ago he had dragged his father out of a tavern in Calvert Lane, and it had required a cold shower and four cups of coffee even to get the old man as coherent and presentable as he was now. He always did love to drink, Frank thought, but since Mom died he's been getting drunk all the time. He's still the finest portrait painter within a hundred planets, but how long can that last?

They were within the walls of the palace now, the horses' hooves clicking on cobblestones. A footman sprinted up to them and bowed.

"If you'll let me take charge of your horses, you can go right in. The Duke is ready to see you."

"Thank you," said Frank, dismounting. He pushed back his straight black hair and set about getting his father out of the saddle. "Hah! Carefully now!" the old man barked as he began to slide off the horse's starboard side. "That's it, now! Feet first, feet first!" Frank caught him and set him upright on the pavement, with a smoothness born of much practice.

The footman regarded the pot-bellied, gray-haired old master with amused contempt. "You're late," he smirked, "but I guess I needn't inquire why."

"No," said Francisco, turning on him savagely. "Not unless it's a part of your modest duties to question the Duke's guests."

"I beg your pardon, sir," said the footman, suddenly meek. "I certainly never—"

"Take the horses," interrupted Frank, having pulled the saddlebags off his mount. The footman took the two sweaty horses away, and Frank led his unsteady parent across the yard to the open doors of the keep. A guard in blue-steel armor, who carried an automatic rifle slung over his shoulder, escorted them up a carpeted flight of stairs and down a hallway, to a pair of doors in whose mahogany surfaces was carved the story of Frankie and Johnnie.

The guard yanked a bell pull on the wall and discreetly withdrew. In a moment the doors were opened by a young, tow-headed page who bowed and motioned Frank and his father into the room.

"Ah, there you are, Rovzar!" boomed the Duke Topo from a splendid tall chair of mosaic-inlaid ebony that was set in the center of the room. His bulky person was enclosed in a baggy pair of blue silk trousers and a green velvet coat. Ringlets of hair, so shiny as to seem varnished, covered his head and clustered about his shoulders.

"Your Grace," acknowledged the older Rovzar. Father and son both bowed. The room was lit by tall, open windows in the eastern wall; bookcases hid the other three walls, and a desk and chair were set in one corner. In the middle of the room, facing the chair in which the Duke sat, was a wooden stand supporting a framed canvas ten feet tall and five feet wide. The canvas was a nearly-finished portrait of the Duke, done in oils. It presented him dressed and seated as he now was, but it conveyed a dignity and strength, even a touch of sadness, that were presently lacking in the model.

"You're looking a bit jaded, Rovzar," the Duke observed. "Feeling all right, I trust?"

"Very well, thank you, and all the better for your Grace's concern," said the old painter. Frank stared at his father, admiring, as he always did, the man's ability to shake off the effects of alcohol when the situation demanded it.

"You think you'll finish it this session?" asked the Duke.

"It's not unlikely," answered Frank's father. "But I can't say for sure, of course."

"Of course," nodded the Duke.

Old Rovzar put his hand on the young man's shoulder. "Okay now, Frank," he said, "you set up the palette and turp and oil while I say hello to the picture." He crossed to the painting and stood in front of it, staring intently. Frank unbuckled the saddlebags and opened the boxes they held. He laid out a dozen crumpled paint tubes and poured linseed oil and turpentine into two metal cups. He unwound a rubber band from a bundle of brushes and set them in another cup. The page, standing beside the sitting Duke, looked on with great interest.

The double doors opened and a slim, pale young man entered. He wore powder blue tights and a matching shirt with ruffles at the throat. A fancy-hilted sword hung at his belt.

"Costa, my boy!" greeted the Duke. "Finished with your piano lesson so soon?"

"I despise pianos," the Prince informed him. "Is he still working on that picture?" He walked over and peered at the canvas closely. "Hmmm," he grunted, before turning and walking to the window. His attitude implied that this painting wasn't bad, in a quaint way, but that he'd frequently seen better. Francisco remembered the Prince's tantrums after he had been told that he was not to be included in the painting—for a week Costa had sulked and, in the months since, tried to make it clear that he regarded Rovzar as an inferior painter.

Frank's father was sketching lightly on the canvas with a pencil, oblivious to the world. What is it that's different about young Prince Costa this morning? wondered Frank. He's quiet, for one thing; usually he made himself tiresome with frequent questions and distractions. One time he had brought a drawing pad and pastels and made an attempt to portray the Duke himself, with much squinting, and theatrical gestures. But now he simply stood at the window, staring down into the courtyard.

Frank's attention was caught by his father's blocking-in of the background. With a few passes of a pencil, the artist's wrinkled hands had converted a patch of blankness into several bookshelves in perfect perspective. He set about defining the shadows with quick cross-hatching.

Suddenly it occurred to Frank what was different about Prince Costa. This was the first time Frank had seen him wearing a sword.

"Where's my number eight camel hair?" asked old Rovzar, pawing through the brushes. "Right here, Dad," replied Frank, pointing out the one in question. "Oh, yes." The painter took the brush, dipped it into the linseed oil, and began mixing a dab of paint.

A loud bang echoed up from the courtyard.

"What's that?" asked the Duke.

Several more bangs were heard, then a series of them like a string of firecrackers.

"By God," said Frank. "I think it's *gunfire.*" He could hardly believe it; guns and powder were so prohibitively rare and expensive these days. Panicky yells sounded now, punctuated by more shots.

"We're beset!" gasped the Duke. Prince Costa ran out of the room, and the Duke took his place at the window. "Troops!" he said. "A hundred Transport soldiers are within the bailey!"

Old Rovzar looked up. "What?" he asked. "I trust my painting won't be interrupted?"

"Interrupted?" shouted the Duke. "The Transports will probably use your canvas to polish their boots!" An explosion shook the palace, and the Duke scrambled back from the window. The pandemonium of shouts, shots, and screams was a mounting roar.

The Duke ran bobbing and puffing across the carpeted floor to the desk. He yanked out drawers and began throwing bundles of letters and documents in a pile on the floor. "How did they get *in?*" he kept whining. "How in the devil's name did they get *in?*"

Frank glanced at his father. "Do we run for it?" he asked tensely. The young page stared at them with wide eyes.

Frank's father scratched his unshaven chin. "No, I guess not. We're better off here than down in that madhouse of a courtyard. Just don't panic. Damn, I hope nobody sticks a bayonet through this," he said, staring at the painting.

The hollow booms of two more explosions rattled the windowpanes. "This attack must be costing a fortune," said Frank. The price of explosives made bombs a costly rarity in warfare, and they were generally used only in times of great need.

The Duke had struck a match and set it to his pile of papers; most of them were yellowed with age, and they were consumed quickly, scorching the rug under them. When they had burned to fragile black curls he stamped them into powder. "What else, what else?" the distraught Duke moaned, wringing his hands.

Suddenly, from beyond the double doors Frank heard a hoarse, triumphant yell, and then heavy-booted footsteps running up the hall toward the room they were in. The page ran to the doors and threw the bolt into the locked position.

The Duke had heard it too and sprang to one of the bookcases. His pudgy hands snatched one of the books from the shelf, and then he stood holding it, staring wildly around the room. The attackers were pounding on the doors now. The Duke's eyes lit on the painting and he ran to it with a glad cry. He stuffed the book—which, Frank noticed, was a leather-bound copy of *Winnie the Pooh*—behind the picture's frame, so that it lay hidden between the canvas and the back of the frame. This done, he ran back to his elegant chair and sat down, exhausted. Frank and the old painter stared at him, even in this crisis puzzled by the Duke's action.

Six bullets splintered downward through the doors, one snapping the bolt and two more tearing through the page's chest. The impact threw him to the floor. Frank's numbed mind had time to be amazed at the quickness of it.

The doors were kicked open and six men stepped into the room. Five of them were brawny soldiers who wore the gray Transport uniform and carried rifles, but it was the sixth, the leader, who held the attention of Rovzar, his son, and the Duke.

"Costa!" exclaimed the astounded Duke. "Not you . . . ?"

Costa drew his sword with a sharp rasp of steel: "On guard, your Grace," he sneered, holding the blade forward and crouching a bit. Bad form, thought Frank, who had spent a good part of his boyhood in a fencing school.

Bad form it might have been, but it was adequate against the Duke, whose only defensive action was to cover his face with his hands. Prince Costa hesitated, then cursed and drove the tempered blade into Duke Topo's heart. He wrenched it out, and the Duke sighed and bowed forward, leaning farther and farther, until he overbalanced and sprawled on the floor.

One of the soldiers stepped to the still-open window and waved. "He's dead!" he bellowed. Cheers, wails, and renewed shooting greeted this announcement. Frank could smell smoke, laced with the unfamiliar tang of gunpowder and high explosives.

The other soldiers seized Frank and his father. "Damn it," old Rovzar snarled. "You apes had better—" He kicked one of them expertly, leaving the Transport rolling in pain on the floor. Another raised his rifle clubwise. "Duck, Dad!" yelled Frank, at which his captor twisted his arm behind his back—Frank winced but didn't yell, fearing that he'd distract his father.

His father had leaped away from the descending gun-butt and made a grab at Costa's ruffle-bordered throat. One of the soldiers next to Frank stepped aside to have a clear field of fire. "*No!*" screamed Frank, twisting furiously in his captor's grasp. The soldier fired his rifle from the hip, almost casually, and the bang was startlingly loud in the small room. The bullet caught old Rovzar in the temple and spun him away from the surprised-looking Prince. Frank, painfully held by two soldiers, stared incredulously at his father's body stretched beside the bookcase.

"Take the kid along with the servants," said Costa. The soldiers, one of them limping and cursing, filed out, carrying the stunned Frank like a rolled carpet. Costa closed the perforated doors behind them. He was alone now except for the three dead bodies, and he looked thoughtfully around the room. He slowly walked to the desk, observing the open drawers and the pile of ashes on the burned carpet. He searched very carefully through the papers that remained in the drawers, but took none of them. He went to the window and put one boot up on the sill, with his hand on his sword-hilt—a dramatic pose, he had been told. In the courtyard three storeys below the day's outcome was clear. The guardhouse was a pile of smoking rubble, crowds of prisoners were being lined up and herded into carts, and the Transport banner snapped and fluttered on the flagpole.

Prince Costa's triumphant laughter echoed between the walls from the lists to the bailey, and the prisoners, all guards or servants or advisers of the old Duke, shuddered or ground their teeth in impotent rage.

CHAPTER 2

Dominion, it was called—a hundred stars in a field five thousand light-years across—and it was the most ambitious social experiment humans had ever embarked upon. It was a nation of more than a hundred planets, united by the silvery nerves of the Transport spaceships, the freighters that made possible the complex economic equations of supply and demand that kept the unthinkably vast Dominion empire running smoothly. Wheat from the fertile plains of planets such as Earth was shipped out to the worlds that produced ore, or fuel, or simply provided office space; and the machinery that was manufactured on Luna or Alpha Centauri III was carried to more rural planets, such as Earth. Planetary independence was a necessity of the past—now no planet's government needed to struggle to be self-sufficient; each world simply produced what it was best suited to and relied on the Transport ships to provide such necessities as were lacking. For centuries Dominion was a healthy organism, nourished by its varied and widespread resources, which the bloodstream of the Transport ships distributed to all its parts.

Frank sat against the back of the horse-drawn cart, hemmed in by a dozen hot, unhappy kitchen servants. They moaned and asked each other questions that none of them knew the answers to: "Where are we going? What happened? Who are these people?" Frank was the only silent one in the cart; he sat where he'd been thrown, staring with intensity at nothing. From time to time he flexed his tightly-bound wrists.

The cart rattled south on the Cromlech Road, making good time since Cromlech was one of the few highways on the planet that were subject to maintenance. Within two hours they had arrived at the Barclay Transport Depot southwest of Munson, by the banks of the Malachi River. The cart, along with fifteen others like it, was taken through a gate in the chain-link fence that enclosed the Depot, across the wide concrete deck, and finally drew to a halt in front of a bleak, gray four-storey edifice. The bedraggled occupants of the carts were pulled and prodded out, lined up according to sex and height, and then divided into groups and escorted into the building. Just before he passed through the doorway, Frank caught sight of the sign above the door: DETENTION AND BEHAVIOR MODIFICATION CENTER.

After many centuries, encompassing dozens of local golden ages, Dominion began to weaken. The fuels—fossil oils from jungle planets, and radium—became perceptibly less abundant. Transportation became increasingly expensive, and many things were no longer worth shipping. The smooth pulse of the import/export network had taken on a lurching, strained pace.

"Name." The officer's voice had no intonation.

"Francisco de Goya Rovzar."

"Age."

"Twenty."

"Occupation."

"Uh . . . apprentice painter."

"Okay, Rovzar, step over there with the others." Frank walked away from the desk and joined a crowd of other prisoners. The room they were in seemed calculated to induce depression. The floor was of damp cement, drains set in at regular intervals; the pale green walls were chipping; the ceiling was corrugated aluminum, and naked light bulbs were hung from it on long cords.

The perfunctory interrogation continued until all the prisoners taken that morning had been questioned and stood in a milling, spiritless crowd. The officer who had been asking the questions now stood up and faced the prisoners. He was short, with close-cropped sandy hair and a bristly moustache; his uniform was faultlessly neat.

"Give me your attention for a moment," he said, unnecessarily. "You are here as prisoners of the Transport Authority, and of Costa, the Duke of this planet, Octavio. Ordinarily you would be allowed a court hearing to contest the charge of treason laid against you, but the planet of Octavio has, as of this morning, been declared under martial law. When this condition is lifted you will be free to appeal your sentence. The sentence is the same for each of you: you are to be lifted tomorrow on a Transport freighter and ferried to the Orestes system to atone for your offenses in the uranium industry. Are there any questions?"

There were none. The situation was deadly clear—the Orestes Mines were a legendary hell feared throughout the Dominion. Frank, his mind only now beginning to recover from the shock of his father's murder, heard his sentence but filed it away without thinking about it.

The situation did not improve. Transportation became more and more sporadic and unreliable. Industrial planets were often left for weeks without

food shipments, and agricultural planets were unable to replace broken ma-
chinery or obtain fuel for what worked. The Transport Company was losing
its grip on the wide-flung empire; the outer sections were dying. Transport
rates climbed astronomically, and the poorer planets were unable to main-
tain contact with the Dominion empire. They were forced to drop out and
try to survive alone. In time even the richest planets began working to be
self-sufficient, in case the overworked Transport Company should, one day,
collapse entirely.

Late that night Frank sat awake in the darkness of one of the Depot
detention pens. His cot and thin mattress were not notably uncomfortable, but his thoughts were too vivid and desperate for him to sleep. The
six other men in the pen with him apparently didn't care to think, and
slept deeply.

My father is dead, Frank told himself; but he couldn't really believe it
yet, emotionally. Impressions of his father alive were too strong—he could
still see the old man laughing over a mug of beer in a tavern, or sketching
strangers' faces in a pocket notebook, or swearing as he drank his black
coffee in the bleak, hungover dawns. Suddenly Frank saw how his life
would be without old Rovzar to take care of, and he fearfully shied away
from the lonely vision.

His destination was the Orestes Mines. That was bad, about as bad as
it could be. The mines riddled all four planets of the Orestes system, and
working conditions ranged from desiccating desert heat to cold that could
kill an exposed man in a matter of seconds; and over everything reigned
the sovereign danger of radiation poisoning. Panic grew as it became clear
to him that he was about to be devastatingly punished by men who had
never seen him before and were totally indifferent to him.

Isn't there anyone who can get me out of this? he wondered. What
about Tom Strand, my best friend? It was in the fencing school of Tom's
father, an interplanetary champion, that Frank had picked up what he
knew of swordsmanship. Could Tom or his father do anything? Of course
not, rasped the logical part of his mind. What could they do to reverse
the decisions of the Transport and the planet government? The idea, he
was forced to admit, was ridiculous.

Panic eventually gave way to a decision. I am *not* going to Orestes, he
thought. I simply am not going. Even though he had no plan to base this
thought on, it comforted him. I am not going there, he told himself again.
I *will* escape.

He got up from his cot and felt his way through the inky blackness to
one of the sleeping men and shook him by the shoulder. The man started
violently.

"Who is it?" he whispered in terror.

"I'm a fellow prisoner," Frank hissed. "Listen, we've got to escape. Are you with me?"

"Oh, for God's sake, kid," the man almost sobbed, "go back to sleep and leave me alone."

"You *want* to go to Orestes?" Frank asked wonderingly.

"Kid—you can't escape. Forget it. Your life won't be real great now, but make an escape attempt and you'll be surprised how sorry you'll be, and for how long."

Frank left the man to his sleep and returned to his cot, his confident mood deflated.

After another half hour of sitting on his ratty mattress, Frank was again convinced of the necessity of escape. Wasn't there a wide ventilation grille set in the center of the ceiling? He tried to remember. Let's see, he thought, they marched us in here, showed us each a cot, and then turned off the lights. But it seems to me I did notice a slotted plate set in the ceiling. I could escape through the ventilation system!

He stood up again. It seemed to be in the *center* of the ceiling, he recalled. He made his way to a wall and counted the number of steps it took to walk its length; then did the same with the other wall. Twelve by eight, he thought. He then went back to the midpoint of the twelve-pace wall and took four paces out into the room, thanking Chance that no sleeping prisoners lay in his path.

By my calculations, he mused, I should now be directly beneath that ventilation grille. He crouched; when he leaped upward with a strong kick, his fingers crooked to catch the vent. Instead, they cracked against unyielding concrete.

He fell back to the floor, strangling a curse. His hands stung, and he could feel blood trickling down one finger. Bit of a miscalculation, Rovzar, he told himself.

He pulled himself to his feet and got ready to jump again, this time only intending to brush the ceiling with his fingers, to feel for the vent. This is what I should have done to begin with, he thought.

After four jumps, muffled by his rubber-soled shoes, he found the vent. His next leap gained him two fingerholds and in a moment he had got a firm grip with both hands. Now what?

Why, he thought, I'll bring my legs up and kick the plate until it comes loose, and then I'll pull myself up into the hole and be off. Right-ho. He drew his legs up, and with a sort of half flip he kicked the plate with one toe. It made hardly any noise, but he was disappointed at how weak the blow was. This time he got swinging first, and then used the momentum of his pendulum motion to emphasize the kick as he flipped again and drove his heel at the grille.

With an echoing clang of broken metal his foot punched completely through the grille. The recoil of the kick wrenched his hands free, but he didn't fall back to the floor; instead he hung upside down, his foot caught in the twisted wreck of the vent.

Shouts echoed eerily through the corridors, and the prisoners below Frank whimpered in uncomprehending fear. An alarm added its flat howl to the confusion. Frank, dangling from the ceiling, pulled at his trapped foot, hoping to be able to return to his cot before the guards arrived. Footsteps thudded in the corridor, and immediately the lights in Frank's cell flashed on, blinding him. The will to move left his body and he relaxed, swinging limp from the mooring of his foot. He heard the door rattle and squeak open, and then something hard was driven with savage force into his stomach and consciousness left him.

Frank came back to wakefulness by degrees, like a length of seaweed being gradually nudged to shore by succeeding waves. First he was aware of a hum of voices and a sense of being carried about. None of it seemed to demand a response.

Then he dimly knew he was sleeping, but it was a deep, heavy sleep, and he did not want to wake up yet even though it sounded as if some people were up already.

Abruptly, a cold finger and thumb pried his right eyelid open. Frank saw an unfocused sea of bright gray.

"This kid's okay," came a loud, gravelly voice. "Throw him over there with that clown who set his bed on fire."

Frank had groggily assumed that the voice was speaking figuratively when it said "throw," but now unseen hands clamped on his ankles and wrists. "Wait, wait—" Frank began mumbling. "Heave *ho!*" called someone cheerily, and Frank found himself lifted from whatever he'd been lying on and tossed sprawling into the air. His eyes sprang open wide and he grabbed convulsively at nothing. He saw the concrete floor rushing up at him and he managed to twist around in midair so that he landed on his hip instead of his head. The sharp, aching pain of the impact was his first *clear* sensation of the morning.

Laughter rang loud in the room, and Frank looked up from where he lay to see what sort of people were amused by this. A Transport captain and four guards returned his gaze with a mixture of humor and scornful contempt in their eyes. All of them wore pistols, and two of the guards held coils of rope.

"Take these two jerks first," said the captain, pointing in Frank's direction. "And tie their hands." The man exited and the four guards walked over to Frank and rolled him over onto his face, then quickly and securely tied his wrists together behind him. They left him lying there and moved on to someone behind him.

"Get up now," one of the guards said. Frank struggled to his knees and then stood up. His stomach was a collage of pain and numbness, and he sagged when he straightened up; the colors of unconsciousness began to glitter before his eyes. He lowered his head and breathed deeply, and the weakness passed. He heard a sigh behind him and turned to see a tall, thin man with graying hair. It must be the guy who set fire to his bed, Frank realized.

"All right, you two, get moving," a guard said. "Out that door."

Frank and his sad-eyed companion shambled out of the little room and, escorted by the guards, made their way down a corridor to an open doorway. Morning sunlight glared on wet asphalt outside, and the air was cold.

Somehow Frank was not very depressed. The light of day had dispelled the fears the night had given him, and his system was buoyed up by the adventurous realization that he was embarking on a perilous journey. Anything can happen, he thought.

The guards prodded the two blinking prisoners outside. Five hundred yards away the silver needle of a Transport ship stood up against the sky, gleaming in the sun like a polished sword. Even though it was the vehicle that was to carry him to Orestes, Frank was overcome with the beauty of the thing.

"Are these our two escapees?" asked a Transport officer who had walked up while Frank was staring at the rocket. He carried in his hand an object that looked like a rubber stamp or a wax seal.

"Yes, sir," answered one of the guards.

"Open their shirts," the officer said. A guard took hold of Frank's shirt-collar ends and yanked them apart. Three buttons clicked on the asphalt. I'm glad this is just an old painting shirt, Frank thought automatically. He heard his companion's shirt being dealt with in the same way.

"Now, boys, this won't hurt a bit," said the officer with a cold smile as he pressed the seal onto Frank's chest and the other man's. The metal felt warm and itched a little, but was not uncomfortable. "There," the officer said. "Now everyone will know at a glance who you are."

Frank looked down past his chin and saw a mark on his chest. It was a circle with a capital E inside it. "Escapee," the officer explained. He turned to the guards. "Get these monkeys aboard. We lift at nine-seventeen." He strode off without another word.

"You heard the man, lads," grinned a guard. "Start walking. Your friends will be coming along as soon as you two maniacs are aboard." Flanked by the arrogant guards, Frank and the bed-burner set off across the tarmac toward the ship. Frank's eyes were becoming accustomed to the daylight and he looked around as he walked. To his right, a hundred yards away, was a chain-link fence topped with strands of barbed wire. Half-a-dozen big tractor motors were stacked against it at one point. Beyond the fence, he knew, was the channel in which the Malachi River surged its way to the distant sea. At his left was visible a cluster of undistinguished gray buildings. Not a really fine view, Frank thought, considering it's probably the last time I'll see this planet. The thought raised a clamoring flock of emotions in him, which he determinedly strangled and put away. It simply would not do, he told himself, to burst into tears out here.

The gray-haired prisoner who paced along beside Frank was acting oddly. He was whimpering, and his wide-open eyes flicked around as if he were watching the quick, erratic course of a wasp. "Are you okay?" asked Frank quietly.

"There's no way," the man said.

"What's that?" asked a guard.

"There's no way!" the man shouted. The guards, sensing a dangerous frenzy, backed away a pace. Frank did, too. The guards were all concentrating their attention on the crazed bed-burner, and it occurred to Frank that since Francisco Rovzar was already branded as an escapee he had nothing to lose by trying it again. He took another step back, so that the guards were all in front of him.

"Oh my God, there's no way!" shrieked the gray-haired man, who now took off at a dead run toward the buildings. At the same moment Frank turned and sprinted, as quietly as he could, toward the chain-link fence and the tractor motors. He heard, without thinking about it, angry calls behind him. Forget it, he thought, they're after that old guy. Keep running.

"Hey, *you!*" sounded an exasperated shout. That's probably me he's yelling at; well, I have to play out the hand now, he thought. He wrung the highest degree of speed out of his pounding legs, ignoring the shortness of his breath and the pain in his stomach. The fence seemed to slowly jerk closer. Vividly, he could picture the guard unsnapping the flap on his holster, lifting out the pistol, and raising it to eye level. Should I weave right and left to spoil their aim? No, that'd slow me down, he thought.

"Hold it right there, kid, or I'll shoot," called one of the guards. Frank covered the last ten feet and leaped, arms still bound, to the oily top of one of the tractor motors; without stopping he sprang up the stairs they formed, and then jumped with all his strength to clear the barbed wire. A gunshot cracked and his body jerked as it fell away, awkwardly, on the other side of the fence.

"You get him?" asked one of the guards.

"Sure I got him," the other guard replied, holstering his gun.

"A lucky shot at this range. You must have aimed high," commented another. "I'll send the grounds patrol to pick up the body. Come on, help me get this guy stowed." The guards picked up the unconscious, bleeding form of the unfortunate bed-burner and strode off toward the ship.

CHAPTER 3

Frank's flying leap ended in a ragged slide down a dirt embankment to a service road below. The breath was knocked out of him, and the side of his head stung where the bullet had creased him. He lay still for a minute or two to get his breath back, but he knew he couldn't rest yet. He struggled to his skinned knees and spit dirt out of his mouth. I've *got* to untie my hands, he realized, looking around desperately for some object with a sharp edge. He saw nothing but the hill and the road.

He got shakily to his feet, but didn't feel able to walk. Blood from his right ear ran down his neck and stained his ruined shirt. I can't take a whole lot more of this, he thought. Looking south, away from the slope, he could see the steep banks of the Malachi. That's where I want to go, he told himself. The Malachi flows right into Munson, and that ancient metropolis has been harboring fugitives for five hundred years.

The grating roar of a jeep interrupted his thoughts. He knew there was no nearby place to hide, so he flopped down on his stomach beside the road, lying on his good ear. A few moments later the jeep rounded the corner and bore down on his lifeless-looking body. It squealed to a halt beside him, its motor still chugging. Frank held his breath.

"Look at him," remarked the driver. "The bullet went right through his head."

"Lemme see," spoke up his partner. "Wow. I wish they'd issue guns to us."

"Hah," replied the driver. "Like to see you try to handle a gun."

"I could do it."

"Yeah, sure. Throw our friend here into the back, will you?"

"Aren't you gonna give me a hand?"

"No, I've got to stay here and keep my foot on the clutch. Hurry up."

"Oh, man," whined the other, climbing out of the vehicle. Frank heard his boots crunch in the dirt as the man walked over to his prostrate form. Rough hands grabbed his shoulders and pulled. I can't keep playing dead, Frank thought, terrified; I *can't*. Any second now they're going to notice.

"This guy's *heavy*," the man complained.

"For God's sake, Howard, he's skinny. Now stop bitching and toss him in here."

Howard lifted Frank by the belt and slipped an arm under his stomach. Then with an exaggerated groan he heaved the limp body up onto his shoulder. Frank managed to keep from tensing any muscles during the maneuver, but couldn't help opening his eyes as Howard flung him into the back of the jeep. There was a spare tire, and he bent a little to let his head land on the rubber; a jack jabbed painfully into his shoulder, but he found himself basically uninjured. He was very tempted to give himself up. I've taken as much as anyone could have expected of me, he thought. All I want is a rest.

With the lurching rattle of engaging gears the jeep got underway. Frank lay face up on the spare tire, his right foot only a short distance from the back of the driver's head. The machine picked up speed, and the driver clanked the stick shift into second gear; after a couple of minutes he pushed it up into third.

Frank risked raising his head. The road took a sharp curve to the left in front of them, and the driver's hand reached out to downshift. Without stopping to think, Frank drew his right leg all the way back and slammed his foot like a piston into the base of the driver's skull. The man's head bounced off the steering wheel and the jeep spun to the right in a bucking dry skid. Off balance from his kick, Frank was pitched over the jeep's side panel; he hit the dirt in a sitting position and slid, taking most of the abrasion on his left thigh and shoulder. When he found himself motionless at last, he decided to die there, right there in the road. I should have died a long time ago, he thought.

He cautiously opened his eyes. The jeep lay on its side a hundred feet away—the tires on the top side were still spinning, and the motor was ticking in a staccato rattle. Frank was about to close his eyes again when he noticed a jagged strip of the hood protruding like a knife. Squinting against dizziness, he got to his feet after overcoming a short spasm in one knee that had him genuflecting like a madman. He limped across the road to the jeep, and backed up against the torn piece of metal, rocking back and forth to saw through the rope binding him. The rhythm of the motion brought to his dazed mind the memory of a song his father used to sing, and after a brief time of rocking in the morning sun he began to sing it:

> "I open my study window
> And into the twilight peer,
> And my anxious eyes are watching
> For the man with my evening beer."

The rope frayed, then snapped, and Frank's hands were free at last. He flexed them to get the blood circulating.

"Who's singing?" came an angry voice. Howard, his shirt torn, lurched around the corner of the upended jeep. His service sword, a short rapier, was drawn. Frank ran around the other side, and saw the driver's body lifeless in the road, face down with his knees drawn up like a supplicant in church. Frank hobbled over to the body and drew the sword from the scabbard on the dead man's belt. Its hilt was a right-handed one, but Frank, being left-handed, held it in his left, trying to grip it with his skinned thumb and forefinger as Mr. Strand had taught him. Awkward, he thought. How good is Howard?

Howard came out from behind the barrier of the jeep; he was running at Frank, his sword held straight out before him like the horn of a charging rhinoceros. Frank parried it, but Howard had lumbered past before Frank could riposte. The big guard turned and aimed a slash at his young opponent's head; Frank ducked the blow and jabbed Howard in the right elbow.

"Damn!" Howard exploded. "Want to mess around, eh? Swallow this!" He jumped forward, thrusting at Frank's stomach. The apprentice painter, who had been through this move a hundred times in the fencing academy, instinctively parried the sword down and outward in seconde, flipped his own sword back in line and lunged at Howard's chest. The point entered just beneath the breastbone, and Howard's forward impetus drove the blade into the heart. Frank watched, both horrified and fascinated, as Howard sagged at the knees and slid away from the streaked blade that had transfixed him. His body went to its knees and then fell forward into the dust of the road.

Frank backed away. Mr. Strand was right, he realized; hardly anybody can really fence. Since guns were rapidly becoming unavailable, the sword was coming back into fashion, but there had not yet been time for fencing strategy to become widely known. Mr. Strand was one of less than five hundred swordsmen in the Dominion who had really made a science of swordplay. Maybe, mused Frank, I was luckier than I knew when I practiced so many hours with Mr. Strand and his son in the academy.

A breath of wind stirred Frank's hair. I can't rest quite yet, he realized. I've got to get down to the Malachi, find something to float on and then just relax while the old river carries me into Munson's antique tangle of canals and alleys.

He half-climbed, half-slid down the embankment on the south side of the road. His ear had stopped bleeding and only throbbed now, but his scraped knees and legs shot pain at him every time he bent them. It was an annoying pain, and it roused in him a powerful anger against the self-righteous Transports who had done this to him. And who killed your father, he reminded himself.

He swore that if the opportunity ever presented itself, he would take some measure of revenge against the Transport and Duke Costa.

He soon came to level ground—an expanse of slick clay soil, littered with rocks and thriving shrubs. He crossed this quickly and found himself standing at the top of a forty-foot cliff; below him, through a bed of white sand, flowed the green water of the Malachi. During the summer the river was a leisurely, curling stream, knotted with oxbows, but it was a spring breeze that now plucked at Frank's tattered clothes, and the river was young and quick.

The painstaking labor of ten minutes got him to the bottom of the cliff. After diving into the cool water and incautiously drinking a quantity of it, he set about looking for objects on which to float downstream. He found two warped wooden doors dumped behind a clump of bushes and decided to use these, one on top of the other, as a raft. If he sat up on it, he discovered, his raft had a tendency to flip over; but a passenger lying down had no difficulties. He tore a wide frond from one of the dwarf palm trees that abounded and used it to shade his face from the midmorning sun. Soon he was moving along with the current, and when he remembered Howard's rapier it was too late to turn back to retrieve the weapon. He shrugged at the loss and drifted on, warmed by the sun above him, cooled by the water below, shaded by his palm frond, sleeping the sleep of exhaustion.

Thus he drifted east, through the Madstone Marshes, under the towering marble spans of the Cromlech Bridge, and through the forests where the Goudy bandits reigned unquestioned. Any eyes that may have spied the makeshift raft felt that neither it nor its passenger looked worth bothering. By mid-afternoon the walls and towers of Munson rose massive ahead.

At the western boundary of Munson, the Malachi divided in two; the first channel, its natural one, took it under the carved bridges and around the gondola docks, across the sandy delta to the Deptford Sea, sometimes called the Eastern Sea. The other channel, built two centuries previously by Duke Giroud, entered a great arched tunnel and passed underground, beneath the southern section of the city, to facilitate the disposal of sewage. The city had declined since Giroud's day, and most of the sewers were no longer in use, but the southern branch of the Malachi River, the branch called the Leethee by the citizens, still flowed under Munson's streets.

Frank was still asleep when he drifted near the ancient gothic masonry of Munson's high walls. Two arches loomed before him, foam splash-

ing between them where the waters parted. The great walls with their flying buttresses dwarfed even the couriers' carracks that sometimes passed
this way, and none of the river scavengers of the west end noticed as an
unwieldy bit of rectangular debris hesitated, rocked in the swirl, and then
drifted through the Leethee arch and slid down into the darkness beyond.

Beardo Jackson tamped his clay pipe and sucked at it with relish,
blowing clouds of smoke up at the stones of the ceiling. Below him in
the darkness the waters of one of the many branches of the Leethee could
be heard gargling and slapping against the brickwork, washing in a dark
tide below the cellars of the city.

He struck another match and held it to the wick of a rusty lantern
beside him. A bright yellow flame sprang up, illuminating the cavern-like
chamber in which Beardo sat perched on a swaying bridge. The light flickered over the walls whose tight-fitted stones were reinforced with timber
in many places; the arched tunnel-openings that gaped at either end of
the bridge remained in deep shadow.

"Morgan!" Beardo called. "Come along, the tide's high!" His voice
echoed weirdly, receding up the watercourse until it reverberated like a
distant chorus of operatic frogs.

A woman appeared at the opening on Beardo's right. She carried a
coil of fifty-pound fishing line; before stepping out onto the bridge, she
looped one end of it around an iron hook imbedded in the wall.

"Don't yell like that," she said. "You never know who might be
around."

"Oh, to hell with that," he sneered. "Everybody within a cubic mile
of here is scared stiff of me." He slapped the sheathed knife at his belt and
laughed in what he believed was a sinister fashion. The woman spat over
the rope rail and stepped out onto the bridge. She was sloppily fat, and
the bridge creaked and quivered as it took her weight.

"Easy, woman," Beardo said. "The bridge was built for frailer girls."
He grinned up at her. The whites of his eyes were almost brown, and his
face, loosely draped over the bones of his skull, was as wrinkled and creased
as a long-unchanged bedsheet. His beard was ragged and patchy, as were
his clothes.

"And what would frailer girls be doing on it?" she asked scornfully.
Beardo rolled his eyes and made lascivious motions with his hands, im-
plying that there were any number of things frail girls might do on it.

"You rotten toad," Morgan snarled, slapping the old man affection-
ately in the side of the head.

"We've no time for fooling around," Beardo declared. "Where's the
hooks?"

Morgan pulled a chain of small grappling hooks from a bag at her belt, and proceeded to tie one of them to the fishing line. She tossed it into the water so that it trailed downstream.

"Okay now, keep your eyes open on this side, so we'll know where to swing the line," Beardo said, facing upstream. "If anything *scares* you, just call me," he added sarcastically. A week ago a dead lion had floated by under the bridge—its hide would have made a fine catch, but Morgan, terrified by the glazed feline eyes, had twitched the trailing hook away from it. Beardo had not yet entirely forgiven her for it.

"Oh, bite a crawdad," she said.

They were silent then, staring intently into the lamp-lit water. Beardo and his woman were, in the understreet slang, "working the shores": scavenging the debris the Leethee brought in from the upper world. Many of the understreet population of Munson made a profitable living at this trade.

Suddenly Beardo stiffened; something was drifting downstream, something that bumped frequently against the brick walls. "Look sharp, girl," he whispered. "Sounds like a piece of wood coming along."

Presently the thing was dimly visible. "It's a midget raft! With a guy on it!" whispered Morgan. Beardo poked her with his elbow to shut her up. The raft, which was indeed a notably small one, rocked forward into the light. Morgan gasped when she saw the passenger, for its head appeared to be a cluster of rigid green tentacles.

"Beelzebub!" she cried.

The figure sat up on the raft abruptly, making hooting sounds. Morgan screamed. The tiny craft flipped over, dumping its rider into the cold black water.

Beardo, who had seen the palm frond fall away, and knew that this underground mariner was only a puzzled-looking young man, slithered under the rope bridge-rail and dropped into the water ten feet below. He caught the floundering intruder and pushed him toward the ladder rungs set in the brick wall. The young man caught the rungs and began to haul himself out of the bad-smelling tide. His black hair was down across his face, and he stared up through it with bloodshot eyes. Morgan wailed and scrambled on all fours off of the bridge; she disappeared into one of the tunnel mouths, still wailing.

The dark-haired youth pulled himself up onto the bridge and sat there shivering. Beardo climbed up right behind and sat down beside him. The old scavenger was smiling and cleaning his hideous fingernails with a long knife.

"And what might they call you at home, lad?" Beardo queried.

"What?"

"What's your name?"

"Francisco Rovzar. Uh, Frank . . . what's yours?" asked the young man.

"Puddin' Tame," answered Beardo gleefully. "Ask me again and I'll tell you the same." The old man giggled like a manic parrot, slapping his thigh with his free hand.

"Where is this?" asked Frank. "Am I in Munson?"

"Oh aye," nodded Beardo. "Or *under* it, to be more precise. What port was it you sailed from, sir?"

"I've been drifting east on the Malachi from the Barclay Transport Depot." Frank wished the old man would put away the knife. He didn't like the look or smell of the ancient stone watercourse, and he wondered just how far under Munson he was.

"Barclay, eh? You a jailbird?"

Frank considered lying, but this old creature didn't look like he had police connections; and Frank desperately needed friends and food and safe lodging. It's almost certainly an error to trust this guy, he thought. But the next one I meet could be a lot worse.

"Yes," he answered. "That is, I was a prisoner until about eight this morning."

"Released you, did they?"

"No. I escaped."

Beardo started to laugh derisively, then noticed Frank's scrapes and bruises and ruined ear. "You *did?*" he asked, surprised. "Well, that's the first time I ever heard of *that* being done. Anyway, Frank, what I really want to . . . uh . . . *ascertain,* is whether or not you have a family that would be willing to pay an old gentleman like myself for your safe return. Do you understand?"

"No," said Frank.

"Ransom, Frank, ransom. Do you have a rich family?" Before Frank could think of a safe answer, Beardo answered himself. "No, I suppose you don't. If you did, they would have bought you out of Barclay. Or maybe the whole family got arrested, hmm?"

Frank shook his head. "No family at all," he said hopelessly. "My father was all I had, and the Transports shot him yesterday."

"Ah!" said Beardo sadly, testing his knife's edge with a discolored thumb. "I'm afraid that narrows down the possibilities for you, Frank my boy."

Do I have the strength to fight old Puddin' Tame? Frank asked himself. I don't think I do. Maybe I could get into the water again.

"Your father and you were thieves, I take it?" Beardo asked, squinting speculatively at Frank's bared throat.

"No!" Frank exclaimed, stung now in his much abused pride. "My father is . . . was Claude M. Rovzar, the best portrait painter on this planet."

Beardo blinked. He was inclined to doubt this, but then saw the paint stains on the ragged remains of the youth's shirt.

"You're full of surprises, Frank," he said. "All right, let's say you *are* Rovzar's son. Why would the Transports shoot Claude Rovzar?"

"I don't know. My father was doing a portrait of Duke Topo yesterday. Transport troops invaded the palace. Costa was with them, and he killed the old duke. The Transports grabbed my father and me, and my father resisted. They shot him."

"You keep saying they shot him. You don't mean that literally, do you?"

"Yes. There was more gunfire that day than I ever heard of, anywhere, in a hundred years. Bombs, even."

"Hmm," grunted Beardo, scratching his furry chin. "There just might be something to all this." He stood up, setting the bridge swaying. "One thing, anyway," he said, "you've earned a reprieve." He slapped his knife back into its sheath. "Come with me. We'll get your wounds cleaned up and feed you. Then you can tell your story to a friend of mine."

Beardo picked up his lantern and Frank followed him into one of the tunnels.

CHAPTER 4

Alarmingly, the tunnel Beardo and Frank followed led *down*. The dim, shifty light cast by the old man's lantern did little to dispel the darkness, and several times Frank heard anonymous scrabbling, splashing and low moans echo out of side corridors. Beardo held his drawn knife in his right hand and tapped it against the damp brick walls as he led Frank along.

"Why are you doing that?" Frank whispered.

"It shows any hole-lurkers that we're armed. Got to let 'em know we mean business."

Good God, Frank thought. I wonder what sort of creatures lurk in these holes. In spite of himself, Frank began thinking of tentacles and green, fanged faces under old slouch hats.

"Good sirs! Good sirs!" came a wheezing voice from the blackness ahead, causing Frank to start violently. "A penny to see a dancing dog?"

"No," rasped Beardo, advancing on the voice. "We don't want to see a dancing dog."

Frank peered ahead over Beardo's shoulder and saw an old person of indeterminate sex, as withered and dark as a dried apple. The figure was slumped against the wall as though it had been thrown there dead, but one upraised skeletal hand held crossed sticks from which dangled a malodorous puppet. Frank looked more closely at it and saw that it was the dried corpse of a dog.

"Just keep walking," whispered Beardo to Frank. "I've seen this one before."

The old puppeteer began to sing, and Frank knew it was a woman. "Tirra lee, tirra lee, dance hound," she crooned, and jiggled the horrible puppet merrily. Beardo stepped around her, smiling ingratiatingly. Frank followed, also attempting to smile.

"Beardo, by the stars!" the old woman exclaimed. "You'll give me some money, now, eh?"

"Certainly, soon as I get some," replied the old man, walking on down the tunnel and pulling Frank by the wrist.

"Soon as you *get* some? Damn your treacherous eyes!" the woman brayed. She struggled to her feet and stumbled after them for a few paces, flailing Frank's back with her mummified dog, before sinking exhausted to the flagstones once more. "A penny to see a dancing dog?" she inquired of the darkness.

Beardo's home was an abandoned section of a spiral stairwell, left over from God-knew-what derelict subway system. The old man hung his lantern on a wall peg and touched a match to three kerosene lamps; the comparatively bright light enabled Frank to see the place in some detail. The shaft was roughly twenty-five feet from stone floor to boarded-up roof, and the ascending iron stairs circled the shaft twice before disappearing beyond the boards of the ceiling. Stacks of books, chipped statues, rusted ironmongery and clothes lined the outer edges of the stairs, with the other half, near the wall, left clear for ascending and descending. In the middle of the floor was a sunken tub in whose murky waters several large toads sported.

"Well, Frankie lad, what think you of the old homestead, eh?" asked Beardo, unscrewing the lid of a coffee jar.

Even in his cold, wet state, Frank could see that Beardo fairly radiated the homeowner's pride, so he answered tactfully. "It's beautiful, Mr. Tame. A regular palace. I didn't know underground homes were so . . . roomy."

"Hardly any of them are, Frank. This is one of the finest dwellings, I believe, in all of Munson Understreet. Oh, and my name is Beardo, Beardo Jackson; that Puddin' Tame business was a joke." The old man put a pan of water over a gas flame, and then turned to Frank, "Well now, off with those old rags and hop in the tub."

"The tub? But . . . there's frogs in the tub."

"Toads. They thrive on the warm water. No poisonous frogs in my home. Hop in."

Come on, Frank told himself. This tub is the least of your worries. He undraped the tatters of cloth from his shivering body and lowered himself gingerly into the tub, which actually was warm. He splashed around for a while with the toads and then crawled out, feeling, to his surprise, considerably better for the bath. The old man dressed and bandaged Frank's bullet-torn right ear.

Beardo had selected clothes to replace his ruined ones and had not spared the finery. Frank donned a pair of purple silk trousers, red leather shoes, and a black shirt with pearl buttons. Over all went a white quilted smoking jacket with tassels and embroidered dragons.

"How do I look?" Frank asked.

"Like a prince. Come on, down this coffee and we'll be off to visit Mr. Orcrist."

Sam Orcrist liked to think of himself as a ruler-in-the-shadows, a confidant of kings, a prompter behind the scenes. He was privy to the secrets of almost everyone, and his unstable fortune was spread about in hundreds of obscure and fabulous investments. Pages in the Ducal Palace left reports for him in certain unused sewer grates; ladies at court passed on to him incriminating letters through waiters and footmen; and children, above and below the streets, were sent by his agents on all sorts of furtive tracking-and-finding missions.

Orcrist entertained often, but selectively. The doors of his under-street apartment were closed to some of the most influential citizens on the planet, and warmly open to a few of the most unsavory.

"Mr. Beardo Jackson and a young man wish to see you, sir," said Orcrist's doorman, standing beside the chair in which Orcrist sat reading a book of Keats.

"Well, don't leave them standing out there for the footpads, Pons. Show them in." He closed his book and took a bottle and three glasses out of a cabinet. He was pouring the liquor when Beardo and Frank entered.

"Beardo!" he said. "Good to see you again. What have you been doing to throw Morgan into a hysterical fright?"

"Good evening, Sam," Beardo replied. "Poor old Morgan mistook my young friend here for an archfiend."

"I see. Who is your young friend?"

"He's Frank Rovzar, the son of Claude Rovzar the painter. And he has an interesting and timely story to tell you. Frank, sit down and tell Sam what happened yesterday."

Comfortable in his new clothes and warmed by Orcrist's brandy, Frank told him about the rebellion at the palace and the deaths of his father and Duke Topo.

"Holy smokes," said Orcrist when Frank finished. "And you're sure it was Transport troops that took the palace?"

"Yes," Frank answered. "Led by Prince Costa."

"I *wondered* why there's been no news from the palace in the last twenty-four hours. They're certainly keeping the lid on this." He stood up. "Pons!"

"Yes sir?" answered the doorman.

"Get up to the land office *fast*, and sell all my holdings in the Goriot Valley. Don't start a run on it, but be willing to take a loss. And for God's sake get there before the office closes. Go!" Pons dashed from the room.

"Don't come back until I no longer own one square foot of farmland!" Orcrist called after him.

He strode to the table and drummed his fingers on its polished surface. "How old is this news, Beardo?" he asked.

"I pulled Frank out of the water less than an hour ago."

"Excellent. To show my gratitude for your prompt action, Beardo, I insist that Mr. Rovzar and yourself consent to be my guests for dinner. You'll sleep here, of course; I'll have Pons show you your rooms when he returns."

Frank was beginning to feel dizzy, and doubtful of his own perceptions. Whatever response he had expected Orcrist to have to his story, this had not been it.

"What's the connection," Frank asked, "between a rebellion at the palace and farmland in the Goriot Valley?"

Orcrist smiled, not unkindly. "I'm sorry if I seem callous about all this," he said. "I'm an investor, you see. About ten years ago Duke Topo, in an attempt to make Octavio an autonomous—that is, self-sufficient— planet, planted and irrigated the entire length of the Goriot Valley. That way we didn't have to import produce. It was a flourishing undertaking, and I am at this moment the owner of much of that farmland. *But* if the Transport has taken control of us, I don't want any part of that damned valley. The Transport doesn't approve of independent planets, and I don't see a bright future for agriculture on Octavio." He tossed off the last of his drink. "And now if you'll excuse me, I have a few other little matters to take care of."

With a stately bow, Orcrist left the room. Beardo crossed to the table and refilled his glass. "A real gentleman!" he smiled, luxuriously sniffing his brandy.

"He certainly is," agreed Frank, to whom, right now, the word "dinner" was like a loved one's name. "It was nice of him to ask us to stay the night here," he added, wondering where he would have slept in Beardo's odd dwelling.

"Ah, well that wasn't so much good manners as *caution,* you see," Beardo said. "Any time someone brings him really hot news he insists that they remain here until the news isn't hot anymore. He doesn't want us telling your story to anyone else." The old fellow sipped the brandy and pulled out his pipe. "And his hospitality, Frankie, is such that no one has ever been known to object to the temporary captivity."

The dinner, which was served an hour later in Orcrist's high-ceilinged dining room, was lavish. A dozen stuffed game hens were piled on a platter in the center of the table, and salads, baked potatoes, toast, cold meats and steaming sauces flanked them. Carafes of chilled wines, red and white, stood next to the roasted hens; Frank was amazed to find out that the whole production was intended only for himself, Beardo, Orcrist, and one other house-bound guest.

"Frank Rovzar, Beardo Jackson, this is George Tyler," said Orcrist as the four of them sat down at the table. "George, Frank and Beardo."

Frank looked across a dish of mustard sauce at George Tyler. He looks like he drinks more than he ought to, Frank thought, though he's still too young for it to really show. Oblivious to Frank's scrutiny, Tyler brushed a lock of blond hair out of his face and speared himself a baked potato.

"I must request, friends, that you do not discuss the respective businesses that have brought you here," said Orcrist. "Not that any of it would provide suitable dinner conversation anyway."

He took a long sip of Chianti, holding it in his mouth to warm it and taste it before he swallowed. "Not bad," he decided. "You and Frank should get along well, George," he said. "You have the artistic temperament in common. Frank is a painter, and George," he added, turning to Frank, "is a poet." The two young men smiled at each other embarrassedly.

"To hell with the talk, I say," put in Beardo, gnawing a greasy hen from whose open abdomen pearl onions cascaded onto his plate. "Mother of God!" he exclaimed, observing the phenomenon.

The dinner progressed with considerable gusto, and by ten o'clock most of the wine and food had disappeared. Frank was feeling powerfully sleepy, though the others seemed to be just blooming, and Beardo had begun singing vulgar songs.

Tyler tossed a clean-picked bone onto his plate. "Not bad fare, Sam," he said. "Nearly as good as what they used to serve at the palace."

"At the palace?" inquired Frank politely.

"Oh, yes," Tyler nodded, a little clumsily. "Didn't old Sam tell you? I'm the true son of Topo."

Orcrist caught Frank's eye and frowned warningly. Don't worry, Frank thought, I won't say anything.

"Oh, hell yes," Tyler went on. "Many's the morning Dad and I would go hunting deer with the game wardens. I had my own horse, naturally, a speckled roan named . . . uh . . . Lighthoof." He drank the last of his wine and refilled his glass. "Oh, and the long evenings on the seaside terrace, the sunset light reflecting in our drinking cups carved of single emeralds! Sitting in our adjustable recliners, fanned by tall, silent slaves from the lands where the bong trees grow!"

"For God's sake, George," said Orcrist.

"Oh, I know, Sam," Tyler said with a broad wave of his hand. "I shouldn't . . . dwell on these things now that I move in lower circles . . . present company excluded, of course. But I long even now for that old life, to mount old . . . Lightboy and ride off on adventures and quests and whatnot."

At this point Frank slumped forward onto the tablecloth, fast asleep.

Frank opened his eyes, but closed them again when he saw that the room was in pitch blackness. Not dawn yet, he thought instinctively. I wonder if Dad is home. A raucous, choking snore from another room made him sit up, completely awake. That's not Dad, he thought; and this isn't my room. Where am I? He felt around on the top of the table beside the bed, and soon had struck a match to a candle.

I'm in one of Orcrist's guest rooms, he realized. And we're underground, so God knows what time it is. He got out of bed and found his gaudy clothes draped over a chair. Odd as they were, he felt better when he was dressed. Now then, he thought, what are Orcrist's breakfast customs?

He sighted the door, and then snuffed the candle and groped to it in the dark. To his relief the silent hallway beyond was lit by wall cressets, and he wandered along it until he came to Orcrist's sitting room.

"Ah, Frank," said Orcrist, who sat in his customary easy chair with a book and a cup of coffee. "Up with the sun even down here, eh? As a matter of fact, I've been waiting for you." He stood up and took two rolls of parchment out from behind a bust of Byron on one of his bookshelves. Then he unrolled them on the carpet, using books to hold the corners down. On one of them had been done a finely shaded drawing of a girl's head; the other was blank.

"What do you think of that picture, Frank?" Orcrist asked.

"I'd say it's one of Gascoyne's best sketches of Dora Wakefield. People used to say he was having an affair with her, but my father never believed it."

Orcrist blinked. "Well, you know your field, Frank, that's certain. Yes, it is a Gascoyne, though I didn't know the name of the model. What I want to know is whether you can, without compromising any principles, *copy* it for me on this blank sheet. Hm?"

"Sure I can," Frank answered carelessly. "Have you got black ink, a little water, and a . . . number eight point pen?"

Orcrist pointed to them on the bookcase. "I'll be back in an hour to get you for breakfast," he said, and left the room, carrying his coffee.

Frank rubbed the sleep out of his eyes and got to work. He lightly sketched the face onto the blank sheet using a dry pen to lay down some guide-scratches; then he dipped the pen in the ink and began carefully mimicking Gascoyne's delicate stippling and cross-hatching. The discipline of his craft took his mind off of the uncertainty of his current situation. Except for the occasional clink of pen-nib against ink bottle, the room was silent.

When Orcrist returned, he found Frank sitting in the easy chair, reading.

"Given up?" he asked with a little annoyance.

Frank handed him the two rolls of parchment. "Which one is Gascoyne's?" he asked. Orcrist unrolled one, looked at it, and replaced it on the table. He unrolled the other one more carelessly, stared at it closely, and then spread both of them out on the floor.

"Given up?" asked Frank.

Abruptly, Orcrist laughed. "Yes, by God," he said. "Which is yours?"

"The one whose ear lobe is showing. I didn't want to do an absolute copy."

Orcrist laughed again and clapped Frank on the shoulder. "Come along to breakfast," he said. "And we can discuss your career possibilities."

CHAPTER 5

Beardo was staring with ill-concealed distaste at a glistening fried egg on his plate. With a petulant jab of his fork he ripped open the yolk.

"There's a sad sight for you, poet," he said somberly.

"Oh, quit playing with it," said Tyler.

Both of them were frowning and squinting, and they seemed to have occasional trouble in breathing.

"Beardo," said Orcrist, leading Frank into the breakfast room, which was cheerily lit by actual sunlight reflected down a shaft from the surface. "Your boy here proves to be a competent art forger. I propose to buy him from you. How does sixty malories sound?"

"You're too generous, I'm sure," smiled Beardo, cheered by this unexpected windfall. "Sixty it is."

Frank was surprised to find that he was a buyable article, but he said nothing.

"How do you feel about that, Frank?" asked Orcrist. "You'd be a licensed art forger, bonded to me. You can have room and board here, plus a good salary, half of which, for the first two years, goes to me. Then when your bond is paid off you keep all of it. Will you take it?"

How can I not take it, Frank thought. It sounds like a good deal, and there's absolutely nothing else I can do. He bowed. "I'd be delighted, Mr. Orcrist. Where do I sign?"

"After breakfast, can't do business before breakfast. Why, gentlemen, you've eaten nothing! Not hungry?" He winked at Frank. Beardo and Tyler shook their heads.

"Well, I thank you for your company anyway. I assume two such busy citizens as yourselves must have many appointments, so I won't inconvenience you by insisting that you stay for lunch."

Orcrist told Frank that they'd get him registered with the Subterranean Companions that night. In honor of the occasion he provided Frank with some clothes of a more sober nature: a suit of brown corduroy, black boots and a black overcoat. "It's not a good idea to be too conspicuous

47

down here," he confided. "If you went out dressed in those other clothes, the first thief that saw you would figure it was Ali Baba himself walking by, and bash you before you could blink."

Frank examined the conservative lines of his new overcoat with some relief. "Who are the Subterranean Companions?" he asked.

"A brotherhood of laborers engaged in extralegal work. A thieves' union, actually. And we've got to get your name on the roll. Freelance work simply isn't permitted."

"Well, I want to do this right," Frank put in.

"Of course you do."

That evening, after a much simpler dinner than the previous night's, Orcrist and Frank set off down Sheol Boulevard, a grand street whose brick roof stood a full twenty feet above the cobblestones. Streetlamps were hung from chains at intervals of roughly fifteen paces, and taverns, fuel stores and barber shops cast light through their open doorways onto the pavement.

"This, I guess you could say, is Downtown Understreet," said Orcrist. "Three blocks farther are the good restaurants. We've even got a couple of good bookstores down here."

"Will we be passing them?" asked Frank.

"Not tonight. We've got to turn south on Bolt after this next cross street."

They walked on without speaking, listening to the sounds of the understreet metropolis—laughter, shouts, clanking dishes and lively accordion music—echoing up and down the dim avenues.

At Bolt Street they turned right, and then took a sharp jog left, into an alleymouth, and stopped. They were in almost total darkness.

"Where are we?" whispered Frank.

"Sh!"

He heard the rattle of keys, and then the scratch and snap of a lock turning. Orcrist's hand closed on his shoulder and guided him forward a few paces. There was a breath of air, and the sound of the lock again, and then a match flared in the blackness and Orcrist was holding it to the wick of a small pocket lantern. The narrow hallway smelled of old french fries. Orcrist put his finger to his lips and led Frank forward, past several similar doors to a stairway.

"Going down," Orcrist whispered.

At the bottom of the stairs, six flights down, Orcrist relaxed and began chatting. "Got to be careful, you see, Frank," he said. "There are people who'd pay a lot for the death of a ranking member of the Companions, so I never come by the same route twice in a row." They were walking along another corridor now, but it was brighter and wider, and Orcrist extinguished his lantern and put it away.

"Why aren't you armed?" asked Frank, who had noticed the absence of a sword under Orcrist's cape.

"Oh, I'm adequately armed, never fear. Ah, and here we are."

They stepped through a high open arch into a huge hall that Frank thought must once have been a church. The pews, if it ever did have any, had been ripped out and replaced by ranks of folding wooden chairs, but the place was still lit by eight ancient baroque chandeliers. A big, altar-like block of marble up front was currently being used as a speaker's platform.

Frank followed Orcrist up a ramp to an overhanging structure that might have been a side-wall choir loft or a theater box. "Make yourself at home," Orcrist told him, gesturing at the dusty chairs and music stands that littered the box. "I've got to count the house." He pulled a pair of opera glasses from his pocket and began scrutinizing the crowd below. Frank sat down. His injured ear was throbbing, and he shifted uncomfortably in his seat.

After about ten minutes Orcrist put the glasses away and turned to Frank. "I'll be back soon," he said. "I've got to give your name to the registrar and pay your first month's dues. Don't leave the box." He waved and ducked out.

Frank leaned on the balcony rail, looked out over the restless throng, and soon saw Orcrist's dark, curly hair and drab cape appear from a side door. He watched him make his way to the speaker's stand and huddle for a moment with one of the men there. Frank's attention was distracted then by a fight that broke out in the middle of the hall, and when he glanced back at the speaker's stand Orcrist was gone. He was still trying to sight him when Orcrist's voice spoke softly behind him.

"Don't look so eager, Frank. Don't be conspicuous." The older man pulled a couple of chairs close to the rail. "Sit down and relax," he said. "This may take a while."

Frank had been expecting great things of this secret, underground meeting of thieves, but soon found himself bored. The speaker, a pudgy man named Hodges, spent the first few minutes exchanging casual jokes with members of the audience. Frank understood none of the references, though Orcrist frequently chuckled beside him. Hodges addressed everyone by their first names, and Frank felt more excluded than he had at any time in the past three days. He felt a little more at home when Hodges read the list of newly-bonded apprentices and he heard "Rovzar, Frank" read out as loudly as any of them.

What would Dad say, Frank wondered briefly, if he knew I was making a living as an art forger? He'd understand. As he once told me, while squinting against the hideous sunlight of a cold morning, "Frankie, if it was easy, they'd have got somebody else to do it."

The meeting dragged on interminably, and just when Frank was convinced that he must fall asleep, a new figure appeared on the speaker's platform. It was a burly old man with a close-cropped white beard, and Frank saw the other officials who were standing about bow as the old man nodded to them.

"Who's that?" Frank asked.

"I thought you were asleep," Orcrist said. "That bearded guy? That's Blanchard. He's the king of the Subterranean Companions. I expected to see him here. He must have heard about the palace rebellion—it's only something big that brings him to one of these meetings."

Blanchard now rapped the speaker's table with a fist. The crowd quieted much more quickly than it had for Hodges.

"My friends and colleagues," he began in a strong, booming voice. "I'm sure many of you have noticed evidences of a concealed crisis in the Ducal Palace." There was a pause while the more literate thieves explained the sentence to their slower-witted fellows. "Well, I am now able to tell you what's going on. Prince Costa has formed an alliance with the Transport Company and, day before yesterday, overthrown and killed Duke Topo." There were scattered cheers and outraged shouts. "We now have a new Duke, gentlemen. It is too early to estimate the effects this change will have upon us and our operations, but I will say this: proceed with caution. The Transport spacers are no longer just drunken marks whose pockets you can pick and whose girls you can abuse. They are now our rulers. They will almost certainly function as police. Therefore I abjure you—" again there was a flurry of interpretation for the less bright thieves "—step carefully; don't cause unnecessary trouble; and keep your eyes open." The old man glared out at the cathedral-like hall. "I hope you ignorant bastards are paying attention. Maybe some of you remember Duke Ovidi, and how he hung a thief's head on every merlon of the Ducal Palace. Those days, friends, may very well be upon us once more."

On the way home from the meeting Frank's ear began to bleed again, and he passed out on the Sheol Boulevard sidewalk. Orcrist carried him back to the apartment, changed his bandage and put him to bed.

Frank tossed a paintbrush into a cup of turpentine and ran his hands through his unruly hair. It's going well, he thought. He'd been trying to get this painting in line for three days and had finally mastered Bate's style. He raised his head and stared at his still-wet painting, then turned and studied the original, hung next to it. I'll have this canvas finished this afternoon, Frank thought, which leaves the problem of darkening it and cracking it so that it looks as old as the original. But that was purely a technical detail, and he didn't anticipate any trouble with it.

The front door swung open and Orcrist strode in. He took off his black leather gloves and tossed them onto a chair.

"By God, Frank," he said, studying the forgery, "you have got the soul of Chandler Bate on canvas better than he did himself."

"Thanks," Frank said, wiping off a brush. "I've got to admit I'm pleased with it myself."

"It was the philosopher Aurelius," said Orcrist, sinking into his habitual easy chair, "who observed that 'the universe is change.' If he'd thought of it, he'd probably have added 'and an art forger's duties vary with the season'."

"Ah. Are my duties about to vary?"

"As a matter of fact, they are." Orcrist poured two glasses of sherry and handed one to Frank. "For three weeks now you've been working away here, and you've copied four paintings and eleven drawings that I've brought you. Where do you suppose those art works have come from?"

"Stolen from museums and private collections," answered Frank promptly.

"Exactly. And whom do you suppose I had do the stealing?"

"I don't know."

"I'll tell you. A cousin of mine named Bob Dill. And two nights ago he was stabbed to death by a zealous pair of guards at the Amory Gallery. They chased him all over the building, hacking at him, and finally brought him down in the Pre-Raphaelite room."

Frank was unable to guess the appropriate response to this story, so he said nothing.

"What with one thing and another," Orcrist continued, "I find it impractical to hire another thief. The fine art market is suffering these days; Costa's damned taxes have taken up a good deal of the money that should rightfully go to people like you and me. The market isn't dead, you understand, just a trifle unsteady."

"So how will you get your paintings now?" Frank asked with a little trepidation.

"You and I will pinch them ourselves," Orcrist announced with a smile and a wave of his glass.

Frank had a quick vision of himself bleeding out the last of his lifeblood on the floor of the Pre-Raphaelite room. "Make Pons do it," he suggested.

"Now, Frank, I know you don't mean that. I knew when I first saw you that you had an adventurer's heart. 'The lad's got an adventurer's heart,' I said to myself." Frank looked closely at Orcrist, unable to tell whether or not he was being kidded. "Besides," Orcrist went on, "I once gave Pons a chance to . . . prove himself under fire, and he absolutely failed to measure up. He's a fine doorman and butler, but he does *not* have an adventurer's heart."

"Oh," said Frank, wondering how adventurous his own heart really was.

"At any rate, Frank, we'll begin tonight. Since it's your first crack at this sort of thing, I plan to start with the Hauteur Museum. It's an easy place."

"I'm glad of that."

"Relax, you'll enjoy it. Now go get something to eat. We'll leave at ten."

As Frank crossed to the door, he heard a soft creak behind it, and when he stepped into the hall he saw the door of Pons's room being eased quietly shut.

The Hauteur Museum had once been Munson's pride, but with the building of several new theaters in the Ishmael Village district to the north, the Hauteur found itself no longer the heart of metropolitan culture. It was still well-thought-of when anyone did think of it, and it could still boast some influential paintings and sculptures, but its heyday was passed.

At eleven o'clock Frank and Orcrist entered its cellar, having wormed their way up a laundry chute that had once, when the Hauteur had been a hotel two centuries before, emptied into a now-abandoned sub-basement. Orcrist had carefully lifted off the mahogany panel that hid the forgotten laundry chute. "We want to replace it when we're done, you see," he told Frank in a whisper, "in case we ever want to come back again."

They stole silently up the carpeted cellar stairs. Their way was lit by moonlight filtering through street-level grates set high in the walls, and Frank realized with a pang of homesickness how long it had been since he had seen real moonlight. I hope the museum has windows, he thought.

The door at the top of the stairs was unlocked, which Frank thought was careless of the owners. The two adventurers swung it open as quietly as they could. Orcrist motioned Frank to wait while he padded off into the darkness of the museum. Frank waited nervously, only now beginning to realize just how much trouble this night's enterprise could lead to. Holy saints, he thought with a chill of real fear, if I'm caught they'll send me back to Barclay! I've still got that tattoo on my chest.

After a few uneasy minutes he heard a thump, then a multiple thud like a bag of logs thrown on a floor. God help us, he thought. What was that?

"Frank!" Orcrist's whisper cut the thick silence. "It's all clear! Carefully, now, go down the aisle on your left!"

When Frank did as he was told, he found himself in the main room. Paintings hung on every side, and he saw with delight a window opening on a quiet street and a deep, starry sky.

"Get away from the window, for God's sake," whispered Orcrist. Frank turned back to the room to see the older man standing over an unconscious uniformed body. "Come on," he hissed to Frank. "There are two paintings over here we ought to get."

Working in silence, Frank helped Orcrist unframe and roll two mediocre Havreville canvases. Orcrist thrust them inside his coat. "See anything else worth carrying?" he asked.

Frank was beginning to relax, and he strolled up and down the dim aisles, peering at paintings and statues with a critical eye. Not bad, most of it, he thought, but none of it seems worth the trouble to forge. I'm not even very impressed with those Havrevilles. As he turned to rejoin Orcrist he noticed, with a thrill of recognition, a small portrait hung between two gross seascapes. He stared intently at it, remembering the hot July day on which it had been painted. His father had been very fond of the model, and had frequently sent young Frank out for coffee or paint or simply "fresh air."

"Anything?" Orcrist inquired impatiently.

"No," whispered Frank in reply. "Let's clear out."

CHAPTER 6

The Schilling Gallery, on which they made an assault four days later, was "not such an easy peach to pluck," as Orcrist was subsequently to observe to Frank. They failed to locate the drain that Orcrist swore would lead them directly into the gallery's office, and they had to bash a hole in the tile floor from beneath with an old wooden piling they found in the sewer. The noise was horribly loud, and they weren't in the gallery five minutes before armed guards were pounding at the doors. Orcrist refused to flee, though, determined to make off with a genuine Monet, which the Schilling had on loan from another planet.

"Let's get the hell *out* of here!" pleaded Frank, who saw the doors shaking as they were battered by boots and sword hilts on the other side. "One of them may have gone to get a key! We don't have thirty seconds!"

"Wait, I found it!" called Orcrist. He carefully took the canvas out of its frame and rolled it. He was sliding it into his pocket when the east door gave way with a rending crack of splintering wood. Four yelling, sword-waving guards raced toward the two thieves.

Frank leaped sideways, grabbed a life-size bronze statue of a man by the shoulder, and with a wrenching effort pulled it over. It broke on the tiles directly in front of the charging guards, and one of them pitched headlong over the hollow trunk, which was ringing like a great bell from the impact of its fall. Frank snatched up a cracked bronze arm and swung it at another guard's head—it hit him hard over the eye and he fell without a word.

"Come on, Frank!" called Orcrist, standing over the jagged hole through which they'd entered. Frank impulsively picked up one of the statue's ears, which had broken off; then he ran toward Orcrist. The other two guards were also running toward Orcrist from the other side of the room, their rapiers held straight out in front of them. Orcrist's hand darted under his cape, and then the front of the cape exploded outward in a spray of fire, and the two guards were slammed away from him as if they'd been hit by a truck. They lay where they fell, their faces splashed with blood and their uniforms torn up across the front. The harsh smell of gunpowder rasped in Frank's nose as he leaped down through the hole after Orcrist.

Twenty minutes later, as they caught their breath in Orcrist's sitting room after a furtive race through a dozen narrow, low-ceilinged understreet alleys, Frank showed Orcrist the bronze ear he'd stolen.

"And what do you mean to do with that?" asked Orcrist, painfully flexing his right hand.

"I'm going to run a string through it, and wear it where my right ear used to be. Like an eye patch, you know."

"An ear patch."

"Exactly," agreed Frank. "How's the Monet?"

Orcrist gingerly pulled the canvas out of his jacket and unrolled it. "No harm done," he said, examining it. "Monet is a durable painter."

"I guess so. Oh, and what the hell was that weapon?" Frank asked in an awed tone.

"That impressed you, did it? That was a two-barreled twelve-gauge shotgun, barrels sawed down to six inches, and equipped with a pistol grip. I think I broke my hand shooting it. Ruined my cape for sure. We're lucky I didn't put the canvas in the line of fire."

Frank sighed wearily. "Mr. Orcrist, in honor of our coup tonight, do you suppose a bit of scotch would be out of order?"

"Not at all, Frank, help yourself." Frank opened the liquor cabinet. Orcrist sat silently, massaging the wrist and fingers of his right hand.

"Oh, by the way, Mr. Orcrist . . ."

"Yes?"

"What becomes of the paintings once they're duplicated here? Do you sell both the original and the copy to collectors?"

"Uh . . . no. If I steal one painting and sell two versions of it, the word would eventually get around. I only sell the forgeries."

Frank waited vainly for Orcrist to go on. "Well," he said finally, "what do you do with the originals?"

Orcrist looked up. "I keep them. I'm a collector myself, you see."

During the following week Frank worked on the forgery of the Monet. It was difficult for him to assume the impressionist style, and he tore up two attempts with a palette knife. As the second imperfect copy was being hacked into ragged strips, Orcrist, sitting in his easy chair, looked up from his book.

"Not making a lot of headway?" he asked.

"No," said Frank, trying to keep a rein on his temper. What a cheap waste of good canvas, he thought. Dad never would have behaved this childishly. Where's my discipline?

"What you need, Frank, is a bit of recreation. Go spend some of your wages. You know the safe areas of Understreet Munson—go have some beer at Huselor's, it's a good place."

"Yeah, maybe I'll do that. Say, what's the date?"

"The tenth. Of May. Why?"

"The Doublon Festival is going on in Munson! On the surface, I mean. I haven't missed it in the last six years! Why don't I take my wages and spend the evening there?"

Orcrist frowned doubtfully. "That wouldn't be a good idea," he said. "You can't really afford to be seen topside yet. You're wanted by the police, you know. Stay underground."

"It'll be all right," Frank insisted. "I'll go when it's dark; and everyone wears masks anyway. You've shown me a couple of safe routes to the surface streets, and I've been to the Doublon Festival a dozen times, so I won't get lost. I won't do anything foolish."

"I'll send a couple of bodyguards with you, anyway."

"No, I'd rather be on my own."

Orcrist considered it for a minute. "Well, it's a bad idea, but I won't stop you." He stood up and crossed to a desk against the wall. "Be back by one o'clock in the morning or I'll send some rough friends to bring you back. Here's ten malories. That ought to buy you a good time."

Frank gratefully took the money and turned to get dressed.

"Wait a minute," said Orcrist.

Frank turned around in the doorway. Orcrist was rummaging in another drawer. "Take this, too, in case of a *real* emergency," he said, holding a small silver pistol. "It only holds one bullet, but it's a forty-five. And don't lose it; the damned thing cost me quite a bit."

"I won't lose it," said Frank, taking the little gun. It was the first time he'd ever held a gun, and he felt ridiculously over-armed.

"The safety catch is that button above the trigger. Push it in and the gun will shoot. Leave it where it is for now. And for God's sake keep it in a secure pocket."

"I will," said Frank. "And thanks. Don't worry, I'll be careful."

After Frank had left the room, Orcrist rang for Pons. "Pons," he said, "young Rovzar is determined to go to the Doublon Festival tonight. I could have forbidden it, of course, but I don't like to operate that way. So I want you to contact Bartlett and . . . oh, Fallworth, and tell them to follow him and keep an eye on him."

"Yes sir."

"No, damn it. Wait a minute." Orcrist scowled. "I guess he's able to take care of himself. Forget it, Pons."

"With pleasure, sir."

Frank dressed in the subdued clothes Orcrist had given him, put on his newly-polished bronze ear, and then left the apartment, the gun and the ten malories each occupying a safe inner pocket. He cut across Sheol to a street that was really little more than a tunnel. After following it for three hundred feet, he turned suddenly to the right, into an alcove that could not be seen a yard away. It led into a much narrower, darker tunnel, and Frank proceeded slowly, his hand on his knife. He still didn't think of the gun as a practical weapon.

Water swirled around his heels, and he was glad when his groping right hand found the rungs of the ladder he'd been heading for. He climbed up it through a round brick shaft whose sides were slippery with moss and flowing water, and eventually came to the underside of a manhole cover. This he pushed up cautiously, peering about carefully before sliding it aside. He quickly climbed out of the shaft and pushed the manhole cover back into place with his foot.

He was now on the surface, breathing fresh night air for the first time in almost a month. The stars looked beautifully distant, and he felt almost uneasy to see no roof overhead. The manhole was several blocks away from Kudeau Street, where the Doublon Festival was held, but he could hear the shouts and maniacal music already.

I've been cooped up too long in that little sewer world, he realized. Let's see how much money I can spend in one night.

He followed the alley to Pantheon Boulevard and headed east down it toward Kudeau Street. Long before he reached it, he was surrounded by masked dancers, and the curbs were crowded with the crepe-decorated plywood stands of vendors. The music was a crashing, howling thing, yelping out of guitars, slide whistles, trumpets and kazoos, and crowds reeled drunkenly down the streets, swaying unevenly to the chaotic melody. The warm night air smelled of garlic and beer.

Frank bought a sequined cardboard mask and a cup of cloudy, potent beer from the nearest booth. After putting on the mask and downing the beer at a gulp, he joined the dancing mob. He linked arms with a groaning rummy on his right and a startlingly fat woman on his left, following Pantheon's tide of revelers as they emptied slowly into the packed expanse of Kudeau Street. The moon was up now, shining full behind the ragged Munson skyline.

After an hour of dancing and drinking, Frank stumbled over a curb and crossed the sidewalk to lean against a pillar and catch his breath. He was somewhat drunk, but he could see a great difference in the Doublon Festival this year; in past years, when he had come with his father, it had been a festive, fairly formalized celebration of the spring.

This year it was something else. Screams that began as singing were degenerating into insane shrieks. The dancing had become a huge game of snap-the-whip, and people were being flung spinning from the end of the line with increasing force. People had stopped paying for the beer. Couples were making frantic love in doorways, under the vendors' booths, even in the street. And over all, from every direction, skirled the maddening noise that could no longer really be called music.

Time for a decision, Frank told himself. Go home now or stay and take whatever consequences are floating around unclaimed. I need another beer to decide, he compromised, and began elbowing his way toward a beer-seller's stand.

Before he reached it he sensed a change in the crowd. People paused, and were craning their necks, peering up and down the street.

"What is it?" Frank shouted to the man next to him.

"Costa!" the man answered. "The Duke!"

Frank looked around but could see nothing because of the crowd. His drunkenness left him, and he felt a cold emptiness in his stomach. *Costa!* he thought. *Here!* He ducked into the nearest building, ran up the stairs, and blundered his way out onto a second floor balcony that overlooked the choked street.

From this vantage point he saw the procession bulling its way through the mob of drunken, torch-waving revelers; he saw the elegant litter being carried at shoulder height and the languid youth who waved from within at the merrymakers. Even from a distance of fifty feet or so he recognized the pale, contemptuous face of Costa, the patricide, the Duke who had had Frank's father killed.

He can't see me in the shadow of the awning here, Frank thought. Even if he could, I'm masked. Instinctively he drew his coat tighter about his chest to cover his damning tattoo, and his fingers brushed the lump under the fabric that covered the gun. Suddenly and completely, he knew what he had to do. The shot wouldn't be difficult at this range, and a forty-five-calibre bullet ought to do the job.

Trembling, he took the gun out of his pocket and pushed off the safety catch. The procession had drawn even with him in the street. Costa was as close now as he would ever be. Stepping back, Frank raised the gun. I *can't,* he thought. There must be twenty guards down there. Some of them have guns, and I've only got one bullet. I'd never get away through this crowd. I *can't.*

He stood there, shaking, with the gun pointed at Costa's face. The procession was slowly moving past. In another few seconds he'll be out of my line of sight, Frank thought.

There was a commotion in the crowd below, and a man ran at the litter and jumped up onto its running board. Frank saw a brief gleam of moonlight on a knife blade. Four quick gunshots broke the continuity of the crazy music, and the man with the knife stumbled to the ground. His weapon fell on the paving stones. He walked lurchingly back toward the crowd, and Frank could see the blood on his shirt. Two more shots cracked, and the man fell sideways onto the street.

Costa leaned out of the litter and waved to show that he was unhurt. The guards cheered, but the crowd almost booed him. An ugly tension was building; Costa and his attendants left quickly.

Frank replaced the gun in his pocket, feeling sick. He returned to Orcrist's underground apartment, stopping twice along the route to throw up.

The next morning he gave Orcrist back his gun and told him about the abortive assassination attempt by the man with the knife."

"I heard about it," Orcrist said. "I knew the man slightly."

"It was a crazy thing to do," Frank declared.

"Yes, it was. Did you hear that Costa has abolished the Doublon Festival? He said it's a 'free-for-all crime fest,' to use his words. It won't even finish out the week, as it normally would."

"It was pretty wild last night. I've been to it a dozen times and it was never nearly as bad as it was last night."

"That's because times were prosperous under old Duke Topo. Times are very bad now and getting worse; that's why the festival was such a madhouse. People figured it was their last chance to enjoy themselves, and they'd do it or know the reason why."

"Times aren't *that* bad, are they?"

"I don't know, Frank. They seem to be. The Transport is a bankrupt organization, but determined not to admit it. The interplanetary shipping lines are collapsing. The Transport seems to have decided to make Octavio its home planet, and so Costa, having sold out to them, is taxing the guts out of the people to support it. The end isn't in sight—and we haven't even hit bottom yet."

CHAPTER 7

Two months later Orcrist once again had occasion to quote Aurelius to Frank.

"You see, Frank," he explained, "when a man proves himself capable, he is likely to be given more tasks. You began as simply an art forger, you'll recall, and then also took on the duties of a quality art procurer."

"Am I about to take on someone else's duties? Did you lose another cousin?" Frank's bronze ear gleamed in the lamplight.

"What a horrible thing to say, Frank. But yes, as a matter of fact, I was thinking of broadening your functions, giving you some experience in another field—now that my art collectors are so tax-strangled and the museums so heavily guarded and our night runs are becoming so few and far between."

"My new field being . . . ?"

"Well, I entertain quite a bit, you know. Pons handles the details quite well, but the kitchen is a chaos. Kitchen boys come and go like sailors in a brothel, and now my chief cook has walked out. So I thought that, in the free time between our night runs and your painting, you might help Pons out with the dinners, cooking and washing up, and all."

Frank swallowed the indignant anger that Orcrist's suggestion raised in him. *Take it easy,* he thought. *Orcrist's employment is all that stands between you and the lean life of a fugitive. He's fed you and taken care of you, and it isn't his fault that the new government has made affluence an archaic word. Orcrist works as hard as you do (harder, probably), and risks his neck as well as your own on the night raids.*

"What do you say?" asked Orcrist, and Frank suddenly realized that the older man was, to his own surprise, embarrassed to be making the request.

"It sounds okay to me," Frank said. "I guess a little kitchen experience is a valuable thing to have."

"Of course it is," Orcrist agreed heartily. "I propose we celebrate it with a couple of glasses of this excellent Tamarisk brandy."

After downing his brandy Frank went to the kitchen to get acquainted with the layout. He found Pons sitting on a stool, nibbling a chunk of Jack cheese. The tall, skinny servant regarded Frank skeptically.

"Don't tell me you took it," he said.

"Matter of fact, I did," answered Frank. "What is it I do?"

Pons stood up and ran his fingers through his graying hair. "Well now, you'll find that kitchen work isn't as easy as painting." He peered at Frank, who said nothing. "But at least it's *honest* work." Frank smiled coldly.

Encouraged by Frank's silence, Pons grinned and took another bite of cheese. "Yessir," he said. "Liquor and books is all very well, but you don't get time for that sort of trash in here. You know what I say?"

"What do you say?"

"I say, if you've got time enough to lean, you've got time enough to clean. Now we don't have to get started on dinner for another two hours yet, so why don't you get a rag and a bucket of hot water and clean off the oven hood? And then after that you can clean out these drains. What?"

"I didn't say anything," said Frank.

"Well, see that you don't. I don't like noisy help." Pons took his cheese and left the room, on his lips the smile of the man who has had the last word.

Now *what,* thought Frank, have I done to provoke all that? He looked helplessly around himself at the kitchen. A big, gleaming oven stood in the center of the room. Around the walls were sinks and refrigerators and freezers. Years of airborne grease had darkened the yellow walls near the ceiling.

With a fatalistic sigh he began looking for a mop, a rag and a bucket.

When Pons returned at four, he criticized Frank's cleaning and asked him if his father and he had been accustomed to living in a pigpen.

"No," said Frank evenly. I will deal with this Pons fellow, he told himself, when the opportunity arises.

"Well, that's what anyone would think, to see the lazy-man job you did on these sinks." He looked around the room with a dissatisfied air. "It's high time we got started on dinner. And let me tell you, sonny, the best way to get on Sam's bad side is to serve him bad food."

Spare me your pompous master-chef act, thought Frank. And I'd like to see you call him Sam to his face.

"He's having eight guests to dinner tonight, and I'm serving them chicken curry. Chop a pound apiece of green onions and peanuts and put them in those silver bowls up there. Also, fill two more bowls with chutney and raisins. Then decant six bottles of the Rigby Chablis, which you'll find in the cooler yonder. Do you think you can handle all that?"

"Time will tell," said Frank with false gaiety, hoping it would annoy Pons, as he set out to find the onions and peanuts.

When the guests had all arrived, the table was set and dinner was ready to be served, Pons strode into the kitchen and grabbed Frank's arm.

"I've got to keep an eye on things here," he said. "You serve the dinner."

"Me? I don't know anything about it! I can't serve the damned dinner!"

"Keep your voice down. Of course you can serve it. I'm giving you a chance to . . . prove yourself under fire, you might say. Here's the wine. Go!"

Frank swung through the kitchen doors into the dining room, carrying a silver tray on which were perched two decanters of Chablis and eight glasses, all clinking dangerously. He had to set the tray down carefully on the tablecloth before he dared raise his eyes to the assembled company.

The first eyes he met were Orcrist's, who looked both surprised and angry. The two white-haired men flanking him looked amused, and their two thin old women regarded Frank with discreet distaste. Bad business, Frank thought, as he pulled desperately at the crystal stopper on one of the decanters. On the other side of the table sat a slender man with slick, gleaming hair; he winked at Frank. Next to him was a good-looking young woman with deep brown eyes and slightly kinky brown hair; very close to her sat a healthy-looking young man who was clearly holding the girl's hand under the table.

Some guests, Frank thought. He'd got the stopper out, poured a half inch of wine into one glass and gravely passed it to Orcrist. This may not be correct, he thought, but at least it's formal.

Orcrist raised his eyebrows, but took the glass. He sipped it and nodded. Frank filled the glass, and then proceeded to fill all the glasses, moving clockwise around the table. When he had finished he set the decanter in the middle of the table, bowed, and fled into the kitchen.

"How'd it go?" asked Pons.

"Not bad. What's next?"

"Salad. In five minutes. Put the dressing on it in four and a half minutes."

As Frank strode out carrying the salad bowl five minutes later, he felt a premonition of disaster. Pons had thrown a handful of garbanzo beans on top of the salad at the last minute, and Frank, foreseeing them rolling all over the table, thought it an unwise move.

I'll serve the pretty girl first, he thought. He walked smiling to her place and, holding the bowl in one hand, reached for the salad tongs with the other. Smooth, he told himself.

Pons had, earlier, set the bowl down in a puddle of salad oil, and now Frank's grip on the bowl slipped an inch. A garbanzo bean rolled off the mound of lettuce and plunked into the girl's wine. She squealed. Her escort turned a face of outrage on Frank, who tried to back away and perhaps get a new wine glass.

"Idiot!" barked the escort as he stood up, shoving his chair violently backward against Frank's leg. The greased salad bowl left Frank's hand, rolled over in the air, and landed on the brown-eyed girl's chest, from there sliding down into her lap. Covered with gleaming lettuce, carrots and garbanzo beans, the surprised girl looked like a tropical hillside.

"For God's *sake,* Frank!" boomed Orcrist after a stunned pause. "Go get Pons!"

Frank hurried into the kitchen. "You take over," he told Pons, and then went to his room, feeling monumentally inadequate.

After the guests had left, Orcrist asked Frank to accompany him on a walk. Frank nodded and fetched a coat. They walked for two blocks along an empty stretch of Sheol before Orcrist spoke.

"Bad show, there, Frank."

"That's true, sir."

They walked on, past another block.

"I am not going to relieve you of your kitchen duties, though. Oh, I know it was an accident! That's not what I mean. I think you should continue to work in the kitchen, under Pons' direction, for the same reason I'd tell you to keep trying to ride a horse that had thrown you, or to keep practicing fencing after you'd taken a bad cut. Don't let these things defeat you, eh?"

"Right," agreed Frank without much enthusiasm.

"Good. Kathrin Figaro's boyfriend wanted to cut your throat, by the way. I told him he'd probably need a bit of help, and he stormed out. Next time, spill the salad on him."

Frank laughed weakly.

"A penny to see a dancing dog?" came a plaintive cry from the alleymouth they were passing. Orcrist stepped aside and handed the old woman some coins before he and Frank continued their walk.

"That was Beardo's mother," Orcrist remarked. "They don't get along real well."

Frank didn't say anything.

The next time he saw Kathrin Figaro he was relaxing in Orcrist's sitting room, having finished his forgery of the difficult Monet canvas. He was dressed in an old pair of jeans and a T-shirt, over which he had thrown the white silk smoking jacket Beardo had given him.

The front door opened just as Frank was pouring himself a well-deserved (he told himself) glass of scotch. Assuming that it was Orcrist, he spoke casually over his shoulder. "I figured you wouldn't mind my taking a glass, sir," he said, and turned around to see Orcrist standing in the doorway with Miss Figaro on his arm.

"You've grown lax in your treatment of kitchen boys, Sam," said Miss Figaro sharply. She stepped forward and slapped the glass out of Frank's hand. It bounced on the carpet, splashing scotch on the bookshelves.

"I hate this sort of thing," declared Orcrist. "Kathrin, he *isn't* a kitchen boy. He's an apprenticed thief, and a junior partner of mine. Frank, pour yourself another glass. Pour me one too. Will you join us, Kathrin?"

"No," she said icily. "Why is he dressed like a hobo mandarin? And why do you have him serve dinner if he's a junior partner?" Plainly, she thought Orcrist was having a joke at her expense.

"I was doing that because we felt I'd be better off for some kitchen experience," explained Frank, who was beginning to enjoy this. "And I'm dressed in my painting clothes. This is a smoking jacket."

"He paints as well, does he?"

"Yes," Orcrist answered. "It's a hobby of his. Still lifes, puppies, sad children with big eyes—you know."

Kathrin looked close to tears. "Sam, if you and this horrible boy are making fun of me, I'll . . ."

"We're not, I swear," said Orcrist placatingly as he put his arm around her shoulders. "Frank, draw something, show her we're not kidding."

"All right." There was a salt shaker on the coffee table, a relic of a bout of tequila drinking the night before, and Frank shook salt onto the dark table top until it had a uniformly frosted look. Then, with his left forefinger, he drew a quick picture of Kathrin. It caught a likeness, and even conveyed some of her apparently habitual irritability.

"There, you see?" said Orcrist. "I wasn't kidding."

"You aren't a kitchen boy?"

"Not basically, no," Frank answered.

"Oh. Well then, I'm sorry I spilled your drink. No, I'm not! You ruined my dress."

"Let's forget all of it," said Orcrist, "and be friends."

"Okay," said Frank agreeably.

"All right." Kathrin still seemed sulky.

The afternoon progressed civilly, and once, when Orcrist left the room, Kathrin turned to Frank with a hesitant smile.

"Could you . . . teach me how to draw, sometime?"

She looks much younger when she smiles, he thought. I'll bet she's about my age.

"Sure," he said.

Rain was somehow falling down the sunlight shaft onto Orcrist's breakfast table. Frank sat watching it drip onto the remains of his scrambled eggs; he was puffing at a pipe and wondering how the devil pipe smokers kept the things lit. Across the table George Tyler was slumped dejectedly in a chair, his blond hair sticking out at odd angles from his head.

Orcrist walked in, carrying a plate of fried eggs and bacon and potatoes. "What's this?" he asked, nodding at the growing puddle of rain water.

"It's raining on the surface," said Frank. "I suppose we ought to put a pan under it." He resumed puffing on the pipe.

"Oh, your plate will do for now," Orcrist said. "What are you trying to smoke?"

Frank waved at a pack of tobacco lying on the table. Orcrist picked it up and stared at it. " 'Cherry Brandy Flavored.' Frank, you can't smoke *that*." He tossed it down. "Let me get you some *real* tobacco."

"And what's *real* tobacco?" asked Tyler irritably. It had been he who'd recommended the Cherry Brandy blend to Frank.

"Something with a lot of latakia in it," Orcrist said. "This fruit syrup stuff is no good for smoking; it's only fit for impressing ignorant girls."

Tyler shrugged, as if to say that that was reason enough to smoke it right there.

"Anyway, I have better things to talk about than bad tobacco," Orcrist went on. "Tomorrow night I'm giving a dinner for ten of the High Lords of the Subterranean Companions. I'm hiring three guys to help out in the kitchen; you and Pons will be in charge, Frank. We're going to have Giant Tacos, Beans Jaimé, and dark beer—I've got Pons out buying supplies now. I think you ought to be the beer steward, Frank; you simply stand by with a pitcher of it and refill any glasses that become less than half full."

"Doesn't sound bad," Frank said. "Will anyone I know be there?"

"No, she won't," said Orcrist.

The next afternoon Frank strolled into the kitchen, where Pons and the three new cooks were already at work. One of the new men was chopping bell peppers on a wooden board; another was stirring a pot of hot sauce; and the third was grating block after block of cheese. On a stool to one side sat Pons, criticizing their work and telling them what needed doing afterward.

"It's about time you got here," Pons said. "Keep an eye on these dopes for a while." He got up and strode out, shaking his head contemptuously.

"Oh, man," said one of the cooks. "Who *was* that guy?"

"His name's Pons," said Frank. "I don't like him either. Do you guys know how to do all this? Because I sure can't tell you."

"Oh, hell yes," said another. "We work in a restaurant together. We've been making this stuff since we were kids. And then old Bon-Bon comes in here and wants to tell me how to cut bell peppers."

"Well, cut them any way you want," said Frank.

The big oven was turned on, and the room heated up pretty quickly, especially when one of the cooks began frying the ground beef in two huge pans. Frank was only doing peripheral jobs, chopping onions and fetching tomatoes, but he soon found himself sweating like a long-distance runner.

"Listen," he said, "I'm ready for a beer. Who'll join me?"

They all assented, and Frank opened four bottles of Orcrist's favorite light beer. He passed these around, and then was amazed at how much more smoothly the kitchen ran when the cooks had bottles of beer beside them. There's some principle at work there, he thought.

The door was kicked open and Pons entered.

"You're letting them *drink*?" he gasped. He snatched all the bottles, which were empty now anyway, and flung them into a trash can. "Sam will hear about this," he snarled at Frank. "You'll be out of a job."

"I don't think so," Frank said.

"Clear out, Bon-Bon," said one of the cooks.

"You've gone too far," Pons whispered. "You can't undermine me. Tomorrow you'll be out on the *street*."

"Time will tell," smiled Frank.

"The guests are here," said Pons in a strangled voice. "Take out fifteen glasses and two pitchers of beer. Now!"

Frank did so, and managed without mishap to present each guest with a glass of the dark beer. There were ten, all older men, and they were dressed in fine clothes and wore decorated swords. When Frank had filled their glasses he stepped back from the table, but Orcrist beckoned him forward.

"Gentlemen," Orcrist said, "I'd like you to meet Francisco de Goya Rovzar, my junior partner." Orcrist introduced Frank to each lord in turn. Frank bowed respectfully to each, and then resumed his stewardship. The lords and Orcrist chatted and laughed among themselves, and Frank listened in from time to time, but found their talk either boring or incomprehensible.

Eventually Pons appeared, pushing a cart on which were set ten plates, each with a huge taco resting on it like a giant, lettuce-choked clam. The assembled lords exclaimed delightedly at the spectacle. Pons served them, and the guests began hesitantly prodding their tacos with forks. Frank was kept busy seeing that the glasses were filled and frequently had to dash to the kitchen for a fresh pitcher.

"Damn fine dinner, Sam," said Lord Tolley Christensen as he threw down his fork for the last time. The other lords all nodded agreement. "And I hope such dinners never become a thing of the past." Again they all nodded.

"Do you know, Tolley," spoke up Lord Rutledge, "I was walking alone the other day or night and an armed policeman, in the Transport uniform, tried to *arrest* me?"

"Times are worse than I thought," said Orcrist. "What did you do?"

"Oh, he drew his sword on me, so I killed him."

"How?" asked Tolley. "As one craftsman to another."

"He took my blade on the outside of his, in the high line, so I did a non-resisting parry and then just spiraled in over his bell guard, then under it, and nailed him."

"He must not have been real sharp," put in Orcrist. "I'd never have given you time to do all that."

"Well, I *am* fairly fast," Rutledge said. "Besides, that's the only move you can make if the other guy takes your blade that way."

"Well," spoke Frank, "you *could* parry and riposte in prime."

"What?" growled Rutledge, shifting around in his chair.

"I said you could have parried him in prime. One, you know."

"What the hell do you mean?"

Frank was beginning to suspect that he shouldn't have spoken. "Never mind, sir," he said. "I'm sorry I interrupted."

"Wait a minute," said Orcrist. "Here, Frank, use my sword. Rutledge, will you let me borrow yours for a moment? Thank you. Now, Frank, *slowly,* show me what you mean."

Frank put the pitcher of beer down on a side table, took the sword in his left hand, and crouched into the on guard position. "All right," he said. "Take my blade in sixte—come in over my sword arm."

Orcrist extended his blade as he was told. When the point was within a foot of Frank's chest, Frank suddenly inverted his sword by flipping his elbow up and deflected Orcrist's blade to the side; then he riposted, thrusting at Orcrist's chest with his arm twisted around so that his thumb and fingers were uppermost.

"That's parrying in prime," he said, holding the position with his point an inch or two away from Orcrist's chest. "It's a bit awkward, but if you use it at the right moment it's unanswerable."

"The boy's making fun of us," growled Rutledge.

"Maybe not," said Orcrist. "Let's try a few thrusts, Frank. Gently."

For the first minute Frank let Orcrist do all the work, and simply parried every thrust without even stepping back. Orcrist's thrusts became faster and stronger, but Frank was able to hold him off effortlessly. He can't really be trying, Frank thought. These attacks are fairly quick, but there's almost no strategy.

"Shall I begin replying?" asked Frank.

"Any time you like," panted Orcrist.

Frank parried the next attack and feinted in quarte, then riposted in sixte to Orcrist's chest, poking him lightly with the point. He then tapped Orcrist's elbow twice in a row, and then did a faultless bind-eight culminating in a full extension lunge. He held the position for a moment; his rear leg straight out behind him, lead leg bent in a ninety-degree angle, weapon arm straight and his sword point pressing a button on Orcrist's coat. Then he relaxed back into the on guard posture. It felt good to get back into the disciplines of fencing—it reminded him of the old days with Tom in the Strand Fencing Academy.

"There is . . . no end to your talents, Frank," Orcrist panted. "Where did you study? Who taught you all this?"

"Jacob Strand, in a fencing school about twenty miles north and ten miles west."

"Hmm." Orcrist sat down and finished his beer. "Do you remember the words of our old friend Aurelius, Frank?"

"Yes, I do. 'The universe is change.' Might he have added 'and talented lads are soon promoted out of the kitchen'?"

"Consider it added," said Orcrist.

BOOK TWO

The Swordsman

CHAPTER 1

Frank delivered a final poke to the man-shaped rubber pad that was nailed to the wall—got him right in the throat!—and put down his sword. He unbuttoned his fencing jacket and sat down in a nearby canvas chair. *Now where the hell is old Rutledge?* Frank glanced at the clock on the wall. *He's ten minutes late.*

Frank stood up, crossed to the open window, and leaned on the sill. He watched the littered tide of the Leethee flow past, its blackness highlighted by dancing glints of light cast by the lamps that hung from the tunnel roof. The river was wide through here; and he sometimes saw festive barges and solitary canoes wend their way up or downstream.

The Rovzar Fencing School had been open for almost six weeks. The location was good (Orcrist had helped him find a good river-view building to rent in a respectable neighborhood), and he already had enough students to pay the rent and keep him busy. Without exception, his students were ranking members of the Subterranean Companions; Orcrist pointed out that there was no reason to teach fencing secrets to strangers.

A chittering screech sounded in the adjoining room, and Frank turned around with a smile as Rutledge entered, carrying his pet monkey on his shoulder.

"Down, Bones!" Rutledge commanded. Bones, a wild-eyed spider monkey, leaped from the lord's shoulder onto a chair and began gnawing the fabric.

"Damn all monkeys," growled Rutledge. He shrugged off his velvet coat and took a fencing jacket out of a closet. "You must have washed these, Rovzar! This one seems to have shrunk."

"It's possible," Frank said. *It's not the jacket's fault,* he thought. *It's beer and pork pie that have tightened the fit.* "Have you been practicing your on guard?"

"Yes, yes. It's invincible." Rutledge flipped a wire-mesh fencing mask over his face and selected one of the practice épées hanging on a wall rack. He flexed the blade a few times and then crouched, the blade held forward and ready. "How's that?" he asked.

Frank put on a mask and picked up his own épée.

"Not bad," he said, critically examining Rutledge's posture. "Let's see if you can maintain it."

He saluted, and they began to bout, starting slow and relaxed. Each point hovered around the other man's bell guard, never getting a clear shot at a wrist or forearm. After a minute, Frank began to let his elbow show beneath, apparently unguarded. He saw Rutledge tense with preparation, and then the lord's blade flashed out at Frank's elbow. Just as he saw him extend, though, Frank went up on his toes and straightened his sword arm, catching Rutledge in the bicep with the sword's covered tip. Rutledge's sword wavered in empty air.

"That's a favorite trick of mine," Frank explained. "Lure him below with your elbow and then go in over the top when he goes for it. You've got to be quick, though, or you'll have a hole in your arm and an opponent who thinks you're an idiot."

"Give me a gun anytime," Rutledge said. "When I was a boy we had guns, you know. Kill a man from across a courtyard! None of this damned personal contact."

"Yes," Frank said, "but a gun doesn't take much skill. Any stable boy could kill you with a gun. But how many people can kill you with a sword?"

"Not many! Especially now that I'm taking your lessons. Your damnably expensive lessons." Frank shrugged. "How do I compare with your other students, Rovzar? I know Orcrist and a few others are studying your methods. Has Tolley come in?"

"No, Lord Christensen doesn't think he needs any help. He told Orcrist that the day he goes to a painter for fencing lessons will be the day he sends Costa his two virgin daughters. Not real soon, in other words. Anyhow, speaking honestly, I'd say you're my most rapidly improving student."

"No kidding?" replied Rutledge in a pleased tone of voice. "In that case have another try at teaching me that eye shot."

The next half hour was spent in showing the elderly lord a particularly vicious bind in sixte that, properly executed, landed one's point forcefully in the opponent's eye. Rutledge was beginning to catch on, and after Frank had three times taken a blow to his mask he called a recess.

"I pity any sewer vagabonds who try to rob you," Frank said. He opened a cabinet and took a bottle of cheap *vino blanco* out of an ice bucket. "Will you join me in some wine, my lord?"

"Good God, yes. Swordplay is dry work."

Rutledge took a glass of wine and gulped half of it right off. Bones climbed up to his belt buckle and made gross smacking sounds, so Rutledge handed the monkey the glass, and the hairy creature drank the rest of it with relish.

"Can monkeys get drunk?" asked Rutledge.

"I suppose so. Want me to give him a glass?"

"Why don't you."

Frank poured a third, slightly bigger glass, and handed it to Bones. The monkey took it to a corner to drink, and Frank poured another glass to replace Rutledge's slobbery one.

"There is a nice feint you can use if your man bends his arm as he retreats," said Frank, crossing to the windowsill and sitting down on it. "Done right, it puts your point into his kneecap. I'll have to show it to you next."

"Why do so few of your moves hit the body, Rovzar?" asked Rutledge. "Seems to me you're just wasting time hitting your opponent in the arm and the knee."

"If your opponent knows anything about swords, you generally can't *get* to the body," Frank told him. "Before your point hits his stomach or chest, his point is buried in your forearm. A full-extension lunge is a beautiful thing to do when you're practicing in a fencing school, but I'd certainly never do one in an alley against an opponent with an untipped weapon."

Frank was suddenly aware of breathing sounds echoing softly behind him, from the river. He leaped off of the sill and turned around, pushing his sweaty hair out of his eyes. Peripherally, he saw Rutledge come up beside him and stare wordlessly out.

The river was jammed. Boats, rafts and logs covered its surface, and every floating thing carried silent, staring passengers. Children huddled in blankets in the bows of rowboats, while haggard old men worked the oars; string-tied bundles and frying pans and guitars were roped in piles on rafts that old women paddled along with boards; sunken-eyed men floated past with their arms around logs, their bodies immersed in water up to their chests. None of these drifters spoke, even to each other.

"What in God's name?" began Rutledge. Bones climbed unsteadily up his master's leg and perched beside him on the windowsill.

"Who are you?" called Frank to the people on the nearest raft. "Where are you all going?"

A man stood up on the raft. He looked about forty, with brown hair beginning to go gray at the temples; he wore overalls with no shirt under them. "We're farmers," he said, "from the Goriot Valley." The echoes of his own voice seemed to upset him, and he sat down again.

"Where are you going?" repeated Frank.

"To the Deptford Sea," answered a woman from a heavily-loaded rowboat. "We can't go overland because we don't have travel permits."

"Give us the monkey," called a boy perched on a log. "We don't have food. Give us the monkey, at least."

"Yes, the monkey, give it to us," came a shout from farther out in the river. In a moment the water-borne fugitives were chorusing madly: "The monkey!" "God save you for your gift of the monkey!" "My boy here hasn't eaten! Throw the monkey to me!"

Frank looked down at Bones, who squatted drunkenly on the stone coping of the window, blinking his eyes at the clamoring floaters. The monkey's stomach was jerking up and down like an adam's apple, and as Frank watched, the beast leaned forward and noisily vomited *vino blanco* into the water.

"Give us the damned monkey! We'll have it! You can't keep it from us!" moaned and wailed the refugees. Frank leaned out and pulled the heavy shutters closed. He latched them, and then slid a bolt through the iron staples.

"Let's close up shop," he said to Rutledge. "You were my last pupil of the day anyway."

They hung up the swords and jackets, blew out the lamps, and locked the front door behind them. The Rovzar Fencing School was in a fashionable understreet neighborhood, so they talked freely and left their swords in the scabbards as they walked. Spicy cooking smells wafted out of restaurant doors, and Frank was beginning to get hungry.

"Have you paid off your bond to Orcrist yet?" Rutledge asked.

"No," Frank answered, "but with the money I'm making from the fencing classes, I should have it paid off in a month or so."

"You'll be getting digs of your own then, I expect."

"Yes. I've been looking at apartments here in the Congreve district, and I think I could afford to live near the school, which would be handy."

They rounded a corner and found themselves facing four uniformed Transport policemen, each armed with a standard-issue rapier. Their faces showed tan in the lamplight, proof that they were new to understreet work.

"Good evening, gentlemen," grinned one of the Transports. "May I see your identification and employment cards?"

"Since when have they been necessary for understreet citizens?" queried Rutledge with icy politeness.

"Since Duke Costa signed a law saying so, weasel! Now trot 'em out or come along with us to the station." Each policeman's hand was on his sword hilt.

Rutledge drew his sword with a salty curse. Frank and the four Transports followed suit simultaneously. One of the Transports lunged at Rutledge, who parried and jabbed the man in the wrist. Bones, terrified, leaped from the lord's shoulder to the ground.

"Nicely done!" called Frank to Rutledge as two of the Transports centered on him. He feinted ferociously at one, and the man retreated a full two steps. The other man aimed a beat at Frank's blade, but Frank dropped his point to elude it and then gored the man deeply in the shoulder. The clanging and rasp of the swords rang up and down the street. Frank stole another glance at Rutledge and saw the lord thrusting furiously at one of his opponents.

"Watch your weapon arm!" Frank shouted. "Hide behind your bell guard! Don't be impatient!" Frank held his two men off by whirling his point in a continuous horizontal figure eight. It was dangerous, but it gained him a breathing space. After a few seconds the shoulder-wounded Transport got angry and ran at Frank in an ill-considered fleche attack; Frank stepped away from the blade and drove his point through the man's neck. The other policeman was close behind, so Frank hopped backward as he pulled his sword free. Bright red blood jetted as the stricken Transport sank to his knees on the street.

"How goes it, my lord?" Frank called as he crossed swords with his remaining opponent.

"I poked one of them in the belly," gasped Rutledge. "Be careful . . . he's crawling around in the middle of the street. Don't let him get you . . . from below."

Frank glimpsed the man, who was on his hands and knees on the pavement, and kept clear of him. Frank tried two feints on his own man, but the policeman was being cautiously defensive—maybe waiting for reinforcements? Frank wondered.

"I can't quite get that . . . sixte bind," panted Rutledge. "How do you . . . take the blade to start it?"

"Watch," called Frank. He hopped forward, took his opponent's sword from below, and then whirled his point in around the other man's bell guard; he lunged, and the point punctured the eye and brain of the unfortunate Transport.

"Thus," said Frank, holding the position for Rutledge's benefit. "Begin it like a standard counter six. And finish with a moderate lunge."

"I see," said Rutledge. Frank straightened up to watch his pupil. After a moment the thief-lord leaped forward, caught the man's blade, and, lunging, spun his point, into the man's eye. The Transport dropped like a puppet with its strings cut.

"Well done, my lord!" Frank nodded. "You see the advantage of practice. Now let's get out of this incriminating street."

Rutledge quickly dispatched the wounded policeman, and Bones, who had been sitting on a curb during the encounter, hopped up on Rutledge's shoulder. Lights had gone on and people were leaning out of windows, but Frank knew none of them would ever tell anything to any authorities. It was entirely possible, in fact, that the local citizenry would dispose of the bodies and weapons, leaving the Transport with, apparently, four more cases of unexplained desertion. Frank and Lord Rutledge strolled away down a cross street as casually as they would if they were leaving a poetry reading.

Frank escorted Rutledge home and then walked thoughtfully back toward Orcrist's dwelling. He was upset, but could not precisely say why. The killing of the four Transports tonight seemed stupid—not cruel or murderous, because those four officers certainly intended to do him harm—simply stupid. Why do I feel that way? he asked himself. Actually, it was quite a brave thing, two against four.

Brave? his mind sneered. You and Rutledge are superior swordsmen. You were safe. It wasn't bravery, it was showing off. You want to know what would have been a brave thing to do? To have pulled the trigger of Orcrist's gun, that night at the Doublon Festival. To have avenged your father.

All the sour black misery of his father's death and his own exile rose up and choked him. Tears stung his eyes; he clenched his teeth and drove his fist against the brick wall of Ludlow Alley. He stood there motionless for a full minute, leaning against the wall; then he straightened up and strode off, impatient with himself for having indulged this maudlin side of his nature.

When he entered Orcrist's sitting room he had forced himself to become quite cheerful. He poured a good-sized glass of scotch, took a deep sip of it, and then set it down while he fetched his pipe and tobacco. Orcrist had brought him a can of good Turkish tobacco, thickly laced with spicy black latakia, and he was beginning to like the stuff. Now he was even able to keep the pipe lit. Soon the pungent smoke hung in layers across the room as he absorbed himself with a book of A. E. Housman's poetry.

"Well, Frank!" boomed Orcrist's voice. "I didn't expect to see you this early. Didn't Rutledge show up?"

"Oh, he was there," answered Frank. "We broke up early, that's all. By the way, it's been an eventful evening. The Leethee, if you haven't yet heard, is *packed* with fugitive farmers from the Goriot Valley, all headed for the Deptford Sea—the south coast, I guess. And then on the way home Rutledge and I were stopped by four Transport cops, and we had to kill them all."

"They were down here?" asked Orcrist. "Understreet?"

"That's right. Four of them, asking for identification cards."

Orcrist shook his head. "Something, I'm afraid, has got to be done."

Frank nodded and put down his pipe. "I've been thinking about it," he said. "The Subterranean Companions are a well-organized group, armed and more-or-less disciplined. What if we recruit and arm a few hundred of these homeless farmers and then overthrow the whole Transport-Costa government?"

Orcrist chuckled as he poured himself a scotch. *"Overthrow* is an easy word to say, Frank."

"But we could!" Frank insisted. "The Transports are having all kinds of financial difficulties—they couldn't maintain a long siege. And Costa is no military genius."

"No," said Orcrist, sipping his drink, "he isn't. But I'll tell you what he is. He's the blood son of Topo, and that's what counts. Even if we did, somehow, take over the palace and kill Costa, we couldn't hold it because we have no one with royal blood to set up as a successor. And that is a prerequisite. The citizens of Octavio may not be fond of Costa, and they aren't, you know, but they're bound up by centuries of tradition. They won't even consider accepting a duke who isn't of the royal blood."

"Ignorant cattle," muttered Frank, aware in spite of himself that he, too, was unable to picture a duke who was not the descendant of a lot of other dukes.

"But," said Orcrist thoughtfully, "we might figure out a way to keep Understreet Munson, at least, free of Transport influence. I'll have to bring the matter up at the next meeting. Anyway, stop bothering your brains with politics and go put on a clean shirt. I've invited Kathrin Figaro over for a late glass of sherry."

Frank stood up. "Righto," he said, heading for the hallway. "Oh," he said, turning, "I was just curious—I don't suppose there's any *truth* to George Tyler's stories about being Topo's son?"

Orcrist shook his head. "Come on, Frank. You've heard his stories. George is a good friend; and a moderately good poet, but a prince he is not."

"I didn't really think so," said Frank, leaving the room.

Just as Frank re-entered, buttoning the cuff of a new shirt, a knock sounded at the door. Frank threw himself into his chair and snatched up his pipe, then nodded to Orcrist, who proceeded to open the door.

"Kathrin!" he said. "Come in. You remember Frank Rovzar?"

"Of course," smiled Kathrin as Frank stood up and kissed her hand.

Orcrist took Kathrin's badger-skin stole and went to hang it up while Frank poured three glasses of sherry.

"There you are," he smiled, handing her one of them.

"Thank you. Was there a fire in here? I smell burning rugs or something."

"That's my new tobacco."

"Oh? What happened to that wonderful cherry stuff you were smoking before? That smelled delicious."

"I think he lost his taste for it," said Orcrist. "Kathrin, tell Frank about your new job."

"Oh, yes. Frank, I've got a job in a dress shop on the surface! I'm a fashion designer. So you see you aren't the only one around here who can draw." Orcrist smiled wickedly and winked at Frank. "What were you reading there?" she asked, pointing at Frank's book.

"A. E. Housman's poetry," Frank answered. "Have you ever read any of it?"

"No, but I love poetry. In fact, I wrote a poem last week. Would you like to hear it?"

"Sure," answered Frank. "Bring it over some time. Would you like some more sherry?"

"No thank you. But I have the poem right here, in my purse." She rummaged about in the purse while Frank and Orcrist exchanged worried glances. "Ah, here it is." Then, in an embarrassingly over-animated voice, she began to read:

> "Love, called the bird of my heart.
> Do you hear it, the sweet song?
> The children go dancing through the flowers
> And I kiss your eyes like the sun kisses the wheat."

After a moment Kathrin raised her eyes. "It's very personal," she explained.

Frank caught Orcrist's eye and looked quickly away. My God, he thought, I can't laugh! He bit his tongue, but still felt dangerously close to exploding. Picking up his glass, he drained his sherry in one gulp, and choked on it. He coughed violently and thus managed to get rid of the most insistent edge of his laughter.

"Are you all right?" asked Kathrin.

"Oh yes," he assured her, gaspingly. "But some of the sherry went down the wrong way."

"Well, what did you think of my poem?"

"Oh, well, it . . . it's very good." Behind her Frank could see Orcrist doing bird imitations with his hands. I will not laugh, Frank vowed. "I liked it."

"I feel poetry should just . . . *flow* from the heart," she went on. "Do you know what I mean?"

"Precisely," nodded Orcrist. "Now, I'm an old man and I need my rest, so I'll be turning in. Why don't you take Kathrin for a ride down the Tirnog Canal, Frank? That'd be pleasant, and I don't imagine any of the Goriot fugitives would have wound up there."

Frank nodded, grateful that the conversation had been steered away from the subject of Kathrin's horrible poem. "That sounds good to me," he said. "Have you ever taken a boat ride down the Tirnog?"

"No," said Kathrin. "Is it safe?"

"Absolutely," Orcrist assured her. "Even if it weren't, Frank is one of the five best swordsmen in Munson Understreet, and maybe on the whole planet. You've got nothing to fear." He fetched her wrap, draped it about her shoulders, and surreptitiously slipped Frank a five-malory note. Frank got his coat and strapped on his sword and they were ready to go.

"So long, Sam," said Kathrin as they were leaving. "At least *Frank* doesn't run down at ten o'clock."

"I envy him his youth," smiled Orcrist as he closed the door.

CHAPTER 2

A night wind sighed eerily down the length of the Tirnog Canal, wringing soft random chords from the many Aeolian harps and wind chimes hung from the low stone ceiling.

Kathrin leaned on Frank's shoulder. Frank put his arm around her—it seemed in some undefined way to be expected of him.

Paper lanterns, red, green and yellow, glowed everywhere, casting a dim fantastic radiance. By their fitful light were visible several ponderous, ribbon-hung barges rocking in the water, each one piloted by a tall, hooded gondolier who carried a long punting pole. Frank waved at the nearest boatman and the man pushed his barge to the padded dock.

"Passage for two," Frank told him, "to Quartz Lane and back."

"Two malories," said the pilot. Frank handed him the five and got change. He helped Kathrin aboard, and they sat close together on the wide leather seat in the bow while the gondolier pushed away from the dock. Frank trailed the fingers of his left hand in the cool water, and eventually put his right arm around Kathrin, who obligingly snuggled up under his chin.

Neither of them spoke as the barge drifted down the tunnel; the only sound was the soft bump of the pilot's pole as he corrected the barge's course from time to time. As the distance grew between them and the dock, the paper lanterns became fewer; soon they were in total darkness. Then, gradually, dim moonlight began to filter through cracks and holes in the ancient masonry that passed by over their heads, for Tirnog Canal, in several places, reached the surface, and the roof that had been built over it in such places was in bad repair. Some of the holes were a foot across, and the stars were plainly visible; and once Frank saw, like a thin chalk line across a distant blackboard, the luminous vapor trail of a Transport freighter hanging in the night sky.

Without premeditation Frank leaned over and kissed Kathrin, and was half surprised to find that she didn't object. Afterward she rested her head on his chest and he thoughtfully stroked her long brown hair.

At Quartz Lane, an abandoned stretch of once stately houses, the pilot laboriously turned the barge around and began working his way back up the slow stream, the thumping of his pole sounding regularly now, like a pulse.

When Frank got back to Orcrist's place he found a courier nodding sleepily in the easy chair. It was after midnight.

"Are you . . . uh . . . Francisco de Goya Rovzar?" the courier asked as Frank shed his coat.

"Yes. Why?"

"I have a letter for you from his majesty King Blanchard, and I've got to deliver it directly into your hands. Here. Now goodnight." Abruptly the courier put on his hat and left.

"Goodnight," said Frank automatically. Blanchard wrote a letter to *me?* He remembered his only sight of the old king, burly and white-bearded and gruff, at the first meeting of the Subterranean Companions he had attended.

He broke the seal and unfolded the letter.

> My dear Rovzar; I would be very pleased if you would
> drop round my chambers on Cochran Street this Thursday
> for the purpose of discussing and perhaps demonstrating
> fencing techniques. I hear from various acquaintances that
> you are very good.   —BLANCHARD

Well, by God, thought Frank. It's quite the social climber I'm becoming. I'll show this to Orcrist in the morning. Right now all I want to do is sleep.

He put the letter on the table and stumbled off to bed. He woke up once during the night when a deep, echoing rumble shook the building; but it had stopped by the time he came fully awake, and so he just rolled over and went back to sleep.

The next morning Frank put on his smoking jacket and wandered out to the breakfast room. The table was empty.

"Pons!" Frank called hoarsely. "Dammit, Pons! Where's my breakfast, you lazy weasel?" He knew Pons hated to be yelled at.

Orcrist entered the room. It was the first time Frank had ever seen him unshaven. Something, clearly, has happened, Frank told himself.

"What's up?" he asked.

"All kinds of things, Frank." Orcrist sat down and rubbed his eyes tiredly. "There was a demonstration last night on the surface, near Seventh and Shank. Shopkeepers or something, a whole crowd, hollering and demanding that Costa break all connections with the Transport. And from somewhere, God knows where, came flying an airplane with the Transport insignia. The damned thing circled the square where this demonstration was taking place, twice, and then dropped a bomb right in the middle of it."

"A *bomb?*" Frank was incredulous.

"That's right. Wiped out most of the shopkeepers, of course, but more to the point it tore a hole through four understreet levels, and caused collapses in five below that. The Companions alone have lost an estimated hundred members. Pons's wife was among the casualties."

"Pons was *married?*"

"Yes, he was. She went insane about four years ago and was committed. He put her in an old asylum up on Seventh; this explosion shook loose the roof of her cell."

"Bad business," said Frank.

"You could say so. Well then—" Orcrist looked up at him, "—any news on the home front?"

"Oh, yes! There is." Frank went into the next room and got the letter from Blanchard. "Look at this."

Orcrist blinked over the letter for a minute, then put it down. "Not bad, Frank," he said. "I guess fencing has been your true calling all along."

"Maybe so." Frank stepped to the kitchen door. "Wait two minutes and I'll make some eggs and toast and coffee," he said.

"Thank you, Frank," said Orcrist. "Why don't you throw some rum in the coffee, eh?"

"Aye aye."

Later in the morning Frank went to see the crater where the bomb had fallen. He approached it from a little alley about two levels below the surface, so that when he stood on the alley's crumbling lip he could look down into a rubble-and-debris strewn valley in which workmen stumbled about, or up at the blue sky framed by the ragged outlines of the crater. Curls of smoke eddied up from the wreckage below, and fire hoses on the surface streets were sending arching streams of water into the abyss.

Six men were in Orcrist's sitting room when Frank returned; they wore muddy jeans and boots, and had a wet, mildewy smell about them.

"Who's the kid?" growled one of them, jerking his thumb in Frank's direction.

"Partner of mine," said Orcrist, who strode in from the hallway, knotting a scarf around his neck. "Hullo Frank. We're going to go drop bricks on a party of Transport sewer-explorers. Want to come along?"

"Sure, I guess so. *What* is it you're going to do?"

"Oh, the Transport cops are puzzled by all the underground tunnels this bomb has revealed. They didn't know the understreet city extended that far. They'd be surprised if they knew how far it does extend! Anyway, they're sending exploring crews down into the crater to follow any tunnels they find and arrest whoever gets in their way. So we're going to go impede them."

"Yeah, I'll help."

"Good. Get a sealskin jacket and boots; there are three branches of the Leethee spewing around down there looking for new channels. And take a good hunting knife out of that closet. There'll be no room for swords, but there's always room for a knife."

Frank quickly slipped into a jacket and boots and put a knitted wool cap on his head. Then, after selecting a sturdy knife, he was ready to go.

The eight of them left Orcrist's place silently and strode away down the low, torch-lit corridors. Bands of furtive, hurrying men were no unusual sight in the understreet city, and Orcrist and his companions caused no comment. They made their way northwest, filing down narrow walkways, going up and down stairs and walking along the sidewalks of big streets. These were areas unfamiliar to Frank, and he made sure to follow the others closely.

After about twenty minutes of walking Orcrist pulled them all aside into a little yard filled with garbage cans. "We split up here," he said. "Lambert, you come with me and we'll circle north and come in from the other side. Poach, you take Frank and go west around the crater. Wister and Colin, try to come up from below. Bob, you and Daryl wait here ten minutes and then go straight in. Everybody got that?"

They all nodded and broke up into pairs. Frank's partner, Poach, was a weather-beaten, middle-aged man with three fingers missing from his left hand. "Okay, kid," he said hoarsely, "follow me and do what I do." He had not looked directly at Frank yet, and did not now—he simply set off down the nearest east-west cross street. The older man had very long legs and a quick pace, and Frank had to trot to keep up with him. An uneven muted roar was becoming audible, and Frank knew it must be coming from the disrupted sections of the Leethee.

After a few blocks they took a right turn, which had them facing north, and Frank saw bright daylight at the end of the street; as his eyes grew accustomed to the glare he saw the jagged, tumbled wooden beams that were silhouetted against the brightness.

"This is it," whispered Poach. "Move slow and don't make no noise." Frank saw that Poach had his knife out, so he took his out too. He looked around, and realized that the last couple of streets had been completely empty. It's like sandcrabs, he thought. You dig a hole, let the sunlight in, and they all burrow deeper down, back into the darkness.

A harsh voice broke the quiet: "Tommy, get over here. They got more tunnels down here than an anthill." There were sounds of splashing footsteps and another voice, presumably Tommy's, spoke. "Captain, the whole floor is swaying on this level, and that damned river is thrashing around only one level below us. I haven't seen one person yet, and I say we should clear *out* of this lousy maze."

Poach made a "wait here" gesture to Frank and set off silently in the direction of the two voices. Frank stood absolutely still in the semi-darkness, clutching his knife and breathing through his mouth in order to hear better. Tommy has a point, he thought absently; the floor is swaying a little. A gray and white cat hurried by nervously, tail held high and eyes darting about. Frank tried to attract it by scratching his fingernails on a wooden gatepost, but the cat, not in a playful mood, didn't stop.

A shrill, jabbering yell was abruptly wrenched out of someone's lungs a block away. "He's killing me, he's killing me, help me for God's sake!" Frank jumped, dropped his knife, picked it up again, and ran off in the direction of the desperate shouting. More yells echoed up ahead: "Look out, Wister, over your head!" "Not *me,* idiot!" "*Get* him, will someone once and for all *get* him?"

Frank rounded a corner, running as fast as he could, and found himself in the midst of it. Two men in Transport uniforms were down and motionless on the street, and Orcrist was chasing a third, waving his knife like a madman. One of Orcrist's companions sat against a wall, white-faced, pressing his stomach with blood-wet hands. Two more Transport cops burst out of an alley at Frank's left, and one of them drove his knife at Frank's chest. The blade ripped his coat, but missed hitting flesh, and before the man could recover Frank drove his own knife into the Transport's side until he could feel the fabric of the man's jacket with his knuckles. The other one clubbed Frank with a blackjack in the left ear, and Frank went to his knees, dropping his knife. The cop raised his own knife, but Poach kicked the man in the stomach and cut his throat as he buckled.

Frank was trying to clear his head and stand up when the angle of the street pavement changed. He had fallen onto a level expanse, but by the time he struggled into a sitting position the street was slanted like a roof. Panicky yells echoed on all sides, so he knew he was not imagining it. The floor is collapsing, he told himself. That's the only explanation.

With a thundering, snapping crash the ancient masonry of the floor gave way like a trap door; Frank tumbled through a board fence, rolled over a collapsing wall and then plummeted through thirty feet of dust-choked air into deep, cold rushing water. The impact knocked the breath out of him and he was pulled far under the surface by savagely pounding whirlpools and undertows. Rocks and lumber spun all around him in the dark water, buffeting his ribs and back. Very dimly, he thought that he would not survive this. He convulsively gasped water, and then was racked by gagging coughs. Even if he could have mustered the strength to swim, he no longer knew which way was up.

He collided hard with a row of stationary metal bars. It must be some kind of grating or something, jammed across the stream, he thought. I could climb it and maybe get my head above water. *Why bother?* said another part of his mind. You've already gone through all the pain of dying—why not get it over with? You've earned your death: take it.

Working by instinct, his mind ordered his arms and legs to pull him upward against the wrenching of the cold water. In a few seconds his head was above the foaming surface and he was retching water, trying with desperate animal gasps to get air into his misused lungs.

He hung there for five full minutes, until the act of breathing did not require all of his concentration. Then he pulled himself along to the right, hoping that this gate, or whatever it was, was braced against the bank; there was absolutely no light, and he had to work by touch. A couple of times he felt the gate slide an inch or two, but it did not pull loose. Eventually he found his shoulder brushing against the wet bricks of a wall—that's all it was, just a brick wall with the rushing flood splashing against it. There was no passageway, so Frank simply hunched there on his perch of metal bars, with one hand braced against the bricks, and wept into the stream.

After a while he gathered his strength and began inching his way across to the other side, clinging tightly to the bars and trying to keep his body out of the water to avoid the wood and debris that were constantly colliding with the gate. Groping blindly in the darkness, he eventually found a rectangular opening that might once have framed a door. He managed to scramble into it and crawl a few yards up the passageway beyond. Then, free from the danger of drowning, he collapsed on the stone floor and surrendered his consciousness.

Someone was tugging at his hair. "Lemme 'lone," he muttered. To his intense annoyance it didn't stop. He dozed, thinking, I'll just wait till they give up and go away. Suddenly he realized that he was cold, colder than he had ever been. I can't sleep, he realized. I've got to get blankets, fast.

He sat up, and heard a dozen tiny creatures scamper chittering away into the dark. Mice, by God! Eating my hair! "Hah!" he croaked, to scare them. He'd meant to yell, but a croak was all he could come up with. He crouched in the stone corridor, clasping his knees and shivering uncontrollably. I'm naked, he noticed. No, that isn't quite right. I've still got my boots on, and my brass ear is hanging around my throat like a necklace. If there was any light I'd be an odd spectacle.

He vaguely remembered his near-drowning and realized in a detached way that he probably needed first aid pretty badly. He stood up on knees that refused to work together, and staggered up the passageway, arms out before him to feel for obstacles. If I get through all this, he thought, I'll stay home the next time Orcrist wants to go on an adventure.

John Bollinger was a religious man and took no part in the sinful society of Munson Understreet. He subsisted on fish and mushrooms and lived in a tiny one-room house that had belonged to his father. He had four books—a bible, a copy of *Paradise Lost,* the *Divina Commedia,* and Butler's *Lives of the Saints.* He always said, even when no one was listening, that to have more books than that was vanity.

He had heard the explosion during the night, but figured it was just a judgment on someone, and he forgot about it. He was looking at the Doré illustrations in his Milton when, the next afternoon, there came a knock at his door.

"Who knocks?" asked John.

There was no answer, aside from a confused muttering.

Rising fearlessly from his table, John strode to the door and flung it open. Confronting him was the strangest apparition he'd ever seen.

It was, as John was later to describe it to his pastor, "the likeness of a young man, naked and blue-colored. He wore curious shoes, and an indecipherable medallion about his neck on a string, and his hair was cut in a barbaric tonsure."

"What seekest thou?" gasped John.

"Clothes, for God's sake. Hot soup. Brandy."

"Aye, come in. Sit down. Of what order are you?"

"What?"

"What order do you belong to?"

"I don't belong to any order," Frank said. Seeing the old man frown, he added, off the top of his head, "I'm an independent. Freelance."

"An anchorite! I see. Here. You can use this blanket to cover your shame. Will you join me in some fish and mushrooms?"

"Will I ever!"

Half an hour later Frank was beginning to pull himself together. The food and strong tea that John had given him had revived him, and he felt capable now of finding his way back to Orcrist's apartment. I wonder if he managed to survive that street-fall? he thought. The last time he had seen Orcrist, he was chasing that Transport *away* from the collapsing street. He must think I've had it, though. I'd better get back quick.

"Thank you for your hospitality to a naked stranger," he said, standing up and wrapping the blanket around himself like a robe. "I will repay you."

"Don't repay me," John said. "Just do the same some day for some other homeless wanderer."

"You bet," Frank said, shaking the old man's hand. "Can you tell me how to get to Sheol from here?"

"We all go to Sheol eventually," said John with a somber frown, "and we'd better be prepared."

"I guess that's true." Poor devil, he thought. Brain warped from a diet of fish. A lesson to us all. Frank crossed to the door and opened it. "So long," he said, "and thanks again."

It was chilly in the tunnels, and Frank was glad to have the blanket. He hurried southeast, numbed feet beating on the cobblestones, and finally did, as John had predicted, get to Sheol, where he turned left. He was wondering what he'd do if some understreet vagabonds were to attack him, because his strength and endurance were very nearly gone. As it happened, though, none did; he wasn't the type of wanderer that would tempt a thief.

After he'd found Sheol the rest of the trip was easy, and within ten minutes he was turning the emergency hide-a-key in Orcrist's front door lock. He swung the door open. The front room was empty, so he stumbled to the bathroom and began putting iodine and bandages on his various cuts and gouges.

Nothing seems to be broken, he thought, wincing as he probed a bruise over his ribs. Not obviously broken, anyway. His left ear was swollen and incredibly painful to touch, so he just left it alone. Finally he stood up and regarded his black and blue, bandage-striped body in the full-length mirror hanging behind the door.

Good God! he thought. What's become of my hair? He ran his fingers through the ragged, patchy clumps of hair on his scalp. This dismayed him more than anything else. Those damned mice *ate* it! I didn't know mice did that. What am I going to do? How can I face Blanchard looking like this? Or *Kathrin?*

He went to his room and dressed. He put on a wide-brimmed leather hat, tilting it at a rakish angle to keep it off his wounded ear. Finally he plodded wearily to the sitting room, poured a glass of brandy and collapsed into Orcrist's easy chair.

CHAPTER 3

Frank woke up to the sound of the front door squeaking open and someone scuffing mud off of boots. Frank tried to stand up, but a dozen
sudden lancing pains made him decide to remain seated.

"Pons?" It was Orcrist's voice. "Pons?"

"Mr. Orcrist!" Frank called.

Orcrist stepped into the sitting room and stared at Frank in amazement. The older man was still dressed as he had been that morning, and
still had not shaved, nor, to judge by his eyes, slept.

"I'll kill Poach," he said. "He swore he saw you and about two hundred feet of Henderson Lane fall into the river."

"Don't kill him," said Frank. "That's what happened. I managed to
climb out of the Leethee after about six blocks."

"Are you all right?"

"No." Frank took off his hat.

Orcrist raised his eyebrows. "Why don't you tell it to me from the
beginning," he said, pulling up another chair. As economically as possible,
Frank explained what had transpired after Orcrist ran off in pursuit of the
fleeing Transport cop. "Did you get him, by the way?" Frank asked. Orcrist
nodded. When the story was finished, Orcrist shook his head wonderingly.

"The Fates must have something planned for you, Frank."

"I hope it's something quiet. How did the rest of you do?"

"Well, let's see. Wister and Lambert went into the river with you, and
are presumed drowned. Bob has disappeared also. Poach is fine. I'm fine.
You've lost your hair. None of the Transports seem to have survived."

"What was the purpose of it? Just to nail some Transport cops?"

"No, Frank, not at all. What we did was . . . set a precedent. We've
got to make it clear to the Transports that they are free to lord it topside,
but have no jurisdiction understreet. If we can make sure that no Transport who comes down here ever returns topside, after a while they'll stop
coming down."

"Maybe so." Frank sipped his brandy. "Is it inevitable that they lord
it in Munson?"

"As far as I can see. Are you still thinking of overthrowing the palace?"

"Sure."

"Oh well. A man's reach should exceed his grasp, and so forth. Would you like a wig? I'm sure I could get one somewhere."

"No, that's . . . well, yes, maybe I would."

During dinner there was a knock at the door, and George Tyler wandered in, grinning, leading by the hand a woman Frank had never seen. She was blond and slightly overweight; her eyelids were painted a delicate blue.

"Good evening, Sam, Frank," Tyler said. "This is Bobbie Sterne. We were just ambling past, so I thought we'd stop in."

"Sit down and have something to eat," said Orcrist. "Pons, could we have two more plates and glasses?"

"Oh, uh, look at this, Sam," said Tyler shyly, handing Orcrist a small book bound in limp leather. Bobbie smiled and stroked Tyler's arm.

"Poems," Orcrist read, "by George Tyler. Well, I'll be damned. Congratulations, George, published at last! This calls for a drink. Pons! Some of the Tamarisk brandy! Sit down, Bobbie, and Frank, get a chair for George." Frank fetched a chair from the sitting room and took the opportunity to make sure his hat was firmly on.

"Frank," said Tyler when he re-entered. "You're limping. And you've got a cut over your eye. Did one of your students get vicious?"

"It's the lot of a fencing master, George," said Orcrist. "Be glad you've got a more peaceful craft."

"Oh, I am."

Pons had, zombie-like, served the brandy, and Bobbie was tossing it down like beer. Tyler took a long sip and smiled beatifically.

"Ah, that's the stuff," he said. "I'll try to publish books more often, at this rate. Say, what do you think of that depth charge last night?"

"Depth charge?" Orcrist asked.

"Don't play the dummy with me, Sam. The Transport used some kind of depth charge to blow out ten levels in the northwest area."

"George, it was four levels, not ten, and it was a regular bomb. They dropped it on the surface to break up a riot. The only reason it did so much damage is that we've dug so many tunnels under Munson that it's like a honeycomb down here." Frank could see that Orcrist was controlling his impatience. "I think if anybody *stomped* really hard on any sidewalk in Munson a couple of levels would go."

"Well, maybe so," said Tyler, not quite sure of what was being discussed. "If I ever claim my kingdom I'll do something about it."

"That's a comfort," said Orcrist wearily.

"You think I'll forget? Just because I'll be living at the palace again? I won't forget old friends, Sam. I'll see to it that nobody steps on any sidewalks over your place."

"Is this a limited edition, George?" asked Orcrist, thumbing through Tyler's book. "It's very handsomely printed."

"Oh, yeah, nothing but the best. It's limited to five hundred copies, and you can have that one. Here, I'll sign it. I'm not the one to say it, but it's likely to be very valuable in years to come."

"I expect it will," said Orcrist. "Thank you."

For a few minutes everyone occupied themselves with the dinner.

"You look tired, Sam," said Tyler, munching on a celery stick. "Been keeping long hours?"

"No longer than usual, George. I must just be—" he was interrupted by a crash from the kitchen. "Would you go see what that was, Frank?"

"Sure." Frank stood up and walked into the kitchen. Pons lay on the floor, unconscious, bright arterial blood gushing from a long slash that ran from his elbow to his wrist. Blood, spattered on the counter and wall, was pooling on the floor.

"Sam!" Frank shouted. He ripped his shirt off and quickly knotted it around Pons's upper arm. Then he thrust the handle of a butter knife under the fabric and began twisting it to tighten the tourniquet. At the third twist the blood stopped jetting from the arm.

Orcrist ran in, stared at Pons for a moment, and ran out again. He was back in five seconds with a needle, fishing line, and the bottle of brandy. He poured the liquor all over the wounded arm, and rinsed his own hands in it. He then threaded the needle with the fishing line and began working in the gaping cut. "Got to try to repair the artery, you see, Frank," he said through clenched teeth. "There it is. Hold the skin there, will you?"

Frank held the wound open while Orcrist sewed shut the cut artery. Everything was slippery with blood and Frank didn't see how Orcrist could tell what he was doing.

"Okay, let's sew the slash closed now," said Orcrist, cutting off the line that dangled from the knot. Frank pressed the edges of the wound together and Orcrist sewed it up as neatly as a seam in a pair of pants. He released the tourniquet, and though blood began to seep out around the stitches, he declared that all was well. He used Frank's torn shirt as a bandage to wrap Pons's arm.

"Will that do?" asked Frank.

"Actually, I don't know," Orcrist answered. "It looks right to me."

Frank looked up. Tyler and Bobbie were standing in the doorway, looking pale and queasy.

"How did it happen?" Tyler asked.

"He cut himself, it appears, with that knife over there," Orcrist said, pointing to a long knife lying next to the stove. "When he fell he knocked over this cart."

"Good Lord. Should I get a doctor?"

"No, George, I don't think so." Orcrist went to the sink and began washing his hands. "I don't really think there's anything you can do here, so if you'll excuse us, Frank and I have a bit of work to do."

"Oh, sure, Sam. Come on, Bobbie."

Frank washed his hands; then he and Orcrist lifted Pons and carried him into his room, laying him on the bed. They heard the front door close as Tyler and Bobbie left.

Orcrist, looking eighty years old, Frank thought, sank into a chair. "This has been a day to try men's souls," Orcrist said. "You and I seem to have survived. I'm going to bed. We can clean everything up in the morning."

Frank stumbled to his own room, fell into bed and was plagued all night by monstrous dreams.

After the grisly mopping up was finished next morning, Orcrist left the house for an hour. Frank spent the time reading Housman's poetry and drinking cup after cup of black coffee. When Orcrist returned he handed Frank a book-sized package. Frank opened it and lifted out the furry object it held.

"What the devil is it?" he asked. "A guinea-pig skin?"

"It's a wig, and you know it," Orcrist said. "Try it on."

Feeling like a fool, Frank pulled the thing over his patchy, bandaged scalp. "How's it look?" he asked.

"Pull it to the left more," said Orcrist. "There, that's good. How's your ear?"

"It doesn't hurt as much today. And I think the swelling's going down. Wait a minute, I've got to see how my brass ear fits with this wig."

Frank went to his room and took his strung metal ear off the bedside table. He put it on over the wig and it fit as well as ever, with the carved ear hanging exactly over the spot where his right ear used to be.

"It's a perfect fit, Mr. Orcrist," he said, returning to the sitting room.

"Yeah, you look like your old self. And I guess you can call me Sam, since you're not a kitchen boy anymore."

"All right." Frank sipped his coffee and wondered how one scratched one's head in a wig. "How's Pons?"

"He was conscious this morning and I gave him some potato soup."

"Is that what they give to people who've lost a lot of blood?"

"I don't know. It's what *I* give them."

"Say, Sam," Frank said, "was it a suicide attempt?"

"I think so. I wouldn't have sewed him up if I was *sure* it was."

"Ah." Frank stood up. "Well, I'd better be off to the school. I've got to start working this stiffness out of me before that appointment with Blanchard day after tomorrow."

"Okay. I may drop in later. I want some practice on that parry in prime you've been trying to teach me."

"Sure. You can even take over the lessons if I find I get too exhausted." Frank put on his coat and shoes, and left.

Frank's first pupil of the day was waiting in the street in front of the school when he arrived.

"Good morning, Lord Emsley," nodded Frank as he unlocked the door. "Sorry I'm late."

"My time is money, Rovzar." Emsley was a short, surly man with a bristly black moustache and bad teeth.

Once inside, Frank lit the lamps and opened the streetside windows; the window that faced the river he left closed, since there were still a few refugees floating down the Leethee.

"Okay, my lord, take an épée and let me see your lunge."

Emsley selected a sword and crouched into an awkward on guard; then he kicked forward with his sword up.

"Extend your arm *before* your lead leg goes," Frank told him. "Otherwise he sees it coming. Do it again."

Emsley did it again.

"Arm first, my lord, arm first. And keep your rear leg straight. Do it again. And again. And again. Good. And again. And—"

"*Damn* you, Rovzar!" Emsley roared. "This is insane! There's no value in all these . . . *calisthenics*. Do you think it matters in a fight whether my leg is straight or my arm moves first? I'll tell you what matters: speed! Listen—I'll lay a wager with you. These ten malories say I can beat you, your style against mine."

The lord flung ten one-malory notes onto the floor.

"Okay," said Frank, picking them up and putting them on the table. "You're on." Damn it, Frank thought. I can't fence today. Every muscle in me is tight as a guitar string. But I've got to show this blustering idiot where he stands. Let me see, what are his weakest points? He doesn't parry well in sixte, when I come in over his sword arm. Let's see if I can do something with that.

"Here," he said, tossing Emsley a mask. He put one on himself and picked up one of the left-handed épées. God help me, he thought as he pulled on a leather glove. "On guard," he said. Emsley lunged immedi-

ately, and Frank parried it; but his riposte was slow, and the lord parried
it without difficulty. Don't be lured into attacking, Frank told himself.
Wait for another one of his stupid lunges.

A heavy knock sounded at the door. "Just a minute," Frank said, turning and raising his mask. Emsley drove his sword at Frank's back, and the
blade flexed like a fishing pole as the padded tip struck a rib. The breath
hissed painfully through Frank's teeth.

"You owe me ten malories, Rovzar!" crowed Emsley.

"Shut up, you ass," Frank said. He crossed to the door and opened it,
and his heart froze. Three Transport policemen stood on the doorstep, and
one of them, a captain, wore an automatic pistol in a shoulder holster.

"Yes, officers?" Frank said.

"Are you Francisco Rovzar?" asked the one with the pistol.

"Yes. Why?" Can I kill all three? he wondered. I don't like that gun.
Emsley will be no help, that's certain, and I'm not in top-notch shape
anyway. Better talk to them.

"Can we come in?" They were already walking in, so Frank nodded
and bowed. "We stopped by yesterday, but you weren't here. We want to
ask you about an incident that took place in the street two days ago. Did
you see or hear or . . . do anything out of the ordinary on that day?"

"Friends of yours, Rovzar?" sneered Emsley.

"Who are you?" asked the captain sharply.

"Christopher Marlowe."

"Write that name down," barked the captain to one of the other officers. The man whipped out a small pad and scribbled in it. "Now get
out of here, Marlowe. Rovzar, maybe you can explain how it is that four
Transport policemen were found killed in the street two days ago."

"No," said Frank. "I didn't hear about it."

"Well, let me fill you in. They were killed in a swordfight. Your fencing school is less than a hundred yards from the spot, so you're impli-
cated. We've come to take you topside for interrogation. Any objections?"

The captain stood a good distance away, with his hand near his pistol.

"Not at all," Frank said with a smile. "I assume you'll provide lunch?"
He hung up the sword and mask casually. I could dive through the river
window, he thought, but that would be a pretty clear admission of guilt;
I'd never dare come back here. I guess I'll have to kill all three. If they get
me topside they're likely to see my tattoo and remember that Francisco
Rovzar who escaped from Barclay six months ago. How long, though,
can I keep killing every Transport who wants to question me?

He turned to the officers cheerfully. "Lead the way, gentlemen," he
said. The captain strode out while the other two officers seized Frank by

the arms and frog-marched him through the door.

"Take it easy, for God's sake," snapped Frank, wincing at the pain in his arm sockets. Four more Transports waited outside in the street, and fell in behind the two who held Frank.

"Only one thing really puzzles me, Rovzar," remarked the captain over his shoulder as the grim procession set off down the street. "Why didn't you change your name?"

"Change my name?" panted Frank.

"Yeah. Did you think we wouldn't check? That we don't keep records? When you jumped over the fence at Barclay and killed those two patrolmen, it was assumed that you'd drowned in the Malachi; but we didn't throw away your file."

Frank didn't answer but cursed inwardly at his foolhardiness. I've had it. They'll ship me off to the Orestes mines, and it will be as if I'd never set foot in Munson Understreet.

A heavy sense of final doom settled over him, and he felt close to tears. He had to forcibly strangle an impulse to beg the captain to let him go.

They turned onto Harvey Way, and Frank knew they must be planning to ascend to the surface by way of the Baldwin sewer. His arms had become numb from his captors' tight grip, and he realized that the time to make a break for it, if there ever was one, had passed.

They had marched a hundred yards down the lamp-lit length of Harvey Way, the soldiers' feet clumping in unison like a monotonous military tap dance, when a sharp explosion sounded up ahead and the Transport captain abruptly sat down on the street. Surprised, Frank looked at the man, and saw blood funneling onto the pavement from a gaping wound in the back.

"It's an ambush," cried the policeman who held Frank's left arm, a moment before a slung stone cracked his forehead and he sprawled on the street. The other man released him in order to draw his sword, and Frank fell helplessly forward onto the sitting corpse of the captain. He heard swords clash behind him, but centered his attention on the task of getting his numb hands to pull the captain's pistol out of its holster. At last he fumbled it out, and rolled over so he could see the fighting. There were four Transports standing in a circle, fighting off about a dozen understreet brigands. Frank waited patiently until he had a clear shot, and then sent ten bullets into the desperately tight police formation. By the time the echoes of the last shot had dissipated, several of the brigands had bolted in terror and every Transport was dead.

Frank dropped the empty gun and scrambled to his feet. One of the bandits thoughtfully fitted a stone into his sling, but a voice barked at him from farther up the street: "Drop it, Peckham. He's one of ours." Frank turned toward the voice and saw Orcrist step out of a shadowed doorway and wave at him with the tiny silver pistol.

"So it was you they were after, Frank! Come on, all of you! Down this alley here."

In spite of his dizziness Frank managed to keep up with Orcrist and his unsavory followers. They fled west, through several of the more dangerous understreet districts, to Sheol Boulevard, and soon they were all filing down the dark stairway under the sign that read "Huselor's."

Huselor's was a big, low-ceilinged bar, lit only by candles in glass jars on the tables. The floor was carpeted and the cool air smelled of gin. Orcrist led his band to a long table in the back, and they sat down silently, looking like a committee of especially disreputable senators.

Orcrist handed each of his hired swordsmen a one-malory note and they all stood up and exited, tipping their hats gratefully. Skilled labor is dirt cheap these days, Frank thought. That can't be a good sign.

When they were alone, Orcrist moved to a much smaller table and waved at the waiter.

"So, Frank," he said in a low voice. "How is it that those boys were leading you off so heavily guarded?"

"Two reasons. They're almost certain I helped kill those four cops the day before yesterday, *and* they know I'm the same Francisco Rovzar who escaped from Barclay six months ago. As that captain said, I should have changed my name."

The waiter padded noiselessly to their table and bowed. "Two big mugs of strong coffee," Orcrist said, "fortified with brandy. Do you want anything else, Frank?"

"Maybe a bowl of clam chowder."

The waiter nodded and sped away. Orcrist sat back with his fingertips pressed together. "That's bad," he said. Frank raised his eyebrows, and then realized that Orcrist wasn't referring to the clam chowder. "I heard, about an hour ago," Orcrist went on, "that a large band of heavily-armed Transports had been sighted down here, so I very quickly rounded up some rough lads, and even brought my pistol along, to go and . . ."

". . . set another precedent," Frank finished.

"Right. And it's a good thing I did. But if they've identified you that thoroughly, you can't relax yet. With the economy as shattered as it is, the Transport is able to buy informers very cheaply, and you never know which alley-skulker might be a spy or assassin."

"Great," said Frank wearily.

"It's tricky, but it isn't hopeless. You've got to go underground again—figuratively this time. Change your name, of course, and your location, and you'll be all right. But you'll have to move fast."

The soup and coffee arrived, and for a while neither man spoke.

"I think I've got a solution," Orcrist said, after five minutes of thoughtful coffee drinking. "I own a boat that's moored in Munson Harbor, just south of the Malachi Delta. It's very near the mouth of the Leethee, so transportation won't be difficult. You could live there. It's got a large dining room below deck that I think you could easily turn into a fencing gym."

"You think I'd still be able to give lessons?"

"Sure. The lords may complain, but they'll make the trip. I think they're beginning to see how much there is to know about the art of swordplay, and how important it is that we learn it before the Transports do. There's a crisis coming upon us fast, Frank, and *we* have to be the ones who are ready for it."

CHAPTER 4

Frank paused in front of the dark glass of a shop window to straighten his wig and his shirt collar. He grinned at himself and walked on, swinging his leather case jauntily, his rubber-soled shoes silent on the damp cobblestones.

Cochran Street, a tunnel bigger, wider and brighter than any he'd yet seen understreet, lay ahead, and he turned left onto its uncracked sidewalk. The sixth door down wore a polished brass plate on which, boldly engraved, was the single name "Blanchard." Frank could feel eyes on him, and realized that he had probably been under several hidden guards' scrutiny ever since he'd turned onto Cochran.

He tucked his light-but-bulky leather case under his arm and knocked at the door. After a moment it was opened by a frail-looking old man with wispy ice-white hair, who raised one snowy eyebrow.

"My name is Francisco Rovzar," Frank said. "I believe . . . uh, his highness is expecting me." The old man nodded and waved Frank inside.

The floor was of red ceramic tiles, and the starkness of the whitewashed stucco walls was relieved by a dozen huge, age-blackened portraits. Torches were thrust into wrought-iron chandeliers that hung by chains from the ceiling.

The old man led Frank down a hallway to a bigger room, high-ceilinged and lined with bookcases. Standing in the center of the room, hands behind his back, stood Blanchard. He wore light leather boots, and his bushy white beard hid the collar of his tunic.

"Rovzar?"

"At your service, sire," said Frank with a courtly bow.

"Glad you could make it. I hear the Transports are interested in you. You know Sam Orcrist, don't you? Would you like a drink?"

"Yes, I do, and yes I would."

"I'm drinking daiquiris. How's that sound?"

"Fine."

Frank leaned his sword case against a wall. "Sit down," Blanchard said, waving at a stout wooden chair in front of a low table. "I'll be back in a second." He left the room and then reappeared immediately, carrying two tall, frosted glasses.

"There you are," he said, taking the chair across from Frank and setting the drinks on the table. "You know, Rovzar, I'm glad you're on our side. Yessir. Our boys were tending to get too smug about their swordsmanship, and now they find out there's a twenty-year-old kitchen boy who can beat 'em—and give 'em lessons, too." Blanchard took a deep sip of his daiquiri. "Damn, that's good. The thing is, you've got to be sharp these days."

"That's true, sir."

"You bet it is. I tell you, Rovzar, it's doggy-dog out there."

"How's that?"

"I say it's doggy-dog out there. The peaceful times are over. Peaceful times never last, anyway. And a good thing, too. They give a man a . . . rosy view of life. Hell, you know how I became King of the Subterranean Companions?"

"How?"

"I killed the previous king, old Stockton. I exercised the *ius gladii*, the right of the sword. It's a tradition—any member who invokes that right can challenge the king to a duel. The winner becomes, or remains, king. But don't get any ideas, Rovzar."

"Oh, no, I—"

"Hah! I'm kidding you, boy. I wish you could have met Stockton, though. A more repulsive man, I think, never lived. Do you play chess?"

"Yes," answered Frank, a little puzzled by Blanchard's topic-hopping style.

"Fine!" Blanchard reached under the table and pulled out a chessboard and a box of chessmen. He turned the box upside down on the table before sliding its cover out from under it. "Which side?" he asked.

"Left," said Frank.

Blanchard lifted the box and chessmen rolled out of it in two side-by-side piles; and the left pile was black.

"Set 'em up," said Blanchard.

Two hours and six daiquiris later Frank was checkmated, but not before he managed to capture Blanchard's queen in a deft king-queen fork.

"Good game, Rovzar." The old king smiled, sitting back. "I've got to be leaving now, but I'll send you another note sometime. Hope you'll be able to drop by again."

"Sure," said Frank, standing up. It was only when he picked up his case that he remembered he'd come to discuss fencing.

That night Frank, wearing a false beard, plied the oars of a rowboat while Orcrist sat in the bow with a lantern and gave instructions.

"Okay, Frank, sharp to port and we'll be in the harbor."

Frank dragged the port oar in the water and the boat swung to the left, through a low brick arch and out into the Munson Harbor. A cold night wind ruffled their hair, and the stars glittered like flecks of silver thread in the vast black cloak of the sky. The boat rocked with the swells, and Frank was finding it harder to control.

"Bear north now," Orcrist said. "It'll be about half a mile." He opened the lantern and blew out the flame, since the moonlight provided adequate light.

The cold breeze was drying the sweat on Frank's face and shoulders, and he leaned more energetically into the rowing. Munson's towers and walls passed by in silhouette to his right, lit here and there by window-lamps and street lights. It's a beautiful city, he thought, at night and viewed from a distance.

"How's Costa doing these days?" he asked, his voice only a little louder than the wavelets slapping against the hull. "Does he like being Duke?"

"He's apparently trying to imitate his father, I hear," Orcrist said. "Topo played tennis, so Costa does too, and his courtiers generally have the sense to lose to him." Frank chuckled wearily. "And he's been seducing, or trying to, anyway, all of the old Duke's concubines. He pretends to savor the wines from Topo's cellar, but hasn't noticed that the wine steward is serving him *vin ordinaire* in fancy bottles, having decanted the good wine for himself. Oh, and this ought to interest you, Frank: he's decided he wants his portrait done by the best artist alive, just as his father did."

"Hah. It's because of him that the best artist isn't alive."

"True. And apparently he's not settling for second best, either."

They were silent for a few oar-strokes. "What do you mean?" Frank asked.

"Well," Orcrist said, "he's let every artist on the planet try out for the privilege of doing the portrait, but so far he's sent every one away in disgust once he sees their work. Your father seems to have set an impossibly high standard."

"It doesn't surprise me. Art, like a lot of things, is a lost art."

Orcrist had no reply to that, and just said, "bear a little to starboard." Frank could see the skeletal masts and reefed sails of a few docked merchant ships, and swung away from the shore a bit to pass well clear of them. Distantly from one of the farther ships he heard a deep-voiced man singing "Danny Boy," and it lent the scene a wistful, melancholy air.

Just past the main basin Orcrist told Frank to head inshore, and in a minute their rowboat was bumping against the hull of a long, wide boat.

It sat low in the water; they were able to climb aboard without paddling around to the back of the craft for the ladder.

"Moor the line to that . . . bumpy thing there," Orcrist said, waving at a vaguely mushroom-shaped protrusion of metal that stood about a foot high on the deck. Frank tied a slip-knot in the rope and looped it over the mooring, before following Orcrist into the cabin. The older man had just put a match to two wall-hung lanterns.

"This is sort of the living room," Orcrist explained; "and you can take that ridiculous beard off now."

Frank peeled it off. "It pays to be cautious," he said.

"No doubt. Through that door is your room—very comfortable, books, a well-stocked desk—and down those stairs is the dining room, another stateroom, and a storage room full of canned food and bottles of brandy. Don't raise the anchor or cast off the lines until I find someone who can give you lessons on how to work the sails."

"Right."

"I guess that's it. There are four good swords in your room—two sabres, an épée and a rapier. There's a homemade pistol in the top desk drawer, but I'm not sure it'll work, and it's only a .22 calibre anyway."

"I'll bring the rest of your things later in the week. If I can, I'll bring the swords and masks and jackets from the school." Orcrist took out his wallet and, after searching through it for a moment, handed Frank a folded slip of thin blue paper. "That's the lease verification. Wave it at any cops that come prowling about. And here are the keys. I'll leave it to you to figure out which lock each key fits."

"Okay. Why don't you . . . bring Kathrin along with you sometime?"

"I will." They wandered out onto the deck again. The moon was sitting low on the northern horizon now, magnified and orange-colored by the atmosphere. "Morning isn't far off," Orcrist said. "You'd better get some sleep." He lowered himself over the side into the rowboat. "Untie me there, will you, Frank? Thanks."

He leaned into the oars, and soon Frank could neither see nor hear him. Frank went below and checked the swords for flexibility and balance—the best one, the rapier, he laid on the desk within easy reach—and then went to bed.

The next few weeks passed very comfortably. Frank read the books in the excellent ship's library, gave more expensive fencing lessons to many of the thief-lords (although Lord Emsley, by mutual consent, was no longer one of Frank's students) and frequently, wrapped in a heavy coat and muffler against the autumn chill, fished off the boat's bow. He often spent the gray afternoons sitting in a canvas chair, smoking his pipe and watching the ships sail in and out of the harbor. He had twice more played chess and consumed daiquiris with Blanchard, and been assured that it was "doggy-dog" out there. Orcrist was a frequent visitor, and Kathrin Figaro came with him several times. She found Frank's exile exciting, and had him explain to her how he would repel piratical boarders if any chanced to appear.

"You should have a cannon," she said, sipping hot coffee as they sat on the deck watching the tame little gray waves wobble past.

"Probably so," agreed Frank lazily. "Then raise anchor, let down the sails and embark on a voyage to Samarkand." His pipe had gone out, so he set it down next to his chair.

"I hear you've become good friends with King Blanchard," Kathrin said.

"Oh . . . I know him. I've played chess with him."

"Maybe when he dies *you'll* be the King of the Subterranean Companions."

"Yeah, maybe so." Frank was nearly asleep. "Where's Sam?"

"Down in the galley, he said. He's looking for a corkscrew."

"Well, I hope he finds one. Want to go for a swim?"

"No."

"Neither do I."

Three miles away, in the low-roofed dimness of Huselor's, two men sat at a back table over glasses of dark beer.

"The thing is, dammit, we've got to keep it in the family. This kid's a stranger, untried, inexperienced."

"I'm not arguing, Tolley," said the other. "I just don't see what can be done about it right now. You could kill him, I suppose, but he's made a lot of powerful friends; maybe if you made it look like the Transports had done it . . ."

"Yeah, maybe. I've got to get this . . . Rovzar kid out of the picture one way or another, though. What you heard *can't* be true—but if Blanchard *is* thinking of naming Rovzar as his successor, then the kid's got to go. I've spent years paving my way to that damned subterranean crown, and no kitchen-boy art-forger is going to take it from me."

"You said it, Tolley," nodded Lord Emsley. "This kid is the fly in the ointment."

Lord Tolley Christensen stared at Lord Emsley with scarcely-veiled contempt. "Yeah, that's it, all right," he said, reaching for his beer.

Orcrist stepped onto the deck, a corkscrew in one hand and a bottle of rosé in the other. He dropped into a chair next to Kathrin and began twisting the corkscrew into the top of the bottle.

"What have you got there?" demanded Frank.

"*Vin rosé,*" Orcrist said. "A simple, wholesome wine, fermented from unpretentious grapes harvested by great, sturdy peasant women." He popped out the cork and pulled three long-stemmed glasses out of his coat pocket. When he had filled them he handed one to Kathrin and one to Frank. All three took a long, appreciative sip.

"Ah," sighed Orcrist. "The workingman's friend."

"The salvation of the . . . abused," put in Frank.

"The comforter of the humiliated."

"The mother to the unattractive."

"The . . . reassurer of the maladjusted."

"Oh, stop it," said Kathrin impatiently. "You're both idiots."

For a few minutes they all sat silently, sipping the wine and watching a fishing boat make its steady way toward the jetty and the outer sea.

"The guide of the lurching," said Frank. Orcrist laughed, and Kathrin threw her glass into the sea and stormed into the cabin.

"The girl's got a horrible temper," Orcrist observed.

"Only when she's upset," objected Frank.

Orcrist and Kathrin left late in the afternoon. Frank waved until their skiff disappeared behind the headland to the south, then went below and fixed himself dinner. He heated up some tomato soup and took it on deck to eat, and then lit his pipe and watched the seagulls hopping about on the few rock-tops exposed by the low tide. When the sun had slid by stages all the way under the horizon he went below to read. He sat down at his desk and picked up a book of Ashbless's poems.

An hour later he had lost interest in the book and had begun writing a sonnet to Kathrin. He painstakingly constructed six awkward lines, then gave it up as a bad idea and crumpled the paper.

"Not much of a poet, eh?" came a voice from the doorway at his left. Frank jumped as if he'd been stabbed. He whirled toward the door and then laughed with relief to see Pons standing there.

"Good God, Pons! You just about stopped my heart." It occurred to Frank to became angry. "What the hell are you doing here, anyway?"

Pons took his left hand out of his coat pocket—he was holding Orcrist's silver pistol. "I followed Sam here," he said in a toneless voice. "I'm going to kill you."

Just what I needed, thought Frank, *a maniac.* He wondered if the gun was loaded—Orcrist had fired it during that ambush a few weeks ago, and he might not have reloaded it. Of course Pons wouldn't know it had been fired.

"You're going to *kill* me? Why?" Frank furtively slid open the top drawer of the desk.

"It's because of you that I've got to kill myself."

"Well, that's real sharp reasoning," said Frank, gently feeling around in the drawer with his right hand. "It wasn't me that put your wife in a second-rate asylum with cheap ceilings."

"It was a good asylum!" Pons said loudly. "Your bomb killed her."

No point in using logic with this guy, Frank told himself. *He's gone round the bend.* At that moment the fingers of his right hand closed on the grip of the small pistol Orcrist had told him would be there. He curled his first finger around the trigger and slowly raised the barrel until it touched the underside of the desktop. He moved it minutely back and forth until he figured it was pointed at Pons's chest.

"And you've got to die for it," Pons said, raising the silver gun.

Frank pulled the trigger of his own gun. There was a muffled bang and smoke spurted out of the drawer, but the bullet failed to penetrate the thick desktop. Pons convulsively squeezed the trigger of *his* gun, and the hammer clicked into an empty chamber. For a moment both men stared at each other tensely.

Frank started laughing. "You idiot," he gasped. "Sam fired that gun a long time ago."

Tears welled in Pons's eyes and spilled down his left cheek. He flung his useless gun onto the floor and ran out of the room. Frank heard him dash up the stairs and out of the cabin; there were footsteps on the deck and then, faintly, he heard the sound of oars clacking in oarlocks.

Perhaps I wasn't as sympathetic as I ought to have been, Frank thought. Oh well; at least I didn't kill him. I'm glad it worked out as painlessly as it did. He thoughtfully closed the still-smoking drawer and picked up his book again.

The sun had climbed midway to noon when Frank's first pupil arrived the next day. Frank sat smoking in a canvas chair by the rail and watched Lord Gilbert's body-servant maneuver the skiff alongside Frank's boat.

Lord Gilbert was a good-natured, very fat man, whose most sophisticated fencing style consisted of taking great, ponderous hops toward his opponent and flailing his sword like a maniac with a fly-swatter. Thirty seconds of this always reduced him to a sweating, panting wreck, and Frank was trying to teach him to relax and wait for his opponent to attack.

"What ho, Lord Gilbert!" called Frank cheerfully. "How goes life in the rabbit warrens?"

"Most distressing, Rovzar," Gilbert puffed, clambering over the gunwale. "Transports keep coming understreet, and getting killed, and are in turn followed by meaner and more vengeful Transports."

"Well, doubtless they'll run out of them eventually."

"Doubtless. And now hundreds of homeless Goriot Valley farmers have settled, or tried to, understreet, and you know how crowded we were even before."

"True. What you ought to be doing, though, is training all those farmers in the arts of warfare, and then you should weld them and the understreet citizenry into an army to wipe out the Transports with."

"Yes, you've been advising that for some time, haven't you? But a farmer is only a farmer, Rovzar, and you can't *really* beat a plowshare into much of a sword."

"Oh well. Speaking of swords, let's go below and see how your parries are coming along."

"Another thing happened, last night," said Gilbert, stopping short. "Orcrist's servant, Pons, died."

Frank stopped also. "He did? How?"

"He walked into one of the methane pits near the southern tunnels and struck a match. I just heard about it this morning."

"Poor bastard. He never was a very *pleasant* person, but . . ."

"You knew him, I see!" grinned Gilbert. "Come on, show me those parries."

Frank worked for two hours with Gilbert, to almost no avail. Finally he advised the lord to carry a shotgun and sent him on his way. Cheerful always, the lord shook Frank's hand and promised to practice up on everything and come back soon.

At about two in the afternoon another boat, wearing the insignia of the harbor patrol, pulled alongside. A tall blond man in a blue uniform climbed onto Frank's deck. "Afternoon," he said to Frank. "Are you the owner of this craft?"

"No sir," said Frank. "I'm leasing it."

"And what's your name?" The man was leafing through papers on a clipboard he carried.

"John Pine," said Frank, using the name he and Orcrist had agreed on.

"I have a Samuel Brendan Orcrist listed as the owner."

"That's right. He's leased it to me. Wait here and I'll get the papers for you." Frank hurried below, found the blue slip and brought it to the man.

The officer looked at it closely and then handed it back.

"Looks okay," he said. "Just checking. Thanks for your time. Be seeing you!" He climbed back into his own boat, got the small steam engine puffing, and with a casual salute motored away across the basin.

When Orcrist visited Frank again, late one afternoon, he brought an ornate envelope with "Francisco Rovzar, Esq." written in a florid script across the front.

"What is it?" Frank asked.

"It's an invitation to a party George Tyler is giving in two weeks. It's in honor of his book being published, I guess. He's invited all kinds of artists and writers, he tells me. More importantly, there'll be a lot of good food and drink."

"Do you think it'd be safe for me to attend? Where's it being held?"

"In George's new place, a big house about fifteen levels below the surface, near the Tartarus district. Yes, it ought to be safe enough; the Transports never venture that deep, and no informers will be specifically looking for you, I don't think. Just call yourself John Pine and all will be well." Orcrist poked two holes in a beer can and handed the foaming thing to Frank. "I'd say you could even bring a young lady if you cared to."

"Good idea. Would you convey my invitation to Kathrin?"

"Consider it conveyed."

It was windy, so they took their beers into the cabin. "Oh, I've got something of yours, Sam," Frank said. He went into his room and came back with the silver pistol. "Here."

Orcrist took it and looked up at Frank curiously. "I noticed it was gone. Where did you get it?"

"Pons brought it here, the night he blew himself up. He tried to shoot me, but there was no bullet in it."

"Poor old Pons. Then he went straight from here to the methane pits, eh?"

"I guess so." Frank sat down and picked up his beer. "He said it was 'my' bomb that killed his wife."

Orcrist nodded. "Did I ever tell you about the time I took him along on a robbery?"

"No. You said you . . . gave him a chance to prove himself under fire, and that he didn't do well."

"That's right. It was about a year before you came bobbing like Moses down the Leethee. Beatrice, his wife, had already cracked up and been committed by that time, of course. Anyway, I decided to take him along on a raid on the palace arsenal; several of the understreet tunnels, you know, connect with palace sewers. Pons was extremely nervous and kept inventing reasons why we should turn back. Finally he worked himself into a rage and turned on me. He accused me of being in love with Beatrice, and of blaming him for her crack-up."

"What made him think *that?*"

"Oh, it was absolutely true, Frank. I was in love with her. I don't know why it was him she married—sometimes I think women secretly, unspokenly prefer stupid, mean men. But all this is beside the point. I called off the robbery then; it was clear that we couldn't work together. And that's the entirety of Pons's criminal career."

"How did he become your doorman?"

"He had no money or friends, so I offered him the job and he took it. He and I had been friends before, you see." Orcrist's beer was gone, and he got up to fetch two more cans.

CHAPTER 5

Frank and Kathrin walked up the gravel path, their way festively lit by lamps behind panes of colored glass. Kathrin wore a lavender, sequined gown that emphasized her slim figure, and Frank wore a quiet black suit with newly-polished black boots. A dress sword hung at his belt in a decorated leather scabbard, but in the interests of security and anonymity he had left his bronze ear at home, and simply combed his newly-grown hair over the spot where his right ear should have been.

Tyler's house was a grand gothic pile, the roof of which merged with the high roof of the street. It looked as though it should have been a long abandoned shrine of forgotten and senile gods, but tonight its open windows and door spilled light and music into the street and up and down the nearby tunnels.

Tyler had been told about Frank's exile-status by Orcrist, so when Frank and Kathrin appeared at the door he introduced them to everyone as "John Pine and Kathrin Figaro." Frank then led Kathrin through the press of smiling, chatting people, shaking hands with several. They found space for the two of them on an orange couch. He immediately took his pipe, tobacco pouch and bullet-shell pipe-tamper out of his pocket and laid them out on the low table in front of him.

"I sense wine over there to the right," he told Kathrin. "Shall I fetch you a glass?"

"Sure."

Frank ducked and smiled his way to a little alcove in which sat a tub of water and ice cubes surrounding at least a dozen wine bottles. He spun them all this way and that to read their labels before selecting a bottle of Sauterne. He uncorked it, found two glasses and made his way back to the orange couch.

"There we are," he said, filling the two glasses and setting the bottle in front of them.

Kathrin sipped hers and smiled happily. "I think it's wonderful that you know a famous poet, Frank."

Frank was about to make some vague reply and remind her that his name tonight was John, when a well-groomed, bearded man leaned toward them from Kathrin's side of the couch. "How long have you known George?" he asked.

"Oh, about six months," answered Frank. "I've never read any of his poetry, though."

"He is the major tragic figure of this age," the bearded man informed Frank.

"Oh," said Frank. He took a healthy gulp of his wine and tried to imagine amiable, drunken George as a tragic figure. "Are you sure?"

"You must be one of George's . . . working-class friends," said Beard, with a new sympathy in his eyes. "You probably never have time to read, right?" He leaned forward still farther and put a pudgy hand on Frank's knee. "*Can* you read?" he asked, in a voice that was soft with pity.

"Actually, no," said Frank, putting on the best sad expression he could come up with. "I've had to work in the cotton mills ever since I was four years old, and I never learned to read or eat fried foods. Every Saturday night, though, my mother would read the back of a cereal box to me and my brothers, and sometimes we'd act out the story, each of us taking the part of a different vitamin. My favorite was always Niacin, but—"

The bearded man had stood up and walked stiffly away during this speech, and Frank laughed and began filling his pipe. He gave Kathrin a mock-soulful look and put his hand on her knee. "*Can* you read?" he mimicked.

"You didn't have to lie to him, Frank," she said.

"Sure I did. And my name is John, remember?" He struck a match and puffed at his pipe, then tamped the tobacco and lit it again. "I hope the Beard of Avon there isn't representative of George's friends."

"Oh, I don't know," said Kathrin. "He looked sort of . . . sensitive, to me."

Tyler himself came weaving up to them at that moment. "Hello, uh, John," he grinned. "How do you like the party?"

"It's a great affair, George," Frank answered. "By the way, I hear you're the tragic figure of this century, or something."

"No kidding?" George said delightedly. "I've suspected it for a long time. Here, Miss Figaro, let me fill your glass. Well, see you later, Fr— John, I mean. I've got to mingle and put everyone at ease."

"Yeah, give 'em hell, George," said Frank with a wave. Kathrin got up, spoke softly to Frank and disappeared in the direction of the ladies' room. Frank sat back, puffing on his pipe and surveying the scene.

The room was large and filled with knots of animatedly talking people. Bits of conversations drifted to Frank: ". . . my new sonnet-cycle on the plight of the Goriot farmers . . ." ". . . very much influenced by Ashbless, of course . . ." ". . . and then my emotions, sticky things that they are . . ."

Good God, Frank thought. *What am I doing here? Who are all these people?* He refilled his wine glass and wondered when the food would appear. There was a napkin in front of him on the table, and he took a pencil out of his pocket and began sketching a girl who stood on the other side of the room.

When he finished the drawing and looked up, the food had appeared but Kathrin hadn't. He looked around and saw her standing against the far wall, a glass of red wine in her hand and a tailored-looking young man whispering in her ear. A surge of quick jealousy narrowed Frank's eyes, but a moment later he laughed softly to himself and walked to the food table.

He took a plate of sliced beef and cheese back to his place on the couch; he had such a litter of smoking paraphernalia spread out on the table that no one had sat down there. When he was just finishing the last of the roast beef, and swallowing some more of the Sauterne to wash it down, Kathrin appeared and sat down beside him.

"'That's pretty good, Frank," she said, pointing at the sketch he'd done earlier. "Who is it?"

"It's a girl who was standing over—well, she's gone now. You'd better jump for it if you want to get some food." He decided to give up on John Pine.

"I'm not hungry," Kathrin said. "Did you see that guy I was talking to a minute ago?"

"The guy with the curly black hair and the moustache? Yes, I did. Who is he?"

"His name's Matthews. Just Matthews, no first name. And he's an artist, just like you."

"No kidding? Well, that's—" Frank was interrupted then by Matthews himself, who sat down on the arm of the couch on Kathrin's side.

"I'm Matthews," he said with a bright but half-melancholy smile. "You are . . . ?"

"Rick O'Shay," said Frank, shaking Matthews's hand. "Kathrin tells me you're an artist."

"That's right."

"Well, here," Frank said, pushing toward Matthews the pencil and a napkin. "Sketch me Kathrin."

"Oh no," said Matthews. "I don't simply . . . *sketch*, you know, on a napkin. I've got to have a light table and my rapidograph and a set of graduated erasers."

"Oh." *A good artist,* Frank thought, *should be able to draw on a wood fence with a berry.* But he knew it wouldn't help to say so. Matthews now leaned over and began muttering in Kathrin's ear. She giggled.

Frank knocked the lump of old tobacco out of his pipe, ran a pipe cleaner through it, and began refilling it. *I'll be damned if I let them run me off the couch,* he thought. A moment later, though, Kathrin and Matthews stood up and, with a couple of perfunctory nods and waves to Frank, disappeared out the back door of the house. Frank lit his pipe.

"Not doing real bloody well, are you, lad?" asked Tyler sympathetically from behind the couch.

Frank shifted around to see him. "No," he admitted. "What's out back there?"'

"A fungus and statuary garden. Lit by blue and green lights."

"Oh, swell."

"Well, look, Frank, as soon as I oust my rotten half-brother from the palace, I'll have Matthews executed. How's that?"

"I'll be much obliged to you, George." Frank got up and wandered around the room, listening in on the various discussions going on. He joined one, and then got into an argument with a tall, slightly pot-bellied girl when he told her that free verse was almost always just playing-at-poetry by people who wished they were, but weren't, poets. Driven from that conversation by the ensuing unfriendly chill, Frank found himself next to the wine-bin once again, so he took a bottle of good *vin rosé* to see him through another circuit of the room. The glasses had all been taken, and someone, he noticed, had used his old glass for an ashtray, so he was forced to take quick furtive sips from the bottle.

He saw Kathrin reenter the room, so he dropped his now half-empty bottle into a potted plant and waved at her. She saw him, smiled warmly, and weaved through the crowd toward him. Well, that's better, thought Frank. I guess old Matthews was just a momentary fascination.

"Hi, Frank," said Kathrin gaily. "What have you been up to?"

"Getting into arguments with surly poetesses. How about you?"

"I've been getting to know Matthews. It's all right with you if he takes me home, isn't it? Do you know, under his sophisticated exterior I think he's very . . . vulnerable."

"I'll bet even his exterior is vulnerable," said Frank, covering his confusion and disappointment with a wolfish grin. "Does he wear a sword? Matthews, there you are! Come over here a minute."

"Frank, please!" hissed Kathrin. "I think he's my animus!"

"Your animus, is he? I had no idea it had gone this far. Matthews! Borrow a sword from someone and you and I will decide in the street which of us is to take Kathrin home."

Frank was talking loudly, and many of the guests were watching him with wary curiosity. Matthews turned pale. "A sword?" he repeated. "A woman's heart was never swayed by swords."

"I'll puncture your heart with one, weasel," growled Frank, unsheathing his rapier. A woman screamed and Matthews looked imploringly at Kathrin.

"Frank!" Kathrin shrilled. "Put away your stupid sword! Matthews isn't so cowardly as to accept your challenge."

"What?" Frank hadn't followed that.

"It takes much more courage *not* to fight. Matthews was explaining it to me earlier. And if you think I'd let a . . . thief and murderer like you take me home, you're very much mistaken."

Everyone in the room had stopped talking now and stared at Frank. He slapped his sword back into its scabbard and strode out of the room, leaving the front door open behind him.

That night after he'd rowed back to the boat, he took a long, very chilly swim in the sea by moonlight, out to the rocks of the jetty. He climbed up onto the highest of them, ignoring the icy wind that twitched his wet hair. Shivering like a drenched cat, he calmly watched the moon peeping at intervals from behind a tattered, back-lit sheet of clouds. Finally he swam slowly back to the boat, where he had a quick glass of brandy and then went to bed.

"Hey, Rovzar!"

Frank opened his eyes. He felt terrible, but it was mainly mental distress; apparently the alcohol and the icy swim had cancelled each other out.

"Dammit, Rovzar, where are you?"

Who the hell is that yelling? Frank wondered. It didn't sound like police, but it might well *bring* some if it didn't stop. Frank rolled out of bed, slid into his pants, grabbed his rapier and stumbled bleary-eyed onto the dazzlingly-sunlit deck. A snub-nosed, insolent-looking young man stood by the stern, dressed in close-fitting tan leather.

"Who the hell are you?" Frank croaked.

"I'm a courier. You're Rovzar, aren't you?"

"Yes."

"Well, here," the courier said, handing Frank a wax-sealed envelope. "Get some coffee into you, pal," he advised. "You look terrible." The young man hopped over the side into his own boat and began rowing away, whistling cheerfully.

Frank sat down on the deck and broke the seal. The letter, when unfolded, read: "Vital meeting of SC Tuesday at 9:00. Important announce-

ment. Mandatory attendance unless specifically exempt by a reigning lord.
—BLANCHARD."

Frank read it over several times and then stuffed it into his pants
pocket. *Coffee,* he thought. *That's not a bad idea.* He picked up his sword,
stood up, and made his unsteady way down the stairs to the galley.

"What I heard was true I tell you, this is it."

Lord Tolley Christensen bit his lip, frowning thoughtfully. "That isn't
certain, Emsley. Don't jump to conclusions." He stared again at the paper
that lay on the table in front of him—it was a duplicate of the one Frank
had received that morning. "Blanchard has got an 'important announcement' to make tomorrow. It might be anything—the Transport, the Goriot
fugitives, the depression—it isn't necessarily the naming of his successor."

Emsley lit a cigar. "Yeah, Tolley, but what if it *is?* And the successor he
names isn't you, but Rovzar?"

"You're right," Tolley admitted. "We can't risk it. Rovzar's got to be
killed."

"Do it carefully, though," Emsley said. "You'll be a prime suspect,
and if Blanchard thinks you did it he sure won't make *you* his successor."

"Blanchard won't have time even to hear about it, I think," said Tolley
with a cold smile. "Have you heard of the *ius gladii?*"

"The what?"

"Never mind. Get out of here, now, and let me think."

Tuesday night was racked with thunder and rain. Frank stood on the
deck under the overhanging roof of the cabin and stared out into the thrashing gray rain-curtains for some sign of the bow-light of Orcrist's rowboat.
The deep-voiced harbor bells and foghorns played a sad, moronic dirge
across the water, and Frank's shivering wasn't entirely due to the cold, wet
wind that whipped at his long sealskin coat. He waved his flickering lantern, hoping it would be seen by Orcrist.

Finally he heard "Ho, Frank!" from the darkness, and a moment later
saw the weak glint of orange light wavering toward him through the rain.
Frank swung his lantern from side to side. "This way, Sam!" he called.

A few minutes later Orcrist's boat was bumping against the bow. Frank
climbed in, holding his oiled and wrapped sword clear of the splashing,
three-inch-deep pool of water in the scuppers. He thrust it inside his coat
and then took the oars and began pulling for the Leethee. The rain was
whipping them too fiercely for speech to seem like a good idea, so the two
men simply listened to the occasional thunderclaps and watched the rain
stream off their hat-brims.

The boat lurched its laborious way around the ship basin and then turned in. After some searching, they found the arch of the Leethee mouth. When they'd rowed a hundred feet or so up its length they took their hats off and Orcrist began bailing the water out of their boat with a couple of coffee cans. The Leethee was deeper and faster than usual, and Frank was soon sweating with the effort of making headway.

"How well do you know Blanchard, Frank?" It was the first thing either of them had said since Frank had entered the boat.

"Oh, I don't know. I drink and play chess with him. Mostly he tells me stories about his younger days. Why do you ask?"

"Your acquaintance with him seems to have caused some jealousy in high circles."

"Oh?"

"That's what I've heard, anyway. Take that side-channel there, it'll avoid most of this current."

Eventually they pulled up to an ancient stone dock and moored their boat in its shadow. "Nobody's likely to see it here," Orcrist whispered. "Come on—up these stairs." Frank buckled his sword to his belt and followed the older man up the cracked granite stairs, slipping occasionally on the wet stone surfaces.

The steps led up to a long, entirely unlit corridor, down which they had to feel their way as slowly as disoriented blind men. At last they reached another stairway and found at the top a high-roofed hall lit by frequent torches, and they were able to move more quickly.

"Say, Sam, I've been meaning to ask you: was the Subterranean Companions' meeting hall ever a church? It sure looks like it was."

"Didn't you ever hear the story about that, Frank? There was a—"

A sharp *twang* sounded up ahead and an arrow buried half its length in Orcrist's chest. Frank leaped to the wall and whipped out his sword, and two more arrows hissed through the space he'd occupied a moment before. Orcrist fell to his knees and then slumped sideways onto the wet pavement. Six men burst out of an alcove ahead and ran at Frank, waving wicked-looking double-edged sabres. Fired to an irrational fury by Orcrist's death, Frank ran almost joyfully to meet them.

He collided with the first of them so hard that their bell guards clacked against each other, numbing the other man's arm; Frank drove a backhand thrust through the man's kidney. Two more blades were jabbing at his stomach, and he parried both of them low, then leaped backward and snatched up the fallen man's sword. Two of the thugs were trying to circle around him, so Frank quickly leaped toward the other three with an intimidating stamp, his two swords held crossed in front of him. All three men extended stop-thrusts that Frank swept up with his right-hand blade, clearing the way for a lightning-quick stab into the throat of the man on the far left; whirling with the move, Frank drove his blade to the hilt into a would-be back-stabber's belly. The other man's blade-edge cut a notch in Frank's chin, but Frank's right-hand sword pierced him through the eye.

Frank backed off warily to catch his breath. Barely five seconds had passed, but four of his opponents were down, three dead and one slumped moaning against the wall. Drops of blood fell in a steady rain onto the front of Frank's dress shirt. The two remaining ambushers approached Frank cautiously, about six feet apart. The man on Frank's right was leaving his six-line open.

Frank tensed; very quickly he leaned forward on his lead leg and then kicked off with his rear leg in a rushing flèche attack that drove his blade into the man's chest and snapped it off a foot above the bell guard. He spun to meet the remaining man, whose point was rushing at Frank's neck, and parried the thrust with his right-hand blade. Frank then drove his shortened left-hand sword dagger-style upward, with a sound of tearing cloth, into the man's heart. After a few seconds Frank's rigid arm released the grip and the body dropped to the pavement.

Hodges stubbed out his cigarette and stood up. The hall was full tonight—more members had shown up than he had known there were. Shouts and whistles and a low roar of talking were amplified in the cathedral-like hall until people had to cup their hands and shout to be heard.

Hodges glanced to his right into the sacristy and saw Blanchard, his hair and beard newly combed, give him a nod. Hodges banged on the speaker's stand with a gavel, but to no avail. He gave it a stronger blow and the head flew off into the crowd. Somebody threw it back at him and he had to leap aside to avoid being hit. He could be seen to be mouthing words like "Shut up, dammit, you idiots!" but in the general roar his shouts couldn't be heard.

Blanchard strode out onto the platform carrying a ceremonial shotgun, and fired it at the ceiling, where a few other ripped-up areas provided reminders of times in the past when this had been necessary. The sharp roar of the gun silenced the crowd abruptly, and the bits of stone and shot whining around the hall were all that could be heard.

"All right then," Blanchard growled. "Let's get down to business. The first thing we've got to get straight is—"

"The question of your successor!" called Lord Tolley Christensen, who stood up now from his fourth-row seat.

"What's the problem, Tolley?" asked Blanchard quietly.

"There's no problem, sire. I'm just invoking a precedent—one you're familiar with yourself."

"That precedent being . . . ?"

"The *ius gladii*."

Hodges stared at Tolley in amazement, and there were shocked gasps from those thieves who knew what was being mentioned.

"All right." Blanchard raised his voice so that everyone in the hall could hear him. "Lord Tolley Christensen has invoked the *ius gladii* and challenged me to a duel. The winner will be your king. Here, two of you move this table out of here. Hodges, get my sword."

Lord Emsley stood sweating in the vestibule. He had posted six experienced, expensive killers in each of the three corridors Rovzar might have taken to get to the hall, and he had little doubt that Rovzar would be killed. Also, he had great confidence in Tolley's swordsmanship—still, he'd be happier when this evening was over.

Blanchard and Tolley now faced each other on the wide marble speaker's stand. They drew their swords and saluted; then they took the on guard position and cautiously advanced at each other.

Tolley tried a feint-and-lunge, Blanchard parried it and riposted, Tolley extended a stop-thrust that Blanchard got a bind on, Tolley released, and they both stepped back, panting a little. The assembled thieves growled and muttered among themselves.

Tolley hopped forward, attacking fiercely now, and the clang and rasp of the thrust-parry-riposte-cut-parry filled the hall. Tolley had Blanchard retreating, thrusting savagely and constantly at the old king. Finally a quick over-the-top jab hit the king in the chest; Tolley redoubled the attack and drove the blade into Blanchard's heart.

Angry yells came from the crowd as the old king fell and rolled off the back of the platform, and several of the thieves leaped up, waving their swords. Hodges, looking grim, raised his hand.

"There's nothing you can do," he said in a rasping, levelly controlled voice. "Tolley Christensen is the King of the Subterranean Companions. The only way to dispute that is to challenge him to a single combat. Are there . . . any members who want to do that?"

There was silence. Lord Tolley's swordsmanship was almost legendary.

"I'll challenge him," came a voice from the vestibule. All heads turned to see who spoke, and Tolley's eyes widened when he saw Frank Rovzar standing in the doorway. Damn that inefficient Emsley! Tolley thought furiously.

Frank shoved the gaping, pale-faced Lord Emsley aside and strode up the central aisle to the altar-like speaker's platform. As he approached he saw Tolley smile—he's noticing my bloody shirt, Frank thought. Good; I hope he overestimates the injury. He swung up onto the platform and nodded politely to both Tolley and Hodges.

"Did you hope to become equal to him by killing him?" he asked Tolley with a wild, brittle cheerfulness. "It didn't work—you're still a Transport-loving slug whom I wouldn't trust to clean privies." Frank knew Tolley hated the Transport as much as anyone, but wanted to enrage him. He succeeded, especially when many of the thieves in the crowd snickered at Frank's words.

"Ordinarily, Rovzar," Tolley said through clenched teeth, "I'd scorn to smear my sword with the watery blood of a kitchen boy. Since you're such an offensive and conceited one, though, I'll make an exception."

Hodges stood up and faced Frank. "Do you mean," he asked wearily, "to invoke the *ius gladii* against his majesty here?"

"Yes," said Frank politely. Cheers sounded in various parts of the hall. "Nail the bastard, Frank!" someone shouted.

Tolley, thoroughly angered, raised his sword and whistled it through the air in a curt salute. Frank unsheathed his own sword, the rapier Orcrist had been wearing, and saluted courteously.

"Go to it, gentlemen," said Hodges, sitting down.

Frank relaxed into the on guard position, with his sword well extended to keep a comfortable distance. He met Tolley's gaze and smiled. "It was you who hired those six bravos to kill me, wasn't it?" Frank asked softly, with a tentative tap at Tolley's blade.

"Emsley hired them," replied Tolley in a likewise low voice. "I told him to. I guess the idiot hired inferior swordsmen." Tolley tried a quick feint and jab to Frank's wrist; Frank caught Tolley's point and whirled a riposte that nearly punctured Tolley's elbow. They both backed off then, measuring each other.

"They weren't inferior," Frank said. "If they hadn't killed Orcrist before turning to me, they'd have earned whatever Emsley paid them."

Tolley backed away a step. "They killed Orcrist?" he asked, beginning to look a little fearful.

"That's right," said Frank.

Tolley took another step back, lowering his point—and then leaped forward, jabbing at Frank like an enraged scorpion. His blade was everywhere: now flashing at Frank's throat, now ducking for his stomach, now jabbing at his knee. Frank devoted all his energy to parrying, waiting to riposte until, inevitably, Tolley should tire. He retreated a step; then another; and then felt with his rear foot the edge of the marble block. Desperately, he parried an eye-jab in prime and riposted awkwardly at Tolley's throat, leaping forward as he did it. Tolley backed off two steps, deflected Frank's thrust and flipped his blade back at Frank's face. Frank felt the fine-whetted edge bite through his cheek and grate against his cheekbone.

He struck Tolley's blade away and forced himself to relax and stay alert, to resist the impulse to attack wildly.

"You're on your way out, Rovzar," grinned Tolley fiercely. Frank drove a most convincing-looking thrust at Tolley's throat—Tolley raised his sword to meet it—and Frank ducked low, still in his lunge, and punched his sword-point through Tolley's thigh. He whipped it out and, grinning, threw aside the older man's convulsive riposte.

"Cut your throat, you bastard, and save me the trouble," hissed Frank.

Tolley stole a glance downward and paled visibly to see the widening red stain on his pants. Frank threw a quick thrust at him and cut him slightly in the arm. Blood was trickling down Frank's cheek and neck, and when he licked his lips he caught its rusty taste.

Tolley ran at Frank now in a fleché attack; the thrust missed, but Tolley collided heavily with Frank and they both pitched off the platform. As they rolled to their feet on the floor, Frank jabbed Tolley hard behind the kneecap, and the lord cried out with the pain.

"Damn you!" the older man snarled, aiming a slash at Frank's head. Frank ducked it and Tolley swung backhand at him again. Frank jarringly caught the sword with the forte of his own and half-lifted, half-threw Tolley away from him.

"It's time for the finish, Tolley," Frank gasped. Sweat ran from his matted hair and dripped from the end of his nose. "Have you ever seen the self-inflicted foot parry?"

Tolley said nothing, but lunged high at Frank, hoping to catch him while he was still talking. Frank carefully took Tolley's blade with his own, whirled it up and then whipped it, hard, down.

Tolley crouched amazed, staring at his foot, which was nailed to the floor by his own sword. Derisive laughter sounded from all sides. Frank drove his own sword with savage force into Tolley's stomach. "This is for Orcrist," he grinned. "And this," he said, with a punching slash that opened Tolley's throat, "is for Blanchard."

Tolley's spouting body arched backward and sprawled, arms outflung, on the floor. His sword still stood up from his foot like a butterfly-collector's pin.

Frank sank exhausted to his knees and panted until he'd begun to get his breath back. A minute later he stood up, pushed his bronze ear back into place and vaulted onto the platform.

"I present King Rovzar of the Subterranean Companions," Hodges called loudly. "Are there any further challenges?"

There were none. Lord Rutledge began clapping, and in a moment the entire hall echoed to the sound of applause and whistling. Frank grinned mirthlessly and raised his bloody sword in a salute. Nobody who'd known him a year ago would have recognized as Francisco Rovzar this savage figure standing above a multitude of cheering thieves, his long, uneven black hair flung back and his face a gleaming mask of sweat and blood.

BOOK THREE

The King

CHAPTER 1

Bright torchlight flickered on the faces of the seven men seated around the oak table. A nearly-empty brandy bottle and a litter of used clay pipes gave testimony to the length of the conference, and one or two of the men were obviously stifling yawns.

"However you argue it," said one of them, obviously not for the first time, "you can't *hold* the palace. You might just be able to take it, as you suggest, with an army of thieves and evicted farmers. But without a prince of the royal blood to set on the throne, you'd be thrown out within the week and your army would be cut to bits and driven into the hills to starve."

"I guess you're right, Hodges," said the man at the head of the table. "We . . . shelve that idea, then. But you haven't given me a reason why you oppose the idea of night raids on the Transport shipment between Barclay and the palace."

"Well," said Hodges doubtfully, scratching his chin, "I guess I don't really *oppose* it . . . but there are two reasons why I don't entirely like it. First, you're saying we should make a direct raid on the Transport, which is bigger meat than the Companions usually go for. Second, it would be on the surface, and our boys aren't used to working without a roof over-head and a sewer or two to scuttle down if things get tight."

"Well, our boys are going to have to *get* used to it," growled the leader. "You know as well as I do what that Transport last week whispered before he died. Their home base, their system headquarters, is what they plan to make of this planet. And do you think they'll allow our little thieves' union to continue when Octavio is nothing but a Transport office and parking lot? Not likely. We've *got* to impede them, as seriously as we can, or we'll all be shipped off to some prison planet within the year."

Hodges shrugged, frowning uncertainly. "That's true," he said. "But the morale won't be good among those who have to go on the raids."

The leader stood up and laid his smoking pipe on the table. The scar of a sword-cut showed paler against his pale cheek, and a glittering bronze ear hung on the side of his head. *Quite a piratical character he looks,* thought

Hodges, *but I wish he'd be more realistic about policy.* "Would they feel better about it," the leader asked, "if the man who led the raid was their king?"

"You can't," said Hodges.

"Would they?"

"Sure. They'd feel even better if God led them in a glowing chariot. But neither one is possible."

"Don't be so . . . hidebound, Hodges. I can lead them, and I will. The next shipment of supplies will be this Thursday night. I'll take ten of our best men and capture the shipment; then we'll all have a late dinner and be in bed before one o'clock. No trouble at all."

"It's a *very* bad idea," Hodges insisted.

"Most good ideas look like bad ones at first," Frank informed him.

The moon was a shaving of silver in the sky, and Cromlech Road lay in total darkness. Crickets chirped a monotonous litany in the shrubbery beside the paved road, and frogs chuckled gutturally to each other in the swamps a mile to the east. The only motion came with the night breeze that swept among the treetops from time to time.

Frank crouched on a thick branch that hung out over the middle of the road, about twenty feet above the asphalt. He wore a knitted wool cap pulled low and a scarf wrapped around his face just under the eyes, and his sweater and pants were of black wool. His rapier hung scabbarded from his belt on one side; a long knife was tucked into the other. He was as motionless as the branch; even in daylight he'd have been hard to see.

Five men, also armed, hidden and silent, waited in the shrubbery on the east side of the road, and five more crouched on the west. None of them had moved or spoken for the last hour, and crickets and spiders had begun to build nests around their boots.

Frank stared at the empty stretch of the road south, only dimly visible to him, and tried to figure out what time it was. We've been out here about an hour, he thought, which would make it roughly nine o'clock now. About a half hour, then, until they come by.

Ten minutes later he tensed—a quiet, distant rattling and whirring was audible and growing momentarily louder. He curled his fingers around his sword hilt and waited, scanning the road more carefully now. The sound, punctuated now and then by coughing or an interval of muted metallic rattling, eventually became recognizable: it was that of a man riding a bicycle.

A moment later Frank saw the dim glow of the bike's headlight; he could hear the man puffing now as he pedaled the thing along, and he heard also, *very* faintly, the long scratch of a sword being drawn. Don't do it, Frank thought furiously. Can't you idiots see that he's a scout, running ahead of the shipment to make sure the way is clear? Frank held his breath, but the bicyclist passed on by the ambush without even changing the rhythm of his breathing. When the sound had dwindled away behind him, Frank let out a soft sigh of relief.

The shipment ought to be along promptly now, he thought; and sure enough, he saw, dimly in the distance, twin pinpricks of light that could only be the headlights of a Transport truck. He took a chance and gave a low whistle to alert his men. They send their scouts damned far ahead, Frank thought. We could have killed that bicyclist easily, and even if he'd yelled the truck is too far behind him to have heard it. Or maybe the bicycle was wired with flares; if we'd knocked it over, a dozen skyrockets would have pinpointed the ambush and likely set us all afire.

The truck was closer now, and he could hear its knocking motor labor up a slight rise. Well, Frank thought, it's all in the lap of the gods now.

Nearer and nearer it came, until, when it was fifty feet in front of him, two steel-headed crossbow quarrels flashed out of the shrubbery, both slanted to the south, and tore into the truck's front tires. The vehicle was doing perhaps fifty miles per hour, so the stop, after the explosive loss of the tires, was a screeching, grinding, sparking slide.

Frank had hoped the truck would stop directly below him—it didn't, quite, so he dropped out of the tree into the downward-slanting, dust-clouded headlight beams and with two blows of his dagger-hilt smashed the bulbs. The driver and two guards leaped out of the cab, brandishing swords at Frank, and were cut down by arrow-fire from the bushes.

Frank whipped out his sword, leaped to the hood and then to the top of the cab. Wooden boxes covered with a tarpaulin filled the truck bed; stretched across several of them was the limp body of another guard— apparently knocked unconscious when the truck was stopped. Even as Frank watched, one of the ambushers sank a dagger into the uniformed body.

Frank's men now dragged the four bodies into the shrubbery while Frank climbed into the cab. He put the gear shift lever into neutral, and his well-trained crew pushed the crippled truck while Frank steered it off the road. The massive vehicle was carried by its own weight several yards into the bushes. Frank's ten men cut branches from nearby trees and draped the truck with them, and aside from the cuts in the asphalt from the tire rims, there were no signs that anything had happened here.

"All right," Frank whispered. "Quick, now, there might be a scout behind them, too. Everybody take one of these boxes and follow me. Forget the rest of them—this time we'll take only what we can carry."

Each of the eleven men shouldered one of the boxes from the truck bed and filed away eastward. After about a hundred and fifty yards, they came to a wider dirt road. Turning right, the party followed it south for a quarter of a mile. Once Frank thought he heard shouts behind them, but it was very faint. The boxes were getting heavy and awkward, but no one spoke or even slackened the pace.

They finally reached the clearing where the eleven sleepy horses were tied. Frank and his men stowed their boxes in the saddlebags, mounted, and galloped away east—a bit awkwardly and unsteadily, for none of them were really competent horsemen.

When the last of the brigands had left the room, Frank turned to Hodges and the four other men at the table.

"Hand me that crowbar, will you, Hodges?" he asked. Hodges passed it to him. Frank pried up the nailed-down lid of the first box and lifted it off. In the box, wrapped in many sheets of waxed paper, were twelve .45 calibre semi-automatic pistols, glistening with oil. In the next box lay a thousand rounds of ammunition and twelve clips.

"Good God!" muttered Hodges. "Open the rest of them!"

Frank quickly opened the next box and found twenty rectangular sponges, rough on one side for scouring. The next box Frank pried apart held flat cans of saddle soap, as did the next two. Six metal bottles of kerosene lay in the next one, and the eighth box was filled with more saddle soap. The last four boxes held, respectively, hand-soap, pamphlets on diabetes, a hundred fountain pens (but no ink) and more saddle soap.

Frank opened a drawer in the table and pulled out his pipe and tobacco pouch. "Well," he said, stuffing the pipe, "the guns and ammunition will be handy. Hell, all of it's handy in one way or another. These scouring sponges, now . . ."

Hodges, who had been looking strangled, now exploded in helpless laughter. "Yeah," he gasped. "These scouring sponges, now." He picked one of them up. "Nothing but the best. Duke's choice!" He picked up two more and began juggling them.

"For God's sake, man," said Frank. "Pull yourself together."

"Sorry, sire," sniffled Hodges, wiping tears out of his eyes. "It's been a long evening."

"For all of us," Frank agreed. "Now listen. We picked them off easily tonight, because they weren't expecting anything—their precautions were minimal and the four guards we ran into were just tokens. Also, the shipment itself seems to have been a . . . fairly minor one. It won't ever be this easy again."

"Right," agreed Hodges. "Next time they'll have a lot of alert, heavily armed guards riding along. So why continue? To corner the market in sponges and saddle soap?"

Frank held a lit match over his pipe-bowl and puffed rapidly on it. "No," he said, tamping it now. "Maybe you've forgotten those twelve pistols. And there are two purposes to these raids—to scavenge things for ourselves and to impede the Transports. And of the two the second is more important.

"Maybe you've also forgotten all those reports of construction going on in the Goriot Valley. They're building offices, barracks, factories for all we know! And when they're finished, more Transports will move in than any of you dreamed existed! How many times do I have to point this out? The Subterranean Companions will be a forgotten joke inside of a year. In the meantime, though, their supplies are being landed at the Barclay Depot and driven up the Cromlech Road to the palace or the valley. If we interfere with those shipments, we put off the day the Transports take complete charge of this planet."

"He's right, Hodges," spoke up one of the previously silent councilors. "It's the least we can do."

"Right!" agreed Frank eagerly, his bronze ear glittering in the torchlight. "It is the least, a mere . . . temporary cure. We have to, eventually, get rid of the Transport entirely, which means, of course, getting rid of Costa as well." He puffed on his pipe for a moment, sending thick smoke-coils curling to the ceiling. "We've got to find an heir—a prince."

"There *aren't* any, besides Costa himself, who has no children," said Hodges with some exasperation. "And you can't simply come up with a likely-looking pretender—you'd have to have documents, proof, things no forger could counterfeit."

"I can't help that," Frank shrugged. "That's what we need."

Tom Strand jogged up the steps of the Transport General Offices' building and grinned at his reflection in the front window as he straightened his tie. Ah, you're a bright-looking lad, Tommie, he told himself. He pulled open the door and approached the stern-faced woman behind the receptionist's desk.

"Uh, hello," said Tom shyly. "I was asked to come . . . that is, I have an appointment with Captain Duprey."

The woman pursed her lips and flipped through her appointment book. "You're Thomas Strand?"

"That's right."

"He's expecting you. Second floor, room two-twelve."

"Thank you." Tom found the stairs after a few wrong turns and soon was knocking on the door of Room 212. He was told to come in, did so, and found himself in a pleasant, sunlit office, facing a smiling man with gray temples and laughter lines around his eyes.

"Tom Strand? I'm Captain Duprey." The officer half-stood and warmly shook Tom's hand. "Sit down, Tom. Will you have some brandy?"

"Yes, thank you." Tom was gratified and profoundly flattered to be on such friendly terms with a Transport officer. *I hope I'm equal to whatever job they have for me,* he thought.

"Well, Tom," said Duprey, pouring two glasses, "you're in a position to do the Transport a big favor. And"—he looked up—"the Transport is not ungrateful to people who do it favors."

"I'll be . . . glad to be of service, sir."

"Good! I knew you were a smart lad when I saw you. I can certainly see we've picked the right man! Here, drink up."

"Thank you, sir." For a moment they both simply savored the brandy.

"Are you loyal to your Duke, Tom?" asked Duprey with a sharp look.

"Oh, yes sir!" Tom had, to be sure, his private doubts and dissatisfactions, but knew when to keep them to himself. "Absolutely," he added with fervor.

"Good man!" Duprey looked ready to burst with his admiration for Tom. "Now," he said, lowering his voice solemnly, "you were, I believe, a close friend of Francisco de Goya Rovzar?"

"Yes," said Tom, mystified by this turn. "He and his father disappeared about a year ago. I heard they were sent to the Orestes mines."

"I'll tell you what happened, Tom. They were in the palace when Costa overthrew Topo's decadent rule, and they resisted arrest. The father was killed and young Francisco escaped into Munson. You've heard of the Subterranean Companions?"

"Yes. They're the ones who've been raiding your supply shipments, aren't they?"

"That's right, Tom. Well, Francisco has become their king and is the instigator of these raids!"

"He's the king?" asked Tom in amazement. "Are you sure? How did he get to become king?"

"I understand he murdered the previous king, which is how succession works with these killers and thieves. Barbaric."

"It certainly is," Tom agreed. "I can see how he'd do well at it, though. My father is a fencing instructor, and Frankie was always his star pupil."

"Is that right? Yes, that explains a lot of things." Duprey flipped open a wooden box on his desk. "Have a cigar, Tom," he said. "Genuine Havanas, all the way from Earth."

Tom took a cigar, glorying in his apparent equality with this space-wise, experienced old soldier. Duprey lit it for him, and Tom puffed at it with an expression of determined enjoyment.

"This brings us right to the point," Duprey went on. "I won't mince words, for I see you're a man who likes to know straight-out what's what. Frank Rovzar is a criminal and a leader of other criminals. He is almost certainly responsible for the deaths of . . . let's see . . . eighteen Transport soldiers, several of them officers, and his raids on our shipments are becoming more costly all the time. You see the position he puts us in?"

"I certainly do, sir."

"Good. Now what I . . . what the Transport asks of you is that you enlist in the Subterranean Companions. We'll provide you with a credible story, of course. Then you can pretend to re-establish your friendship with him; get close to him; and then, quickly and mercifully, execute him. You'll be acting as a representative of the state, naturally, and when you return from this valuable mission you'll be given a high position in our company—as well as a cash reward for Rovzar's death. It's a fairly dangerous adventure, I know, and many men would fear to take opportunity's somewhat bloody hand. But, unless I'm mistaken, you're made of sterner stuff."

Tom gulped his brandy, trying hard to mask the uncertainty inside him. *Even for a high position in the Transport,* he thought, *can I coldly kill old Frank? Still, if I turn Duprey down I'll likely wind up in jail myself.*

"I'm always ready to do my country's bidding," Tom said with a pious look. "I'll do my best, sir."

"I knew you were our man!" said Duprey with the sort of smile one saves for a true comrade.

Unlike Blanchard, Frank made it a point to attend as many meetings of the Subterranean Companions as he could. He liked to keep up on the news and to learn as much as possible about the workings of the organization he'd become king of. Generally he sat to the side, smoking thoughtfully, only occasionally speaking up to add something or ask a question of Hodges.

Tonight he squinted curiously through a haze of latakia smoke at Hodges, who had just claimed to have an announcement to make about "the deceased king, Tolley Christensen."

"After the duel in which Tolley Christensen was killed," Hodges read from his notes, "his sword was picked up, together with the sword of King Blanchard. The two swords were observed to cling to each other. Upon investigation, Tolley's sword proved to be magnetized. This is a trick expressly forbidden in the bylaws, and therefore I declare that Tolley's admittedly brief reign was won by unfair means, and is, because of that, invalidated. Henceforth, then, our present King Francisco Rovzar is to be remembered as the successor to King Blanchard, with none between."

Frank felt a quick panic. *That means that Tolley wasn't king when I killed him,* he thought. *Therefore, technically, I'm not really the king now. Damn it, Hodges, I wish you'd cleared this with me before announcing it.*

Oh hell, he thought. *Even if they do appoint someone else, I can always pull the* ius gladii *out of the hat again. And they'll know I will, so they won't try it even if they think of it.*

A magnetized sword, eh, Tolley? Were you that scared of Blanchard? In the legendry and superstition of the understreet thieves, a magnetized sword was reputed to be much deadlier than an ordinary one; but Frank couldn't see that it would make any difference. *It just might,* he thought, *make getting a bind a little easier, and it might make your parries a little quicker—but it would do the same for your opponent, too.*

Frank suddenly snapped out of his reverie. Hodges was now reading the names of newly-bonded apprentices. "What was that last name, Hodges?"

"Uh . . . Thomas Strand."

"Thank you."

Thomas Strand! Could it be my old buddy? Frank wondered. *I'll have to check the lists after the meeting and see where this Strand is staying. It would be great to have Tom down here. Since Orcrist was killed, I don't have a really close friend in this understreet antfarm—only George Tyler, I guess; and maybe Beardo Jackson.*

Eventually Hodges declared the meeting adjourned, and the crowd broke up into departing groups arguing about where to go for beer. Hodges was shuffling his papers together and a handful of young apprentices were waiting for the nod to drag out the ladders and snuff the lights.

"Hodges," Frank said. "I think I know one of the new apprentices. Let me—"

"Frank!" came a voice from below him. "Your majesty, I mean."

Frank looked down and grinned to see Tom Strand standing in front of the first-row seats. Frank jumped down from the marble block and slapped him on the back. "When the hell did you fall into the sewer world, Tom?"

"A couple of days ago. I saw you kind of blink when the emcee read my name. But Frank, you look ten years older! You've got a metal ear! And how did you cut your face? Shaving?"

"We've both got long stories to tell, I'm sure. I'm taking off, Hodges. Oh, and I'd like to see you tomorrow at ten in the council room; there's a detail or two of protocol I want to check with you on."

"Right, sire." Hodges leaped down from the platform and ambled into the sacristy.

"Come on," Frank said. "I know where we can get some beer." As they walked out he waved to the boys, who trudged off to the closet where the ladders were kept.

"Tolley killed Orcrist and Blanchard, both of them friends of mine, so I killed him. Afterward I found that that had made me the new king. And here I am. So how is it that you've become one of my subjects?"

Tom mentally ran through the story Duprey had provided him with. "Well, Frank, my old girlfriend, Bonnie—remember her? Of course you do—Bonnie and I were out getting drunk one night, and a Transport cop came over and said to her, "Drop creepo, here, baby, and try a *real* man." Well, I told him to, you know, buzz off, and he punched me in the face, so I hit him with a bottle and he fell right over, like he was dead."

He's lying, Frank thought—or at least exaggerating. Oh well, if he wants to look brave, I won't hinder him.

"There were about six other Transports there, and they went for me, swords out. I've never been scared by swords, you know that, but I figured six of 'em were too many, so I headed out the door."

"What about Bonnie?"

"Hm?"

"Bonnie. You left her there?"

"Oh . . . no, no. I knew the guy that owned the place, see, and I knew he'd look after her. Anyway, I ran out of there and headed for Munson. I didn't have any place to stay, and Munson in the winter isn't the right town for sidewalk-sleeping, so I crawled into a sewer, followed it along, and found a whole city down here."

"You were lucky you did. Munson on the surface is a Transport nest. Who's your sponsor?"

"An old guy named Jack Plant. Know him?"

"Slightly." Frank frowned inwardly. Plant was a perpetual whiner and complainer, and had in the past been vaguely suspected of having made deals with the surface police. "I'll get you a good position so you can pay off your bond quickly."

"Thanks, Frank. But I don't want you doing me favors just because I'm your friend."

"Don't worry. I never let personal feelings interfere with what's got to be done. Never. But getting you a job isn't any trouble. Finish your beer, now, and I'll show you the way back to Plant's."

After Frank had left, Tom sat drinking weak coffee in Plant's front room. I can't kill old Frank, Tom thought, even if he is a criminal. The poor devil's had a horrible time and has to live his whole life underground in a sewer. Of course it isn't *that* bad—and he's living high, by sewer standards.

Maybe, Tom thought, I could *pretend* to kill him. I could buy a slave of roughly Frank's build, and then cut the slave's head off and dress him in Frank's clothes and tell Duprey that it was Frank. Then I'd have to do something with Frank . . . maybe I could sell him into slavery in the Tamarisk Isles. I'd have to cut out his tongue, I suppose, but that's better than being killed. I guess it would probably be best to blind him, too—can't have him coming back, after all—but that's *still* better than being killed.

Yes sir, Tom smiled to himself, that's what I'll do. That way I get the Transport post Duprey promised me, and I don't have to kill Frank. Hell, he'll probably be happier, dumb and blind in the sunny Tamarisk Isles.

"Okay, Hodges, that wasn't it. Send in the next one." Frank leaned back in his chair and wished he had his pipe.

The door opened and a thin, well-dressed man entered the room. His suit was clean and meticulously pressed, but looked a bit threadbare around the cuffs. He had apparently combed his hair recently with some kind of oil.

"Please sit down," said Frank. "You are related to the royal family, I believe?"

"That's right," the man nodded.

"What is your connection?"

"My father was the rightful duke, and Topo had him killed so he could marry my mother."

"Your father was Duke Ovidi?" Frank asked.

"That's right. Topo had him killed."

"How?" Frank had always understood that Ovidi had died after falling, drunk, down a flight of stairs, thus leaving the dukedom to his brother Topo.

"My father was sleeping, and two scoundrels that Topo had hired snuck up and poured poison in his ear. Then Topo married my mother and took the title of Duke. But now I think it's time that I claimed my kinship and threw Topo out. I've been having visions—"

"Yes, yes," said Frank hastily. "Visions. I see. Well, thank you for your time. If anything develops, we'll get in touch with you."

The man stood up uncertainly and ambled out of the room. A moment later Hodges leaned in. "Another blank?" he asked.

Frank nodded.

"Nut or fortune-hunter?"

"Nut, for sure," said Frank. "The guy doesn't know Topo's dead, even."

"Well, I've got six more out here. You want 'em now or save 'em to see tomorrow?"

"Oh, tomorrow, I guess. We've *got* to find an heir, Hodges."

"If you say so, sire."

Frank waited until Hodges had got rid of the six other pretenders to the throne, and then went downstairs and put on his coat and sword.

"Going somewhere, sire?" Hodges asked.

"Yeah; I'm meeting a couple of friends on the boat."

"Be careful."

"Always, Hodges."

Cochran Street was empty as Frank closed the door behind him. The air was chilly, and foul with fumes that were filtering up from some low-level swamp or stagnant branch of the Leethee. He pulled his coat tighter about him and strode off rapidly toward his dock. After insisting that his boatman and two guards remain where they were, Frank untied a small rowboat and took off down the Leethee. The river was flowing quick and smooth, but the choppy water and erratic evening wind of the harbor slowed him down. When he reached the anchored boat another rowboat was already moored to it.

"Frank!" someone called from the deck. "Get up here with the key, for God's sake!"

Frank tied his rowboat to a mooring ring and climbed aboard the larger vessel. George Tyler stood shivering on the afterdeck, clutching a wine bottle as if it were a threatened baby. Frank unlocked the cabin and they both hurried inside.

"Get the heater lit," gasped Tyler. "I've been out there for an hour."

"You have not."

"Well, nearly. Who's this friend I've got to meet?"

"His name's Tom Strand. He was my best friend before I came understreet."

"Oh." Tyler struck a match and lit the lamps. "Say, Frank, I'm sorry about what happened at my party."

"Forget it, George. I'd say Kathrin and that Matthews dimwit are made for each other."

"I guess so. They certainly see a lot of each other, anyway." Tyler slumped into a chair. "Say," he said, "where is Sam's grave? I never thought to ask, but now I'd like to go and . . . pour some wine on his last resting place, or something."

"He doesn't have a grave," Frank told him.

"You didn't bury him?"

Frank pulled the cork out of George's wine bottle. "Not exactly. I dragged his body back to our boat and then went on to that meeting we'd been heading for. Afterward I rowed out past the jetty and tied a heavy chain around him and let him sink in the outer sea." He handed Tyler a glass of wine.

Tyler frowned for a moment, and then nodded. "You did the right thing, Frank. Bodies buried understreet always pop out sooner or later on a lower level. Here's to his shade!" He tossed off the wine.

Frank drained his, too, and flung the glass hard at the narrow starboard window, which shattered explosively outward, spraying the deck with tinkling glass. Tyler flung his through the jagged hole into the sea.

"Hey, take it easy!" someone called from outside. "Frank, is that you?"

"That must be Tom," Frank said, walking to the door. "I was beginning to worry about him."

Frank went out on deck and showed Tom where to tie his boat, then helped him aboard and opened the cabin door for him.

(Two hundred yards away a tall, blond man in the harbor patrol uniform lowered his binoculars. He looked pleased as he took up the oars and began pulling toward the south.)

"This is George Tyler, Tom, one of the great poets of our age," Frank said. "George, this is Tom Strand. Will you have some wine, Tom?"

"Sure. I can never afford any on an apprentice's wages."

"Maybe you can do better than that," said Frank, pouring two new glasses for Tyler and himself. "I have a position for you."

"Oh?" Tom took his glass and sat down. "Doing what?"

"Training my troops in fencing. They—"

"*Troops?*" Tom asked incredulously.

"That's right. I've been organizing these thieves and a lot of the homeless Goriot farmers into an army. I'm beginning to get them into some kind of shape, but they know nothing about real fighting. I've been giving groups of them some basic lessons in stance and parrying and all, but I need someone who can be a full-time instructor. You're probably as good a fencer as I am; why don't you take the job? You'll have your bond paid off in no time."

Tom stared into his wine. *An underground army,* he thought. Duprey will be damned grateful when I tell him. "Sure," he answered, looking up. "It sounds fine to me."

"Terrific. You can start the day after tomorrow. I'll have Hodges get a group of the best ones together in the meeting hall."

They soon finished the wine and opened a bottle of Tamarisk brandy; the sight brought tears to Tom's eyes.

"Easy, Tom," Frank said jovially. "I guess it's been a long time since you've had good brandy. Relax. Real soon you'll be able to buy all the fine brandy you want."

"I know," said Tom.

CHAPTER 2

A fly was circling, in the aimless way of flies, in and out of a beam of morning sunlight in Duke Costa's throne room, annoying him mightily. Three hard-eyed, leather-faced men stood in front of him and watched impassively as the powdered and jewel-decked Duke flung books at the insect.

Finally one of them spoke. "Your grace," he rasped. "Why have you called for us?"

"What? Oh. You're the assassins, right?"

The three men exchanged cold looks. "We served your father in many ways," spoke up another of them.

"I know. But right now it's only as assassins that I want to see you. Now listen closely, I hate repeating myself. The King of the Subterranean Companions is a young man named Francisco Rovzar. He owns a large boat in the harbor, just north of the ship basin; and he spends time there, I've heard, when he wants to relax after doing whatever horrible things he does—interfering with the government, mostly. Anyway, I want you to kill him. I'll pay you the same rate my father did."

"Double it," growled one. "The malory isn't worth a sowbug's dowry these days."

Costa frowned and pressed his lips together, but nodded. The three men bowed and filed out of the room.

They're insolent boys, Costa thought. *I probably should have had them seized and flung into a dungeon (I wonder if I have any dungeons?). But no, I'll let them kill Rovzar first. It will be fun to mention, off the cuff, of course, to those serious-minded Transports that I've succeeded where they've failed, and had Rovzar killed without their tiresome help.*

Tom Strand lifted his mask so that it sat on his head like a conquistador's helmet. "Okay," he called to the thirty sweating men lined up in the hall. "Advance, advance, advance, retreat, advance, *lunge!*" His students leaped about awkwardly, thrusting their swords in all directions.

"Well, that's pretty bad," Tom said. "Let's call it a day. But be back here tomorrow—I'll teach this stuff to you guys or kill you all trying."

The thirty thieves sheathed their swords and swaggered out of the hall, clearly pleased with themselves. Tom threw his mask onto the floor, sheathed his own sword and hurried out after them. He decided he didn't have time to change out of his white fencing clothes.

He made his furtive way down a little-used alley that opened onto a stairway, which he followed down two flights. Moored to an ancient stone dock was a small skiff, in whose bottom lay two oars, a wide-bladed axe and a bound and gagged man. Tom hopped in, shoved the tied man aside, loosed the rope and pushed away from the dock with an oar.

"So far so good," he whispered nervously to the terrified prisoner. "Frank will get there about an hour after you and I do. Ha ha! You're helping me into a high-paying Transport job, pal, so I guess the least I can do is kill you quick."

The boat skimmed smoothly down the torch-lit Leethee tide, and none of the scavengers and beggars they passed gave the skiff a second look. Soon they passed through the last stone arch and found themselves in the harbor. The sun was only a hairsbreadth clear of the ocean's horizon, and the sky was a cathedral of terraced red-and-gold clouds against a background of pale blue.

"We're timing it well, my friend," Tom grinned, turning the boat north. "Old Redbrick's ship ought to be just lowering anchor beyond the jetty. I'll kill you (begging your pardon), knock out poor Frank, cut out his tongue and eyes and row him out to the ship. Redbrick will give me a hundred malories and take Frank away to the Tamarisk Isles. I'll take your headless body to Duprey, and tell him it's Frank, and he'll give me a job. Everybody does well except you, I guess. And, hell, a slave is probably happier dead anyway, right?" The slave moaned through his gag. "That's right," agreed Tom.

He worked the boat north, around the anchored merchant ships, until Frank's boat came into view. He pulled alongside it, relieved to see no other boats moored there.

"Up you go," Tom said cheerfully, hoisting the slave like an awkward piece of lumber onto the deck. Tom followed, carrying the axe. "Okay, you just lay there for a minute," he said. "This is complicated, I admit, but if we all do our parts it'll work out fine."

The slave turned his face despairingly to the cabin wall. Tom shrugged, put down the axe and went to the door, which was locked; he kicked it open and hurried into Frank's room, where he picked up a gray shirt, a sword, a pair of shoes and a pair of white corduroy pants. He bundled these together, and went out on deck again.

The bound slave still faced the wall, so Tom quietly set the clothes on the deck and picked up the axe. He raised it over his head, aiming at the man's neck. Then he swung it down with all the force he could add to the thing's own weight, and he crouched as he struck to keep the blow perpendicular. He stood up a moment later, rocked the blood-splashed axe blade loose from the deck-wood it had bitten into, and flung it overboard. The severed head he tied in a canvas bag weighted with two sextants, which he also tossed over the side.

He cut the ropes loose from the body and stripped it of its clothes, and then pulled Frank's pants and shirt onto it. The shoes were difficult—he pushed them and pounded on the slave's feet, but to no avail. He finally tossed the shoes into the sea. The sword clipped easily onto the belt, and Tom stood up dizzily.

Good God, he thought, suppressing a very deep nausea. What horrible things people sometimes have to do. Oh well: I'll enjoy the future luxury all the more for this present ugliness. He picked up the slave's blood-stained clothes, wrapped a large fishing sinker in them, and threw that bundle, too, into the water. It's a messy ocean floor tonight, he thought crazily. I wonder how often the cleaning lady comes.

He stumbled to the bow and sat down in one of the canvas deck chairs to await Frank's arrival. The sun was in Tom's eyes; no matter how he blinked and shifted his gaze he frequently got an eyeful of glare. Black spots floated through his vision. For this reason he didn't notice the approaching rowboat until it was only about fifty yards away.

"Oh no," he muttered. He stood up and waved, and then dashed back behind the cabin, crouched beside the headless body and rolled it over the rail into the sea. "I'll fish you out again real soon," he said softly to it. Then he ran back to the bow and waved again, smiling broadly.

"That's him," said one of the three men in the boat. "Look at him waving at us, all dressed in white. He must have mistaken us for someone."

"Yeah," agreed another. "I wonder why he ran away when he first saw us, though? Do you think it's a trap?"

"I don't know," said the third. "Best not to get too close, anyway. Move in ten yards more and I'll pitch a bomb at him."

A minute later the third man stood up, lit the fuse of a shot-put sized bomb and hurled it at the larger boat. Tom still stood on the bow, waving. A moment later an obscuring explosion tore a hole in the cabin and flung pieces of lumber spinning through the air. The roar of the detonation echoed off the shore, and a cloud of smoke and wood splinters hung over the blasted vessel.

"Let's circle and look for the body," growled the man in the stern. The little rowboat made an unhurried circle around the smoking boat, and near the stern they found floating the headless body of the slave. They pulled it aboard.

"That's him all right. Odd the way the bomb just took his head off and left the rest of him untouched, though."

"Who cares?" said another. "It's him. Look, there's one of his shoes floating there. I've seen bombs do that. Let's get this body back to Costa quickly, and get paid." The other two nodded, and the one at the oars began leaning into his work.

An hour later Frank wearily tied up his own rowboat next to Tom's at the stern and climbed aboard. "Tom?" he called. "Sorry I'm late. Business, you know. Tom?" It was still light enough to see, and he looked around the stern. The cabin door is open, he noticed. Tom must have fallen asleep below. Did he *kick* the door open? Then he noticed the wide blood stains on the deck and whipped out his sword.

"Tom!" he shouted. "Where are you?" He leaped inside the cabin—and stared at the chaos he found. The bulkhead between the cabin and his own stateroom was split; the air was thick with the smell of gunpowder; his bed and desk lay shattered in the broken doorway, and stretched across this wreckage was a naked and clearly dead body. Frank crossed to it warily, and stared at the face.

He was just able to recognize it as Tom Strand's.

Frank backed out of the cabin and sat down heavily on the deck. My father, he thought. Orcrist. Blanchard. And now Tom. I'm poison to my friends, beyond doubt.

After a while he stood up and stared out to sea, where a ship beyond the jetty was unfurling its sails and tacking south.

It must be the Transports who did this, Frank thought. They must have found out I was coming here frequently, and thought Tom was me. He went below and carried four bottles of Tamarisk brandy into the cabin, then broke them on the floor. After he dropped a lit match into the aromatic puddle and heard it *whoosh* alight, he strode out onto the deck, climbed into his rowboat and cast off.

Hodges lit a cigarette nervously. He liked times of quiet prosperity, leisure to spend untroubled days with his family and cats. It upset him to scent doom in the air, and tonight it almost masked the tobacco reek in his nostrils. He watched gloomily as Frank poured himself a fifth glass of scotch.

"Gentlemen," Frank said, "remember that you are . . . only my . . . *advisors.* I will listen, have listened, to your timid cautions and warnings, and I don't believe there's *any* course of action you'd favor. I've told you my idea, and you haven't yet given me a good objection."

Hodges leaned forward. "Your plan, sire, is to try out for the job of painting Costa's portrait and to kill him once you get close to him. Right?"

"That's right, Hodges. You've got it."

"Well, Mr. Hussar has pointed out that you'd be killed yourself, almost immediately."

"I might not," Frank said, taking a liberal sip of his drink. "That doesn't matter, anyway. The main thing is to get rid of Costa."

"Ah. But who would they replace him with?"

"I don't know. A relative, if he has any—though God knows I can't find any. Who cares? It would be a change, anyway."

"Maybe not," Hodges answered. "Costa is only a figurehead for the Transport government. Kill him and they'll get another mascot. If you could kill the whole Transport there'd be a change—but killing poor idiot Costa would do nothing but give you personal vengeance, which a king can't really afford."

"Well, dammit, Hodges, I've got to do *something*. Every day we lie quiet, the Transport gets stronger. What's being done to stop them? I—"

"Sire," Hodges said, "Hemingway said never confuse motion with action. I think—"

"*I* think," said Mr. Hussar, leaning forward, "that perhaps we ought to discuss Mr. Rovzar's claim to be our king."

Hodges let the cigarette smoke hiss out between his teeth. Everyone had stopped talking, so the sound of Frank's sword sliding out of its sheath was clearly audible.

"How do you mean, Hussar?" asked Frank with a smile.

"Put your sword away," Hussar snapped angrily. "Tolley wasn't king when you killed him. Isn't that right, Hodges? Therefore, you can't claim the *ius gladii* precedent. Therefore you're not our king." Hussar sat back. "I wouldn't have brought this up," he added, "if you hadn't exhibited signs of alcoholism and insanity."

"Hodges," Frank said. "A point of protocol: what is the procedure when someone calls the king's qualifications into question?"

Hodges answered wearily, as if reciting a memorized piece. "The person is free to prove his allegations by engaging the king in personal combat. Sorry, Hussar."

Frank stood up, suddenly looking much soberer. His sword was in his hand. "Now, then, Hussar, what about these allegations?"

Hussar pressed his lips together angrily. "I withdraw them, sire," he said.

There was a long pause. "All right," Frank said finally. He sheathed his sword and sat down, looking vaguely puzzled and defeated. "I . . . I guess you're right, Hodges. A kamikaze attack on Costa personally would accomplish nothing." He had another sip of scotch. "What we've got to do, I guess, is keep building our army and keep looking for a ducal heir. We have the strength right now to take the palace—especially since we captured that dynamite shipment en route to the Goriot Valley two days ago; all we need now is a genuine prince." He drained his glass. "Keep sending the claimants to me, Hodges. Maybe if we don't find a real one we can come up with a convincing fake."

"Aye, aye," Hodges said. "Gentlemen, I pronounce this meeting adjourned." Everyone except Frank stood up and began shouldering on coats and bidding each other good night. They all filed out, leaving Frank alone in the room. Two of the lamps had gone out, the candles were low in their sockets, and the clink of the bottle-lip on the glass-edge, and the gurgle of the scotch sluicing into the glass, were the only sounds.

Heavy music resounded in Kelly Harmon's huge living room, and most of the guests were dancing wildly. Harmon lived in the finest district of Munson Understreet, and his parties, which had become legendary in the belt-tightening days of Costa's reign, were said to be the gathering place of all the truly worthwhile people in Munson, above or below the surface. The music, provided by a trio of crazed trumpet players, was so loud that the knocking at the door could only be heard by the people actually leaning against it. They pulled the door open and a tall, dark-bearded man edged his way inside, waving an invitation, and was soon absorbed into the crowd.

The music and dancing slowly mounted in intensity to a feverish and frenzied climax, after which the dancers began reeling to their chairs and gulping drinks. Kathrin Figaro whirled like a spun top to the last choppy bars of one song, and collided with a table, knocking over a lamp.

"Whoops!" she giggled. "Time for a rest, I think." She weaved away from the dance floor to the only empty chair, at a back table at which the bearded man was sitting. "Can I join you?" she asked breathlessly. He looked up at her and, after the briefest hesitation, nodded.

"Thank you." She slid into the chair and looked at her table-mate. Long black hair was cut in uneven bangs across his forehead, and his eyes hid in a network of wrinkles under his brows. The black beard didn't quite hide a long scar that arched across his cheek. "Do I know you?" she asked politely, privately wondering how this derelict had got in.

"Yes," he said.

Kathrin looked at him uneasily. "Who are you?"

"John Pine."

Kathrin looked blank, and then startled. "*Frank* . . . ?" she whispered. He nodded.

"But I heard you were dead—they hung . . . *somebody's* headless body, dressed in your clothes, from the palace wall a week ago." He shrugged impatiently. "When did you grow the beard, Frank? I don't like it."

"My name, *please,* is John Pine. The beard's fake."

"Oh." She lifted two glasses of champagne from the tray of a passing steward and set one of them before Frank. "Isn't it terribly risky for you to be here? Did you come to see me?"

"No," he said. "I didn't know you'd be here. I came because I was bored." He sipped the champagne. "Harmon has been sending me invitations to these affairs for months, and I decided to take him up on one."

"Will I see you at more of these, then?" she asked brightly.

"No. I'm not much of a party man, as you doubtless recall. And it *is* too risky a thing to make a habit of."

She tasted her drink thoughtfully. "Are you still king of the . . . you-know-whos?" He nodded. "I heard about how you got it. It sounded very brave." He looked at her skeptically. "I don't see Matthews anymore, John. He treated me horribly, just . . . horribly. Do you think," she went on, lowering her eyes, "there's any chance of us trying it again?"

Yes, he thought. "No," he said.

"But I've—"

"Don't embarrass both of us, Kathrin." He stood up. "There's nothing to say. I shouldn't have come to this. I'm sorry." He stepped around the table, pushed his way through the crowd to the door and disappeared into the eternal understreet night.

The yawning page boy plodded around the room, refilling the oil-reservoirs of the lamps from a can he carried. The job done, he returned to his chair, began nodding sleepily and was soon snoring.

George Tyler refilled Frank's wine glass and then his own; his aim had deteriorated during the evening, and he poured a good deal of it onto the tabletop.

"Frank," George said carefully, "don't try to pretend with *me* that this is an . . . altruistic action you're contemplating. You *know* that it isn't Costa that's strangling this planet. He's just a . . . pitiful puppet . . . within whom moves the cold, steely hand of the Transport." Pleased with his metaphor, Tyler chuckled and gulped his wine. "*And* it isn't even personal revenge, lad, that's goading you to kill the poor geek. Not entirely, anyway. Want to know what it is?"

"What is it, George?" Frank asked obligingly.

"It's suicide, Frankie," said Tyler sadly. "You want to die. No, don't get rude with me; I'm a poet, I'm allowed to talk this way. If you go grinning up to the palace gate with a knife in your paint box, it may look like a gallant bid for revenge, but *I'll* know. It will be a suicide attempt, disguised as desperate vengeance to fool everyone, yourself as well, maybe."

"George, you are so full of crap—"

"Yeah, you say that. But you're my last friend since Sam got it, and now you're *eager* to get killed. And all because that half-wit girl ditched you for Matthews."

"That isn't it, George. Not much of it, anyway."

"Aha! You admit it's suicide, then?"

"I'm not admitting anything, dammit. I'm humoring a raving drunk."

"Well, *there's* a judgment. But all right, I won't bother you anymore."

For a full five minutes they drank in silence.

"Someday I'll be restored to my former exalted state," Tyler muttered, half to himself, "and then I'll set all this right. I'll have Costa sweeping the gutters, and then you won't have to kill him."

"George," said Frank levelly, "I have been trying very hard, for weeks, to find a real claimant to the ducal throne. Throughout that time I have admired your tact in not burdening me with your own . . . delusions in that line. If there is (and there *is*) one thing I don't want to hear, it's another crackpot telling me he's the true prince."

"I'm sorry, Frank," Tyler said. "You're right, you don't need that." He emptied his glass. "I don't really believe all my stories, either, so you needn't think I'm a crackpot. It's just my poetic nature letting off steam."

"I didn't mean you're a crackpot, George. I spoke . . . heatedly, without thinking." Frank opened the table drawer and felt around in it, but his pipe was missing. "Where *did* you come up with all those stories about being Topo's son, anyway?" he asked.

"I made them up, mostly," Tyler said. "And my mother used to tell me I was. I was an illegitimate child, you see. I'll bet all unwed mothers tell their sons they're the secret offspring of royalty."

"Yeah, probably so. Not a good idea, in the long run, if you ask me." Frank poured out the last dribble of the bottle. "Page. Hey, page! Another bottle of this. A cold one."

The page nodded and scampered away.

"It was a bedtime story, you see," Tyler explained. "She was a scullery maid, at one time, in the palace, so when she was fired she hinted to everybody that Topo was the real father of her illegitimate brat. I always liked the story, that's all."

"Didn't she ever give you a reason why the Duke didn't acknowledge you as his son?" asked Frank, curious in spite of himself.

"Didn't need to. What self-respecting duke would admit to having a child by a scullery maid? Besides, she was fired and moved understreet, soon after I was born. But wait—" Tyler squinted thoughtfully "—I remember now. She always did tell me that Topo had written up an official birth certificate for me, acknowledging me as his blooded son. Costa, the story says, was a spoiled kid even then, and Topo wanted to have the option of leaving the dukedom of Octavio to me. Hah!"

The wine arrived and Frank twisted a corkscrew into the bottle.

"Not just his son—his favorite, too, eh?"

"Yeah, it's delusions of grandeur, I admit. She was real convincing about it, though. Even told me once where Topo had hidden the birth certificate."

"Oh?" said Frank. "Where?"

"In a copy of *Winnie the Pooh*. Frank! That's good wine!"

Frank had dropped the bottle, and pieces of wet glass spun on the floor. The page leaped up to fetch a mop and broom. "Never mind that," Frank told him. "Get Hodges for me. Tell him to summon a full council, at once. Yes, I know it's three o'clock in the morning. A full council, you hear? Immediately! Run!"

The page darted out of the room.

"Frank," said Tyler uncertainly, "are you all right?"

"For the first time in months, George."

An hour later twelve irritable lords sat around the table, their eyes squinting, their hair oddly tufted, and half of them in incorrectly-buttoned shirts.

"What is this, Hodges?" rasped Hussar. "More delirium tremens?"

"You're treading on thin ice, Hussar," said Hodges softly. "His majesty will be here in a moment to explain the reason for this meeting."

"We probably haven't been hijacking enough brandy to suit him," giggled Emsley.

"I'll discuss that with you afterward, if you like, Emsley," said Frank, who had silently entered the room. "Come on in, George."

Frank and Tyler took the two empty chairs at Hodges's left. "All right, gentlemen," Frank said, "I've found an heir—a genuine one, as a matter of fact. He's an illegitimate son of Topo, and I know where to find a birth certificate, signed by Topo, acknowledging him as a son."

The lords stared at him skeptically. Even Hodges looked doubtful, knowing that Frank had not interviewed any claimants since the last meeting. "And who is this lost prince?" asked Hussar, with a look of long-suffering patience.

"It's George Tyler," Frank said, knowing full well the response that declaration would have. It did. After a moment of stunned silence all the lords burst into howls of laughter.

"*Tyler?*" gasped Emsley. "Get some black coffee into you, Rovzar."

"Black coffee?" queried Frank with a quick smile. "Why black coffee, my lord?"

"Because you're drunk," Emsley replied carelessly, not seeing the snare.

"That will do, I think," Frank said, "especially in front of thirteen witnesses. You will do me the honor, Lord Emsley, of meeting me in East Watson Hall tomorrow morning at ten?"

Emsley paled. He glanced at Hussar, who was staring at the tabletop, and then at Frank. "But I—" he began. Frank raised his eyebrows. "All right," Emsley said weakly. "Ten o'clock."

"Now back to more important things," said Frank. "George, tell them about your bedtime story."

Tyler awkwardly outlined the story his mother used to tell him, and told them where she'd claimed the birth certificate was hidden.

"And I know where that copy of *Winnie the Pooh* is, gentlemen," said Frank. "I was with Topo when he was killed, and just before the Transports kicked down the door, I saw where he hid it."

"Where?" asked Hussar.

"In the throne room. For the time being I'll keep to myself the exact hiding place. Now pay attention, here is what we'll do: I'll assume a disguise and apply for the job of painting Costa's portrait; I'm confident that I'll get it. Once in the throne room I will quietly remove the *Winnie the Pooh* from its concealment, make an excuse to visit a bathroom, and blow a loud whistle down the bathtub drain."

"And what will that do?" asked Hussar with exaggerated politeness.

"It will summon our army, which will be waiting in the sewers under the Ducal Palace. They will dynamite, from beneath, all the bathrooms, janitor closets and laundry rooms in the ground floor of the palace, and attack through the resultant holes. Our army is large and adequately trained, as you all know, even though it's made of thieves and farmers. I don't think there's any doubt that we can take the palace. And with an acknowledged prince to set on the throne, we can hold it."

There was a thoughtful silence. "I think it's good," said Hodges finally. "I think it'll work."

"If you've got it right about this birth certificate," said Hussar cautiously, "I agree."

The others all nodded their somewhat qualified approval, except for Emsley, who looked nauseous.

"With George on the throne we'll be able to evict the Transport from Octavio," Frank said. "They won't go cheerfully, but they haven't become strong enough to openly oppose the government. In a year they *would* be strong enough. I suggest, therefore, that we mount our attack on the day after tomorrow, first to strike before they get any stronger, and second to prevent them from hearing about it in advance."

"This seems hasty, your majesty . . ." began Hodges.

"It's quick, Hodges, but it isn't hasty. Now send me maps of the palace sewers, and their connections with the understreet sewers. You'll all be hearing from me tomorrow (later today, I should say), so be where I can reach you. And Hodges," added Frank as they all stood up, "since it looks like I'm going to get no sleep tonight, bring me a pot of black coffee, will you?"

For the next three hours, Frank studied multi-level sewer diagrams and drawings of the palace, making copious notes and drinking quantities of coffee. Finally he threw down his pen and rubbed his bloodshot eyes.

"I think I see how we'll do it," he said to Hodges, who was lighting his twelfth cigarette since the meeting. "The palace sewers all run into a long watercourse that joins the Leethee near the Bailey District. That's the most direct route, and it shouldn't be hard for you to get the army organized there. Then you run them up the line and into the pipes that connect with the palace. The pipes are all five feet high and probably well-built, since they date from the time of Duke Giroud. Then you'll just wait for the whistle."

"Sounds good to me, sire," said Hodges a little sleepily.

Frank sat back and drained his most recent cup of coffee. "Hodges?"

"Yes, sire?"

"Was the Subterranean Companions' meeting hall ever a church?"

Hodges blinked. "Uh, yes. A couple of hundred years ago some philanthropist built two churches understreet. He later disappeared—some say he ascended bodily into heaven, some say he fell into the Leethee." Hodges took a long puff on the cigarette and exhaled slowly. "So one of his churches became our meeting hall, and one, to the northwest, was converted into a cheap hotel. It was destroyed, incidentally, when that bomb took out four levels last year. The place had two carved-iron gates out front, said to have been cast by some sculptor of note. They both fell into the Leethee flood when the explosion kicked the place apart. Haven't been found yet."

"Ah." Frank reached for the coffee pot. "Well, I've got to figure out the arrangement of our troops, Hodges, but you can go home. Get some sleep; we'll all be busy as hell later today."

"Right. Thank you, sire."

CHAPTER 3

Thirty miles northwest of Munson—separated from the city by slums, suburbs, small cities and, eventually, the most wealthy neighborhoods on the planet—stood the Ducal Palace, a grim fortress of centuries-old stone under the bright banners that waved from its walls.

The sun had made dust of the spring mud, and the merchants who thronged the gate and courtyard wore veils across their noses and mouths. Street musicians fiddled and clanged at every corner, storytellers babbled to rings of children, and palace guards fingered their sweat-damp sword grips and squinted irritably at the crowds. The place was a carnival of smells: garlic, curried meat, dust, sweat, hot metal and exotic tobacco.

Under the barbican, across the bridge and through the gate plodded a tall man on a gray horse. The man wore a ragged brown leather jacket and a white cape, and had wrapped a length of white cloth around his head and across his lower face, so that only his cold blue eyes, a glimpse of a scar and a lock or two of black hair showed. He was unarmed, and carried only a wooden box slung behind him on the saddle.

Whichever way it falls today, Frank thought, *this is the end of a circular road I've traveled for a year. It's been a busy year, too—I've been an art forger, a thief, a kitchen boy, a fencing teacher and a king of thieves. I've fallen in love, and climbed out of it. And I've seen more deaths—of friends, enemies and strangers—than I want to think about.*

He nudged his tired horse across the crowded courtyard to the steps of the keep.

"What's your business, stranger?" asked the guard, a red-faced man in the ubiquitous Transport uniform.

Frank unwrapped the white cloth from his head and shook back his hair. An artificial moustache clung to his upper lip. "I've come to paint the Duke's portrait," he said. "I understand he wants it done."

"Yeah, that's true, he does. Leave your horse here and go down the hall inside. Third door on your left. Are you armed?"

"No. I'm a painter."

"Well, open up your box and let me see."

Frank unstrapped his battered wooden box and handed it to the guard, who set it down on the dusty pavement and flipped up its lid. He rummaged about for a few seconds in the brushes, crumpled tubes and bottles, and then closed it and gave it back.

"Okay," he said. "Go on in. Third on your left."

Frank dismounted and let a footman lead his horse away, then picked up his box and walked up the steps into the keep. The third door on the left opened easily when Frank turned the knob, revealing a counter behind which a dozen people sat at paper-littered desks. An old man shambled up to the counter.

"You're applying for the custodial position?" he asked.

"No," Frank said. "I've come to paint Duke Costa's portrait."

"Oh. Okay. Wait on that bench for a moment."

Five minutes later a grinning, slick-haired clerk approached. "You've brought your portfolio, yes?"

"No," Frank said, "but I'll draw you in two minutes."

The man raised an eyebrow. "Go ahead."

Frank took a chewed pencil from a pocket in his leather jacket. He laid his box across his knees and quickly sketched the man, using the side of the box for a surface. The drawing was quick and graceful, shaded with the fine cross-hatching of which his father had been master.

"Hm," said the official, peering at it. "Not bad. But can you paint? It's a painting he wants, you know."

"Paint. Sure." Frank took three tubes of paint, all shades of brown, out of his box and squeezed blobs from them onto the bench. He dipped a brush in one and went to work on the wall. In five minutes there glistened on the ancient plaster a portrait, done in the style of Goya, of the slick-haired clerk.

"Well," said the clerk. "You've got the job, assuming the Duke likes your work, which I think he will; but I'm afraid I'll have to fine you five malories for defacing government property."

"Take it out of my salary," Frank said. "When can I start on the portrait?"

"Anytime, I guess. I'll have a guard escort you to the throne room, and you can discuss it with the Duke himself. Uh, what's your name?"

"Richard Helder," Frank told him. The clerk scribbled it on a piece of paper, then handed it to a guard.

"Just follow him, Mr. Helder," the clerk said. Frank nodded his thanks and followed the guard upstairs.

The throne room, as Frank noticed when he was finally admitted, had changed considerably during his absence. The bookcases and desk were gone, replaced by overly colorful tapestries, the throne had been painted, and the year-old, unfinished Claude Rovzar portrait of Duke Topo was nowhere to be seen.

Duke Costa, a little redder of face and ampler of belly, was sitting on the throne and staring at a sheaf of star-maps. "Who's that?" he asked the guard, pointing at Frank.

"An artist," said the guard. "Richard Helder. Briggs passed him."

"I'll be with you in a moment," Costa smiled, returning to his star-maps. Frank nodded and sat down in a chair by the entrance. He glanced at the doors and saw, dimly under the new paint, the unevenness of the putty filling in the old bullet holes.

The rise and fall of Duke Costa, Frank thought. Or maybe the rise and fall of Frank Rovzar. This is the room our fathers died in.

Under this building, he thought, staring at the floor, crouches, silently, my army. It would be an interesting development if the army *wasn't* down there—if they've simply stayed home, as Emsley told them to do yesterday, just before I killed him.

Idly, as he waited, Frank did a couple of sketches of Costa in profile on the reverse side of the paint box.

Finally Costa flung the maps aside. "Mr. Helder?" he said. "I understand Briggs likes your work. He's not too easily pleased. What were you drawing there, just a second ago?"

Frank walked forward and showed the Duke the profiles.

"Not bad," Costa said with a critical squint. "I like the style. Did you ever study the works of Rovzar?"

"What artist hasn't?" replied Frank.

"Just so," nodded Costa. "When can you begin?"

"That depends," said Frank in an artificially casual voice. "You see, the only canvases I have are small—fit for paintings of children, or kittens, but hardly Dukes. I can order a canvas, of course; but with the interplanetary shipping system in the state it's in, God knows when it would come." He hoped Costa was unaware that canvases were made on Octavio. "Uh . . . you wouldn't happen to *have* an old canvas, a painting, lying around, that I could paint over? Something roughly ten feet by five feet?"

"By God, I have!" laughed Costa. "Hey, guard!" he yelled. "Bring that picture in here! The big unfinished one!" He grinned at Frank. "You, sir," he said, "are to have the privilege of painting over a genuine unfinished Rovzar."

Frank raised his eyebrows, but didn't say anything.

The painting was brought in, still on the original easel. It was dimmed with dust, and something greasy had dripped down the left side of it, but

Frank easily recognized his father's work, and the sight of it brought back memories of the old man with more force than anything else had in a year.

The guards bowed and withdrew. Frank took a rag out of his paint box and gently wiped off the canvas. There, looking nobler than Frank had ever seen him look in life, sat Duke Topo. Frank reached out and ran his fingers over the fine brush strokes.

He turned to Costa to speak, but saw the Duke, suddenly pale, rising from the throne and pointing a trembling finger at him. "I . . . I was told you were dead," he whispered.

"You've got me confused with someone," said Frank levelly.

"No, no. Your drawing style—I should have guessed immediately." The Duke slid his jewel-hilted rapier out of its velvet scabbard and then ran at Frank with the weapon held over his head like an axe. Frank snatched up the paint box and caught the descending blade with it; the sword stuck, and Frank roughly levered it out of Costa's grasp. He kicked the Duke in the stomach and Costa dropped to the floor. Frank wrenched the paint-smeared blade loose, raised it—Costa cowered under an upflung arm—and brought it down across the face of the painting, slashing the canvas open from top to bottom.

"Guards!" bellowed Costa, scuttling away from him like a frightened beetle. "I'm being killed!"

Frank reached in behind the split painting and seized the book, then ran to the door just as it was flung open by the first of four sword-waving Transport guards.

Frank drove the paint-colorful rapier at one of them, who parried it hard, flinging drops of color at the wall. The *Winnie the Pooh* was in Frank's right hand, so he hit the man in the face with it. A sword tore a gash in Frank's right shoulder, and he twisted around and cut the throat of the guard who held it. Then he was through them, and running to find a bathroom. He impatiently peeled off the itchy false moustache and flung it to the ground.

"Get him! Get him!" screamed Costa. "He's insane!"

Frank ducked into one room and surprised a half-dozen women who were tacking typed pages onto a bulletin board; he fled them and their panicky, guard-drawing screams and dashed down another hallway. Blood from his shoulder spotted his cape and ran down his arm onto the leather binding of the book he held.

Ahead of him a guard appeared from around a corner. The man raised his arm and a bang sounded as a strip of plaster beside Frank's head turned to powder. Frank convulsively kicked open the nearest door, ran through the room beyond it and, whirling his cape over his head, leaped through the closed window.

He fell, together with a rain of shattered glass, through fifteen feet of air onto a pavement, rolling as he landed to minimize the impact. He tore his cape off, picked up his book and colorful sword and looked around. He was in an enclosed garden; tables stood among the greenery, and astonished people were flinging down forks and getting to their feet; two guards, swords out, strode toward him.

Frank desperately picked up a chair from beside a nearby table and tossed it through the largest ground-floor window, which burst inward with a hideous racket. Frank leaped through it, hearing the shouts of guards from all sides. I'll never get to a bathroom now, he thought dizzily. They've got me surrounded.

He was in a bar-lounge occupied only by a sparse mid-morning crowd. He vaulted over the bar, scattering glasses and ashtrays, and sent the bartender sprawling with a blow of his sword-pommel. Then, lying under the bar sink, he fumbled in his pocket and put a powerful whistle to his lips, and blew it with all the strength he could wring out of his lungs directly into the floor-drain.

"Where is he?" called someone excitedly.

"He's hiding behind the bar!" howled the bartender, who had run off while Frank was blowing the whistle.

"All right, Pete, bring your boys in from the left, and we'll go in from the right. We may be able to get him alive."

Frank blew his whistle twice more, cupping his hands around the drain to aim the noise downward.

"The Duke's right," someone called. "He *is* crazy. He's trying to play music back there."

Frank took hold of his sword, stuffed the book in his shirt and stood up. A dozen of them. Here's where I die, possibly. "What'll it be, gents?" he asked with a smile.

They charged—and simultaneously the wall behind them exploded into the room like a gravel pile kicked by a giant. Frank was hurled backward into a display case full of bottles, and two of the Transports landed on top of him. After the debris had stopped falling he flung their limp bodies aside and struggled to his feet, coughing in the dust-foggy air. He heard the roars of two more explosions; and a third; and a fourth.

The silhouettes of men moved behind the rubble of the wall. "Hey!" Frank called, waving his sword. "This way, Companions! I'm Rovzar!"

The men cheered and ran to him, led by Hussar. "Should have known I'd find you in the bar," the lord grinned.

"We've got to get upstairs," Frank said. "Costa's up there. Come on." Every second, more men were climbing out of the hole in the foundation where the ladies' room had been, but Frank impatiently hustled the first ten out of the bar and up the first flight of stairs they came to.

They met three guards on the stairs; two died and the third fled upstairs, hotly pursued. Yells, cheers and explosions echoed up and down the embattled corridors. Frank's band of Companions took off after the fleeing Transport, but Frank concentrated on his search for the Duke. After a few minutes of running and dodging he saw, at the end of a corridor, the two doors bearing the scarred Frankie-and-Johnnie bas-relief. He ran toward them and launched a flying kick that ripped the bolt out of the wood on the other side. The doors slammed inward, knocking over a Transport guard and startling six others. Behind them all stood Costa, radiating both fear and rage.

"There he is, idiots!" he yelled. "Get him, quickly!"

Frank ran at the six guards and, with only a token preparatory feint, drove his point through one man's throat. He parried a downward-sweeping blade with his right arm, and winced as the edge bit through the leather jacket into his skin; then he riposted with a quick jab between the ribs and the man rolled to the floor, more terrified than hurt. Two Transports now engaged Frank's blade while a third man ran in and swung a whistling slash into Frank's belly. The impact knocked Frank off his feet and the guards cheered as their adversary fell.

"Finish him, finish him!" screeched Costa, waving a rapier he'd picked up.

The foremost guard raised his sword as if he were planting a flag, and drove it savagely downward into the floor, for Frank had rolled aside. Pausing only to hamstring another guard, he scrambled catlike to his feet. His shirt was cut across just above the belt, and the *Winnie the Pooh* had been chopped nearly in half.

Costa, beginning to worry about the outcome of the skirmish, tore down one of his gaudy tapestries and opened a door it had hidden. Frank saw him step through it, and swung a great arc with his blade to make the Transports jump back a step—like most novice swordsmen, they were more fearful of the dramatic edge than the deadlier but less spectacular point—and then leaped for the secret door, catching it a moment before it would have clicked shut. He hopped through before the four remaining guards got to it, and shot the bolt just as they began wrenching and pounding on the door from the other side.

He turned; a narrow stairway rose before him, and he could hear Costa's quick steps ahead and above. Frank gripped his sword firmly and loped up the stairs two at a time. He was very tired—near exhaustion, really—and he was losing blood from his right shoulder and forearm; but he wanted to settle the issue with Costa before he rested. He kept thinking about the night at the Doublon Festival when he had seen Costa's face over the barrel of a pistol, and had failed to pull the trigger.

At the top of the stairs stood an open arch that framed a patch of the blue sky. Leaping through it Frank found himself on the slightly tilted red-tile roof of the palace. The stairway arch he'd come out of stood midway between two chimneys that marked the north and south edges of the roof. Resting against the northern chimney was Costa, staring hopelessly at the spot where, before all the explosions started, a fire escape had stood.

Frank slowly walked toward him, and Costa stood clear of the chimney and raised his sword in a salute. After a moment of hesitation, Frank returned the salute. Plumes of black smoke curled up into the sky from below, and the roof shook under their feet from time to time as more bombs went off within the building.

Neither man said anything; they paused, and then Costa launched a tentative thrust at Frank's face. Frank parried it easily but didn't riposte— he was in no hurry and he wanted to get the feel of the surface they were fighting on. The tiles, he discovered as he cautiously advanced and retreated across them, were too smooth to get traction on, and frequently broke and slid clattering over the edge.

Frank feinted an attack to Costa's outside line and then drove a lunge at the Duke's stomach; Costa parried it wildly but successfully and backed away a few steps. A cool wind swept across the roof, drying the sweat on Frank's face. His next attack started as an eye-jab but ducked at the last moment and cut open the back of the Duke's weapon hand. That ought to loosen his grip, Frank thought, as another explosion rocked the building.

Costa seemed upset by the blood running up his arm, so Frank redoubled the attack with a screeching, whirling bind on the Duke's blade that planted Frank's sword-point in Costa's cheek. The Duke flinched and retreated another step, so that he was once again next to the north chimney.

"Checkmate, Costa," Frank said, springing forward in a high lunge that threatened Costa's face; Costa whipped his sword up to block it— and Frank dropped low, driving his sword upward through Costa's velvet tunic, ample belly and pounding heart.

The transfixed Duke took one more backward step, overbalanced and fell away into the empty air, the jeweled sword still protruding from his stomach.

Frank stood up and brushed the sweat-matted hair out of his face with trembling fingers. Time to go below, he thought; too bad Costa took both swords down with him.

He turned to the stairway arch—and a final, much more powerful explosion tore through all three stories beneath him and blew the north wall out in a dissolving rain of bricks. The whole north half of the roof crumbled inward, and Frank, riding a wave of buckling, shattering tiles, disappeared into the churning cloud of dust and cascading masonry as timbers, furniture, sections of walls and a million free-falling rocks thundered down onto the unpaved yard of the list.

EPILOGUE: The Painter

Kiowa Dog and his friends were bored. The scaffolding around the north end of the palace was fenced off, so they couldn't play there. It was too hot and dusty to play tag or knife-the-bastard, so they sat in the shade of a melon cart and flicked pebbles at the legs of passing horses.

"Let's *do* something," said Cher-Cher.

"Like what?" asked Kiowa Dog lazily.

"We could go explore the cellar."

"I'm sick of your damned cellar," Kiowa Dog explained.

"Well, we could climb—holy cow, Kiowa, look at this guy!" Cher-Cher pointed at a bizarre figure leaving the keep and heading slowly for the open palace gates.

It was a man, riding in a small donkey cart because his left leg had been amputated at the hip. His age was impossible to judge—his thick hair was a youthful shade of black, and his body was that of an active young man, but his lined face and scarred cheek implied a greater age. He wore a bronze ear, and it glittered and winked in the sunlight as the cart bumped over the cobblestones.

"What circus are you from, Jack?" yelled Kiowa Dog.

"Juggle for us! Dance!" giggled Cher-Cher.

Frank didn't hear the children's calls. He sat back in his cart, enjoying the sunlight and the glow of the wine he'd had with breakfast. He reached behind to make sure his supplies—his new paint box, several canvases, four bottles of good rosé from the ducal cellar—were still strapped down in the shaded back of the cart, and then lightly flicked the reins. The donkey increased his pace slightly.

It hasn't been smooth and it hasn't been nice, he thought, this circle I've walked for a year—but it's closed now. He remembered his father's saying: "If it was easy, Frankie, they'd have got somebody else to do it." Well, Dad, it must be easy, because I think they're getting somebody else to do it.

157

On a second floor balcony of the keep, a man in a blue silk robe watched the donkey cart's progress toward the gate.

"So long, Frank," he whispered.

"I beg your pardon, your grace?" spoke up the page standing behind him.

"Never mind," Tyler snapped. "Uh . . . bring me the Transport file on Thomas Strand, will you?"

The page bowed and sprinted away down a hall.

I guess you were right to leave, Tyler thought. There's nothing left for you here, above or below ground. Maybe there is a life for you in the hills, as you said.

Tyler pounded his fist once, softly, on the railing. You should have thought of it, Frank. Gunpowder and dynamite are more valuable than gold. Where else would a stupid, suspicious man like Costa store it but in the palace basement? And then your ignorant understreet thugs come up from below with their own explosives . . . I've never seen a book as ruined as that *Winnie the Pooh* was when we dug it and you out of the wreckage: cut, ripped, smashed and blood-soaked, but still carrying intact its precious document.

The page returned, holding a manila folder. "Thank you," Tyler said, dismissing the boy with a wave. He opened the file and read Captain Duprey's notes and reports. After a few minutes of reading he nodded, as if the file had confirmed certain suspicions, and struck a match. The folder was slow to catch fire, but burned well once it did, and a few moments later Tyler dropped the blackened, flickering shreds and let the wind take them.

"I won't take any of your friends from you, Frank," he said. "Especially the dead ones."

The crowd in front of the Ducal Palace bored Frank Rovzar, and he kept his eyes on the hills beyond. I could ride east, he thought. The Goriot Valley is being farmed again, and the country is lush with vineyards and hospitable inns and friendly peasant girls.

He smiled, deepening the lines in his cheeks. No, he thought, it's the western hills for me, the occasional towns among the yellow fields and the gray-brown tumbleweed slopes. It's a dry region but it's my father's country, and it's there, if anywhere, that I'll be able to practice the craft I was born and named for.

To my parents, Noel and Dick Powers

An Epitaph in Rust

Often there's a whisper that I hear in shadowed streets.
A breath of desperation from the tall, far-seeing clouds
Or gasp of outrage from a manhole cover—something meets
Between the earth and sky, in pain, and if the shifting crowds
Can sense it, their response is only in their frightened eyes.
The very breezes pick their way among the alleyways
As if afraid of something in the gray December skies,
Or listening to the heartbeat of these hollow latter days.

Ride on, Messiah—there's no place for you behind the wheel.
You've come too late to sell your closing chapters, for our hands
Have written us an epitaph in rust, on dusty steel.
We're pulled aside and served with debts and overdue demands
By angry, ragged shapes that once were us; and when we pay
We'll wait in neatly ordered lines to sign our souls away.

—from the unpublished
Poems of Rufus Pennick

BOOK ONE

Rufus Pennick

CHAPTER 1
Brother Thomas

When the carillon of bells rang out across the valley to herald matin prayers, Brother Thomas struck the rusty lock off the door of the monastery's highest tower, and swung it open. He stepped cautiously out onto the flat stone blocks of the tower's roof and groped his way through almost total darkness until he touched the crumbling parapet; a cold night wind swept up the valley from the south, and he shivered as he opened his robe to lay down his two bundles.

Up from below him floated the solemn voices of the Brothers of St. Merignac at their midnight prayers. I hope they're all too sleepy to notice my absence, Brother Thomas thought. God knows *I've* never been very alert at matins.

He knelt down and untied his bundles. The first held two flexible sticks that fitted together to form a long, tapering rod with a heavy cork butt. A series of metal rings, descending in size toward the tip, ran along the top side of it. He pulled a fishing reel out of his pocket, clamped it onto the rod's grip and carefully drew the line through the rings. Finally he tied a gleaming steel hook onto the end of the line and leaned the rod against the parapet.

The other package was simply two wooden sticks wrapped in a diamond-shaped sheet of string-reinforced black paper. Brother Thomas tied the sticks together in a cross, flexed them, and then stretched the paper over them like a skin, fitting the string perimeter into notches cut in the ends of the sticks.

Not bad, he thought, as he gently punched the fish-hook through the front of the kite, looped it around the crossed sticks and drew the barbed point out again. With any luck, my days at this monastery are numbered.

He stood up and peered down over one of the cracked stone merlons; the high chapel windows threw streaks of colored light across the grass of the garden, and the vineyards beyond rustled in the darkness. The very picture of routine calmness, reflected Brother Thomas with satisfaction.

From another pocket he took a cheap rhinestone necklace, which he knotted around the hook. Then he lifted the kite, let the wind take it, and slowly played out the fishing line as the kite rose bucking and swinging into the night sky. After he had let out about fifty yards of line he sat under the parapet to avoid the worst of the wind, and simply waited.

Come on, he thought. Bring me a rich one. One with a discerning eye—not too discerning to like rhinestones, though.

The wind seemed to Brother Thomas to carry a hint of the smells of the city; a faint, aromatic smoke blended from the chimneys of a hundred restaurants, forges, bath-houses and incinerators. It was infinitely more alluring than the damp-earth, pine-sap and incense odors of the monastery.

A faint sound of flapping and chittering was audible above the sighing of the breeze, and he gripped the rod more tightly. His chest felt hollow and his fingers trembled a little. I hope they're not too noisy, he thought.

Then the rod lunged in his hands and the reel whirred as yards and yards of line were pulled rapidly up into the sky. His lightly-pressing thumb felt the spooled line diminishing by the second. He'd better get tired quick, he thought, or I've lost two dollars worth of thirty-pound test.

The line hissed out for an eternal half-minute, and then paused. Immediately he clicked on the drag. The thing seemed to be circling now, high above, as Brother Thomas stumbled about on the dark tower-top, trying to reel in as steadily as he could. The thing in the sky resisted, but with ever weaker and more spasmodic efforts.

"Damn me! Damn me!" came a shrill cry from above. "What gives? What gives?" Thomas started so violently that he nearly let go of the rod. God in heaven, he thought; they can talk. I wish this one wouldn't.

"Leggo, Jack. Lemme go. It wasn't me, Jack." The flapping, protesting creature was now only a few feet over Thomas' head, and the young monk jerked the rod downward to fling the vociferous flier to the stone floor.

"Hoooo!" the thing wailed despairingly. *"Wooo-hooooo!"*

"Shut up, goddammit!" hissed Thomas. "I'm not going to hurt you!" Thomas grabbed the little bird-man by the spindly legs and awkwardly removed the hook from the thing's webbed hand. Still holding on, Thomas reached into the warm pocket of the bird-man's kangaroo-like pouch and pulled out a handful of bright, hard objects. "There!" Thomas told it. "That wasn't so bad, eh? Now take off!"

He tossed it into the air and it spread its wings and thrashed away into the night, calling back childish insults and obscenities.

Thomas wiped his sweating forehead with his sleeve and listened intently. No apparent commotion, he thought—but all this racket *must* have been heard by someone. He quickly scooped up the loot he'd taken from the flier's pouch and dropped it all into the pocket of his robe. Don't panic, he told himself. Sneak back to your cell, crawl into bed and deny everything.

Nodding at the wisdom of his own advice, he hurried down the narrow, curling tower stairway, his fishing rod and kite in one hand and the fingertips of the other brushing the damp stone wall to keep him away from the unrailed inner edge. He was panting nervously, and the echoes in the tower made it sound as if a pack of exhausted dogs had taken refuge there. God, he thought—I'm making enough noise for ten men. I'd better hurry.

He tried to take the steps two at a time; immediately his sandaled feet slipped on the uneven mossy blocks and he rolled painfully down the last twelve steps, skinning his knees and smashing his kite and fishing pole to splinters.

"God *damn* it!" he muttered when, at the bottom of the stairs, he got his breath back. It had taken him six months of furtive work to make that fishing rod. He was about to get to his feet and continue his flight when the silence was abruptly broken.

"This blasphemy, Brother Thomas," came a harsh voice, "while deplorable in itself, fades to insignificance before your more serious crime." The owner of the voice slid open the door of a dark lantern he carried, and Thomas found himself looking up into the half-angry, half-sad face of Brother Olaus, the abbot, who stood in the open doorway.

Thomas paled. "Brother, please," he said quickly and desperately, "don't hand me over to the police. Give me penances, I'll scrub the sacristy floors for a year, but don't—you *can't*—let them cut my hands off. Look, the fishing rod broke, I can't do it anymore. If you—"

"I'm sorry, Thomas," the abbot said. "There's nothing you or I can do about it now. Our duties are clear. This . . . this calamity may, I hope, turn out in the end to have been your key to salvation." The abbot looked down at the shivering monk with something like sympathy. "Try to see it in that light. Try—"

Thomas hit him, hard, in the stomach, and the old abbot dropped to the dewy grass like a broken piece of lumber. Thomas opened his hand and let fall a fist-sized piece of the fishing pole.

"Hey!" came a voice across the dark lawn. Running footsteps could be heard from the direction of the chapel, so Thomas turned and hobbled in the opposite direction, toward the vegetable garden and the south wall.

"Stop!" called one of his pursuers. "Stop in the name of God!"

Thomas instinctively slid to a halt. A moment later he was running again, cursing himself impatiently.

He was in among the vegetables now, in total darkness, tripping over tomato vines and putting his feet through watermelons. Chilly mud splashed his legs and clogged his sandals.

A half dozen outraged monks followed him cautiously; they assumed he was a bandit, probably armed, and possibly accompanied by vicious henchmen, so they hung back and contented themselves with shouting admonitory bits of Scripture at him.

Thomas lurched through the last of a row of bean-trellises and collided with the rough bricks of the wall. He tried to climb it, but gave up when the bricks cracked apart under his fingers. The monks, beginning to doubt his stature as a menace, were throwing rocks at him now with rapidly improving accuracy.

Thomas yelled as a well-flung cobble caught him in the ribs. I can't linger here, he realized. He got down on his hands and knees and scuttled along the base of the wall, searching for one of the drainage pipes that passed through it at irregular intervals. He cut his finger deeply on a stray bit of broken pottery and blundered through several complicated spider webs, but found one of the pipes and, urged to haste by the thrown rocks that were tearing into the vegetation all around him, scrambled head first into the narrow, slippery, downward-slanting shaft.

The monks soon found his escape-route and were fiercely thrusting a couple of tree branches into the pipe mouth when Brother Olaus limped up and told them to be quiet. "He's gone . . . you idiots," he gasped. "Back to your cells, now, move. I'll . . . inform the police in the morning."

Still not certain what had happened, the monks shrugged, laid down the branches and trudged back to the main building. Soon the last of the monastery's lights was put out and the silence was, except for occasional faint sounds like voices and laughter in the sky, complete.

The air was sharp with pre-dawn chilliness, and Thomas' nose and throat ached every time he took a breath. His first impulse was to thrash his way through the grapevines to the front gate of the monastery and pound on it until someone let him back in; they would turn him over to the police in the morning, but at least he'd be able to sleep warm until then in the piled straw on the floor of the detention cell.

No, no, he told himself, trying to muster some confidence—this is adventure. The whole world is laid out and waiting for you if you can just get clear of these damned trees and wait till the sun comes up. After a few moments of indecision he took his own word for it and plodded away through the darkness, whimpering softly as the cold penetrated every seam in his robe.

He tried to move steadily south, toward Los Angeles, but thickets and creeks and ravines twisted his course so frequently that after a while he had no idea which direction he was facing. I may wind up in the Hollywood Reservoir, he thought, or even back at the monastery. I've got to get my bearings.

He had been colliding frequently with pine branches and trunks, and now decided to climb one of the trees and look for the lights of Los Angeles to guide him. He peered up at the branches silhouetted against the dim purple sky, trying to judge which tree was bare enough to serve well as a ladder and crow's nest, and chose a tall one whose limbs seemed to be solid and evenly spaced.

He went up it quickly, glad to be free of the dew-soaked, clinging underbrush, and was soon straddling a comfortable branch fifty feet above the ground. He peered around intently, trying to get his tired eyes to focus on the dim, blurry landscape. He could see no lights, but half a mile away a gray streak curved through the forest. The Hollywood Freeway, he thought, with the first surge of real confidence he'd felt that night; I'll follow it south and be in the city by sunrise.

He hopped and swung his way back down the tree, thinking cheerfully of the breakfast he would buy with the money he'd taken from the bird-man. Bacon for sure, he thought. Scrambled eggs—no, an omelette, by God. And beer. And—

"Take it slow now, son, and keep your hands where we can see 'em," came an odd, quacking voice below Thomas, startling him so that he missed the next branch and half-leaped, half-fell to the bed of matted pine needles ten feet below him.

He scrambled painfully to his feet, and then froze when he saw he was surrounded by short, stocky figures. Children? he wondered dizzily.

A match flared alight in the gnarled hand of one of them, and Thomas saw that they were dwarves—a bearded, ragged crew, with mean-looking knives thrust into the belts of their leather tunics.

"A monk!" observed the one with the match. "Up in a tree, chatting with God in the middle of the night!" The other dwarves laughed uproariously in falsetto voices and slapped their knees. "Well now," the leader went on, "what we want to know—right, boys?—is whether you've got some tobacco. Quick, now, no lies!"

Thomas blinked and gulped. "Tobacco?" he answered automatically. "No. I don't smoke. Sorry."

The dwarves growled and muttered, and a few unsheathed their knives. Thomas looked around for an escape route, and saw none. "Look," he said desperately, "I'll get some and bring it back. There's some at the monastery—good stuff, Cavendish. I'll be back before the sun clears the hills."

The dwarves frowned, scratched their beards and exchanged shrewd glances. "Ah," piped up the leader again, poking Thomas in the ribs, "but how do we know you'll come back? Eh?" The other dwarves nodded, pleased that their leader had so succinctly expressed the problem.

"Here," Thomas said, trying to seem sure of himself. "Hold my rosary until I get back." He untied the long rosary—a hundred and thirty-three polished wooden beads knotted along a light rope—that encircled his waist, and handed it to the leader. "It's collateral," he explained.

"I thought you said it was a rosary," the leader said.

"It is, dammit," said Thomas with some exasperation. "Collateral means I let you hold it so you know I'll come back."

"Ah!" said the dwarf, nodding wisely. He considered the idea for a moment. "Well, it sounds okay to me. Whoever heard of a monk without his rosary? We've got him over a barrel, eh, boys?" His fellows nodded and grinned delightedly. "We'll wait here. You sure you can find your way back?"

"Yeah, I come here all the time," said Thomas, edging away. The sky had lightened during the discussion, and he could see well enough to sprint away quickly as the dwarves huddled around their leader, examining the rosary with great interest.

I've lost my badge of office, Thomas thought. I'm no longer a monk—just a battered young man in a ripped-up brown robe. The thought scared him a little, and brought home to him, as nothing else had done, the realization that he really had stepped out from under the stern but protective wing of the church. The sun was nearly up, though, and the empty blue vault of the sky promised a warm day. The birds were setting up a racket in the trees as Thomas trotted along a path below them, craning his neck for a glimpse of the freeway.

Finally he burst through a tangle of oleander bushes, showering himself with dew, and saw its concrete bulk rising up out of a stand of junipers, the high white rim already lit by the sun. Thomas recalled reading that it was called the Hollywood Freeway only locally, and was known as Route Five to the hardy merchants who drove their donkey-borne cargoes along its ancient track from San Francisco to San Diego. There were even legends that it stretched further, north to Canada and south into Mexico.

He climbed a young sapling, edged out along a bending branch, and then dropped onto the surprisingly wide concrete surface of the freeway.

As soon as he stood up he felt leagues removed from the monastery. Worldly, adventurous-looking debris was scattered along the edge of the old highroad, and cast long, sharp shadows across the lanes—the charred remains of an overturned cart were fouled in the railing at one point, and donkey skeletons, broken wheels and rusted sections of machinery lay everywhere, as if strewn, Thomas thought, by some passing giant. He even found a rusty sword, its blade broken off a foot above the bell guard, and carried it with him until he noticed tiny bugs infesting the rotted leather grip.

The heel strap on his left sandal had snapped sometime during his frantic exodus, and he was having difficulty now in walking. He put up with it for a while and then sat down, annoyed at the delay, to see if it could be tied up or something. His repair attempt only served to break the strap off entirely, and he was about to fling the wretched, mud-caked sandal away, and proceed barefoot, when he remembered seeing a three-inch length of wire among the loot he'd taken from the bird-man a few hours ago. He emptied his pocket—and stared for the first time at the plunder he'd risked his hands and possibly his life for: a cheap ring, several bottle caps, a few gum wrappers, some broken glass, eleven one-soli coins, and the wire.

Good God, he thought, stunned with disappointment; buying breakfast will use up nearly my entire haul. I can't afford to stay in Los Angeles even one day. What can I possibly do?

Well, fix the sandal, for one thing, he told himself. And then use your wits. A young, well-educated man like yourself ought to be able to get by in the city. Did you see how I handled those dwarves?

With a confidence born of naiveté and the cheery sunlight, he whistled as he twisted the wire onto his sandal, slipped it on, and then continued his southward trek.

He had walked about half a mile when a rattling and creaking behind him made him stop and look back. A horse-drawn cart was coming along at a leisurely pace, and its white-bearded driver waved amiably to Thomas, who waved back and smiled.

"Good morning, brother!" called the driver when he reined in beside Thomas. "It's no trouble, I hope, that's got you on foot?"

"No trouble, no," said Thomas, brushing the dark hair out of his eyes, "but it is slow travel. I'd be much obliged for a ride into Los Angeles."

"Sure, hop aboard. Careful of the box, there, it's black powder." Thomas climbed up onto the driver's bench and sat back comfortably on the passenger's side, glad to rest his legs. The bed of the cart was filled with wooden boxes over which a tarpaulin had been roped.

"What's your cargo?" asked Thomas, peering back at the boxes as the cart got under way.

"Guns, lead and powder, brother," replied the old man. The wrinkles around his eyes deepened, and Thomas knew he was grinning even though the bushy white beard hid his mouth. "I know you're a good lad," he added, "but do me the kindness of looking at the back-rest you're leaning on."

Thomas stared at the old man, and then sat up and turned around. In the center of the passenger's side of the back-rest was a metal-rimmed hole big enough to put his thumb into. The wood immediately around it was blackened as if by smoke.

"Uh . . . what is that?" asked Thomas cautiously, not leaning back.

"The barrel of a gun, son," the driver told him with a dry chuckle. "Throws .50 calibre hollow-point slugs. Take it easy, I won't shoot it. It's just there so we can trust each other."

"Oh." Thomas sat back gingerly. "Have you ever had to use it?" he asked after a while.

"Oh, yeah." The old man spat meditatively. "Going through Agoura last summer, a hitchhiker pulled a knife and said I was a war-monger and he was going to kill me so kids could play on the beaches, or something like that. It blew him right over Aeolus' head," he said, nodding at the horse.

The sun had warmed the air and dried Thomas' robe, and the even rocking of the old cart was making him sleepy. He was determined to resist it, though, and sat up straighter. "What's that over there?" he asked, pointing at a marble shrine glittering in the new sunlight on a hill to the left.

"That's the old Odin Temple," the driver told him. He glanced at Thomas. "You're not from around here?"

"Well, yes," Thomas said. No harm in telling him part of it, he thought. "I'm from the Merignac monastery, though—I grew up there—so I haven't learned much about the area. They're cloisters, you know."

"Hm," said the old man, nodding. "I knew they made wine and cheese, but I sure never knew they handled oysters." Thomas didn't try to explain. "So what'll you do in L.A.? Work in one of Broadway missions?"

"No," said Thomas carelessly. "I figure I'll wander down to San Pedro and sign aboard a tramp steamer. See a bit of the world." He'd given his situation some thought, and this seemed the wisest course.

They were well into Hollywood by now, and Thomas could see the crazily leaning roofs of houses sticking up like fantastic hats above the freeway rail. Barking dogs and screaming children could be heard from time to time, and rickety wooden stands had been set up along the edge of the freeway, selling everything from cool beer and tacos to horseshoes and axle-grease. Crows flapped lazily by or huddled in secretive groups along the rail.

"Getting into civilization now," the driver observed. "A tramp steamer, eh? Good job for a young man, if you're tough. I was a deck hand on the *Humboldt Queen* back in—Jesus—forty-seven, I guess, when Randall Dowling was wiping out the Carmel pirates. Wild times, I tell you."

Thomas would have liked to hear more, but the old man had lapsed into silence. "What brings you and your guns into L.A.?" he asked.

"Oh, I sell 'em to the city government," the driver said. "Mayor Pelias wants every one of his android cops to carry a real firearm, not just the traditional sword-and-stick. He's the gunsmith's patron saint."

"Android cops?" Thomas asked. "What do you mean?"

"They *didn't* tell you much in that monastery, did they?"

The traffic—bicycles, rickshaws and many horse-drawn carts—had grown fairly thick, and suddenly broke into a disordered rout for the right-hand lane when someone began blowing strident blasts through a horn somewhere behind them. A hundred feet up the road a mounted merchant attempted to vault his panicky horse right over a slow-moving rickshaw, and a crew of roadside laborers had to rush in and clear away the wreckage and moaning bodies, and cut the throat of the crippled horse.

"What in hell is going on?" Thomas cried. "Why's everybody moving over?"

"Hear that horn?" the driver asked as he calmly worked his cart in between two beer wagons and set the hand brake. "That means a gas-car's coming."

The *blaap, blaap, blaap* of the horn was very loud now. Thomas could see nothing to the rear because of the tall beer truck, and kept his eyes on the empty left lane.

All at once it had appeared and sped past, and the racket of the horn was slowly diminishing ahead. Thomas had got only a quick glimpse of a big, blue-painted metal body, on thick rubber wheels, carrying a driver in the front, a passenger in the rear and a red-faced man in a makeshift chair on the roof, blowing like a maniac into a long brass trumpet.

"Holy Mother of God," said Thomas in an awed voice. "What did you say that was? A lascar?"

"Gas-car," the driver corrected, amused to see Thomas so impressed by it. "That'll be some city official, probably Albers from Toluca Lake. An emergency in town, I guess."

Traffic was slowly untangling itself and moving on now, and Thomas sat back thoughtfully. "Tell me about these android cops," he said.

"Oh yeah." They were passing under the Sunset Boulevard bridge now, and Thomas stared curiously at the beggars in its shade who were calling to passing vehicles and coughing theatrically or waving crippled limbs to excite pity. "A few years ago," the driver said, "Mayor Pelias decided that his police force was no good. He was paying them a lot, but nothing was getting done, you know? So he started brewing androids and using them on the police force. He caught a lot of criticism for it at the time— androids had only been used for roadwork and construction before that, and everybody said they weren't near smart enough to be cops. But some scientist figured out how to implant a little box they call a PADMU in the androids' heads, and it lets 'em think and do things almost as well as a human cop, and more reliable. So pretty soon he converted entirely to android. Saves a whole lot of money, 'cause androids are cheap to produce in quantity, and they don't need a salary, and they eat grass and hay like cows." The old man laughed. "You should see them grazing. A whole field full of naked guys on their hands and knees, eating grass."

"Wow," Thomas said. He was quiet for the rest of the ride, wondering what sort of world it was for which he'd traded the quiet halls and familiar disciplines of the Merignac monastery.

Just inside the high city wall they pulled over to let a Customs officer check the cargo for contraband liquor ("Fusel oil in the Oregon vodka," the officer explained), and Thomas hopped down from the bench and walked around to the driver's side.

"Thanks for the lift," he told him. "It would have taken me till noon to get here on foot."

"Yeah, it would have," the old man agreed. "What's your name, anyhow?"

"Thomas."

"Well, Thomas, I'm John St. Coutras." He stuck out his hand, and Thomas stepped up on the rear brake pedal and extended his own hand to St. Coutras. Immediately there was a deep boom, the cart lurched, the horse neighed and reared and the Customs officer dropped his clipboard. A cloud of raspy gray smoke hung in the air, and in the ensuing silence Thomas could hear bits of stone pattering to the pavement on the other side of the courtyard.

"You stepped on the rear brake pedal, I believe," St. Coutras said.

"Uh . . . yes." They completed the delayed handshake. Smoke, Thomas noticed, was dribbling upward from the hole in the passenger's back-rest. "That's how you shoot it, huh?"

St. Coutras nodded.

"What the hell have you got? A cannon?" brayed the Customs man, who had by this time found his voice. "You bastards aware that shooting firearms inside the walls is a felony? Hah? Jesus, I'll—"

"It was an accidental discharge," St. Coutras explained calmly, "which is just a misdemeanor. But here," he said, reaching into his pocket, "let me pay for the wall repair." He handed the officer several coins.

"Well, all right, then," the man muttered, shambling back to his little plywood office. "Can't have that sort of thing, you know; I'll let you off with a warning this time . . ."

"Gee, I'm sorry about that," Thomas said. "I'd pay you back, but—"

"Forget it, Thomas. It's good community relations to give Customs men money."

"Oh. Well . . . thanks again for the ride." Thomas waved, and then walked through an arch out of the shadowed courtyard into the full sunlight of Western Avenue.

CHAPTER 2
A Day in the City

The waiter, after giving Thomas a long, doubtful look, led him down the aisle to a narrow booth at the back of the restaurant.

"There you are, sir," he said. "Would you care for coffee?"

"Yes," Thomas said, "and a ham and swiss cheese and bell pepper omelette, and sourdough toast, and fried potatoes with onions, and a big glass of very cold beer."

The waiter slowly wrote it all down on a pad and then stared at Thomas, plainly doubtful about the young man's finances, but intimidated by the monk's robe.

"I can afford it," said Thomas haughtily. He waved the man away.

As soon as the waiter walked off Thomas dipped into his water glass the first finger of his left hand, which he had gashed deeply the night before. He wiped the dried blood off with his napkin. Looks all right, he decided. It'll leave a scar, but I guess it's clean.

Most of the restaurant's booths were empty, which struck Thomas as an odd state of affairs at roughly eight o'clock in the morning on such a nice day. I hope there's nothing wrong with the food, he thought.

A tiny, leaded-glass window was set in the wall next to his left ear, and he hunched around in his seat to be able to see outside. There was a congested line of vehicles moving north on Western; out of the city, Thomas realized. The carts all seemed to be filled with chairs and mattresses, and he saw men pulling several of them, strapped into harnesses that were meant for horses. A policeman was walking down the line, and the people in the carts were pulling sheaves of papers from their pockets and letting him look at them. Sometimes he would keep the papers and make some person move his cart out of the line and return into the city. Thomas remembered that St. Coutras had said all the cops were androids, and he tried to look more closely at this one, but the wavy window glass prevented him from seeing anything clearly,

Six young men were walking rapidly up the Western sidewalk, holding long sticks. They sprinted the last hundred feet to the policeman and clubbed him to the ground from behind. For a full twenty seconds they crouched above the uniformed body, raining savage, full-arm blows; then they ran away in different directions. Thomas had expected the people in the traffic line to say or do something, but they had just watched the beating disinterestedly. After a few minutes another policeman appeared and began calmly checking their papers.

Thomas turned back to his table, frowning and upset. Do androids feel pain? he wondered. The replacement cop didn't seem bothered by his predecessor's fate, Thomas thought—why should I be? Haven't I got enough problems without having to worry about the well-being of some creature that was brewed in a vat?

At that moment his beer arrived, followed closely by the food he'd ordered. He felt a little queasy about eating until he took a long sip of the cold beer, and then his hunger returned in force. He wolfed the food and washed it down with another glass of beer.

When he finished he had forgotten the unfortunate android and was leaning back, feeling comfortable and wondering whether or not to buy a cigar. After a while the waiter appeared.

"What do I owe you?" asked Thomas, reaching into his pocket.

"Forty solis."

Thomas smiled. "No, really."

"Forty solis," the waiter repeated slowly, moving to block Thomas' exit from the booth.

Thomas' smile disappeared. "Forty solis for one breakfast?" he gasped. "Since when? Brother William told me you can get a good *dinner* for ten."

"Brother William hasn't been to town for a while, apparently," the waiter growled. "The Los Angeles soli has been dropping ever since last summer." He grabbed Thomas by the collar. "Listen, brother—if you *are* a monk, which I doubt; where's your rosary?—you're lucky we'll take solis at all, after Thursday morning. Most shops are closed, won't take any currency till they see where it stands. Now trot out forty solis or we'll be using your lousy hide to wash dishes with tonight."

"Oh, all right then!" Thomas said indignantly, pushing the waiter's arm away. "Here." He reached into his pocket again with his right hand, and with his left picked up his water glass and splashed its contents into the waiter's face. While the man's eyes were closed Thomas punched him in the stomach and then grabbed him by the hair and pulled his dripping face down hard onto his breakfast plate. Bits of egg flew, and the waiter yelled in pain.

Thomas shoved him aside and dashed up the aisle. The cashier, a blond girl in a frilly apron, stepped into his path but then stepped back again when he roared fiercely and waved his arms at her.

His escape looked good until two burly, unshaven men in stained
T-shirts and aprons appeared from the kitchen and stood in front of
the door. "Grab the bastard!" yelled the waiter, who, blood running down
his chin, now advanced on Thomas from behind.

"Oh, Jesus," moaned Thomas in fright.

A well-to-do family filled a booth by a window nearby; there was an
older gentleman, his stocky wife, three children and, under the table, a
poodle in a powder-blue dog sweater. They all watched Thomas with
polite interest, as if he'd just announced that he was going to do a few
juggling tricks.

"I'm sorry, I really am," Thomas yelled, and picked up their dog with
both hands, raised it over his head and pitched it through the window.
Taking a flying leap and setting his sandaled foot firmly in a plate of sau-
sages on their table, he dove head-first through the jagged-edged casement.
When he rolled to his feet on the glass-strewn sidewalk outside he saw the
dog huddled against the wall, terrified but apparently saved from injury
by the idiotic sweater.

"Your dog's okay!" Thomas yelled back through the window. He felt
bad about having done that. The two big men in aprons rounded the
corner of the building, one armed with a long fork and the other with a
spatula. Thomas turned and ran down the block, jogging sharply right
on a street called Sierra Vista and then left into a nameless alley. It led him
eventually to another big street, and he followed it south, only walking
briskly now that the vengeful cooks had been left far behind.

Anton Delmotte sipped at his tomato juice and shuddered.

His boss, sitting across the table from him, looked up. "What's wrong
with you?" he asked unsympathetically. "Did my breakfast disagree with
you?"

"Oh, no, Bob." Delmotte twisted his wrinkled face into an ingratiat-
ing smile. "The breakfast was tip-top. As always."

"Yeah," Bob grunted absently, returning his attention to the papers
before him on the table. "Better than you deserve."

Delmotte didn't answer. He took another deep sip of the red juice
and managed to swallow it with no change of expression. When Bob
left the room a few minutes before, Delmotte had tiptoed furtively to
the liquor cabinet with the glass of tomato juice, hoping to find some
vodka or gin to fortify it with. Bob's returning footsteps had sounded on
the stair before he'd found any, though, and he'd had to make do with
peppermint schnapps.

A short, rat-faced man now leaned in the rear door, his ragged beard
and greasy sweatshirt presenting an incongruous contrast with the simple

colonial elegance of the dining room. "That kid from Bellflower died during the night," he said. "I *said* he was sick. We'll be lucky if the rest of 'em don't come down with it."

Bob let a long sigh hiss out between his teeth. "Okay," he said. "Tie him up under the wagon and we'll cut him loose once we get moving. He's not still in with the others, is he?"

"No, boss. I've got him under a couple of boxes out back."

"Good. Get the rest of them in the wagon. We'll be moving out at eleven." The man nodded and withdrew. Bob turned to Delmotte, who had drained the tomato juice. "You swore that kid was okay," he said. "Not that I should ever take your word for anything."

"Oh, hell, Bob," Delmotte protested nervously. "He looked all right. Good muscles, clear eyes. You'd have sworn yourself that it was just a cold."

Bob stared at him. "Maybe. But you're the one that did swear it. And Alvarez ordered fifty, not forty-nine." He stood up and walked to the window, squinting out at the street. "We leave in about two hours. If you haven't found a replacement for the Bellflower kid by then, we're leaving you behind."

"Wha . . . ?" Delmotte turned pale. "Leave me behind? You—I couldn't get out of the city alone, Bob. I'd starve for sure . . . but you're just pulling my leg, aren't you? Hell, yes. You'd never maroon *me,* not after all these years. You know as well as—"

"I'm not joking." Bob still stood at the window, looking out. "I wouldn't miss you. All you do these days is drink and throw up." He turned to the old man. "Two hours, Pops. You'd better get busy." He crossed to the table, picked up his papers and left by the rear door.

Delmotte, trembling wildly, tottered to the liquor cabinet and, wincing, took two deep swigs of the schnapps; then he went into the kitchen and returned with a pot of hot coffee, which he set on the table. A small, cork-stoppered bottle of clear fluid stood on the bookshelf and he fumbled it open and emptied it into the coffee.

"Recompense," he kept muttering. "A cold, cold recompense."

He scuttled to the window and peered out, and a crazy spark of hope woke in his rheumy eyes. Back to the bookcase he went, grabbed five volumes at random, and then wrenched open the street door and darted outside.

As he'd moved deeper into the city, Thomas had been increasingly puzzled by the air of unspecified tension that he felt hanging over the sunlit streets; most shops were closed, a surprising amount of broken furniture and old crockery littered the gutters, and the few people he saw moved in groups of at least two, walking fast and glancing uneasily up and down the boulevard.

It's Friday now, Thomas thought. What *was* it that happened Thursday morning?

Another fugitive appeared now—an old man, dashing out of a doorway up ahead with a stack of books. Poor man, Thomas thought. All alone, fleeing from whatever it is that everybody's scared of, trying to hang onto a few treasured books. Even as he watched, the old man stumbled, scattering the books across the sidewalk and into the gutter.

"Let me help you with those," Thomas said, running over to him. He picked up the volumes, brushed them off and handed them back to the old man.

"Thank you, lad, thank you." he wheezed. "A kind soul in this cold metropolis. Come inside and let me give you some coffee."

"No, thanks," Thomas said, wondering why the old man smelled so overpoweringly of peppermint. "I've got to be in San Pedro by sundown, and it's a long way, I hear."

"True, lad, true! So long that ten minutes of good conversation over a cup of coffee won't matter a bit." He put his arm around Thomas' shoulders and turned him toward the open door.

"Really," Thomas protested. "It's kind of you to offer, and I'm grateful, but I—"

"All right." Tears stood in the old man's eyes. "Go, then. Leave me to the dusty loneliness from which suicide is the only exit. I . . . I want you to keep these books. They're all I own in the world, but—"

"Wait a minute," Thomas said, bewildered. "Don't do that. I'll have a cup of coffee with you, how's that? I'll have two."

"Bless your heart, lad."

Delmotte led the ragged young man inside, reflecting, even in this tense moment, how much the lad resembled his long-dead son, Jacob. Jacob would never have let Bob treat me this way, he thought.

"Sit down, son," he said as jovially as he could, pulling out a chair that faced the door across the table. "Ah, there's the coffee. Drink up."

Thomas sat down reluctantly. "There's no cups," he pointed out.

Delmotte sagged. "What? Oh, yes. You couldn't drink it right out of the . . . ? I suppose not. Wait there, I'll fetch a cup." He went into the kitchen, stopping first at the liquor cabinet to lower the level of the schnapps another inch. "Medicine," he explained.

As soon as the old man was gone, Thomas lifted the lid of the pot and sniffed the dark liquid within. It had a sharp, sweet smell.

Delmotte reappeared, waving a cup proudly. "Here you are, Jacob," he said.

"Thomas. Thomas is my name."

Delmotte wasn't listening. He was pouring coffee into the cup and humming softly to himself. "There you are," he said, pushing the cup toward Thomas.

"I don't want any." Thomas tensed his weary legs for a dash out the door.

"You'll drink it, though, won't you? You've always been my obedient son—not like Bob."

That does it, Thomas thought. He leaped up and bolted around the table toward the door; but the old man, with surprisingly quick reflexes, sprang from his chair as Thomas rushed past and seized him around the waist.

"Bob!" Delmotte shrilled. "I got one, I got one!"

Thoroughly terrified now, Thomas drove his elbow into the old man's face. Delmotte dropped to the floor and Thomas ran outside and pelted off down the street.

After a moment Bob stepped out onto the sidewalk, his mouth twisted with impatience and exasperation as he raised a pistol to eye level.

The bullet tore across Thomas' right side before he heard the shot, and sheer astonishment made him lose his footing and fall to his hands and knees on the pavement. The second shot, with a sound like a muted bell, punched a hole in a pawnbroker's sign over his head.

"Help, I'm being murdered!" he yelled as he scuttled up the sidewalk on all fours, like a dog. Another bullet zipped past his ear, and then he was around the corner. He got to his feet, breathed deeply for a few seconds and then trotted away down another street that stretched south.

After a block or two he noticed that blood was trickling down his side under his robe and being absorbed by his loincloth. I suppose I can't afford to bleed to death on the way, he thought impatiently. He ducked into an alley, stepped modestly behind a stack of cabbage crates and, lifting the skirts of his robe, tore away the already tattered hem.

The wound was about two and a half inches long. It was not deep, though it seemed willing to bleed on indefinitely. Thomas held a wad of fabric against the gash and then tied the threadbare brown hem-strips across his middle so that they pressed on the makeshift bandage. The cloth blotted black with blood fairly quickly, but not so quickly as to indicate a torn vein or artery.

His bandage in place, he slumped against the brick wall at his back and heaved a long sigh. When he focused his eyes again, he saw a boy of about ten years glowering down at him from an open second-floor window.

"Uh, hello there," Thomas said.

The child frowned deeply.

"Say," Thomas went on, "can you tell me what happened yesterday? Why is everybody so frightened?"

"They blew up Mayor Pelias," the boy answered after a pause. "Twice, early in the morning. It woke me up."

"He's dead, then?"

"No." The boy stepped away from the window.

Thomas considered and then dismissed the idea of calling him back. He made sure his robe was as neat as possible, and then stepped out onto the sidewalk again and resumed his journey. He was on Western again, he noted, and a number of signs agreed that Wilshire was the big street that lay half a block ahead. I wonder how close San Pedro is now, he thought. I wish I'd brought a map.

He strode on with a firm jaw and lots of determination, but after half an hour of walking he slowed. His forehead, despite the hot sun and his heavy robe, was dry, and a powerful nausea was opening its hand in his abdomen. The glare on the buildings and sidewalks made his eyes water, and squinting helped only a little. Sunstroke, he thought dizzily— or maybe it's fever, infection from my bullet-wound. I've got to rest, get out of this sun.

Pico was the next cross-street, and he turned right, noticing a closed stagecoach station only two buildings away. Its door was recessed a good fifteen feet from the sidewalk, and he looked forward to sitting down and resting in the shaded hall—maybe I'll even take a short nap, he thought.

Thomas turned into the cool hall, and was halfway to the locked door at the end when he saw the man already sitting there.

"Oh. Hi," Thomas said, halting. In the sudden dimness he was unable to see the man clearly.

"Howdy, son," came a mellow voice. "Sit down, make yourself at home. The shade's here for everybody."

"Thanks." Thomas leaned back and slid down the wall into a sitting position.

"What brings you out of doors?" the man enquired. A paper bag rustled and Thomas heard swallowing. "Like a bit of scotch?"

"No, thanks," Thomas said. "I'm a stranger in town. Just passing through, as they say. What *has* happened to the mayor, anyway?"

"He's had a stroke, the story is, after two bombs bounced him out of bed yesterday morning, one ten minutes after the other. I think he's dead, and they don't want to let on. They figure the city would *really* go to the dogs if it got out that he'd kicked off."

"Would it?" Thomas asked drowsily. "Go to the dogs, I mean."

"Yeah, probably," the man said. "The people would try to wipe out the androids, and the androids'd fight back, and then San Diego or Carmel

would send an army against L.A. while none of us were paying attention."
He sucked the scotch. "I don't know. Who cares? I don't care. Do you
care?"

"Not me," Thomas said agreeably. "I don't care."

"Right! Have some scotch."

"No . . . well, okay, maybe I will." The man handed him the bottle
and Thomas opened his robe and poured some of the liquid on his stiff-
ening bandage. It felt wonderfully cold on his feverish skin, and smelled
so invigorating that he gulped a mouthful of it.

He handed it back to his companion. "Thanks."

"How'd you get cut?"

"I was shot at," Thomas told him. "Some crazy old man tried to serve
me poisoned coffee, and I ran, so he shot at me. Three times."

"I'll take care of him," the man said with a reassuring nod.

"You will?" Thomas asked curiously.

"Sure. I think I'll take care of the whole damn city. I've had my eye on
'em for a long time. Sin everywhere you look. Dope, whores, murderers—
do you know what I saw the other day?"

"What?"

"A screwdriver. There were these two girls, see, photographs, in the
plastic handle. They had black bathing suits on, but when you turn the
screwdriver upside down the bathing suits slide off, and the girls are naked. That's the kind of thing I'm talking about."

"Oh, yeah." Thomas nodded and eyed his companion uncertainly.
The man was big, with a puffy, ruddy face, and eyes that hid between
thick eyebrows and sagging pouches.

"You're just passing through, you say?" he asked. Thomas nodded.
"Well, I'll hold off till tomorrow night before I unleash them old seven
angels of doom, okay?"

"Okay. Much obliged." I'd be well advised to leave now, Thomas felt,
and got to his feet.

"Taking off so soon?"

"'Fraid I have to," Thomas said.

"Okay. Listen, if you get in any jams, tell 'em the Lord of Wrath is a
buddy of yours."

"Will do." He waved and walked back out to the sidewalk. I hope
San Pedro Harbor isn't too much further, he thought. I don't think I could
ever get used to this city life.

The sun was well on its way down the afternoon side of the sky when
Thomas crossed Park View Street and found himself in MacArthur Park.
He had been walking all day, and his wound was throbbing, so when he

flopped down on one of the wooden benches he began considering the feasibility of spending the night right there. The tall buildings around the park were softly lit by the golden light, their eastern sides and inset windows shadowed in pale blue. Very pretty, he thought—but I feel the evening chill coming on. I'll need newspapers to stuff inside my robe for warmth.

An armed street vendor was pushing a cart along Sixth Street. "Get yer red-hot mantras right here, folks. Can't meditate without a mantra of your own. We got 'em, you want 'em."

"Hey!" Thomas called. The merchant stopped and looked up the grassy hill to Thomas' bench. "Can you eat those things? Mantras?" It had occurred to him that it might be some sort of Mexican food.

The street vendor simply stared at Thomas for a few seconds and then moved on, repeating his monotonous sales pitch. Oh well, Thomas thought. I probably couldn't have afforded one, anyhow.

He had sat back on the bench, and was trying to muster the energy to get up and look for newspapers when he became aware of muffled laughter behind him. It was the first sign of mirth he'd heard since parting ways with St. Coutras that morning, and he turned around curiously.

A young man of roughly his own age—possibly a year or two younger—was leaning on a tree trunk ten feet behind him. He was dressed in brown corduroy pants and coat, with leather boots, and his unruly hair was as red as a new brick. He saw that Thomas had noticed him, so he gave up on trying to conceal his laughter and fairly howled with it. Thomas stared at him, beginning to get annoyed.

"Ho ho," said the red-haired one finally. "So you're going to eat a mantra, hey. With proverb jelly and a side order of gregorian chant, no doubt."

"It's not food, I take it," said Thomas stiffly.

"Hell, no." The young man walked over and put one foot up on Thomas' bench. "It's a chant that you say over and over in your mind when you're meditating. Like . . . one-two-three-four-who-are-we-for, or Barney-Google-with-the-great-big-googly-eyes."

"Oh." Thomas tried not to look chagrined.

"Where are you going, anyway? I've been following you ever since Beverly. A young monk with no rosary, soaked in blood and reeking of whiskey—an unusual sight, even these days. I'm Spencer, by the way."

"I'm Thomas." They shook hands, and Thomas found that his anger at being laughed at had evaporated. "I'm trying to get to San Pedro," he explained. "How much further is it?"

"An easy twenty miles," Spencer said. "Maybe more. Catch the Harbor Freeway about eight blocks east of here and then go south till you fall into the ocean. What's in San Pedro?"

"I'm going to sign aboard a tramp steamer," Thomas said, a little defensively.

"Oh. Where are you going to spend the night? On this bench?"

"I was thinking of it."

Spencer stared at him and then burst out laughing again. "You're lucky I came by, brother," he said. "I don't even want to *hint* at what'd happen to you if you slept here. This isn't like sleeping in the orchard out back of the chapel, you know." He sat down beside Thomas and lit a cigarette with an unnecessary flourish. "They give you any education at your monastery?" he asked after puffing on it for a few moments.

"Yeah," Thomas said. "In some things."

"Ever hear of Shakespeare? William H. Shakespeare?"

"Sure."

"Ah. Well, the Bellamy Theatre, over on Second Street, is putting on *As You Like It*, which this Shakespeare wrote. I'm in it, I'm one of the actors, and I could find you a place to sleep at the theatre. We all sleep there."

"That'd be great," said Thomas eagerly. It was already getting cold, and the prospect of sleeping on a bench was quickly losing its charm.

"Come on, then," Spencer said, hopping to his feet and flinging away the cigarette. "If we move fast we can get there in time to grab some food."

Thomas needed no further encouragement.

The few shopkeepers who had opened their doors were locking up now. The evening wind was tossing bits of paper along the sidewalks and carrying, from time to time, the sound of sporadic gunfire from distant streets. Thomas thrust his hands into his pockets and shivered.

"You're broke, aren't you?" Spencer asked. "Uh . . . have no money, that is."

"Well, I've got eleven solis, but that's it. Yeah, I'm 'broke' all right."

"Were you robbed?"

"No, that's all I came with."

"*What?* You—"

"Wait a minute, wait a minute," Thomas interrupted. "It's not quite as stupid as it sounds. I didn't plan on doing it this way."

"How *did* you plan on doing it? And what are you doing, anyway?" Spencer lit another cigarette. He let it hang on his lower lip and then squinted through the smoke.

"Running away from the Merignac monastery, up in the hills." Thomas answered. "I was an orphan, you see, so the monastery kindly indentured me to work for them until I turned twenty-five—which is four years from now—in exchange for room and board and education."

"And you're making a . . . premature exit."

Thomas nodded.

"And you grabbed the collection basket one morning, and jumped over the wall, and then discovered there was only eleven solis in it."

Thomas laughed ruefully. "That's almost right," he admitted. "I made a kite and a fishing pole, and last night I went sky fishing." ("Jesus," Spencer muttered.) "Those bird-men make their nests up at the high end of the valley, you know, and the monastery lies right in their flight-path. I've heard they grab bright, glittery objects like coins and jewelry, and carry 'em home in their pouches to decorate their nests; so I figured if I caught about ten of them, over a period of a month, say, I'd have enough money to fund my escape."

"Did you know . . . *do* you know what they do to sky-fishers?"

"Yeah. They cut their hands off. Seems a little extreme to me."

"Well, sure. All the penalties are extreme. But the government claims those bird-men are tax collectors, see. They've got big nets set up by the Hollywood Bowl, and they catch them, empty their pouches, give 'em a little food and then send them on their way. It's a government monopoly. Anytime you catch one yourself, it's the same as holding up a tax collector at gunpoint."

"Oh." Thomas thought about it. "Then I really was robbing from the collection basket."

Spencer snapped his fingers, sending his cigarette flying at a rat who had poked his nose timidly from behind a collapsed and abandoned couch; he missed, but the shower of sparks sent the rat ducking back into the shadows. "And all you got out of it was eleven solis."

"That's right," Thomas said. "I was caught by the abbot the first time I did it. Did you know those bird-men can talk? And yell? So I had to punch the abbot and take off immediately."

Spencer shook his head wonderingly. "You're lucky to have got this far. Sky-fishing, punching old priests—and how did you get so bloody?"

"I was shot—relax, I don't think it's serious; just plowed up the skin— by a madman. And I've been having adventures all day. I was chased by gangs, some guy gave me wrong directions for San Pedro, so I was walking north on Vermont for an hour, and—"

"I get the picture," Spencer said. "Well, the Bellamy Theatre is just around this corner. We can get you some hot soup, a clean bed and a solid roof to sleep under." He clapped Thomas on the shoulder. "Relax, brother," he said. "Your troubles are over."

They picked their way for a few yards down a cobbled alley that reeked of Chinese food ("Restaurant next door," Spencer explained) and then climbed a swaying wooden stairway that brought them to a narrow balcony overlooking the alley. Two ruptured, rain-faded easy chairs and a mummified plant in a pot gave evidence of some long-ago attempt to make the balcony habitable, but the only occupants at present were two surly cats.

"This way," said Spencer, leading Thomas around the chairs to a plywood door set in the brick wall. He knocked on it in a three-two sequence.

"Who is it, for Christ's sake?" came an annoyed female voice. "The door ain't locked."

Spencer pulled the door open. "It's *supposed* to be locked," he complained. "Gladhand said you're only supposed to open it when somebody gives the secret knock."

Thomas followed Spencer inside and found himself in a red-carpeted, lamp-lit hallway, looking at a short, dark-haired girl wearing a brown tunic and leotard.

She stared at Spencer for a moment and then, with exaggerated caution, leaned out the door, peered up and down the length of the balcony, pulled the door closed and bolted it securely. "Don't we have a dresser or something we could lean against it?" she asked innocently.

"Save your cuteness for somebody else, will you, Alice?" said Spencer. "Now sober up, I want you to meet somebody. Thomas, this tawdry baggage is Alice Faber. Alice, this is Thomas, a friend of mine. He needs a place to sleep tonight."

"My God," Alice exclaimed, looking at Thomas for the first time. "He's all bloody! You're all bloody! Did somebody knife you?"

"No," said Thomas, embarrassed. "I . . . uh, was shot at. There was this old guy with an armload of books, and—"

"We'll have to get you cleaned up," she interrupted, taking him by the arm. "I won't do it, but Jean will. I get sick if I see blood. Really. *Jean!*"

"I'll see you later," Spencer said. "When the girls get through with you, there's somebody you've got to talk to."

"Okay," Thomas said, and allowed Alice to lead him down a tightly curving stairway to another, wider hallway.

"She's probably in the green room," Alice said "Hey, Jean!"

"Yeah?" came a lazy call.

"Come out here and clean up this young man who's been shot! He'll bleed to death right here if you don't move fast."

"I'm not bleeding," protested Thomas.

A tall, thin girl leaned out of a doorway. Her tired, sarcastic expression turned to alertness when she saw Thomas swaying in the hall, leaning on Alice's arm and looking pale and exhausted in his ragged, blood-streaked robe.

"It's not as bad as it looks," Thomas said. "The bullet just creased me, really . . ."

The sudden shift to the warmth in the building from the chilly air outside had made him dizzy, and he wasn't sure what he was saying. Jean was standing in front of him now, he noticed, and had apparently asked him a question. Probably asked me my name, he thought; he was still trying to pronounce "Thomas" when her face slid away below him and the back of his head struck the floor.

CHAPTER 3
The Misunderstanding in
Pershing Square

"Well now, Spencer. What's this I hear about you taking in a stray monk? What if—" The voice became softer. "Oh, is that him?"

"Yes, sir," came a whisper. "I figured he might be your Touchstone."

"Well, let's not jump the gun here. Let's see . . . he looks okay, I guess. Is he smart?"

"He's read Shakespeare. And he's adrift completely—has some crazy idea of going to San Pedro and becoming a sailor."

"Hmm!" An odd, slow bumping-and-sliding sound was repeated several times. "Hand me my cigars, would you Spencer? Thanks." There was the scratch and hiss of a match being struck.

It was the sharp smell of tobacco fumes that finally pulled Thomas up into complete wakefulness. He opened his eyes, and found himself staring at a great stone head that rested on a shelf only a foot away from him. It was bigger than life-size, and although the forehead and part of the thick, wavy hair were chipped, and the nose was broken off entirely, Thomas could see that it was a fine piece of craftsmanship. The shelves above and below the head were cluttered with bundles of colored paper, a stack of cardboard swords with tinfoil-wrapped blades, a number of grotesque wooden masks, and piles and piles of crumpled, glittery cloth.

"Oh hell. I admit I'd have done just what you did, Spencer. Of course with our luck we'll no sooner get St. Francis here really good in the role than Klein will reappear."

"Don't be pessimistic."

"I have to be, I'm the manager." Thomas heard the ponderous bump-and-slide again. "Has he eaten anything within the last couple of days? He looks like one of the old Nevada atrocity posters."

Thomas sat up slowly, scratching his head. "You *did* say something about soup," he reminded Spencer.

Standing next to Spencer he saw a burly, bearded, bald-headed man with a thick cigar clamped in his teeth. The man was propped up awkwardly on a pair of crutches, and Thomas knew then what the bump-and-slide sound had been.

"Spencer told me your name," the man said, "but I've forgotten it. Francis? Rufus?"

"Thomas," supplied both young men at once.

"Oh, that's right." He poled his bulk laboriously across the room and thrust his hand toward Thomas. "I'm Nathan Gladhand."

Thomas shook the muscular paw, and Gladhand lowered himself into a wicker chair. "Jean said you'd be unconscious until morning," he said, laying the crutches on the floor beside him.

"It was the mention of food that snapped me out of it," Thomas said, hoping that wasn't too broad a hint.

"Get him some soup, will you, Spencer? And bring a bottle of cognac and three glasses." Spencer darted out of the room.

"Where are we?" asked Thomas, peering around at the high-ceilinged chamber. A flickering lantern nearby illuminated endless piles of poles, plywood and boxes.

"In the theatre basement," Gladhand said. "You can sleep here. Listen," he added, fixing Thomas with a direct stare, "I don't mind helping a distressed traveler—I've been one myself, often enough—but I won't keep freeloaders." He held up his hand to silence Thomas' protests. "What I'm trying to say is—you're welcome to stay as long as you like."

"That's what you were trying to say?"

"Let me finish, will you? What I mean is, you can work here."

"Oh. Doing what?"

"That depends. Spencer says you've read Shakespeare. Who else have you read?"

"Oh . . . Byron, Kipling, Baudelaire, Ashbless . . ."

"You go for poetry, eh?"

"Yes, sir. I, uh . . . hope to publish some poems of my own, sometime."

"Of course you do." A tarnished brass woman stood with upraised arms beside Gladhand's chair, and he tapped his cigar-ash onto her head. "Spencer may have mentioned that I'm putting on *As You Like It* here. We're supposed to open two weeks from now, on the twenty-second, and the guy that was playing Touchstone left the day before yesterday. Just walked out."

"You want me to play Touchstone," Thomas said.

"Right. Not that I'd even consider you, of course, if experienced actors were available." He blew smoke toward the ceiling. "Which they aren't.

You'll get no salary, but you get room and board, which is not something to snap your fingers at, these days."

Thomas shrugged, and noticed for the first time that he was wearing a long woolen bathrobe. "I'll do it," he said. "Where are my clothes, by the way?"

"Your robe we burned. The sandals we gave to an old Olive Street beggar named Ben Corwin. We'll give you new clothes, don't worry about it."

Spencer angled his way into the room, a steaming bowl and a bottle clutched in one hand, three glasses in the other, and a folding table wedged under his arm.

"Jacques," Gladhand pronounced it *jay-queez,* "meet the new Touchstone."

Spencer set up the table and put the soup, bottle and glasses on it. "By God," he said, handing Thomas a spoon he'd carried in his pocket, "it's good to have you aboard."

"Thank you," smiled Thomas, taking the spoon with as formal a bow as he could manage.

Gladhand leaned forward and poured an inch of the brandy into each glass. "Any business at all today, Spencer?"

"No. The welfare board was locked and *guarded,* the permit bureau never opened their gates, the employment office was the same way, and even the breadlines were gone." He sat down on a box and sipped the cognac. "I'll try it tomorrow, early. It can't stay this way for long."

"What do you do, Spencer?" Thomas asked, stirring his hot chicken broth to cool it off.

"I hold places in lines." Seeing Thomas' puzzled look, he went on. "Hand-outs, jobs, housing, medicine . . . you have to wait in long lines for those things nowadays. I have a friend who does clerical work for the police—she's human, let me add, not an android—and she tells me in advance what's being given out, and where. I get there early, let the line get to be about three blocks long, and then sell my place to the highest bidder. The people in the tail end of the line know whatever it is will be gone before they get to it, see, so they walk up and down the column, offering to buy places."

"Don't the people around you undersell you sometimes?"

"Not often. They're in line because they need whatever's being given away, see? They can't afford to lose their places." He grinned at Thomas over the rim of his glass. "You want to come with me tomorrow? The prices should be goddamn high by then, and if we have two places to sell, we could make enough to buy a fancy dinner somewhere. I'll even dig up a couple of girls to impress. How's that sound?"

Thomas, to his horror, felt his face get hot and realized he was blushing. He covered it by lowering his head and busying himself with his soup. "Sounds good to me," he muttered. "Fine soup, this." Until today the only female humans he'd seen had been a handful of haggard old nuns who did the laundry at the monastery, and the prospect of impressing a couple of girls filled him with a kind of excited terror.

"Good!" Spencer hopped up and Gladhand winced to see the young man toss off his brandy in one gulp. "I'll amble over to Evelyn's place, then, and get the scoop on where the lines will be. See you tomorrow, early."

Thomas nodded and Spencer was gone.

Gladhand sat back in his chair with a long sigh. "Stick by Spencer," he said after a thoughtful pause. "He acts crazy sometimes, but he won't ditch you and he knows this city better than . . . he knows it very well." He carefully pinched out his cigar with two fingers and put it in his shirt pocket. "Don't go outside by yourself, at least for a while. The police would probably take interest in someone with a gun-shot wound, and there's plenty worse than the police out there. Wait'll you know your way around a bit more." Thomas nodded. "Finish your brandy, now, I haven't got all night to spend down here."

Thomas drained the last trickle of it. "That's nice," he breathed when he'd swallowed it.

"You like that, do you?"

"Yes sir. Hennessey, isn't it?"

Gladhand stared at him. "Yes," he said. "And how is it that you've acquired a taste for Hennessey?"

"The Merignac monastery had a very well-stocked cellar," Thomas explained.

"I see." Gladhand reached down and picked up his crutches. "Just shove your table over there when you finish," he said. "That couch you're sitting on will, I've been assured, turn into a bed if you pull this out. Whether it does or not, there are blankets and a pillow here. *Try* to remember to put the lantern out before you turn in."

"Aye aye."

"See you tomorrow." Gladhand levered his body erect, picked up the bottle and clumped out of the room. Thomas listened until he could no longer hear the theatre manager's progress, and then set to work on the soup.

The bird-creature kept pulling itself clear, leaving Thomas with the weary, finger-cramping job of reeling it in still another time. He couldn't remember why he had to catch it, but he knew it was desperately important that he do so, and becoming more urgent with every passing second. He suspected that the creature's face was changing, but he couldn't be certain since by the time he pulled the thing near enough to look at, he had invariably forgotten what it had looked like the time before. It was coming closer again, now, unwillingly, tugging harder than ever. Its face was obscured by the thrashing wings, but after a moment they became transparent and blurred away, and Thomas was able to see clearly.

It was a girl. Her face was white as Jack cheese, and huge, wide as a sail and rippling as if it were under running water. The eyes were empty black holes, and the mouth, which was slowly spreading open, was an infinitely wide window upon a cold universe of vacuum.

Thomas withdrew convulsively, opened his eyes by sheer rejection of sleep. He was trembling and afraid to move, but aware that he was lying on a couch, and that he'd been dreaming. After a while he remembered where he was, and the musty stale smells, the odor of old dust, ceased to bother him.

When Spencer shook him awake, the first gray light of dawn was slanting in through ventilation grates set high in the walls.

"Here's some clothes," Spencer said quietly. "Everybody else is still asleep, so don't knock anything over."

Thomas nodded and began groggily struggling into the jeans, flannel shirt and rope-soled shoes. "I smell coffee," he whispered.

"Yeah, here." Spencer handed him a steaming cup and he sipped at it until he could think clearly. "Not bad," he said.

"I put a little rum in it. Now come on, the police are going to dispense ration numbers today from Pershing Square. Sequentially, so the early birds get the low numbers."

Thomas stood up and finished the warm coffee in one long gulp. "What's so great about low numbers?"

"Well, the city has only got so much credit, see." Spencer fitted a cigarette into the corner of his mouth. "The low numbers are sure to be covered, but a shopkeeper would be real doubtful about accepting a ration ticket if the number was more than, say, five hundred." He snapped a match alight with his thumbnail, grinned proudly, and waved the flame under the cigarette. "Let's go," he said. "The *L.A. Greeter* comes out in twenty minutes, and this ration number business is going to be on the front page. In half an hour Pershing Square will look like Hell's courtyard on the Day of Judgment."

The stately old Biltmore Hotel stood aloof over the milling herds of people that choked Pershing Square. The midmorning sun had begun to dry the grass, and a lot of people were sitting down, some under little tents made of the blankets they'd been wrapped in when they had arrived, early in the chilly morning.

The people in the first two hundred feet of the line, on the east side of the square, weren't sitting, though; they were on their feet and tense, ready to repel the frequent attacks of desperate late-comers. There had, hours earlier, been a few old and crippled people in the front section of the line, but they had long since been forcibly weeded out.

"I don't like this," Spencer muttered to Thomas. "I'm afraid we might just have to duck out of here and go home."

"Why?" Thomas was astonished. "We're numbers fifty-six and -seven, for God's sake! And we've had to fight off people to keep these places."

"Shh. That's just it. They're trying to *take* our places instead of buy them. I'm afraid if we offer to sell out we'll be killed in the . . . ensuing stampede." He lit a cigarette, puffed on it once, and flung it to the ground. "Look at that crowd back there. I know they're going to rush us again."

Thomas looked back nervously. Many of the people on the grass were standing now, and looking at the front of the line. "Yeah," he agreed. "And a lot of them have sticks."

A high-pitched screech grated out of the loudspeakers mounted on the stucco walls of the Welfare Dispensation Building, followed by a voice made tinny by amplification: "Ten o'clock news. Ten o'clock news. Although Mayor Pelias has not yet recovered from the stroke he suffered a little more than forty-eight hours ago, his physicians are optimistic about his chances of a full recovery. The search for the would-be assassins who planted bombs in his chambers continues round the clock, and police chief Tabasco is confident that the . . . malfeasors will be apprehended within twenty-four hours." The speakers clicked off with a snap that echoed across the square.

"The guy's name is Tabasco?" Thomas asked, incredulous.

"What?" Spencer turned to him impatiently. "Yes. Tabasco. A lot of times they name androids after kinds of food and drink. From the old days, when they tried to breed 'em for food. Shut up, now, this is looking bad."

A large group of men was walking leisurely toward the front of the line. They all carried sticks, and Thomas remembered the android he'd seen beaten yesterday. "Let's get out of here," he whispered to Spencer. The other people in line shifted uncertainly and began picking up rocks.

Spencer nodded tensely. "In a second," he said. ". . . *now.*" He grabbed Thomas' arm and bolted out of the line, running toward the south side of the square. The men with sticks took that as a signal, and charged; immediately the air was rent by yells and the defenders of the line sent a hail of hard-flung stones into the ranks of the attackers. Nearly everyone in the square began to run toward the fighting, hoping to be able to improve their positions in the churning mob that could no longer be called a line.

Spencer and Thomas skirted the fighting and managed to dodge and duck their way across the lawn to the sidewalk of Sixth Street, where they paused.

"This is incredible," Spencer panted, looking back. "I've seen rough lines before, but *this* . . ." He shook his head. "There'll be people killed."

"Holy Mother of God," Thomas muttered, "look at that." He pointed west, at a troop of police that were trotting in formation north on Olive, blocking off the western edge of the square. They all carried rifles at the ready.

Spencer drew in his breath sharply between clenched teeth. "We can't rest yet," he hissed. "Come on." He dragged Thomas across Sixth Street, waving and nodding to the carts they held up, and then both of them ducked behind the solid brick shoulder of a bank.

The rattle and pop of gunfire broke out as Spencer was scurrying up a fire-escape ladder mounted on the bank's alley-side wall. Thomas followed him, taking the rusty rungs as quickly as he could, although his wound was stinging and his lungs felt ready to shut down entirely. If we don't stop to rest very soon, he thought, I'm going to pass out.

To his relief Spencer crawled out onto the lowest of the fire-escape balconies that faced Sixth, and a few moments later both of them lay panting on the close-set bars, watching the chaos in the square.

The android police had not moved in; they simply stood in an orderly line along the Olive Street sidewalk and fired volley after volley into the rapidly thinning crowd. At first a few people walked toward the police, their hands raised, but they were quickly chopped down by the unflagging spray of bullets, and no one followed their example.

People clattered past beneath Thomas, shouting with panic and rage, and he could see, to the north, a similar rout surging east on Fifth. In a few minutes the square was emptied, though the receding tide had left dozens of sprawled figures littered across the green lawn. A horn was sounded, and the firing ceased immediately. The fog of white smoke that hung over the western edge of the square began to drift away on the wind.

"Don't move until they're gone," whispered Spencer. There were tears in his eyes, and he wiped them impatiently on his sleeve. Thomas simply stared between the iron bars of the railing at the square below, trying desperately to explain to himself how and why this had happened. There must be a reason, he kept thinking. There *must* be.

The police unhurriedly slung their rifles over their shoulders, regrouped in the empty street and marched away south in a jogging step. When the echoes of their boots on the asphalt had died away, Spencer stood up.

"Let's go," he said. He leaned down and shook Thomas' shoulder. "Let's *go*. We're already running on luck—we can't afford to push it by hanging around."

Thomas nodded and got to his feet, and they swung back down the ladder to the pavement. Scattered moans and yells from the square told of a few whose wounds were not immediately fatal; and some of the people who had fled were beginning to peer fearfully from behind nearby buildings to be sure the police had really left.

"Where to?" Thomas asked, looking nervously up and down the sidewalk. His nostrils flared at the acrid smell of gunpowder, which hitherto he'd only associated with fireworks the monks had shot off on holy days and Easter.

"Back to the Bellamy," Spencer answered. "But first let's go visit Evelyn. I want to find out more about this ration number give-away."

"I thought you said she works at the police station . . . ?"

"Yeah, she does. We'll have lunch with her somewhere. Don't worry," he added, seeing Thomas' worried look, "they're not going to shoot us just for walking into the station house."

"Yeah? Yesterday I'll bet you wouldn't have thought they'd shoot us for standing in Pershing Square."

"Well, that's true. But twice in one day would be too outrageous. Come on—aren't you getting hungry?"

Thomas glanced at the bodies lying on the grass across the street, their collars and skirt-ends flapping in the breeze. "I . . . don't know," he said.

"Don't look at them, goddammit!" Spencer rasped. "You know what happened, so don't keep looking at it. Now let's *go*."

Thomas nodded. "Sure," he said. "Sorry."

They had been walking for several blocks with pawnshops, vegetable stands and bars to their right and a high, sturdy wooden fence to their left. Bright new barbed wire glittered along the top of it.

"What is this, anyway?" asked Thomas quietly, jerking his thumb toward the fence.

"Grazing land," Spencer answered. "Extends east to San Pedro Street, north to Olympic and south to Pico. And this here, Main, is the western edge."

"What do they graze th—" Thomas began, and then remembered St. Coutras' words of the day before. "Not . . . *police?*" he whispered.

Spencer nodded.

Thomas tried to imagine hundreds of policemen, stark naked, cropping grass on their hands and knees. Do they wear their caps? he wondered.

Now that would be a truly weird sight—the sort of things nightmares are made of.

"Do they wear their—" Thomas suddenly choked on suppressed laughter.

"What?"

"Their . . . *hats!*" Thomas gasped, and whispered, "Do they wear their hats when they're grazing?"

"Christ, no," Spencer said. His face twitched between impatience and amusement.

"It'd be a . . . hell of a spectacle," Thomas said carefully. "A million naked guys in policemen's hats, eating grass." Spencer snickered in spite of himself. "The city could sell tickets, repair its credit. People would love it." He did an imitation of a citizen loving it.

In a moment both young men were laughing uncontrollably, tears running down their cheeks. A few people walking by on the opposite sidewalk gave them contemptuous glances, clearly supposing them to be drunk.

"Pull . . . yourself together . . . for God's sake," giggled Spencer. "The goddamn . . . police station is just around this corner, on Pico." They straightened up and did their best to assume solemn expressions. Thomas was surprised to find that he felt much more cheerful and confident than he had five minutes ago—the laughter, childish though it had been, had got rid of the dry, metallic taste of tension in his mouth.

They rounded the corner and pushed through two swinging doors below a weather-beaten sign that read LOS ANGELES CENTRAL POLICE STATION. Maps and indecipherable documents were tacked up on the walls of the waiting room above the backs of the old tan couches that lined three of the walls. The place smelled of old floor wax.

"Something I can do for you gents?" enquired an officer behind the counter that stretched across the fourth wall. Thomas looked at him curiously—the officer's face was placid and unlined, with a somewhat low forehead and a wide jaw.

"Uh, no thanks," replied Spencer. "We just want to see someone in the bookkeeping section."

"Evelyn Sandoe?" the policeman asked, with a little V of a smile.

Spencer nodded, his face reddening.

"Ah, young love!" pronounced the officer, turning away.

Spencer made a rude gesture at his back. "Come on," he said to Thomas, and led the way down a hall lit by genuine electric bulbs.

"He was an android?" Thomas whispered.

"Sure. Jesus, I hate the way they . . . fake human feelings." Spencer shuddered. "I wish they didn't build them to look like people. What's wrong with, I don't know, horses, maybe, or monkeys. It's just too creepy when they talk and smile."

They passed a number of doors. Spencer finally opened one, and they stepped into the room beyond it, and were confronted by ranks of girls at gray metal desks, sorting, stamping and filing papers. Thomas followed Spencer down an aisle and stopped beside him at the desk of a pretty, curly-haired girl in a brown sweater.

"Hullo, Evelyn," Spencer said to her. "My friend and I were wondering if you'd care to join us for lunch."

She looked up, startled, and then spoke with a casualness that Thomas felt was not genuine. "Spencer! I didn't expect you. Lunch?" She glanced at the wall clock. "Okay. Doris, I'm clocking out. Cover for me for ten minutes, will you?"

Evelyn stood up and took Spencer's arm, and the three of them left the building by a side stairway. They walked quickly down Pico away from the police station.

"Jesus, Spencer," Evelyn whispered breathlessly. "I was afraid you were killed. Forty armed police were sent out to put down a riot in Pershing Square. Were you there? They just came back a little while ago, and they said they had to open fire on the crowd."

"That's what they did, all right," Spencer said. "Yeah, we were there. This is my friend Thomas, by the way. Thomas, Evelyn." They nodded to each other. "There's a few things I want to find out about all this. Let's stop somewhere. Are there any restaurants open?"

"I hear Pennick's is," Evelyn said.

"Pennick's it is, then."

Pennick's was a cafeteria a few blocks away; Thomas spent ten of his eleven solis on a roast beef sandwich and a cup of watery beer. Evelyn and Spencer had the same, and the three of them took a table in the back corner.

"So what *happened?*" Evelyn asked as soon as Spencer had taken a sip of beer.

"We were in a good position in line," Spencer said, "but it was a spooky line. The people behind tried to *take* our places. It began to look like we'd have to risk losing teeth to keep our positions, and we didn't really want ration numbers anyway, so we ducked out just as the fight started. Then all these cops arrived and just started pouring bullets into the square."

"They claimed they gave everyone a chance to leave peaceably," Evelyn told him.

"I didn't hear anything like that," Spencer said. "In fact, we saw them shoot down a lot of people that were trying to give themselves up." He had another pull at the beer. "The thing that worries me is this:

the police showed up—what would you say?—about ten seconds after
the first rock was thrown, and they started shooting no later than five
seconds after that. They were trotting up Olive, with their rifles at the
ready, while everything was still more-or-less peaceful."

"Yeah . . . ?" said Evelyn slowly.

"Yeah. I think they were going to shoot up the crowd in any case. The
fact that a fight happened to be going on just gave them a better excuse
than they'd planned on."

"What would they want to do that for?" Evelyn asked skeptically.
"That sounds paranoid to me."

"I don't know why they would," Spencer said, "but that's how it looked."

Thomas nodded. "I'd have to agree," he said. "It looked like that's
what they'd planned to do from the start."

"Jesus," Evelyn exhaled, and reached for her glass. "Well, to answer
your soon-to-be-asked question: no—I haven't heard or seen anything
that'd support your suspicion. Maybe their PADMUs have all shorted out
at once, and they've all gone crazy; the other big news today was—"

"PADMUs?" Thomas interrupted.

"Priority and Decision-Making Units," Spencer explained. "What was
the other news?" he asked Evelyn.

"Oh, some monk who ran off from the Merignac monastery. There
are more murders and robberies and arson going on lately than we can
even file, and what are they wasting all their time on? Chasing a monk."

Thomas drained his beer in one gulp and wiped his mouth with a
trembling hand.

"That is odd," Spencer agreed. "Why are they so hot to get him?"

"I don't know. I just know they're all looking for him. His name's
Thomas, as I recall, and they're looking for him around MacArthur Park.
Somebody thinks he saw him there."

"Maybe they *are* all going crazy," Spencer said. "Be careful at the
damn station house." He stood up, wrapping his sandwich in a napkin
and sliding it into his coat pocket. "We gotta go, Ev. I'll see you tonight."
He leaned over and kissed her.

"Okay," she said. She waved at Thomas. "I'm sorry. What was your
name again?"

"Rufus Pennick," he blurted automatically.

"Huh! Any relation to this place?"

That's where I got the name from, Thomas realized with some panic.
"Uh, yes," he said quickly. My great-uncle used to own it, I believe. I don't
know if he still does or not. Haven't kept in touch."

"I know how that is," Evelyn nodded. "I haven't seen my family in
two years. Good meeting you. Later, Spence."

The two young men stepped out of the restaurant door and onto the sidewalk. Thomas started to speak, and then noticed that Spencer was shaking with suppressed laughter.

"What in hell is so funny?" he demanded testily.

Spencer coughed and straightened his face. "Nothin', Rufe," he drawled.

"Yeah? Well, I'd like to see what you could come up with on the spur of the moment."

"Ladies and gentlemen, Rufus Pennick—of the restaurant-baron Pennicks, you know," said Spencer in a ridiculous British accent.

"Jesus. Will you stop? The L.A. police are devoting their lives to catching me, and you're kidding around."

Spencer sobered. "You're right. What have you done, anyway? They wouldn't go to *this* much trouble for a . . . cannibalistic child molester who spent his weekends blowing up old ladies with a shotgun."

"I don't know. I told you I was sky-fishing. And I punched Brother Olaus—maybe he died . . . ? I can't really picture that from just one sock in the belly, though. And I ran out of a restaurant yesterday morning without paying for breakfast . . . oh, and I threw a poodle through a window." He grinned. "Those are my sins, father."

"Go to hell, my son. This doesn't figure, though. None of that stuff would be enough to get 'em really interested, even if old Brother Olaf *did* die. Especially these days, with Pelias in a coma and riots in the streets." He scratched his jaw. "I wonder what it is they *think* you've done."

The Bellamy Theatre, seen by daylight, was a good deal larger than Thomas had imagined last night. Its broad entrance, crowded now with gawking people, took up nearly a third of the two-hundred block of Second Street, and rose upward for three storeys in a grand display of balconies, tile-roofed gables and rust-streaked concrete gargoyles.

Spencer saw the knot of people around the entrance and quickened his pace. "What now?" he muttered. The crowd parted for the two purposeful-looking young men and a moment later Thomas saw, lying on the pavement, the body of the girl, Jean, who had cleaned and bandaged his wound the night before.

She was clearly dead. The left half of her skirt was drenched in blood and her head lolled at an unnatural angle. Someone had straightened her limbs, but her eyes remained open and, Thomas thought, puzzled-looking.

"What the hell happened?" Spencer asked sharply.

Gladhand rolled forward in a wheelchair. "She was in Pershing Square," he said, "when the police opened fire on the crowd. This gentleman—"

he nodded toward a heavy-set man in overalls, "—brought her back here."

"She was alive when I found her," the man said humbly. "She told me to take her here. Only she died in the back of my cart."

"Who are all these people?" Spencer asked, waving at the rest of the crowd. They grinned in embarrassment and shuffled their feet.

"Spectators," Gladhand said.

Spencer shoved one of them in the arm. "Get out of here, you bastards," he spat.

"See here," began one. "You can't—"

"I can break your teeth, slug. Get *out* of here!" The crowd began to break up indignantly. "Sweep on, you fat and greasy citizens!" he shouted at them.

"Thank you, Spencer," said Gladhand. "That's what I was trying to get across when you arrived." The theatre manager was speaking calmly, but he was pale and breathing a little fast. "Come in, sir, and have some brandy with us," he said to the man in overalls.

"Uh, okay," he said. "Here, I'll carry her inside for you." He bent down and picked up Jean, one arm under her knees and the other under her shoulders. Spencer led him inside and helped him lower the body onto a vinyl-covered couch.

Thomas followed, pushing Gladhand's wheelchair. "Thank you, Thomas," Gladhand said.

"Rufus," Spencer corrected.

"Now wait a minute," Gladhand protested. "Last night you—"

Spencer winked at him and shook his head; the theatre manager shrugged. "Thank you, Rufus."

"I'll get brandy," Spencer said, and bounded up a carpeted stairway.

The man in overalls sat down on a wooden chair and rubbed his hands together nervously. "I'm Tom Straddle," he said. "I grow stuff."

"I'm Nathan Gladhand, and this," with a wave at Thomas, "is apparently Rufus."

Straddle's head bobbed twice. "I come along after the cops was gone," he said. "They was lots of people dead on the grass, but she was on the sidewalk, and movin'. So I picked her up and she said take her to the Bell'my Theatre, so I did."

Spencer returned with the brandy and glasses, and Gladhand poured it. When everybody had a glass, he raised his. "For Jean," he said evenly.

Thomas repeated it and took a long sip.

"You two didn't see her there?" Gladhand asked Spencer.

"No," he answered awkwardly. "It was a huge crowd. She told me she was going to paint the Arden set all day today."

"Yes, that's what I thought, too."

"Them cops must have gone crazy," Straddle put in. "Shootin' all them people."

"Yes," said Gladhand. "Well, I see you've finished your brandy, Mr. Straddle, so I suppose we shouldn't keep you any longer. Thank you again for bringing her back here. Let me—sir, I insist—give you something for going out of your way to help us."

Straddle accepted a handful of coins and shambled out.

"Deal with the, uh . . . remains, will you?" Gladhand said, waving vaguely at the couch. His voice was, with evident effort, quite calm.

"Sure," Spencer answered quickly. He and Thomas lifted the body and carried it through the inner doors and down the center aisle to a narrow storeroom under the stage. They returned silently to the lobby, wiped off the couch with a number of paper towels, and sat down.

"What happened at Pershing Square, Spencer?" Gladhand asked thoughtfully.

Spencer described in detail the events of the morning, and shared with the manager his guess that the police had intended from the beginning to fire on the crowd.

"It certainly is inexplicable," Gladhand observed when he'd finished. "You'd think Tabasco would keep his androids quiet now, with old Joe Pelias in whatever kind of comatose state he's in. Ever since Hancock killed himself six years ago, Pelias has been the main champion of the androids. Why are they running amuck the first time he's not there to defend them?"

"They liked him?" Thomas asked.

"Oh, I suppose so, if androids like anybody," Gladhand said. "Sure, they liked him."

"Well," said Thomas slowly, "maybe it's revenge."

No one spoke for a moment, then Spencer muttered, "Jesus. *There's* a thought."

"Rehearsal is cancelled for tonight, Spencer," Gladhand said briskly. "Post that fact where everyone will see it, will you? And Rufus, you can tell me what became of a young man named Thomas, who, as I recall, slept here last night."

CHAPTER 4
A Night at the Blind Moon

Later that afternoon Thomas was slouched comfortably in one of the sprung easy chairs on the alley-side balcony. He was leafing through his script of *As You Like It,* lazily underlining the Touchstone speeches, and sipping from time to time at a glass of cold vin rosé that stood on a table within easy reach.

After a while he became aware of a voice from the alley below, getting nearer and louder. Soon he decided it was a song that the unseen person was trying to render, and he listened for words. "Bringing in the sheep; bringing in the sheep," the cracked old voice rasped. "We all come re-*joi*-cing, bringing in the sheep."

Now clumping labored steps sounded on the stairs to the balcony, and Thomas laid the script aside and stood up. "Who is that?" he asked.

A crazy-eyed, ragged-bearded face, shadowed under a cardboard hat, poked up over the top step and squinted suspiciously at Thomas. "Who," it countered, "is *that?*"

"I'm, uh, Rufus Pennick. I'm an actor here. Now—"

"Oh, that's all right, then." The old man grinned reassuringly and lurched his way up the remaining stairs to the balcony. "I'm Ben Corwin," he said, holding out a stained, claw-like hand which Thomas shook briefly. Ben Corwin, Thomas thought; where have I heard that name?

The old man slumped into the other chair. After a moment he spied the glass of wine and drained it in one gulp. "Ah, good, good, good," he sighed. He fished a little metal box out of his pocket and flipped open its lid. "Snoose?" he asked.

"I beg your pardon?"

"I said, would you like a bit of snoose?"

Thomas peered distastefully at the iridescent brown powder in the box. "No, thanks."

"Suit yourself." Corwin put the box down and then lifted his feet in his hands and rested them on the wobbling table. He was wearing battered sandals, and Thomas noticed, on the left one, a bit of wire where the heel-strap should have been. My old sandals! he thought. This is the beggar they gave them to. Corwin picked up the snuffbox and took a liberal pinch of the brown dust, spread it on the back of his hand, and then inhaled it vigorously, giving both nostrils a turn.

"Ahhh," he sighed, sagging in the chair. His head fell back and his jaw dropped open, and a noise like snoring issued from his mouth. Thomas tried to go on with his script-marking, but found that the balcony had, for the moment, been robbed of its charm. He went inside.

He wandered downstairs to the greenroom and found Spencer knotting a plaid scarf about his throat. "Rufus!" Spencer said. "I was looking for you. Me and a couple of the guys are going over to the Blind Moon to have a few beers. Come along." His cheeriness had about it a quality of suppressed hysteria.

Thomas considered the invitation, then nodded. "Okay," he said. "What's snoose? Snuff?"

Spencer looked at him sharply. "Why? You haven't bought any, have you?"

"No. There's a gentleman on the balcony, though, whom it has rendered unconscious."

"Ben Corwin? Sure. He takes it all the time. The stuff was invented by androids, and they're the most common users of it. It's real bad business— a mixture of snuff, opium and fine-ground glass."

"Glass? Why glass, for God's sake?" Thomas shuddered, remembering the gusto with which Corwin had inhaled the stuff.

"It makes tiny cuts in the skin so the opium goes right into the bloodstream. Trouble is the glass does too. It does incredible damage to the body, they say—blindness, insanity, heart trouble, even varicose veins. Snoose fans never live long." He shook his head. "Most people just jam it up under their lip, but old Ben snorts it. Sometime he's going to blow his nose and find his brain in his hankie."

"He didn't look like that would upset him a whole lot."

Spencer grinned. "Yeah, it probably wouldn't." He pulled a black knitted cap over his red hair. "Get your coat and come on," he said.

In the lobby two young men were waiting for them. "Rufus, meet a couple of fellow-thespians," Spencer said. "This," an amiable-looking youth with lanky blond hair, "is Jeff Kyler, and that one," a dark, short man in burgundy-colored pants, "is Robert Negri. Jeff, Robert—Rufus Pennick."

Thomas said hello to them and detected, he thought, a trace of reserve in their answering nods. Oh well, he said to himself; I'm a green newcomer, an intruder thrust into the intimacies of their craft. I'd probably be a little stand-offish too, if I was in their place.

"Shall we walk or drive?" Jeff asked.

"Too many maniacs running around loose lately," Negri growled. "Let's drive."

"Right," Spencer agreed. "I'll bring the car around front." He ducked down a hallway.

Thomas remembered the machine that had rocketed past him on the Hollywood Freeway the day before. "A gas-car?" he asked, following the other two out of the building.

"The body of one," Jeff said. "It's a derelict we found in the hills one day. Spencer put wooden wheels on it and took the old motor out. We all painted it and cleaned it up, and now it's the neatest little wagon you ever saw."

Thomas nodded, tried and failed to think of something to say, and nodded again. "You, uh, heard about the business in Pershing Square this morning?" he asked.

"Never discuss your casualties," Negri snapped.

"It's too soon to talk about her," Jeff explained more kindly.

"Ah," Thomas said softly, trying not to look disconcerted. A close-mouthed crew, these actors, he thought. The clopping of a horse's hooves on pavement broke the awkward silence, and then the car rounded the corner onto Second from Broadway and pulled up to the curb.

"Hop in, gentlemen," Spencer called from the driver's seat.

Thomas stared at the vehicle. It was a streamlined, albeit dented here and there, metal body, painted gold. A burly old horse was harnessed to the front bumper, and the reins extended from his bit to Spencer's hands through the space where a windshield must once have been. The wheels were sturdy oaken disks rimmed with battered bands of iron.

"Quit gawking and come on," Spencer said. Thomas got in beside him and the other two got in back. The seats were transplanted theatre chairs, upholstered in red velvet, with cast iron flourishes for arms.

"An impressive vehicle," Thomas commented.

"Hell yes," Spencer said, snapping the reins. "If you like, I'll let you have a try behind the wheel."

"Behind the wheel?"

"The steering wheel. This ring here. That's how cars were meant to be steered, see, by turning it. Behind the wheel means, you know, in the driver's seat."

"Oh," said Thomas. "Sure. I'd like to, sometime."

"Not today, huh, Spencer?" Negri pleaded. "I don't feel so good, and I sure don't need any extra shaking up."

"You never feel so good," Spencer told him as he turned the rig north on Spring Street.

Thomas sat back in his seat and watched the passing pageant of the late afternoon sidewalk. Here a heavy-set man was selling day-glo velvet paintings of nudes; there a young man and his girlfriend sat against a wall, passing back and forth between them a bottle in a paper bag; a dog scampered past, hotly pursued by a gang of kids waving sticks; the city, in short, was relaxing into character again in spite of the undisclosed malady that had struck its mayor.

The golden car attracted its share of attention, and by the time they mounted the buttressed bridge over the Hollywood Freeway they had acquired an escort of young boys who ran alongside and begged for rides. When they got too numerous or insistent Spencer would punch the rubber bulb of a curled brass horn mounted on the side of the car, and the boys would scatter.

North of the freeway Spring was called New High Street; the buildings were older here, and the passersby tended to be Mexican or Oriental. The last street inside the city wall was Alpine, and Spencer pulled the car to a curb half a block short of it. "We've arrived," he told Thomas.

A sign dangling on a chain ten feet over the sidewalk was the place's only distinguishing feature—its heavy, paneled door and small-paned windows might believably have hidden anything from a barber shop to a used book store. The sign bore a drawing, done in Doré-like detail, of a cratered moon with a mournful mouth and nose, but no eyes; below the picture were the words *The Blind Moon of Los Angeles.* Spencer opened the door with a courtly bow and his companions filed inside.

The dark interior smelled of musty wood and tobacco smoke. Negri weaved his way around occupied tables to an empty one against the wall, and the four of them sat down. Spencer had just lit a cigarette when a girl sidled up to the table.

"Hiya, Spence," she said. "A pitcher for ya this evening?"

"That'll do for a start," he answered. She made a got-it gesture and wandered off toward the bar. "Well," Spencer said, turning to Jeff and Negri, "how did you boys spend the day?"

"Who is this guy, anyway?" countered Negri, jerking a thumb at Thomas.

"Rufus Pennick," Spencer said evenly. "He's a friend of mine, and of Gladhand's—and he's doing Touchstone in the play. And I, for one, don't care how you spent your goddamned day."

"No offense meant," Jeff told Thomas with a placating smile. "It's just that some people might call what we've been doing illegal, and we don't know you."

"It's all right," Thomas assured him hastily. "I certainly don't want to . . . nose in on any secrets of yours."

"Well, it's nothing *dirty*, or anything like that," flared Negri.

"I didn't think it was," protested Thomas.

"Jesus, Negri," snapped Spencer. "can't you—"

"I just didn't like the look on his face. Like he thought we were fruits, or something."

"I don't think you're fruits," Thomas asserted, wondering what in heaven's name Negri meant by the term. "I swear."

"Well," growled Negri grudgingly, "okay then."

The beer arrived, and the tension of the moment quickly dissolved as Spencer sluiced the foaming stuff into four glasses the girl had set on the table. They soon had to signal her to bring another pitcher, and by the time the second one was empty they were all taking a more tolerant view of the world. Spencer even smoked his cigarette all the way down, which Thomas had not yet seen him do.

A girl passed through the room after a while, lighting miniature candles that sat in wire cages on the tables. Thomas looked around curiously at the smoke-dimmed pictures, posters and photos that were hung or tacked all over the walls.

"What are all these pictures?" he asked, waving his sloshing beer glass in an all-inclusive circle.

"Oh," Spencer sighed, leaning back, "posters announcing old art openings, musical revues, plays. There's a sketch of Ashbless, over the bar, done by Havreville in this very room, sixty years ago. Right over your head is—" he jerked his hand and overturned his glass, splashing beer across the table. "I'm sorry," he said, whipping napkins out of a metal dispenser and throwing them on the spreading puddle. "I must have had more than I thought. Only cure for that is to have more still." He waved to the waitress and pointed to their only half-emptied pitcher.

"Dammit, Spence," laughed Jeff, "wait'll we finish one before you order another."

That's odd, Thomas thought. I could almost swear he spilled that beer intentionally. What had he started to say when he did it? Oh yes: *right over your head is—*. Whatever he was going to say, he apparently thought better of it. Thomas waited for a few minutes, and then turned as casually as he could and looked over his shoulder.

Framed on the wall behind him was a photograph of a young couple in outlandish clothes embracing passionately. Even on his brief acquaintance, Thomas recognized them—the man was Robert Negri and the woman was Jean, whose body he and Spencer had carried into a storeroom that afternoon. The photo's caption was, *She Stoops to Conquer; Gladhand, Bellamy Theatre.*

Thomas quickly turned back to the table and, had a long sip of beer, but when he raised his eyes Negri was scowling at him.

"That was taken last year," the dark-haired actor said. He drained his glass and refilled it sloppily. "I was in love with her."

"Oh, come on, Bob," said Jeff. "We all were."

The new pitcher arrived, and Spencer began loudly reciting "The Face on the Barroom Floor" in an attempt to change the subject. When he'd rendered all the parts he knew, Thomas let go with "Gunga Din," punctuating the ballad by pounding his fist on the wet table-top. There was scattered applause from the other tables when he finished, but Negri still stared moodily down at his hands.

"When we finish this one, let's head back," Spencer said. "This must be the fifth or sixth—"

"No," said Negri, looking up with an odd light in his eyes. "It's too early to head back."

"Oh?" asked Spencer cautiously. "What do *you* think we ought to do?"

"What Jeff and I were doing this afternoon," Negri said. "Blowing up blimps."

"Oh, Jesus," muttered Spencer.

"We were just doing it for laughs then, from the top of the fence," Negri went on. "We didn't know they'd killed her. Now we've got a reason to do it."

"Somebody fill me in," Thomas said. " 'Blowing up blimps' means . . . ?"

"Well," said Spencer wearily, "androids, as you know, are plant-eaters. And sometimes they swell up with methane gas, same as sheep do. They look just like balloons—or like they're about to give birth to a small house. The healthy cops take 'em to the infirmary when they begin to look like that, and a doctor pokes 'em with a long needle and lets all the gas out. Then after a couple of days they're all right again."

"Right," agreed Negri almost cheerfully. "And what we do is climb the fence and shoot flaming arrows into the swelled-up ones."

"You're kidding," said Thomas flatly.

"No sir. You hit them right, and spark all that gas, and they just go up like bombs."

"And that's what you want to do tonight?" Thomas asked.

"Yeah." Negri sucked at his beer. "*I* don't happen to think it's right that a girl like Jean should get killed by a bunch of androids and not be avenged. Goofus here," he said, pointing at Thomas, "didn't know her, so I can't expect him to give one measly damn about her murder. And maybe you two don't happen to remember what she was like—how she was when you were in trouble, or depressed. Maybe you think it's best that she be forgotten as quickly as possible. She'd like that, huh? Oh sure. She was never a fighter or anything when she was alive, was she? Nothing like that.

Jesus! She's probably getting sick in hell right now, to see you guys drinking beer and reciting poetry when her body isn't yet cold." He stood up unsteadily. "Well, *I'm* going to go send a few androids to kingdom come for her. You guys stay here and . . . make sure the goddamned breweries don't go out of business." He turned toward the door.

"Bob," said Spencer slowly. "Wait a minute." He got to his feet. "I— I'm with you."

Jeff leaped up and pitched backward over his chair, having got his foot entangled in it. Negri and Spencer helped him up and brushed him off. "Count me in," he gasped dizzily.

"Wait here for us," Spencer said to Thomas. "We ought to be—"

"Hold it," Thomas said. "I'm going with you. Who was it," he asked, carefully enunciating each word, "that bandaged me up last night? Jean. I can't sit here while you guys go avenge her."

"He's right," Negri said. "Pennick, you're not the slob I thought you were."

They shook hands all around, drank off the last of the beer, and stumbled out the door into the chilly Los Angeles evening.

Making a fist to keep his barbed-wire-torn finger from bleeding— will that finger ever get a proper chance to heal? he wondered—Thomas loped across the grass after Spencer, stepping high so as not to trip over anything in the darkness. He saw Spencer's silhouette disappear behind the wall of a bungalow, and followed him into the deep shadow. Negri and Jeff were already waiting there.

"Okay," Negri whispered when Spencer and Thomas had caught their breath, "now listen: the infirmary is to our right, just past the—"

"Hold it," Jeff said. "If we're doing this for Jean, it ain't right to just blow up some sick ones."

Thomas couldn't see him in the blackness, but raised one eyebrow questioningly. "Oh?"

"He's right," Negri whispered, smothering a hiccup. "We've got to take on the barracks."

Spencer heaved a sigh. "Okay," he said.

"Okay," Thomas agreed. He did wish he could have some more beer first. Maybe they'd find some in the barracks. "Do androids drink?" he asked.

"Naw," answered Negri. "They've got snoose. Now pay attention: the barracks, as I recall, is over there, ahead of us and to the left. I think the armory is off to the side, in a shed. We'd better go there first and grab some guns. Follow me and keep low."

The four of them scuttled furtively across a little lamplit courtyard and then trotted for a hundred yards in the shadow of another building and halted at its far corner. Negri pointed at a low plywood structure that stood between them and the next long building. A bright light was mounted over a screened window in front, and threw the shadow of the padlock across the door like a diagonal streak of black paint.

"That's the armory," he whispered. "We'll dash over there, one at a time, and stay on the dark side. Then we'll pry the screen off a window and Pennick here, being the skinniest, will climb in and hand weapons out to us. After that we'll move on to the barracks, shoot a dozen or so of the bastards, and climb the far fence and head home. Sound okay?"

Everyone allowed that it did, Thomas with some reservations. The beer fumes were beginning to leave his head, and he couldn't remember why coming here had seemed such a good idea.

"Take it away, Rufe," Spencer said, patting him on the back, and Thomas sprinted across the open space into the shadow of the shack. One by one the others followed. it was the work of a minute to lever the screen from the window, and a moment later Thomas was hoisted up and supported horizontally in the air by six hands, his head thrust into the window.

"Can you see anything?" Negri hissed.

"Nothing clear," Thomas whispered back over his shoulder. "Listen, though—roll me face up, and let me get my hands up here, and I think I could climb in." They carefully rotated his tense body until his back was to the ground. He angled both arms in through the narrow window and locked his fingers firmly around a pole that seemed to be firmly moored. "Okay," he said nervously. "Now when I say *go*, you shove me in. Gently! I should jackknife through and land upright on the floor." He gripped the pole even tighter, made sure again that he could picture how this would work, and then gasped, "Go."

They pushed him through, the pole came free in his hands, and he tumbled upside-down over a wheelbarrow and into a rack of shovels. The clatter and clang was appalling, and it took him nearly thirty seconds of thrashing about even to get to his feet. He bounded for the window, and tripped over a bottle of some sort that shattered resoundingly.

Spencer poked his head in the window. "Weapons, for God's sake!" he shouted. "Now!" His face disappeared again.

Thomas flung four shovels through the window and then dove through it himself, rolling as he fell and landing painfully on his shoulder. He leaped up immediately, and was momentarily surprised to see that not one of his companions had fled.

Spencer thrust one of the shovels into his hands. He saw that lights had gone on in the building ahead, and a half-dozen figures were clustered in the doorway. "All right, hold it right there!" came a call.

"Run back the way we came," Spencer snapped, and all four of them did, still carrying their shovels. *Bang.* A bullet spanged off the concrete a hundred feet to the right. Another broke a window ahead of them and two more whistled through the air. Thomas' legs pounded on and on, even when each breath seared his lungs and abraded his ribs, and he could see the rainbow glitter of unconsciousness playing around the borders of his vision.

Androids were designed to run faster than the average man, but they also had a tendency toward sluggishness when suddenly awakened, and none of these considered it worthwhile to leave, unbidden, their warm barracks in order to pursue such bandits as would lay siege to the gardener's shack. They simply stood in the doorway and emptied a revolver at the fleeing figures.

Spencer, leading the way, saw the sentry first; the android was loping toward them terrifyingly fast, with its head low and its hand fumbling at the flap of its holster. Thomas saw Spencer leap toward the galloping thing, whirling the shovel over his head like a long battle-axe. The edge of the descending blade cracked into the android's shoulder, and Spencer and the sentry were both knocked off their feet. Thomas ran toward them with his own shovel held over his head.

The android leaped up with bestial agility and finally fumbled the pistol out of its holster as Spencer rolled to his feet three yards away, ready to attempt a last charge at the thing. At that moment Thomas' rush arrived from behind the android—he swung the poised shovel down upon the creature's skull with every bit of strength the evening had left him, and then tumbled past in an involuntary somersault across the pavement.

Jesus, no more, he thought as he struggled up on his hands and knees, fighting a strong nausea that gripped his stomach. There was a clank of metal breaking metal, and a sound like a dropped coin. "In here," somebody hissed, and somebody else hauled Thomas forcibly erect and gave him a shove forward. He tripped through an open door and sprawled full length across the floor beyond. He lay there while the door was shut behind him, trying simultaneously to recover his breath and control his stomach.

"Old Rufo there . . . isn't as tough as he thinks," someone panted.

"Go to hell. He . . . killed that android, didn't he?" came a gasping whisper from somebody else. "So far tonight he's the only one who has."

Thomas rolled over and sat up. "The spirit," he pronounced carefully, "is willing, but the flesh is drunk and exhausted." Negri, Jeff and Spencer, still carrying their shovels, were slumped against the walls of the little room. "Where are we, anyway?"

"I think this is the service entrance for the infirmary," Negri answered. He held up his hand suddenly, and thudding footsteps raced past outside the door. "We can't relax yet. They might notice the busted lock any time. *Uhh,*" he gasped, standing up, "let's see where this inner door will take us."

It was an aluminum door with rubber insulation around its edges; it wasn't locked, and swung open at Negri's first tug. The room within was lit by dim red lights, and smelled of steam and disinfectant. They filed inside, and saw a number of chest-high vats lined up against the wall. Thomas' dim hope that this might be a winery of some sort evaporated when he peered through the clear plastic cover of one of them.

"Damn my soul!" he whispered. "There's a guy in there!"

The other three joined him and looked down at a smooth human body that was suspended a few inches below the surface of the cloudy liquid in the vat.

"We're in an android brewery," Spencer said. "I didn't know there was one here."

"Who's this guy look like to you, Spence?" asked Jeff. "He looks familiar to me."

"Yeah," Negri agreed suddenly. "I've . . . seen that face."

Thomas peered at it again, but it didn't especially look like anyone he'd ever seen. He wandered over to another vat. "Whoever it is," he said, "he's over here, too."

There were a half-dozen vats in the room, and a quick check revealed that the nearly-completed occupants of all six were cast from the same blueprint.

"I wish I could remember who it is that they all look like," Negri said, frowning.

"Should we kill them?" Jeff asked.

Spencer looked at him skeptically. "How? This is obviously shatter-proof plastic—even with these shovels it'd take five minutes to splinter through one of them. And I don't see any valves we could fool with. We don't have time. Come on."

They left the room through another metal door, and found themselves in a hallway. It seemed chilly after the steamy heat of the vat room, and Thomas wondered wistfully when—and if—he'd see his theatre-basement bed again. Spencer led them down the hall in the direction that led away from the barracks. The floor was carpeted, and the corridor was dimly lit by electric bulbs that hung in globes of frosted glass. The disinfectant smell was here, too, but rivaled by an odor reminiscent of stables and animal cages.

The corridor split in a T, and they followed the left-hand branch, which ended, after a hundred feet, at a door whose chicken-wire-reinforced window showed only darkness beyond. "This just may lead outside," Spencer whispered, holding up crossed fingers as he turned the knob.

At that moment the door at the far end of the hall was flung open by a gang of gray-uniformed androids who uttered glad shouts and bore down upon the four half-fuddled actors.

Spencer whipped the door open and leaped through after his three companions, whirling on the other side to lock it by twisting a disk on the knob. The air was stuffy and still, and he realized they were in another room. "Turn on the lights!" he barked. "We've got to get out of here."

Thomas' groping hand found a switch; he flipped it on and the room was abruptly flooded with illumination.

Sitting up on their blanketless beds, blinking and whimpering at the sudden light, were what appeared to be nine grossly obese naked men. "Lights out!" one of them squeaked, and the rest took up the cry like a flock of parrots: "Lights out! Lights out!"

"You three hold the door," Spencer snapped. The androids on the other side were already kicking and pounding on it. "I've got an idea."

While Thomas, Negri and Jeff tried to pull on the doorknob and duck the splintering glass of the crumpling window, Spencer raced to the door at the far end of the room, which proved to be, as he'd expected, locked. He dragged the nearest bed over to it and lifted one end so that the whimpering occupant was spilled squashily onto the floor in front of the locked door. Then Spencer ran back to his companions, whipping off his shirt.

The reinforced window-glass had been punched nearly out of its frame, and android hands were reaching through and plucking at the young men's hair and shirts. "Hurry, Spence!" Thomas gasped.

Spencer wrapped the head of one of the shovels in his shirt, and then fished a matchbook out of his pocket and struck a match to the fabric. It was slow to take the flame, but after a few door-pounding, glass-splintering seconds it began to flicker alight.

Spencer turned to the far door, raised the shovel over his shoulder and, running forward, flung the makeshift spear at the bloated android on the floor.

It arced through the still air, spinning lazily and trailing smoke, and then thudded into the creature's distended belly. There was a muffled bang, a flash of light and a cloud of acrid smoke, and they heard the door bounce on concrete outside.

"Let's go," Spencer panted; unnecessarily, for the other three had already released their door and were following him at a dead run toward the empty, smoke-clouded doorway, while the remaining occupants of the beds gibbered, "Lights out! Lights out!"

When Thomas burst out through the doorway, practically on the heels of Negri, the first thing he noticed was the temperature—the night air was hot and dry, blowing from the east. He followed his companions as they ran across the dark lawn, cringing, as he ran, in anticipation of the tearing impact of a bullet in his back.

"Get *moving*, Rufus," Spencer gritted, seizing Thomas by the shoulder and pulling him along. Jeff grabbed his other arm, and Thomas found himself being nearly carried toward the fence.

Hard footsteps pounded on the lawn behind them, but the four of them had reached the fence now, and helped each other scramble and fall over it several seconds before the androids arrived and began shooting their pistols through the boards.

"Give yourselves up," the androids called calmly as their bullets hammered at the splintering boards of the fence. "Give yourselves up." When they had emptied their revolvers, one of them climbed onto another's shoulders and peered through the strands of barbed wire at the empty stretch of Main Street beyond. A few lights had gone on in nearby buildings, but no one came outside to investigate the shooting. The android looked up and down the street, peered at the sidewalk below, and sniffed curiously at the hot night wind as if hoping to catch the fugitives' scent.

"They're gone," he said finally. He leaped down and they holstered their guns and plodded back across the grass toward the buildings.

On the other side of the street four figures darted out of a shadowed drugstore doorway and fled silently away.

"Hey," Thomas said drowsily. "This isn't the Bellamy Theatre."

"You don't miss a lot, do you?" growled Negri. "We're back at the Blind Moon."

"Why? Aren't we ever going to get to sleep?"

"We've got to establish our alibi," Spencer explained as they turned into the alley that led to the bar's rear door. "We've got to give people the idea that we've been here all evening."

"Evening?" Thomas protested. "It must be nearly dawn."

"It's only a quarter to ten," Jeff said. "I saw the city hall clock about five minutes ago."

"Jesus." Thomas shook his head in dull wonder and followed Spencer into the rear of the kitchen. It was empty except for a teenage boy who stood at the sinks, languidly running a wet rag over dishes and dropping them into the water.

"What were you doing out there, Spence?" the boy asked.

"Getting a bit of fresh air, we were," Spencer told him. The four of them filed past and stepped through the kitchen door into the crowded, noisy, smoke-layered public room. They managed to find a table, near the door, and sat down with relaxed sighs.

Spencer immediately bounded to his feet. "My God," he gasped. "I was supposed to meet Evelyn at nine under Bush-head. I'll see you later. Or tomorrow." He opened the door and sprinted away down the sidewalk.

"Bush-head?" Thomas echoed as the door banged shut.

"It's a statue of Mayor Pelias down by the mission church," Jeff said. "About three years ago, when he began to get really unpopular, somebody looped a rope around the statue's head and tried to pull it down. All that happened was the head broke off. A year or so later—ah, the beer already! Thank you, miss—a year or so later somebody wired a big tumbleweed onto the neck-post; so everybody calls it Johnny Bush-head."

"Huh." Thomas poured himself a beer and sipped it thoughtfully.

"Want to throw some darts?" Negri asked Jeff. Jeff nodded and they stood up and moved away, taking the pitcher with them. Thomas idly traced designs in the dampness on his glass.

A minute or so later, a paunchy old man with wisps of gray hair trailing across his shiny, mottled scalp sat down across from Thomas. "All right if I join you?" he asked hesitantly.

He was carrying a glass and a new pitcher of beer, so there was some sincerity in Thomas' voice when he said, "Certainly, certainly."

"Thank you. Here, let me fill your glass."

"Much obliged."

"Not at all." He leaned back and set the pitcher down. "You're a friend of Spencer's?" Thomas nodded. "A fine lad, he is," the old man went on. "Are you an actor too?"

"Yes," Thomas answered.

"I'll have to make it over to see the play. One of Shakespeare's best, I've always thought."

Thomas looked at him. "Really? I much prefer . . . oh, *Lear,* or *Macbeth,* or *Julius Caesar.*"

The old man blinked. "An educated man, I perceive! Allow me to introduce myself. I am Gardener Jenkins." He cocked a hopeful eyebrow at Thomas, then lowered it when Thomas showed no recognition of the name. "I was—still am, in a way—a professor of philosophy at the University at Berkeley."

"Oh," said Thomas politely. "What brings you so far south?"

Jenkins pulled a pint bottle of bourbon out of his pocket, uncorked it and topped off his glass of beer with the dark brown whiskey. He sipped it and nodded with satisfaction. "What? Oh, yes. I'm at work on a . . .

very big *project*, you see, research that couldn't be done at Berkeley." He chuckled ruefully. "And it couldn't be done here, either, I discovered."

Thomas looked more closely at him, noticing now the puffy face and broken-veined skin of the long-time alcoholic. "Oh?" he said, curious about the scholarly old rummy.

"Indeed. Have you ever heard of J. Heinemann Strogoff?"

"Wait a minute," Thomas said. "Strogoff. Yeah. He was a scientist—right?—and he did a lot of genetic research, and died about ten years ago. I read a pamphlet about him. *Loki Ascendant,* it was called."

"Good God, son, where did you see a copy of *that?* I thought mine was the last extant copy outside of a few monastic libraries."

"My grandfather had one," Thomas said quickly. "Lost now, I'm certain. Anyway, it said a lot of horrible things about Strogoff."

"Well, sure. It was published by the Church, and the clergy was very hostile toward Strogoff's work."

"What was his work, exactly? The pamphlet talked about . . . 'soulless constructs,' I recall—"

"He was a biologist and a philosopher. His evaluation of Locke is still considered the definitive one. But what he's famous for, and what set the Church against him, is his work with artificial and mutated species. The tax-birds, the forest dwarves, the sewer-singers, even the androids—all the weird, semi-rational creatures you find in and around the southern California city-states—were developed by Strogoff and his successors." He took a sip of his fortified beer.

A fight at the bar distracted Thomas for a moment. This place certainly isn't restful, he thought. I wonder if I could find my way alone back to the Bellamy. I guess not. Maybe I'll go sleep in the car, though.

He turned back to his companion. "So how has the study of Strogoff brought you here?" And to this, he added to himself.

"I was—am—editing the *Collected Letters of J. Heinemann Strogoff.*" He rolled the title off with evident relish. "I'm nearly finished, too." Jenkins frowned deeply. "Two days before he died, Strogoff wrote a letter to Louis Hancock, who was then the major-domo of Los Angeles. I found part of the carbon of that letter—just a torn-off piece—in the Berkeley collection of Strogoff's papers. It . . . it seemed, from what sense I could make of it, that Strogoff was threatening Hancock. And pleading with him, too, at the same time. Anyhow, I figured the complete letter definitely belonged in my book; it was probably the last letter he ever wrote, for one thing." Thomas refilled his glass from Jenkins' pitcher, and shook his head when the old man raised the whiskey bottle invitingly. "So," Jenkins went on, "I came to L.A. four years ago. Figured I'd look up Hancock and talk him into letting me make a copy of the complete letter. Hah! Hancock was two years dead when I got here. Killed himself. And his papers were locked in the city archives, where they still, I suppose, are."

"Won't they let you see them?" Thomas asked.

"No. Christ knows why—clerks just think that way, I guess. I've made a hundred requests, phrased a hundred different ways. The University even wrote to Pelias, asking him to give me access. No dice."

"And you've just stayed on."

Jenkins nodded. "That's right. After a while those bastards at the University terminated my contract. And me with tenure! So I stayed. Money ran out and I got a job on the *Greeter*. I'll head back up to Berkeley sometime, pick up my stuff and publish the book somewhere else. But . . . there's no hurry." The level of his drink had lowered, and he refilled it with the bourbon. "No hurry," he repeated vacantly.

Thomas nodded doubtfully. "I'll see you later," he said, getting laboriously to his feet.

"Yeah, take it easy," Jenkins said with a wave.

Thomas looked around at the crowd, but failed to see Jeff or Negri. He walked outside, found the car, and curled up in one of the back seats. The warm eastern wind that was sifting fine dust over the dark streets had kept the car from becoming chilly, and Thomas sank immediately into a deep sleep.

CHAPTER 5
The Girl at the Far End of the Row

As soon as he awoke, Thomas knew he was sick. His nose was completely stopped up, his mouth was dry from having breathed through it all night, his throat hurt when he swallowed, and he had a small, tight headache under his left ear.

"Creeping Jesus," he moaned thickly, rolling over. I'm in my bed at least, he thought. He forced his eyes open and found himself staring at the stone head on the shelf. "Good morning," he croaked at it.

Once he stood up he felt a little better. He slid into his shirt and pants and padded barefoot to the greenroom. Spencer was there, talking to a half-dozen people Thomas didn't know.

"Damn, look what shambled out of the swamp," Spencer grinned. "Mornin', Rufe."

"G'morning." Thomas slumped into a chair.

"You sound awful," spoke up a pretty, auburn-haired girl. "Got a cold?" Thomas considered it, then nodded. "It's this Santa Ana wind," she said. "Comes in from the desert."

"Gang, this is Rufus," Spencer said. "Rufe, I won't run through everybody's names, because you wouldn't remember them anyhow. This is the guy," he remarked to the others, "who split the skull of the android that was about to put a bullet into me."

They nodded and looked at Thomas more respectfully. The auburn-haired girl crossed the room and sat on the arm of his chair. "Would you like some breakfast?" she inquired.

"Um . . . coffee," Thomas said. "Thank you. Hot, with sugar."

"You just sit there and rest, hon. I'll bring it." She scurried out of the room.

"Well, Rufus," said a tall, hearty-voiced young man with short-cropped hair, "I understand you are, to a certain extent, one of us." A couple of the others shot sharp looks at him.

"Yes," answered Thomas, too tired to care whether there had been sarcasm in the man's sentence.

"Say," put in a girl across the room. "How's Pelias? Does anyone know?"

Several people shrugged. "Somebody told me," said Thomas, "that he's probably dead, and the government's scared to admit it."

"That may be," nodded the short-haired man. "Hell, it's been three days now since the, uh, resistance guerrillas detonated those two bombs in his house. The administrators may well be holding a corpse and stalling for time."

"I never permit political talk in the greenroom, Lambert, as you know," said Gladhand, who had propelled his wheelchair in the door. "In our line of work it's an unaffordable luxury." He looked around at the group. "And speaking of our line of work, everybody had better remember to be at the noon rehearsal today. We'll have two newcomers—Rufus here, and hopefully a girl to play Rosalind." Everyone shifted uncomfortably. Jean must have been doing Rosalind, Thomas realized. "Where's Alice?" the manager went on. "Not here? Well, when she shows, have her finish nailing up the Arden set. Rufus, why don't you come along with me. I'll pick the new girl and then explain everything to both of you at once."

The girl returned with Thomas' coffee; he thanked her and then followed Gladhand down the corridor, taking cautious sips of the hot brew.

"I sent a boy to the *L.A. Greeter* office last night," Gladhand said over his shoulder. "Had him put an ad in this morning's paper. 'Actress wanted, for the part of Rosalind in *As You Like It.* Apply at the Bellamy Theatre, 10 A.M.' With the city in its current uproar, I have no idea what kind of response it'll draw. Might be nobody, might be every female north of Pico."

They took a side hallway that led between two heavy curtains and eventually out onto the stage. The house lamps were lit and three broad, scrimmed spots illuminated the stage. Jeff stood in the central aisle, near the lobby doors.

"Have we got any, Jeff?" Gladhand called.

"Yes sir, a good dozen."

"Trot 'em in." The theatre manager turned to Thomas. "By the way, uh, Rufus, I want to have it established that no further escapades like last night's will take place. Spencer told me about it. I can see your motivations, but nothing like that must ever recur. I've already spoken to him and Robert and Jeff. I hope I make myself clear?"

"Yes sir," said Thomas, embarrassed. "It won't recur."

"Good lad! Now look sharp, I may want your advice on these young ladies."

A gaggle of women entered and walked uncertainly down the aisle. "If you'll all just sit down in the front row, ladies, we'll commence," Gladhand said loudly. The women filed along the row and found seats.

Thomas regarded them curiously, in spite of feeling semi-undressed without his shoes on. Several were obviously too fat, and a couple looked too old to him, though he admittedly had no idea what could or could not be accomplished with makeup. That skinny little girl there might do, he thought, or—then he noticed the girl at the far end of the row.

She had a round face, with black bangs cut off in a line just above her heavy-lidded eyes. She didn't chat with the others, simply watched Gladhand and Thomas with an air of wary amusement. She wore a gray sweater, over the neck of which was folded the collar of her pale blue blouse.

"The first thing," said Gladhand, wheeling to the edge of the stage, "that I should make clear is the fact that I pay no salaries. My actors live on the premises and receive room, board and clothing by way of payment."

"How's that going to feed my kids?" queried a broad-shouldered woman in a hat.

"Ma'am, I'm afraid it will not. The position I offer is suitable only to an unattached person with no pressing responsibilities."

The woman in the hat, and several others, stood up, picked their way out of the row and strode impatiently up the aisle. One paused at the door to make a rude gesture. Six remained sitting, and a couple of these looked doubtful. The expression, though, of the girl at the far end had not changed. I think she's the one for it, Thomas decided.

"Well," said Gladhand, "now that we're weeded down to a manageable number, tell me about yourselves. You first." He pointed at the over-made-up girl who sat nearest the aisle.

She stood up. "Well, sir, I feel a . . . creative urge within me that demands expression in the theatre, treading the boards. I have too vast a soul, you see, to keep it to myself. In a manner of speaking, I am Life. To me—"

"Please," said Gladhand firmly. "That's enough."

"Enough for what?" she asked.

"Enough for me," he replied irritably. "Get out of here."

She left indignantly, with *sotto voce* observations to the effect that certain people were crippled in more ways than one. So long, Life, Thomas thought.

The self-descriptions of the next few women were very subdued, and Thomas soon stopped listening and stared at the girl in the gray sweater. After a while he became aware that she was staring back at him, and he blushed and looked away.

"And yourself, miss?" Gladhand said politely, turning finally to her.

She rose. "I saw your ad in the *Greeter,*" she said, and shrugged. "I've never acted before, so you know I haven't developed any prejudices or bad habits. I have read the play, at least. And I have no previous jobs or commitments to prevent my starting directly."

Gladhand nodded, and wheeled himself into the middle of the stage. He beckoned to Thomas, who hurried over to him. "What do you think, Rufus?" the theatre manager asked solemnly.

"Jesus, sir," Thomas answered under his breath. "Take the girl in the gray sweater. She's . . ." He hesitated.

"Yes?" pursued Gladhand with a half-mocking smile. "She's what?"

"She's probably the best actress of them," finished Thomas defensively.

"Nonsense. That one I ordered out was probably the best actress." He threw up one hand in a surrendering gesture. "But—I must have people I can work with. Okay. I'll take her."

"Sir? Why didn't you have an audition for Touchstone's part?"

"I didn't have to. You dropped in at the right moment, and seemed adequate." Gladhand rolled forward. "The truth is," he whispered over his shoulder, "I hate auditions. I never really know what to do."

He was at the edge of the stage again. "Ladies, it will not be necessary to do readings. I have made my choice. The ones not chosen may pick up free tickets to the performance from the young man by the door there. And the part of Rosalind, I've decided, goes to you." He pointed to the girl who was Thomas' choice. The others got to their feet and shambled out.

The girl in the gray sweater stepped to the stage, and resting one hand lightly on the edge, vaulted gracefully up onto it. Thomas noted that she was wearing faded black corduroy pants. She was somewhat short, and her figure was full but certainly not plump.

Gladhand bowed somehow in his wheelchair. "I am Nathan Gladhand, and this is Rufus Pennick," he said. "You are . . . ?"

"Cleopatra Pearl," she said.

"Cleopatra Pearl," Gladhand repeated gloomily.

"My mother thought it sounded sharp," the girl said apologetically. "I can't help it. Call me Pat."

Gladhand brightened. "Pat it is. Well, Pat, Rufus here is a newcomer to our company like yourself, so I'll explain our rules and customs to both of you at once." He plucked a cigar out of his pocket and struck a match on the wheelchair arm. "First *(puff puff)*, know your lines. I realize you two haven't had a chance to, yet; but starting tomorrow I will expect every actor to have his or her lines down pat, so we can spend our time on movement and inflection and things like that. Second—what I say is law. You may make suggestions from time to time, but you may never persist in disagreement. Third—nothing is beneath an actor's dignity.

Everybody builds sets, hangs lights, paints backdrops, goes next door to fetch chop suey and eggrolls. Let's see, what am I on, fourth? Fourth—there are no fights within my troupe. In the event of a fight, both parties are expelled, no matter who it might be." He pinched the cigar out and replaced it in his pocket. "And there's no smoking in the auditorium. That's all the rules I can think of for now. If any more occur to me I'll let you know. There's a rehearsal in about an hour; you two needn't participate yet, but you should watch. I'll see both of you later. Rufus, show her around."

"Aye aye." Thomas led her away into the wings while Gladhand wheeled himself off in the opposite direction. "Actually," Thomas confessed to her, "I don't really know my way around the place yet. I've only—"

"You've got a cold, haven't you?" she interrupted.

"What? Oh, yes. Haven't been taking care of myself this last couple of days. Anyway, I can show you the greenroom—which is painted yellow, by the way; I guess it used to be green. That's the only landmark I know, so far. Maybe you and I could explore—"

"What did you do before you came here, Rufus? Where did you live?"

"I—" *I can't tell her I was a ward of the local cloistered monastery,* he realized. *She'd recoil. And I ditched that identity, anyway.* "I was a student at Berkeley," he said. "I got expelled, though, for punching the dean one night, so I signed aboard a tramp steamer and came to Los Angeles. Oh," he added, "and I'm a poet in my spare time." *That much, at least, was true.*

"A *poet?*" she echoed, her voice a blend of doubt and awe, as if he'd claimed that he'd been brought up by wolves.

"Well, yes," Thomas said, a little disconcerted. "A few sonnets and things. I haven't been published yet."

They walked on, silently, to the greenroom. "This is where everybody seems to congregate," he told her, though the only one there at present was Negri, who was combing his hair in front of a mirror. "Bob," Thomas said, "this is Pat Pearl. Pat, Bob Negri. Pat is taking the Rosalind part."

Negri turned around and gave the girl a long, interested up-and-down look. "Well, hello," he said with a slow smile.

"I'll show you the rest of the place, Pat," Thomas said quickly, taking her arm.

"That's all right, Rufus," she said. "We can explore later. Right now I'd better get my stuff out of my cart. It's parked out back and somebody's likely to grab it."

"I could help you carry it in," Thomas pointed out.

"No, it's only one bag. I'll be okay." She waved and strode away down the hall.

"*There's* a piece," commented Negri. "I wouldn't kick *her* out of bed."

Thomas looked at him sharply. "Jesus, Negri. You sure adapt quickly."

"What do you mean by that?"

"Give it some thought."

Thomas left the room angrily and walked out to the lobby. Bright sunlight glittered on the asphalt of Second Street outside the windows, and Thomas stepped out onto the sidewalk for some fresh air.

Spencer was slouched against the wall, smoking a cigarette. "You've got no shoes on, Rufe," he observed.

"You're right." Thomas leaned on the wall too. "I don't like Negri."

Spencer squinted through the tobacco smoke. "I hear the new girl's real pretty," he said.

"True." Thomas relaxed and looked up and down the street. "Say, did you ever find Evelyn last night?"

"Yeah. Finally convinced her that I hadn't intentionally stood her up. Lied like a bastard, too. I couldn't tell her the truth."

"I suppose not. Gladhand wasn't real pleased about last night, was he?"

Spencer grinned. "Oh, he didn't really mind so much. When he's fatherly-stern you know he's not genuinely upset. He just doesn't want his people to get killed running off on drunken inspirations."

"Oh." A beer truck rattled past, pursued by a gang of little boys. The city seems to be about its usual business, Thomas thought. "How's Pelias?" he asked. "Have you heard?"

"Yeah. The official word is—give up?—he's still in a coma."

"I didn't know you could be in a coma this long."

"Oh, sure. Three days isn't the world record. I think he's alive," Spencer said, "because Lloyd, the major-domo, hasn't named a successor, and he hasn't tried to take the office himself, either. I'm sure he'd have done one or the other if Pelias was dead." Spencer pointed over the rooftops at a trailing plume of smoke that stood out sharply against the blue sky. "Roughly Alameda and Third Street, I'd guess. And I heard exchanges of gunfire three times this morning, in the south. Somebody'd better take charge pretty soon."

Thomas nodded helplessly. "Uh . . . will there be a funeral or something for Jean?" he asked.

"No. Not for us, anyway. She has some folks in Glendale, and Gladhand had her body sent out there."

For a while, neither of them spoke, and then Thomas turned to re-enter the theatre. "You heard right," he said. "The new girl is real pretty."

CHAPTER 6
The Dark-Rum Queen

Two seats to Thomas' right, Gladhand puffed on a cigar and regarded the people on stage through narrowed eyes. The short-haired man, Lambert, whom Thomas had met earlier in the greenroom stood with Alice in the foreground; behind them were a young man and woman Thomas didn't know, and, holding a script, Pat Pearl.

They'd begun rehearsing the fifth scene of Act Three. Phebe, played by Alice, was unsympathetically explaining to Lambert's Silvius that she wished he'd stop bothering her with his wooing.

"That's good," called Gladhand. "Just the right amount of impatience. Silvius, try to look anguished, will you? Dumb, sure, but anguished too. All right, now, Rosalind, walk over to Phebe."

Pat stepped forward, and Thomas envied her air of self-possession. Gladhand had decided that his two new players ought to at least walk through their parts, reading from scripts, and Thomas feared that he'd bungle even that. He remembered uneasily the panic that had always assailed him when he'd been called on to serve Mass as a boy.

Rosalind, through Pat, was now advising Phebe at length to take Silvius at his word. "Sell when you can: you are not for all markets," she told her finally. It was a long speech, but Pat read it well and with conviction.

"Not bad," said Gladhand.

The scene moved on, and it developed that Phebe had now fallen in love with Rosalind, who was to be, in the actual performance, disguised as a man. Needlessly complicated, Thomas thought. And it's just not credible that Rosalind's disguise could be as convincing as the plot demands.

"Hold it, Rosalind," Gladhand interrupted. "Do that last line again, but look at Phebe when you say it. You were looking out here at us."

Pat nodded and repeated the line, looking this time toward Phebe: "I pray you, do not fall in love with me, for I am falser than vows made in wine."

"That's how it ought to go," the theatre manager nodded.

At five o'clock they had run through the scene several times—with Pat looking at her script only once or twice the last time—and had begun work on the first scene of Act Four. Thomas, sitting with his feet on the back of the seat in front of him, heard with relief the five distant notes of the city hall clock.

"That's plenty for today," Gladhand said, struggling up onto his crutches. "I'm feeling more optimistic about the damned play now than I have in a week. I think you're all beginning to relax into it."

Most of the lights were put out, and the actors broke up into groups and wandered offstage. Thomas tried to intercept Pat, but she was talking and laughing with Alice, and didn't see him. Jeff was sliding the plywood flats back into the wings, and Thomas waved to him. "Jeff!" he called. "How does one get dinner around here?"

"One follows the east hall—" Jeff pointed, "—all the way to the back. There's a dining room."

"Much obliged."

Thomas followed the stragglers down the hall and wound up sitting at a long wooden table, wedged between Lambert and the girl who'd brought him coffee this morning. Pat, he noticed with a hollow, despairing sensation, was sitting next to Negri, who was performing some trick with his fork and spoon for her amusement.

"You're Rufus?" the girl on Thomas' right asked.

"That's right."

"I'm Skooney," she said. "Here, have some of this stew. Greg, pass the pitcher, Rufus didn't get any beer."

"Thank you," Thomas said automatically, his attention focused on Pat and Negri.

"I'm the gaffer," Skooney said.

Thomas reluctantly turned to her. "The what?" He had thought gaffers worked on fishing boats.

"I'm in charge of the lights. Did you know we've got some real electric lights? Gladhand set up a generator out back. There are only two other theatres in the whole L.A. area that have electric lights."

"Well," said Thomas, "I'm glad I'm starting out at the top." He took a deep sip of beer and set to work on the stew, still casting occasional furtive glances down the table.

A little later Spencer wandered through the room, and leaned over Thomas' shoulder. "Meet me on the roof when you get done," he whispered, filling a spare glass with beer. Thomas nodded and Spencer, after exchanging a few rudely humorous insults with Alice, left the room.

*   *   *

Beneath the high, cold splendor of the stars, the winking yellow lights of Los Angeles looked friendly and protective, like a night-light in a child's bedroom. From the streets below the broad concrete coping of the roof there echoed from time to time the rattle of a passing cart, or the long call of a mother summoning her children.

Spencer flicked his cigarette out over the street when he heard Thomas' footsteps on the stairs.

"Is that you, Rufus?"

"Yeah. Wow, what a view." The Santa Ana wind was still sighing its warm breath from the east, and Thomas took off his coat.

"No kidding. Listen, I was talking to Evelyn today, and I casually asked her if they'd caught this escaped monk, Thomas."

"What did she say?" asked Thomas, with the sinking feeling of one who's been reminded of a lingering disease.

"She says they're looking for him day and night. They're not even looking for the guys who bombed Pelias as hard as they're looking for you. No charges have been mentioned, though." Spencer lit another cigarette. "Are you *sure* you haven't forgotten something? Something you saw or heard, maybe?"

Thomas shook his head helplessly. "There's some mistake," he said. "Maybe some other monk named Thomas ran off from some other monastery on the same day I did."

Spencer inhaled deeply on his cigarette, then let the smoke hiss out between his teeth. "They said the Merignac, remember?"

A deep, window-rattling boom shook the roof, and part of a building several blocks away collapsed into the street. Flames began licking up from the rubble.

"The rent on that place just went down, I believe," Spencer said.

Thomas could see, silhouetted by the mounting flames, people appearing on the surrounding roofs, waving their arms and dashing about aimlessly.

"What was that building?" Thomas asked, leaning on the coping and staring out at the conflagration.

"Oh, a city office bombed by radicals," Spencer answered, "or a radicals' den bombed by city officers. I just hope it doesn't spread real far on this wind. Do you hear any bells?"

Thomas listened. "No."

"Neither do I. The fire trucks aren't out yet. If they appear within the next couple of minutes, we'll know it was some administrator's house or office. If it was a troublesome citizen's house they probably won't get there before dawn."

They watched without speaking. Five minutes later they'd been silently joined at the roof-edge by five other members of the troupe, but no fire trucks had made an appearance at the scene of the fire.

"Maybe we ought to organize a group to go help put it out," someone suggested. "If it gets to the buildings next to it the whole city'll go up."

"No," said Negri. "Look, they've got it under control. When the roof collapsed it killed most of it. See? The whole thing's darker now. The only stuff burning now is what fell in the street."

"We'll have to read about it in the *Greeter* tomorrow," Thomas said. "Find out what happened." Everyone laughed, and Thomas realized his statement had been taken as a joke.

"Did you *see* the damned paper this morning?" Jeff asked him. "You know what the headline was? Pelias has been bombed, you know, and the androids are running amuck, right? So here's the headline: ALL-TIME HIGH FROG COUNT IN SAN GABRIEL VALLEY."

"They're right on top of things," Thomas observed. The fire really was dimmer now, and the actors moved away from the roof-edge.

"You bet," Jeff agreed.

"I read that," Spencer said. "Apparently the summer wasn't as hot as it usually is, so the Ravenna swamps didn't dry up this year. The frogs didn't all die, like they usually do—they just sat around and multiplied all year long, so now the valley's choked with 'em. I was thinking that some enterprising businessman should drive up there and pack a few tons of frogs in ice, and run them down to Downey or Norwalk and sell them for food."

"You're a born wheeler-dealer, Spence," said Alice.

Thomas spied Pat still standing by the coping, watching the diminishing fire. He walked over and leaned on the wall next to her. She was sniffling and wiping her nose with a handkerchief.

"You aren't catching my cold, are you?" he asked.

She sneezed. "No," she answered.

"Hey," came a jovial voice, and Negri interposed himself between Thomas and Pat. "Running off with my girl, are you, Rufus? Come on, Patsy, I want you to meet some people." He put his arm around her shoulders and led her back toward the rest of the group.

Thomas stared after them for a moment, and then strode angrily toward the stairs.

"Rufus." Thomas stopped. Gladhand had got up the stairs somehow, crutches and all, and now sat in a wicker chair in the far shadows. "Come over here a moment," the theatre manager said.

Thomas picked his way over a litter of two-by-fours to where Gladhand sat. Another chair stood nearby, and he sank into it. "Weird evening," he said. "With this wind and all."

Gladhand nodded. "Several hundred years ago it was considered a valid defense in a murder trial if you could prove the Santa Ana wind was blowing when the murder was committed. The opinion was that the dry, hot wind made everybody so irritable that any murder was almost automatically excusable. Or so I've heard, anyway."

Thomas pondered it. "There might be something to that," he said.

"No," Gladhand said. "There isn't. Start sanctioning heat-of-anger crimes and you've lost the last hold on the set of conventions we call . . . society, civilization."

He sat back and pressed the tips of his fingers together. "Some things, Rufus, cannot be avoided. They will happen no matter what efforts you make to prevent them. Once, when I was much younger, I was at a girl's house with some friends. It was about noon, and we were all standing around the piano, singing and drinking lemonade. After a while I glanced down and saw, to my horror, that the fly of my trousers was unbuttoned. I've got to divert their attention, I thought desperately, long enough for me to rectify this potentially embarrassing state of affairs. Thinking quickly, I shouted, 'My God, will you look at that!' and pointed out the far window. They turned, and I buttoned my fly. But now, I noticed, they were regarding me with . . . surprise and loathing. Puzzled, I crossed to the window and looked out." Gladhand sighed. "On the front lawn were two dogs engaged in the most primal sort of amorous activity."

The theatre manager shrugged. "It was inevitable, I guess, that I would suffer embarrassment that day—and by fighting it, resisting it, I only managed to bring down an even greater embarrassment on myself."

"You mean there's no use in resisting anything?" Thomas asked doubtfully.

"I didn't say that. The trick is, you see, to know which you are: the inevitable consequence or the doomed resistor. Though as a matter of fact—take my word for it!—you can't know until it's too late to change, anyway."

Thomas nodded uncertainly.

"So!" concluded Gladhand briskly, "go rejoin your fellows. It's too hot a night to spend inside."

By the time the moon was high in the heavens most of Gladhand's troupe was on the roof, sitting in deck chairs, propped against chimney-pots, or simply sprawled full-length on the tarpaper. Lanterns and wine had been brought up from below, and Spencer was striking chords on a guitar.

Thomas noticed approvingly that Negri had downed his sixth glass of wine, and was now getting to his feet to make a quick trip downstairs.

"I'll be back in a flash, Sugar-Pie," he told Pat, and lurched away toward the stairs. Thomas casually strode over and sat down where Negri had been.

"Hello, Rufus," Pat said, a little wearily.

"Hi, Pat." A kind of hopeless depression descended on him. *I've got nothing to say,* he realized. *Why are Negri and I bothering this girl, anyway? Oh, come on,* he protested to himself; *all I've done is sit next to her. It isn't* me *calling her Sugar-Pie.*

"Let's go see if the fire really did go out," Pat suggested, getting up.

"Good idea," Thomas said. They walked out of the uneven ring of lantern light to the rough, time-rounded stones of the coping. The city lay spread out before them, as clear as a toy held at arm's length. The glow of the fire was gone completely. Distantly came the echoes of three quick gunshots.

"A wild, unholy night," Thomas observed. Pat said nothing. "Where are you from, Pat?" he went on.

She sighed. "Oh, I come from quite a distance, the same as you. I'm the youngest of a very large family, and the smartest, so my parents sent me to the city."

"To make good," Thomas said.

"Or whatever."

"Where the hell . . . ?" came an angry shout from behind them. Thomas turned to see Negri striding furiously toward him across the roof. "All right, Pennick," he spat, "you're a little slower than everyone else, so I guess you've got to be told what's what. Listen, and save yourself some trouble. Pat is my girl. And no—"

"I'm not your girl," Pat said.

"Shut up," Negri snapped. "I'll decide. So, Pennick, if—"

"*You'll* decide?" Thomas repeated, angry and laughing at the same time. "You heard her, Negri. She isn't interested. What do you plan to do, cut your monogram in her forehead?"

Negri cocked his fist back, and it was seized firmly from behind. "You two aren't going to forget the no-fighting rule, are you?" smiled Spencer, releasing Negri's arm.

"Uh, no," Negri admitted. "But I'm challenging this toad to a duel, to decide once and for all whether Pat is my girl or not."

"How can a duel decide *that?*" Thomas protested. "You mean automatically if I lose—"

"Go ahead, Rufus," Pat interrupted.

After a tiny pause, Spencer shrugged. "Okay, a duel, then. Jeff, set up the table."

The rest of the actors cleared a circle in the center of the roof, and set the lanterns so that the area was well-lit. Chairs for spectators were ranged around the perimeter, and Gladhand stumped over and lowered himself into a front-row seat. "This should be instructive," he remarked.

Spencer walked into the circle and raised his hands for silence. "Quiet," he said, "while I explain to Rufus and Pat how our duels work. On the table Jeff is trying to set up, you'll notice, is a chessboard. What Rufus and Bob are going to do is play a game of chess—the chess-pieces, though, will be different-sized glasses. One duelist's glasses will be filled with red wine, the other's with white. When you capture a piece, you must drink it. One loses by passing out or being checkmated."

Jeff had set up the table and two chairs, and was now placing glasses in the chessmen's places. The pawns, Thomas noticed, were shot glasses, the bishops and knights fairly capacious wine glasses, the rooks tumblers, and the queens full-sized beer schooners. The kings were represented by conventional wooden chess pieces, and Jeff held these until the color choice should be made.

"Sit down, gentlemen," Spencer said. "In each of my hands is a cork, one from a Zinfandel, one from a Chablis. Rufus, right or left?"

"Hold it," said Negri. Thomas looked warily across the table at him. "Take the damn wine away. That's for kids. We'll duel with rum, light and dark."

An interested murmur arose from the assembled actors. Clearly this had not been done before. Spencer turned uncertainly to Gladhand, who shrugged and nodded.

"Okay," said Spencer, "Jeff, give the wine to the spectators and dash below for four bottles of rum."

Thomas looked past Negri and saw Pat sitting in the first row. She smiled at him. I've got to win this, he thought.

"Bob's been drinking all night," called someone in the crowd. "Rufus is nearly sober. It ain't fair."

Gladhand spoke up: "Rufus has a bad cold, which will doubtless be a handicap equal to Bob's degree of drunkenness. Besides, Bob is the challenger, and is familiar with the strategies of wine-chess."

Jeff came clattering back up the stairs with four bottles of rum under his arm. He handed them to Spencer, who uncorked them, held the corks tightly in his fists, and turned to Thomas. Thomas tapped one fist, which opened, revealing the dark cork.

"Rufus is black, Robert white," Spencer said. He filled Thomas' glasses with the dark rum while Jeff filled Negri's with the light. Finally they both stepped back, leaving a daunting array of drinks gleaming in the lamp-light on the table. "Your move, Bob," Spencer said.

Negri edged his king's pawn forward two squares. Thomas replied with the same. Abruptly, Negri's queen was slid out of the ranks all the way across the board to the rook's fifth place.

Thomas saw the trap immediately; he had last fallen for it before he was ten. Negri hoped Thomas would advance his king's knight's pawn one square in an attempt to drive the enemy queen away. If he did, of course, Negri's queen would leap three spaces to her left, taking Thomas' first-moved pawn and, inevitably with the next move, would dart invulnerably in and capture Thomas' rook.

Thomas automatically reached forward to move his knight to his king's bishop's third—and paused. What if, he wondered, I let him have the rook? I could move my queen's knight up to the bishop's third when he takes the pawn, as if I'm threatening his queen; and then when he takes the rook I could hop the knight back down in front of my king, which would bar his queen from decimating my ranks any further. And it would leave him with a tumbler and a shot glass worth of dark rum in him.

Thomas withdrew his hand and looked closely at Negri. How much can he put away, I wonder? He's already had a good amount of alcohol this evening—and his mouth is tending to sag, and his eyes aren't focusing perfectly. By God, I'll try it.

Thomas advanced the knight's pawn.

"Hah!" barked Negri as he slid the queen over and tapped the shot glass that was Thomas' first-moved pawn. He snatched it up and tossed it off, smacking his lips. "Not bad," he announced, setting the glass aside. "I believe I'll have some more."

Thomas obligingly brought his queen's knight forward, allowing Negri's queen to take his king's rook. A mutter of dismay and approval passed over the spectators as Negri drained Thomas' rook-glass. "Ahh!" he exclaimed. "How does your queen taste, Pennick? I mean to find out."

Thomas moved his queen's knight to his king's second square. Negri made as if to take Thomas' king's knight, then noticed that it was protected by its twin.

"You can't stop me, Pennick," he said, and took instead Thomas' rook's pawn. He drank it in one gulp, but set the empty shot glass too close to the edge of the table, and it fell when he let go of it.

A few people in the crowd giggled, and he shot a venomous look in their direction. "Go to hell, Jeff," he barked.

"Take it easy, Robert," Gladhand spoke up. "You know better than to yell at an audience."

Thomas now moved his king's knight to his bishop's third, threatening Negri's queen; she withdrew, and the tension was relaxed for the moment. Thomas had lost two pawns and a rook—but his men were opening out fairly well, and he had his unmolested queen's side to castle into if need and opportunity should arise. And Negri, to Thomas' well-concealed satisfaction, was beginning to look really drunk—frowning at the board in a passion of concentration, and pushing the curly hair back from his forehead with rubbery fingers.

A stray gust of the warm wind flickered the lanterns and, for a moment, blew the heavy rum fumes away from Thomas' face. He looked up, caught Pat's eye and winked. She winked back, and he felt suddenly proud and brave, as if he was facing Negri at misty dawn somewhere, settling the question with sabres.

The game progressed slowly, with Thomas drinking a piece—slowly, and in several swallows—only to avert direct danger or to press a certain advantage. Every few moves he tried to sacrifice a pawn, or an occasional bishop or knight, to increase the watery, fuddled look in Negri's eyes.

"He's trying to get you drunk, Bob!" came a call at one point. Negri's derisive laughter at that sounded genuine, but he glanced furtively at the tally of empty glasses along the sides of the table; and then smirked confidently to see how many more of Thomas' glasses had been emptied than his own.

Despite Thomas' stay-sober strategy, he found himself having to work at keeping all the threats, protections and potential lines of attack clear in his mind. I've got to mount that checking attack with my bishop and queen, he thought a little dizzily. I'd like to get my rook into position to back them up, though. Can I? Sure, but it'll take . . . three moves. Can I count on Negri not to put me in check—or interfere with my queen and bishop—for three moves?

He regarded Negri suspiciously. What if he's pretending to be drunker than he really is? I've got to chance it, he thought, and moved his rook.

Negri moved a pawn out of its home row.

Thomas moved his rook the second time.

A bishop-full of light rum advanced from Negri's ranks and came to rest, threatening Thomas' beer-schooner queen, on a square that was protected by a pawn and a knight.

Thomas' heart sank. There goes my whole plan, he thought. With my queen moved I won't be able to salvage any part of it. Did he do that simply to foul me up, or is there another purpose? He stared carefully at the board—and it was all he could do to stifle a gasp of horror.

Negri's bishop was now in a position to take the pawn behind which stood Thomas' modest wooden king—and a forgotten white knight stood by to back the move up. He's going to do that next, Thomas realized. It won't quite be checkmate, but that probably won't be long in following.

The silence was absolute, and Thomas fancied he could hear the sweat running down his neck into his collar.

There's only one slim hope, he thought. If it doesn't work, all I'll have done is hand him the game. And Pat, too, he reminded himself.

He moved his rook the third time.

There were a few gasps and groans from the crowd, and Negri looked both surprised and pleased. "You're drunker than I thought, Pennick," he said slowly. Thomas watched him closely, almost able to read the sluggish thoughts that reeled through the narrow spotlight of Negri's consciousness. He's puzzled, Thomas thought, that I ignored his threat to my queen; and he's wondering whether to take her or pursue his planned attack. Negri looked up sharply, and Thomas crossed his eyes slightly and hiccupped. I've got to make him think I'm drunk, he thought—that I didn't even see the threat. Come on, Negri. Take a certain queen instead of an uncertain checkmate.

"I said I'd taste your queen, Pennick," Negri said finally, tapping her with his bishop. Thomas tried to look surprised and dismayed.

The queen was heavy, and Negri lifted her with both hands. He peered dazedly for a moment into the amber depths of the glass, then took a deep breath and set it to his lips.

Everyone on the roof watched tensely as Negri's adam's apple bobbed up and down and the bottom of the glass slowly rose. The color had drained from his face, and beads of sweat stood out on his forehead, but still he kept methodically gulping the heady brown liquor. Finally he drained it— flung the empty glass away—shuddered—and slid unconscious from his chair to the tarpapered floor.

Spencer hopped up and, with an upraised hand, silenced the quick rush of cheers and boos. "Rufus," he said, "you've lost your queen. Do you choose to resign?"

"No," Thomas said.

"Then since your opponent is unconscious, you are clearly the winner."

There was more cheering and booing, and a brief scramble for the remaining glasses on the board, and then Thomas got up and walked out of the ring of light to gulp some fresh air.

"Rufus."

He turned around and saw that Pat had followed him. "Thank you," she said, and kissed him, a little awkwardly. As far as he could recall, it was the first time anyone had ever kissed him, but he was drunk enough not to get flustered.

"You're welcome," he said. "I didn't really *do* anything, though. Just fed him rum until he passed out."

"No, no," she protested. "I was watching closely. You calculated just how much alcohol you could let him have without losing the game yourself. It was fascinating. What *does* alcohol do to your brain, anyway?"

"Haven't you ever had any?"

"No. My family was—what's the word?"

"Teetotalers," he supplied, and she nodded. "Well," he said, "alcohol, enough of it, wrecks your ability to concentrate. It's like trying to run down a familiar hallway that's suddenly dark, and cluttered with a lot of boxes and old bicycles and fishing poles. Or like the first day of a cold, when you're dizzy and light-headed and can't remember what the correct answer to 'Good morning' is."

"I hear every drink destroys ten thousand brain cells. Why do . . . why do people *get* drunk, anyway?"

"Well, not everybody drinks to get drunk. Just a little every now and then is very pleasant. And, hell, the loss of a few thousand brain cells here and there—who counts?"

She stared at him with a total, undisguised lack of comprehension. "I don't understand people," she said. "It's late; I'm going to turn in. See you tomorrow." She turned toward the stairs. "Oh, and thanks again for . . . rescuing me."

"You're welcome again. Good night."

Now what, he asked himself when she'd disappeared, happened there? She obviously doesn't approve of drinking; but she doesn't quite disapprove, either—she simply can't understand it. Oh well, he thought, she seems to like me. After all, I risked a whole truckload of brain cells to save her from being Negri's Sugar-Pie.

With a shiver of blended surprise, pleasure and apprehension he realized that he was, as the saying goes, falling in love with her.

BOOK TWO

Nathan Gladhand

CHAPTER 7
A Bad Dinner at the Gallomo

Late in the afternoon of the next day, rumors began to reach the city—the merchants on the long coast run from La Jolla and Oceanside told of hundreds of campfire lights glimpsed in the valleys south of El Cajon, and of streaks of smoke and raised dust on the southern horizon during the day. At sunset the inevitable suspicion was confirmed by the Escondido mail rider: General Alvarez of San Diego had mobilized his army and was marching north.

During the next two days details trickled in—agreed, contradicted and amplified each other—until the full situation was clear. Alvarez was advancing up route five with a force of a thousand men and eight siege-mortars.

Los Angeles' buffer states Santa Ana and Orange sent ambassadors racing to the city to beg troops for the defense of their borders—and were reluctantly denied aid by major-domo Lloyd, who was said to have turned them away with tears in his eyes. Souveraine of Santa Ana declared that he couldn't, unsupported, defend his unwalled city, and that he'd side with Alvarez when the time came. Smith of Orange came to the same decision, with, as he put it in the letter he sent to Lloyd, "incalculable reluctance."

Thursday morning dawned clear and warm, for the Santa Ana wind was still surging in off the desert. One week exactly had passed since the bombing of Mayor Pelias' chambers; and the crowds that gathered around the news-loudspeakers sent despairing groans up into the cloudless blue sky when it was announced, once again, that the mayor was still unconscious.

Blaine Albers glanced contemptuously down at the clamoring crowd twenty storeys below him and, pushing open the window, flicked the ash of his cigar out at them. "You haven't answered my question, Lloyd," he said quietly, turning back to the room.

Across the table an old man sweated and stared hopelessly at the litter of ashtrays and scattered papers. "I can't tell you," he whispered.

"He's dead, isn't he?"

"No. He's under a . . . doctor's care, and he might—honestly—recover any day. Any hour."

The four other men in the room shifted impatiently in their seats, and one stubbed out a cigarette.

"Listen," said Albers, "even if he'd come out of it an hour ago it might have been too late." He struck his fist on the table. "Aside from the police, we have no army! Had you realized that? Our draft program is impossible to enforce. The few men we get desert the first time you take your eyes off them. We can't afford mercenaries. What, Lloyd, do you have to suggest?" His voice had risen during this speech to a harsh yell.

"Find . . ." the old man quavered, "find Brother Thomas."

"*Why?* What the hell is the connection between Pelias and this delinquent monk?"

Lloyd sagged. "I can't tell you."

Several of the other men sighed and shook their heads grimly.

Albers spoke softly. "Lloyd, I'm sorry to have to say this. Tell me, now, where Pelias is, and what this monk Thomas has to do with the situation; or we'll question you with the same methods we'd use on any criminal."

Lloyd was sobbing now. "All right," he said finally. "You win." He stood up slowly and crossed to the window. "God help us all," he said, and quietly rolled over the sill and disappeared.

For a full ten seconds no one spoke; then Albers went to the window and looked out. The section of the crowd directly below was churning about with, perhaps, more energy than it had shown before. Aside from that, the view had not changed.

"That," he said to the others, "is the second time one of our majordomos has killed himself. His predecessor, Hancock, you know, hanged himself in his bedroom six years ago."

The others nodded dumbly. "What can we do now," one asked, "besides grab some ready cash and run for Bakersfield?"

"Idiot," Albers said. "It's not time to run yet. Alvarez couldn't get here before Sunday even if he was already across the Santa Margarita River, and he isn't." He scratched his chin thoughtfully. "But our hold on the city just went out the window. We've got no authority at all, now."

"Maybe we could claim to know where Pelias is hidden?" suggested one of the others.

"No. Tabasco, damn his android eyes, almost certainly *does* know. He probably knows whatever the secret about this monk is, too."

"What *could* that monk have or know that they could want so badly?" wondered the one he'd called an idiot.

"I don't know," Albers answered softly. "But I'd say if we want to keep any hand at all in this game, *we'd* better find him before Tabasco's police do." He flung himself into a chair. "We'll worry about that a little later," he said. "Right now, show that gun dealer in, Harper."

Harper stood up and went to the door. "Come in here," he said when he opened it.

A moment later a tall old man with a white beard and mane strode into the room. He was dressed in sun-faded dungarees, and puffed furiously on a battered corncob pipe. "Look here, boys," he growled, "if you want to make a deal, then let's talk. If not, I'll be on my way. But I'm not going to wait one more—"

"I apologize, Mr. St. Coutras," Albers said. "It was not our intention to keep you waiting. Sit down, please."

St. Coutras took a seat and rapped the still-smoking tobacco out of his pipe onto the floor. "All right," he said. "Do you want the hundred Brownings or not?"

"We do," Albers said. "We've decided we can pay you a hundred solis per rifle."

"Goddamnit, I said a hundred and fifty. I can't go below that and make a living."

"What kind of living do you think you'll make if Alvarez takes this city?" hissed Harper.

"The same as now," the old man replied. "Everybody needs guns."

"He's right, Harper," Albers said. "Shut up." He looked intently at St. Coutras. "Would you take the difference in bonds?"

The old man considered it for a full minute. "I'll take a hundred in cash and a hundred in bonds per rifle. That way, you'll be sure of getting good merchandise from me, since I'll have a ten-thousand-soli stake on your side of the table. If Alvarez takes the city, he's sure not going to honor any bonds issued by his predecessors."

"Good point," Albers nodded. "Okay. Hastings, draw up the papers. And Harper, you get busy on tracking down that damned runaway monk. Get some details on *why* he left the monastery. It occurs to me to doubt old Lloyd's story that the kid stole the season's wine-money."

"Runaway monk?" St. Coutras repeated curiously.

Albers frowned. "Yes. He . . . uh, has some information we need."

"His name isn't . . . Thomas, is it?"

Hastings' pen halted in mid-air; Harper froze halfway out of his chair. Albers slowly lit another cigar. "Why?" he asked. "Have you met a runaway monk named Thomas?"

"Yeah. A week ago. Last Friday morning. Gave him a ride into town."

"That'd be our boy, all right," Albers said.

"Have you seen him since?" Harper asked quickly.

"Nope."

"Where did you drop him off?" Albers asked.

"The north gate," St. Coutras answered. "On Western Avenue. Why, what's he done?"

"We have no idea. But somehow he's the key to a lot of desperately important questions. Would he remember you?"

"Sure."

"Kindly?"

"Yeah, I think so."

"Good." Albers took a long, contemplative pull on his cigar. "Do you have an apprentice or partner or somebody, who could bring the guns in without you?"

"Maybe. Why?"

"I want you to stay here and smoke this blasted monk out of whatever hole he's hiding in. We're pretty sure he hasn't left the city, but the police haven't been able to get any leads on him at all. What we'll do is check with the monastery and find out what his interests and skills are, and then send you to places where he's likely to show up. And when you see him, grab him. We'll give you as many men as you like to help."

"I'd be working with the police?" St. Coutras asked doubtfully.

"No; as a matter of fact," Albers said, "you will, practically speaking, be working against the police. We don't want Tabasco to get hold of the monk."

"Hmm. This post pays well, of course?"

"Of course. And carries a five-thousand-soli—cash!—bonus if you bring him in."

"Well, I'll give it a try," the old man said. "I've done weirder things."

"Good," Albers said, with his first smile of the day. "We'll have a rider to the Merignac monastery and back by three this afternoon, and you'll be able to start searching before sundown. You'll—"

"I get a thousand a day to look for him," St. Coutras remarked.

Albers' face turned red, but his smile held its ground. "That's right," he said levelly. "Where are you staying?"

"At a friend's place. Never mind where. I'll come back here at four-thirty. See you later, gents." He got up, clamped his pipe in his mouth and left the room.

"I don't like his attitude," Harper complained. "Are you really going to pay him all that money? I think you promised him more than the city owns."

"He'll be paid, all right," Albers rasped. "We'll give him a few dozen of his own bullets, in the head."

Harper grinned and nodded, and was about to speak when a girl leaned in the door. "Police Chief Tabasco is here to see major-domo Lloyd," she said.

"Send him in," Albers said. "None of you say anything, hear?" he added to his four companions.

Police Chief Tabasco was tall, with fine blond hair cut in bangs over his surprisingly light blue eyes. His face was pink and unlined. When he stepped into the room he made the five men look scrawny and unhealthy by comparison.

"Where is major-domo Lloyd?" he asked.

"Well," Albers said thoughtfully, "to tell you the truth, he's dead." Harper didn't interrupt, but clearly wanted to. Tabasco raised his golden eyebrows. "You see," Albers went on, "he admitted to us that Mayor Pelias is dead, and then immediately regretted betraying that secret, and leaped," he waved at the open window, "to his death."

"You're lying," Tabasco observed calmly. "Pelias is alive, and Lloyd knew it. He and I looked in on the comatose mayor earlier this morning. You killed Lloyd, correct? Why?"

"Oh, hell," Albers said, sitting down. "Okay, I guess Pelias *is* alive. No, we didn't kill Lloyd. I threatened him with torture if he wouldn't spill a few secrets, and he dove out the window. Look, Tabasco, if we're going to govern this city, there are several things we've got to know. First, where is—"

"You're not going to govern this city."

"Oh? Who is, then? Pelias? Lloyd? Alvarez? *You?*"

"Why not me?" Tabasco asked quietly.

Albers leaned forward. "Are you getting delusions of humanity? Listen, the people of this city would rather have a trained dog for mayor than a damned grass-eating, vat-bred android. Don't you know that? You creatures are just barely put up with as policemen. If—"

"Excuse me for interrupting," Tabasco said, a little heatedly. "But I would remind you that I control—absolutely—the only armed force available to Los Angeles, whereas you have nothing, not even—"

"I've got Thomas," Albers said.

"Who?"

"Thomas. The monk from Merignac. I have him."

"You're lying again," Tabasco said, but his eyes were lit with desperate hope.

"Believe that, if you like," said Albers carelessly. "I've got him, anyway. And I don't need you."

"I knew you were lying," Tabasco said, the hope leaving his eyes. "If you really had him you'd know how much you *do* need me. And you'd know better than to sneer at androids. I want all five of you out of the city by sundown tomorrow. I'll instruct my officers to shoot any of you on sight after that. Do you understand?"

"Why, you filthy—we're the—you can't tell the city council to—"

"I'll assume you do understand. Goodbye, gentlemen. May we never meet again."

Peter McHugh put down his coffee cup and newspaper and stood when he heard booted feet pounding up the stairs.

"That you, John?" he called, his hand hovering over a .38 calibre revolver lying on the wicker table beside him.

"Yes," came the answer, a moment before John St. Coutras burst into the room.

"Up and saddle the horses," the old man barked. "If we move quick we can get out of this doomed city with no trouble."

"What? Wait a minute. What happened at city hall? You didn't hit anybody, did you?"

"No. But I got Albers to agree to so many crazy payments that I *know* he means to kill me. Hell, he even offered me a thousand a day to look for some monk. If we can get outside the city walls within the next hour, we—"

"Hold it. Listen to me. I got another offer for the guns. A hundred and fifty apiece."

St. Coutras halted. "You *did?* From who?"

"I don't know his name. We've been dealing through an intermediary, a red-haired kid named Spencer. But the offer's genuine, I'm convinced. We'll deliver the crates through the sewers, from north of the wall."

St. Coutras ran his fingers through his beard ruminatively. "This is a hundred and fifty *cash* we're talking about?" he asked in a more quiet tone of voice.

"Nothing but. The kid wanted to give me five thousand down, right there. Had it in a knapsack. I told him I'd have to see you before I could take it."

"*Well,*" The old man sank into a chair. "Is there any more of that coffee?"

"Coming up, boss."

Thomas looked critically at the final couplet of his sonnet while he chewed on the back end of his pen; after a few re-readings of the poem he decided it would do, and slid the paper into the box he'd appropriated for his personal belongings. The first eight lines of it he'd written the night before, in a bleak mood brought to a head by eight consecutive cups of black coffee and three stout maduro cigars, and enough of the mood had carried over to the morning for him to write the last six lines immediately upon awakening.

He had stood up, stretched, and was pulling on his pants when a loud crack sounded from the floor above him. Splinters and dust whirled down through one of the beams of morning sunlight.

He bounded upstairs to the stage, where he found Gladhand and five villainous-looking men staring at a small, ragged hole in the polished wood of the stage. Smoke was still spiraling up from it.

"What the hell," Thomas said, unable to come up with anything better, but feeling that he ought to say something.

"Oh, good morning, Rufus," Gladhand said. "Nothing to be concerned about, that explosion. Just a special-effect device we're testing."

"*More* special effects?" For four days now Gladhand had been consulting furtive men—"technicians," he called them—and buying dozens of sturdy, heavy wooden boxes that he stored carefully in the basement. He'd explained, in answer to Thomas' questions, that the boxes contained the wherewithal for various spectacular special effects he intended to use during the scene in the play in which the god Hymen appears.

Gladhand now nodded vaguely. "Oh, yes. I've decided to have a few miracles and apparitions and such things take place when Duke Frederick gets converted by the holy man in the wilderness."

"But that's only referred to. How will—"

"I've written in a new scene so as to have it take place on stage. Plot's too rickety otherwise. Look, I'm pretty busy right now, but I want to talk to you later. Meet me . . . on the alley balcony right after the noon rehearsal, okay?"

"Okay."

Thomas wandered to the dining room and wheedled a late breakfast of coffee and sweet rolls from Alice, who had already begun to put everything away. He sat down at one of the long tables and gulped the oily coffee. After she'd rinsed out the pots and wiped down the counters, Alice sat down beside him with her own cup of coffee.

"You're a late sleeper these days," she remarked, looking through her purse for a cigarette. "How are you and Pat getting along these days?"

"Horrible."

"Oh, you had a little fight? Well, don't worry, it—"

"We didn't have a fight," Thomas said. "We never have fights. We just have . . . bafflements. Each of us is certain the other's lost his or her mind."

"Well, maybe you two just aren't meant for each other."

"Yeah," Thomas admitted, trying not to gag as he sipped at the coffee. "Logically speaking, that's true. But when we do get along—and we do, sometimes—it's the greatest thing that's ever happened to me."

"Which is most common? Getting along or not getting along?"

"Oh, not. By a long shot."

Alice shook her head with mock pity. "De course ob de true luhv nebbah did run smoooth," she leered in some badly-imitated dialect, as she picked up the two empty cups and walked bizarrely into the kitchen.

Thomas stared after her and then slowly got to his feet and went below to put his shoes on.

Ten minutes later he was sitting in the greenroom, going over his lines with the girl Skooney, who obligingly read all the other parts. After a while Pat came in and sat down, and Thomas regarded her warily out of the corner of his eye, trying to get a clue to her current mood.

"You're not paying a hundred percent attention to this," Skooney said.

"Oh, I think I've got it down pretty well already. Thanks, Skooney."

"Anytime," the girl said, getting up to leave.

"Morning, Pat," he said when Skooney was gone.

"Hi, Rufus," she answered with a friendly smile. Aha, Thomas thought; she's in good spirits. And in the morning! Absolutely unprecedented. The feeling that had spawned his sonnet began to evaporate.

"Hey, noon rehearsal in five minutes," Lambert called, walking through the hall.

Thomas inwardly cursed the interruption; but then reflected, after Pat had blown him a kiss and darted out of the room, that the rehearsal call had probably saved him from unwittingly puncturing her good mood. Anything, it seemed, could cast her into heavy depressions or smoldering anger—a kiss at the wrong time, the lack of a kiss at the right time, a careless sentence, a carefully considered opinion—and her good cheer was always slow to return.

It's too bad she's the first girl I ever really knew, Thomas thought. I have no way of knowing whether all girls are this way or if she's unique. I wonder if every guy heaves an instinctive sigh of relief when he's kissed his girl goodnight, and the door is shut, and he can go relax by himself?

The noon rehearsal went quickly. Gladhand wasn't watching as closely as he usually did; his corrections were infrequent and brief, and he had the actors skip over two scenes that he didn't feel needed any work. The theatre manager seemed preoccupied, and kept staring into space and running his fingers through his thick black beard.

By one-thirty everyone was wandering offstage and deciding whether to eat in the theatre or at a restaurant somewhere, and Skooney was switching off her treasured lights.

Ben Corwin was sitting on the balcony when Thomas got there. The old man's moustache, beard and shirt were dusted with brown powder, and he was sneezing and sniffling so hard that he could only wave and blink his wet eyes at Thomas by way of greeting.

"That stuff is going to kill you," Thomas remarked. "Why don't you drink, instead?"

Corwin managed to choke, "Good enough for androids . . . good enough for me."

Thomas sat down, wishing he had a really cold beer. This blasted desert wind is getting tiresome, he thought. I'll never lose this cold while it keeps up.

The plywood door dragged open after a minute or so, but it was Spencer, not Gladhand, who stepped out onto the balcony.

"Howdy, Rufus," he said. "Clear out of here, Ben. Important conference coming up out here. You've got to move on." The old man uttered an obscene suggestion. "Will you leave for a five-soli bill?" Spencer asked, pulling one out of his pocket and holding it just out of reach of Ben's waving, clutching hands.

Finally the old man struggled to his feet. "Give it here," he said clearly.

"It's yours," said Spencer, letting him take it. "Go buy yourself a bottle of your favorite white port." Muttering incoherently, Corwin tottered down the stairs.

"A conference?" Thomas inquired as Spencer sat down.

"Yeah, sort of. I'll let Gladhand explain."

The door grated open again and Gladhand wobbled out on crutches, closely followed by Negri. "Two more chairs, Bob," the theatre manager said. Negri ran to fetch them, and in a moment the four of them were seated facing each other.

"There's something it's high time you learned, Rufus," Gladhand began.

"Before it's too late, sir," Negri said, "reconsider. It's crazy to trust—"

"We've been through this, Bob," Gladhand said, a little impatiently. "Be quiet."

"Sir," Negri pursued, "might one—"

"Might one bugger off, Negri?" Gladhand said angrily. "Robert, you see," he went on calmly, "doesn't want me to tell you. He doesn't trust you, Rufus."

"I have no idea what's going on here," Thomas said, truthfully.

"Let me explain," Gladhand said. "We are a theatre company, are we not? Right. But, lad, that's not all we are. The Bellamy Theatre is a front—no, that's not quite right—is the secret, uh, center of the only organized resistance force in L.A. My employees are guerrilla soldiers as well as actors."

Thomas blinked, and then nodded slowly, trying to assimilate the idea. "That explains one or two odd remarks and looks," he said. "Ah! And those 'special effects' are really weapons?"

"Some of them," Gladhand nodded. "Some of them really are special effects devices. Don't get the idea that the play is simply a mask, a cover. Our guerrilla efforts are no more important than our dramatic ones." He lit a cigar. "Would you leave us, Robert?"

Negri raised his eyebrows incredulously.

"Leave us," Gladhand insisted, and Negri stalked inside, pausing to give Thomas a look of pure hate. "You showed good . . . aptitude," Gladhand continued, "in that foolish raid on the android barracks last week. I'd have taken you into our confidence right then, if it weren't for the fact that the police were devoting so much time and effort to catching you. I was afraid you'd be seized at any time, and so for security reasons I kept you in ignorance of the . . . other half of our activities."

"And . . . what changed your mind, sir?" Thomas asked.

"Things are quickly coming to a head. A crisis nears. Major-domo Lloyd committed suicide this morning; Alvarez has certainly reached the Santa Margarita River by now; and every two-bit politico south of Glendale is trying to take the reins of the city. I need every good man I can get, and it would be the exaggerated caution of a madman for me to keep you in the dark any longer. By the way, do you gentlemen recall those half-matured androids you saw under glass in that secret android brewery last week?" Thomas and Spencer nodded. "Well, Jeff told me at the time that the face they all wore looked familiar. Today it struck him whose it was. He swears it was the face of Joe Pelias."

"Good God," Spencer said. "Replacements, in case the real one dies?"

"I believe so," Gladhand nodded. "They'll be mature in another week, I'd judge, if they were already recognizable. We can't waste time, you see."

"Yes," Thomas said. "What is it you're hoping to do? In long-range terms, I mean?"

"Kill Pelias—it was our bombs that nearly did him in last week—and institute a new government, hopefully in time to defend the city against Alvarez."

"What sort of new government?"

Gladhand shrugged. "A better one than this Pelias has given us. I know of a man with an unarguably valid claim to the mayor's office. We will, I hope, manage to establish him when Pelias is finally disposed of."

Thomas pondered all this. "Were you the ones who made that assassination attempt on Pelias ten years ago?"

Gladhand smiled oddly. "No. That attempt was certainly none of our doing. Anyway, our organization has only been in existence for eight years."

"Does Pat know?" Thomas asked. "Is she in this?"

"Yes. I told her about it two days ago. She's in."

"Well, what can I do to join? Sign something in blood? Scalp a cop?"

"No, none of that. We're very informal in that respect. Take my word for it that you're a member. I did want to tell you all this today, though, so that you could help Spencer out tonight. He's going to make the final arrangements on a purchase of a hundred rifles, in a bar called the Gallomo. I'd like it if he wasn't alone, and you two seem to work well together."

"Sure, I'll go along," Thomas said. "How are we going to get all those rifles back here, though?"

"We won't," said Spencer. "We're just going to make a down payment, assuming the guns haven't already been sold. Delivery will be in a couple of days, through the sewers."

"I'll want you both to carry pistols," Gladhand said. "Just in case, you know." He picked up his crutches. "In the meantime, get some lunch, and Spencer can fill you in on the details." He swung himself erect and re-entered the building.

Four hours later Thomas was doing his best to eat a particularly gristly beef pie. "The drinks here might be okay," he told Spencer, "but the food is vile."

"Well, hurry up and finish it," Spencer said. "The guy's supposed to be here in ten minutes, and you've got your face in a goddamned pie."

The pie had begun to cool off, and things were beginning to congeal in it, so Thomas pushed it away. "If things get rough we can throw it at somebody," he said.

"Yeah, and—don't turn around. He's here. Good. That means we outbid city hall."

Thomas slowly picked up the pitcher and refilled his beer glass. "Is he coming over here?" he whispered.

"He's getting a drink first. Making it look unplanned, I suppose. Ah, here he comes."

Peter McHugh sat down and nodded to Spencer. "Who's your buddy?"

"A colleague," Spencer said. "He's okay. City hall didn't go for it?"

"Oh, they claimed to, but my partner suspected they didn't really intend to pay him. He's got good instincts for that kind of thing."

"Where is he?"

"He's out in the wagon; he'll be in in a minute. You've got the five grand?"

Spencer nodded and nudged the knapsack under the table with his foot.

"Good, good." McHugh took a sip from the glass of wine he'd brought to the table. "Not bad," he observed. "How's the food here?"

"Terrible," Thomas said, pointing at the pie.

McHugh peered at it. "Oh, yeah." He looked up. "Here's my partner now," he said.

Thomas didn't turn around, so he didn't see the new arrival until he sat down. "Mr. St. Coutras!" he said in surprise when he got a look at the white-bearded old man.

"You two know each other?" McHugh asked, puzzled.

"My God, it's Thomas the famous runaway monk," St. Coutras said. "You're with these guys?" he asked, nodding at Spencer.

"I am now," Thomas told him. "I certainly wasn't when I met you. And my name is Rufus, please."

"Hah! Rufus? Oh well, whatever you say."

"They've got the money," McHugh said impatiently.

"Okay," St. Coutras said. "Now listen," he said to Spencer. "Pick up the guns Saturday, that's the day after tomorrow, under the third manhole on New Hampshire south of the wall. That's right above the city college, near Vermont."

"I know where it is," Spencer nodded. "When Saturday?"

"Eleven at night. Be there, we won't wait around. If—"

McHugh half stood up, reaching quickly in his coat. A loud bang sounded behind Thomas and McHugh was kicked backward over his chair, the gun he'd reached for spinning across the floor.

"No one else is going anywhere, are they?" inquired a cultured voice from behind Thomas' shoulder. Four smooth-faced android policemen surrounded the table as Albers picked up McHugh's chair and sat down.

Thomas, from where he sat, couldn't see McHugh's body. Spencer could, though, and looked sick, scared and angry.

"Foolish of you to miss our appointment, St. Coutras, old boy," Albers smiled, taking a sip of McHugh's wine. "Very tolerable Petite Syrah," he remarked. "Is the food equal to it?"

Thomas pointed mutely at the congealed pie. "Yes, I see," Albers said with a shudder. "At any rate—these two young men, then, must be members of our own Los Angeles resistance underground! What are your names?"

"Edmund Campion," Thomas said.

"Dan McGrew," said Spencer.

"Uh huh. So you thought you'd sell to a rival market, eh, St. Coutras? That's known as treason, my friend. You'll be hanged and we'll appropriate your guns. For nothing. And you lads will be hanged, too, never fear—after a few days with the city interrogator, naturally." He picked up the wine glass again, then froze. He turned a sharp stare on Thomas. "What did you say your name was?" His voice was like a slap in the face.

"I forget," Thomas said. "It was a phony name anyway."

"I know that. You just said the first name that popped into your head, didn't you?"

Puzzled and terrified, Thomas simply nodded.

"Right," Albers grinned. "Edmund Campion. The name of a . . . *saint*. Let's see—you're the right height, dark hair . . ." He leaned forward and stared at Thomas more closely.

Through his tension and fear Thomas felt a taste of relief. At least it's over, he thought. Now I'll find out why they've been hunting me with such determination.

"This is him, isn't it, St. Coutras?" Albers said. "Thomas, our long-sought fugitive."

St. Coutras shook his head. "Wrong, Albers," he said. "Are you going to grab every dark-haired young man who thinks of saints when he's in trouble? You bastards are really grabbing at straws."

"Hmm." Albers frowned thoughtfully. "Of course you'd *say* that in any case, to keep your bargaining position . . . What the hell. We'll take all of you in for a little intensive interrogation, hey? Maybe even send a coach to Merignac, bring back a monk who could absolutely identify this damned Thomas. Up, now, and march outside. Put that down, you monster," he added to one of the androids, who had furtively picked up the pie.

Five horses were tied to a rail in front of the Gallomo, next to the old gun-runner's cart Thomas had ridden to the city in, a week ago. One of the androids frisked the prisoners, removing a pistol apiece from Spencer and Thomas and a short, large-calibre sleeve-gun from St. Coutras.

"Handcuff the prisoners," Albers directed the android, "and lay them in the back of the old man's cart."

The cold metal rings were clicked viciously tight around Thomas' wrists, and then the android lifted him as easily as an armful of lumber and dropped him face down into the empty bed of the cart. A moment later St. Coutras and Spencer were dropped in on either side of him.

"Stay loose, lads," the old man gasped. "They haven't got us in the pan quite yet."

Thomas could see no basis for hope, but felt a little better for St. Coutras' words.

"All right," came Albers' voice. "You three follow us back to city hall—and don't forget to bring the spare horses, idiots. You—you'll drive the rig and I'll ride along to watch our little guests."

The cart rocked on its creaking springs as Albers and one of the androids climbed up onto the seat. "Don't look up, friends," Albers said, "but rely on it that I am staring down at you with a revolver in my right hand. I can't afford to kill any of you yet, but I sure won't hesitate to blow off an arm or two. Okay, Hamburger or whatever your name is, move out."

Thomas heard the snap of the reins, and the cart lurched and rattled as it turned out of the parking lot and east onto Beverly. In a moment followed the snare-drumming of hooves on cobblestones as the five horses fell in behind.

"What time is it, Captain?" inquired St. Coutras politely.

"Shut your filthy hole, traitor," Albers snapped. "Step on it, will you?" he said to the android driver, and Thomas felt the cart's speed increase. He glanced over at St. Coutras, and the old gun-runner winked at him.

The cart leaned and creaked as it weaved to pass slower vehicles. The steady roar of the cobbles under the wheel-rims had risen in pitch. "Don't stop for him," Albers snarled. "Go around! There, grab that space! *Oh yeah?*" he shouted to some outraged driver they'd cut off. "*Well, how'd you like to*—oh Jesus, look out!"

The cart's brakes squealed and Thomas was thrown forward.

"Hit the back brake!" St. Coutras called out commandingly, "or we're doomed!"

A deep, hollow *boom* shook the cart to its axles, and immediately St. Coutras was up on his knees. "Run for it, Aeolus!" he howled, and butted his white-maned head into the driver's shoulder. The horse leaped forward in a sudden burst of speed and the android, off balance, pitched off the bench into the street.

The old man frantically wrestled his manacled hands under his legs as the driverless cart picked up speed. When, a second later, he'd got them around in front of him, he vaulted onto the driver's bench and caught the flapping reins.

"Go, Aeolus, darling!" he yelled to the horse.

Thomas rolled over and managed to drag his own hands around to the front. "Have you got a gun?" he shouted to St. Coutras. "They're coming up fast behind us."

The driver held the reins in his teeth for a moment while he groped under the bench; there was a wooden *click* and he came up holding a pistol. Thomas took it and turned around.

The three android riders were terribly close, and even as Thomas raised the pistol one of them got off a shot at him which almost burned his cheek as it passed. Thomas fired full into the rider's face, and the android rolled off the back of its horse. The other two fell back a little.

Thomas' next shot went wide as St. Coutras wrenched the speeding cart around a tight corner. Spencer was sitting up, looking tense but cheerful. A bullet splintered the bench over his head and he ducked low. "Careful of those bastards, Rufus!" he yelled.

Thomas nodded, and squeezed off a shot at the nearer rider. It tore a hole in the android's arm, but didn't slow it down. Thomas' next shot crippled its horse, and mount and rider tumbled across the street in a tangle of thrashing limbs.

"Only one more!" Thomas called.

This one stood up in the stirrups now, raising its pistol in both hands for one well-aimed shot. Thomas centered the android in its sights, and both guns roared simultaneously.

Thomas spun violently back into the cart bed, his gun whirling away into the street, as the last android clutched its exploded belly and rolled off its horse.

Spencer grabbed Thomas' shoulder. "Where are you hit?" he demanded.

"My hand," Thomas whispered through clenched teeth. His whole left hand was a blaze of pain, and he feared more than anything to look at it. He could feel hot blood running up his wrist and soaking his sleeve.

"Head for the Bellamy Theatre," Spencer called to the driver.

"Screw that, son," St. Coutras replied, not unkindly. "Our best bet is to head for the gate muy pronto, and get out of this maniac city before they hear about this and lock us in."

"Well, look, my buddy here's bleeding like a cut wineskin; at least drop us off here."

"Okay." St. Coutras reined in in front of a dark shop, and Spencer helped Thomas out of the cart.

"Listen," the old man said. "When Albers was blown out of the cart your five thousand went with him. But I'm willing to write that off as taxes if you still want the guns."

"We do," Spencer said.

"Good. No change in the delivery plans, then. Thomas?"

"Yes?"

"You're a good lad to have at one's back in a fight. Hope I see you again."

Thomas was pale and trembling, but managed a smile. "Thanks," he said. "We were lucky to have you in the driver's seat."

"We owe it all to Aeolus. Here." He tossed a box from under the seat to Spencer. "First aid. See you Saturday, boys!" He flicked the reins and the cart rattled away up the street.

Thomas and Spencer stepped into an alley. "Hold out your hand," Spencer said. He poured alcohol all over Thomas' injured hand and began wrapping it in a bandage. "This ain't easy to do when both of us are handcuffed," he remarked.

"How's it look?"

"Oh, you won't die of it, I guess."

"Do the bandages have to be that tight?"

"Yes." When he'd laboriously tied a knot and bitten off the slack, Spencer patted him on the back. "That'll do for now. We're close enough to the theatre to be able to walk back. If we pass anyone, just keep to the shadows and sing as if you were drunk, and with any luck at all they won't notice the cuffs."

CHAPTER 8
The Head in the Box

The front of the Bellamy Theatre was dark; the cluster of gargoyles and decorated balconies were homogenous blurs in the huge shadow that was the building. Then a match was struck on a second-floor balcony, and held to the end of a cigar. The flame flared up as the smoker puffed, revealing for a moment the bushy beard, bald head and deep-set eyes of Nathan Gladhand. The match was abruptly whipped out, leaving only the dull red pinpoint of the cigar tip.

Gladhand looked anxiously up and down the dark, empty expanse of Second Street, and listened carefully as the city hall clock struck six-and-a-half.

Suddenly someone began singing, a few blocks to the west. No, two people. Incongruously, for it was only October, it was a Christmas carol in which the two slightly hysterical-sounding voices were raised.

> *O little town of Bethlehem, how still we see thee lie,*
> *Above thy deep and dreamless sleep the silent stars go by . . .*

It's got to be them, he thought; pretending to be drunk. Or maybe they are drunk. He could see them now—weaving along the nearer sidewalk and leaning on each other—and, further behind them, a tall figure following. The theatre manager reached into his coat pocket and rested his hand on the butt of a shoulder-holstered pistol. As he watched, though, the man following entered a hotel, and the two young men walked the last block and a half alone. When they were directly below, Gladhand leaned over the balcony rail.

"Spencer! Rufus!" he called quietly. "Is all well?"

Spencer looked up. "Yes and no, sir."

"Come up here and tell me."

Two minutes later they sat in canvas chairs on the balcony, sipping gratefully at glasses of cold beer.

"All right," Gladhand said. "Tell me. What happened? How did Rufus hurt his hand?"

"That guy McHugh is dead," said Spencer. "Four cops and Blaine Albers followed him to the Gallomo, killed him and were going to arrest us. Albers even figured out who Rufus really is. It looked bad, need I say. That old guy St. Coutras, though, tricked the android that was carting us away into setting off a hidden gun which blew Albers right out of the cart. St. Coutras drove like a madman while Rufus leaned out the back and shot all three pursuing androids. The last one shot him in the hand."

"How bad is it?"

Spencer started to speak, stopped, then tried again: "The first finger's gone completely. Sorry, Rufe. The rest's okay, though the thumb may be sprained."

"Are you left-handed, Rufus?"

"Well—yes sir."

"Ah. That will be difficult. I'm sorry." He turned to Spencer. "And the guns?"

"Delivery at eleven P.M. Saturday. No trouble there."

"Well, thank God for that, anyway. Rufus, go below and have Alice fix you some food. And don't think your heroism and self-sacrifice have gone unnoted. Spencer, escort him there, if you would, and then come back here."

Spencer led Thomas away, and took him downstairs to the greenroom, where Alice, Pat and Lambert were playing some card game.

"Alice," Spencer said, "see what Rufus will have, and get it for him, will you? He's a casualty."

"Jesus, have you been shot again?" Alice exclaimed. "My God. You want some food or something?"

"Some soup," Thomas said slowly, "would be nice. Thanks, Alice." He sat down as Alice scampered away. Pat, he noticed, was looking at him with an expression almost of hostility.

"What happened to you?" she asked.

"I got . . ." He was suddenly very tired, and enunciating each syllable was a real effort. "I got my finger—" he waved his bandaged hand "—shot off in a gunfight with some androids. And then Spencer and I had to sing Christmas carols—" With no warning he found that he was crying. Almost as soon as he noticed it he was able to stop.

"For God's sake," Pat said, standing up, "talk to me when you've managed to pull yourself together." She walked out of the room.

"Wow," said Lambert softly. "Anybody ever accuse you of masochism, Rufus?"

As far as Thomas could recall, this was the first time Lambert had called him by his first name. He grinned weakly. "It's only these last few days they'd have had any cause to," he answered.

"I mean," Lambert went on, "I've pursued some cold ladies in my time, but this girl of yours is a whole new category. Do you always go for girls like that?"

Thomas shrugged. "She's the first girl I ever . . . went for."

"Honest?" Lambert shook his head. "God knows where you'll go from here."

Alice returned with a pot of steaming clam chowder and a tall mug of beer. "I ran into Spencer in the hall," she said. "He tells me that Gladhand has advanced our opening night to Wednesday the twentieth."

"Wow," said Lambert uneasily. "Less than a week away.'"

"Yeah," Alice agreed. "Apparently he's going to step up the pace of the rehearsals, to compensate.'"

"Is that . . . code or something?" Thomas asked. "Does 'opening night' mean the day we spring our coup on city hall?"

"No, it's really opening night," Lambert said. "Gladhand made it clear, didn't he, that the play is no shuck? Of course, there might be a clue here; he might be planning to mount the attack sooner than he originally meant to, and is moving the opening-night date up so the two won't interfere with each other. Who knows? He might even be planning to overthrow city hall *before* the play opens. He'd never let on, in any case."

Thomas' hand hurt, and he had difficulty in getting to sleep. When he finally did drift off he was plagued again with the sky-fishing dream. Again he reeled the resentful flier closer and closer, again saw the great white face, and knew for one awful moment whose it was; then it changed into the face of the stone head beside Thomas' couch, which in turn became the face he'd glimpsed on the creatures in the vats in the android brewery. He woke at dawn, and lay there for an hour, tired and sick, and disgusted with his own subconscious mind.

He stood up, finally—and found, when his vision cleared, that he was lying full length on the floor beside his couch.

"What was that?" came a familiar voice. "Rufus? Are you all right?"

Thomas got to his knees and shook his head to clear it. "Yeah," he said clearly. "It's okay. That you, Pat?" He forced himself to forget the horrible white-cheese face from his dream.

"Yes." She was standing beside him now, and helped him to his feet. His hand, he noticed, had bled during the night, and his sheets were spotted with brown.

"Do you love me, Pat?" he asked dizzily.

She thought about it. "Yes," she said finally, "I guess I do."

He nodded. "I love you, too," he said. "Let's go get some breakfast."

"Right," she said. "Better not waste any time," she added. "Rehearsal's at eight."

"Eight?" he echoed. "Instead of noon?"

"As well as noon. Opening night's been rescheduled. Didn't you hear?"

"Oh yeah. I remember now. Wednesday."

"Right. Hurry up, now. Everybody's probably gobbling up our share."

When they got to the dining room, though, they found that breakfast had been held up until they arrived. As he and Pat sat down, Spencer and Jeff trooped in with platters of scrambled eggs and sausage and bacon, followed by Skooney, who carried in both hands a huge jug of orange juice. There was the usual babble of conversation, and no mention was made of the events of the previous evening. Thomas noticed, though, that the trace of condescension was gone from people's voices when they spoke to him now. I'm a full-fledged member at last, he thought. And all it cost me was a finger. He looked around for Negri but didn't see him.

He barely managed to swallow a mouthful of egg before having to sneeze violently into his napkin. "Does the damned paper have any idea when this Santa Ana wind will quit?" he asked.

"Yeah, matter of fact," Spencer answered from across the table. "A big tide, or whatever it's called, of cold air is sliding south down the San Joaquin Valley, I read. It ought to cancel this heat a bit."

"Won't that cause tornadoes?" Alice asked. "I read somewhere that causes tornadoes."

"It might, up around San Gabriel or San Fernando," Jeff said. "Not here, though."

The hall doors were pushed open, and Gladhand propelled his wheelchair into the dining room. "Where's Negri?" he asked.

"Haven't seen him all morning," Alice answered. Everyone else shrugged or shook their heads in agreement.

"He might even be buying breakfast somewhere," Spencer said. "He does, sometimes."

"I don't think he is today," Gladhand said grimly. "The idiot tacked this note on my door last night. Listen: 'Sir—the killing of individual androids, while doubtless praiseworthy in its own small-scale fashion, can at best—' oh hell, I won't read the whole murky thing. The upshot is—" he looked around helplessly, "—he says he's gone off to, singlehanded, kill Police Chief Tabasco."

Thomas happened to glance toward Pat as Gladhand finished, and saw her turn pale. He was surprised, and felt a twinge of reflexive jealousy;

would she, he wondered, be that concerned if it was me out risking my life? Was she last night, when it *was* me?

"Good God," Spencer said, getting to his feet and flinging down his napkin. "How long's he been gone?"

"Possibly as long as . . . eight hours," Gladhand said.

"God help us," Spencer muttered. "Rufus—no, never mind. Jeff, you and Lambert run to the basement, quick, and drag as many of the bomb and gun crates into the deep cellar as will fit. Hide the rest of them, or camouflage 'em; throw old costumes in on top of the incriminating stuff." Jeff and Lambert hurried out.

"Right," Gladhand said. "If any of you own personal guns, fetch them and give them to Jeff. And then get the hell back here; rehearsal is beginning at eight—that's . . . nine minutes from now—as planned. Everybody is to be there, no excuses. Rufus, you'll read the Orlando part as well as your own."

"What's all this?" spoke up a pig-tailed girl whose name Thomas had never caught. "Can't we help Negri somehow? He's risking his life for us."

"He's risking *our* lives for the sake of his outsize pride," Gladhand shouted. "You all know my rules about individual, unauthorized sallies against the enemy. And Negri was reminded of them only last week. What if he's caught? They'll torture him, or shoot him up with scopolamine or sodium pentothal, and he'll tell them everything he knows. I'm praying he's been killed, and that the police are unable to identify him. If they do identify him they'll be knocking on our front door five minutes later— or, more likely, kicking it down."

All the actors pushed away from the table and left the room. "Rufus," Gladhand said, "go to the lobby and keep an eye out for cops. If none appear in the next five minutes, get on stage for rehearsal."

"Aye aye," Thomas said. He caught Pat's eye, made a brief, mock-despairing sign-of-the-cross, and sprinted for the lobby.

"Okay," Gladhand barked from his front row seat. "Curtain. Scene two."

A girl walked out on stage, looked around and shrugged. "I pray thee, Rosalind," she began, then halted. "Uh, sir?" she said hesitantly, trying to shield her eyes from the glare of the lights. "Rosalind's—Pat's not here."

"What?" Gladhand roared. "*Find* her! I—"

"Here I am," Pat said lightly, running down the carpeted center aisle.

"Where were you?" The theater manager's voice was ominously low.

"I was trying to find Jeff, to give him my gun," she said. "I thought I had plenty of time to make my entrance. I'm sorry, sir. Won't happen again."

Gladhand nodded wearily and scratched his beard, looking like an overtime clerk who notices another figure that must be included in an already complicated equation. "Get on stage," he said quietly. "Your entrance has only just arrived."

They had reached the beginning of Act Four when the police arrived.

"Hi!" came a voice from the lobby doors. "You there, you actors! Where's your boss?"

Gladhand shifted around in his seat and stared for a moment at the two android policemen who stood in the doorway. "I'm Nathan Gladhand, the manager," he said. "Skooney! House lights only!"

The auditorium lights went on and the stage lights dimmed as six policemen filed in and strode down the aisle to where Gladhand sat. The actors gathered curiously at the front of the stage.

One of the policemen carried a cardboard box, and now pried up the lid. "Did you know this person, sir?" the android asked, lifting out of the box by the curly hair a severed human head.

Gladhand frowned. "Put it away," he said in a rasping voice. The android lowered the head back into the box. "Yes, I knew him. That's Robert Negri, one of my actors." A low mutter of horror and anger arose from the stage; Thomas' eyes darted to Pat, but she showed no particular dismay now. "How," Gladhand asked, "did this happen?"

"This young man walked into the police station and requested to see Chief Tabasco. When officers asked him to submit to a search, he produced a pistol and menaced them. Two officers were killed before we managed to kill the young man. We brought the body to Chief Tabasco, who, being a connoisseur of the dramatic arts, recognized him as one of the Bellamy Players."

"I see," Gladhand said. "His . . . girlfriend was killed in the . . . misunderstanding in Pershing Square on Saturday. Perhaps, in his grief-crazed state, he blamed Chief Tabasco for her death."

The android nodded. "That seems most likely," he agreed. "We must, though, be thorough. Do you have any objections to the notion of us searching your theatre?"

"Of course not," Gladhand said. "Would you like a guide?"

"No."

"In that case we will go on with our rehearsal."

The officer smiled at him. "Will your actors function well, immediately after a . . . piece of news such as this?" He held up the box and shook it.

"Probably not," Gladhand answered shortly, "but I'd rather have a bad rehearsal than call a halt so they all can brood on it."

"Ah. Good point." The android bowed and led his fellows back up the aisle to the lobby.

"Okay, goddamnit," Gladhand snapped. "Onward. Spencer, tell us again about your 'humorous sadness.' Skooney! Lights!"

The rehearsal moved on leadenly and without verve, and by the time they'd finished the police had left, taking Negri's head with them.

"Albert says they never even entered the basement, sir," Spencer said when the troop had gathered in the greenroom. "So I guess we're okay. We weathered this one:"

Gladhand looked uncertain. "They made a very cursory search," he said slowly. "I've seen them be far more thorough with far less cause."

Spencer shrugged. "It's hopeless to look for logic in the behavior of androids," he said.

"Is it, Spencer?" the theatre manager asked softly. "Is it, entirely?"

The noon rehearsal left Thomas exhausted and obscurely depressed, and when the actors dispersed at one-thirty he gravitated toward Pat. She was standing by the edge of the stage, intent on wiping her nose after a sneezing fit, and she jumped when Thomas touched her on the shoulder with his uninjured hand.

"Oh, it's only you, Rufus," she said when she'd whirled around. "What do you want?"

This isn't quite, Thomas thought, the way I'd expect to be spoken to by a girl who loves me. "Let's go up to the roof," he said, trying to keep the dullness he felt out of his voice. "Catch whatever cool breeze there may be."

She considered it for a moment. "Okay," she said.

They walked in silence up the three flights of stairs, and Thomas held the roof door open for her. The daylight was overpowering after the dimness of the stairwell, and Thomas was squinting through watering eyes as he dragged two canvas chairs to the roof coping and he and Pat sat down. The vast, empty blue vault of the sky seemed to Thomas to have been arranged as a contrast to show up his own unimportance, and he saw with relief that the sapphire uniformity of the heavens was flawed by a dirty smudge of rainclouds over the mountains to the north.

His eyes were adjusting to the brightness, and he glanced at Pat, who was staring out over the maze of cobbled streets and gray-shingled roofs that was Los Angeles. God, she's pretty, he thought helplessly. The black hair fringing around her smooth jawline in the wind, the curve of her tightly-blue-jeaned leg braced against the bricks in front of her. What makes you think, he asked himself contemptuously, that you could possibly have any future with a girl like this? Guys like Negri get these girls.

Negri didn't get this one, though, he reminded himself.

"Awful," he said, "what happened to Negri."

"Oh," she waved her hand dismissingly, "he was a jerk." She looked at him and smiled. "You know that."

"Yeah," Thomas admitted.

"He was just trying to make what you did last night look . . . small-time." She draped her hand with careless affection over his arm. "You guys were really up the creek there for a little while last night, weren't you? Before you managed to kill Albers and get away. The penalties for outright treason must be considerable."

"There was some talk of hanging," Thomas admitted, "and even of torture. But I think Albers had something else in mind for me personally."

"Oh? Like what?"

"Well—it's a long story, Pat, and to start it I've got to say I lied to you last week, when I told you where I came from."

"You're not really from Berkeley?"

"No, I grew up not ten miles from here—not twenty, anyway—at the Merignac monastery. I ran away from there last week. And my name isn't Rufus Pennick. It's Thomas. Anyway, Spencer tells me the police have been looking for me ever since I entered the city, though neither of us can figure out why. Last night Albers realized I was this escaped monk Thomas that everybody's after, and he wanted me for that reason—whatever it is—rather than for gun-running."

Pat seemed tense, and he patted her hand reassuringly. "But Albers is dead now," he told her, "and you and Spencer and Gladhand are the only ones that know I'm Thomas. So I'm safe again."

"Well, that's good," she said. Then she shook her head, and Thomas noticed in her eyes an expression of hopelessness he'd never seen there before. "Oh, but for how long, Rufus? How long will you be safe? And what can conceivably become of us?"

Thomas put his arm around her shoulders. "It isn't that bad," he said softly. "They aren't omnipotent. And I'll tell you what's to become of us— we'll get married when all this political foolishness is over with."

She buried her face in his shoulder and said nothing.

Thomas stroked her fine hair and stared thoughtfully at the vista of rooftops stretching away as far as he could see to the south. I wonder what would have happened if I'd reached San Pedro, he thought. He tried to picture himself dashing about the deck of a steamer, stripped to the waist and tanned the color of an old penny—but the absence of Pat from the daydream made it unconvincing.

After a while, four gunshots sounded a few streets away, and Pat jumped. "God, that's a recurrent sound these days," she said.

"Yeah," Thomas agreed. "And you never find out who was shooting, or being shot at."

Pat stood up and stretched. "I've got to go," she said. "Some of us girls are going out for ice cream this afternoon."

"Ice cream?" Thomas didn't know what that was.

"Yeah. I'll see you later. Rufus," she said gravely, "I love you. Do you believe that?"

He looked at her intently. "Yes."

"Good. See you later." She loped to the stairway door and disappeared. Thomas carried his chair away from the edge into the shadow of a beach umbrella, and sat down and went to sleep.

CHAPTER 9
Deductions in Room Four

The rays of the late afternoon sun, slanting under the rim of the umbrella, glared against his eyelids and woke him up. He got to his feet and rubbed his eyes, feeling disoriented and apprehensive.

The only person in the greenroom, he found when he'd shambled down the stairs, was Gladhand, who was drinking scotch. Thomas dropped himself into one of the chairs.

"Where is everybody?" he asked.

"Spencer and Jeff and Lambert are off on a bit of official business," Gladhand said. "You're exempt from all that till your hand heals. Most of the girls went off to eat snacks somewhere. I'm sitting here drinking."

Thomas nodded. "If it's all right with you, sir, I think I'll go have a solitary beer or two at the Blind Moon."

"Sounds like a valid course. Here." He reached into a pocket and handed Thomas a ten-soli bill.

"Thank you, sir."

"The girls took that ridiculous car, but I believe you'll find at least one horse out back."

Thomas left the building by the rear entrance, and did indeed find a horse in one of the stalls—a sturdy creature of indeterminate breed that winked at him when he patted its nose. He saddled the beast with only moderate difficulty, mounted it, led it out of the back lot and rode slowly east on Second for a block and then turned left onto Spring. The horse seemed as lazy as Thomas, and clopped along at an easy pace.

Only a few people were out, sitting against buildings or slouching along the old sidewalks. The slightly cooler wind of evening carried smells of frying meat and spicy sauces, and Thomas realized most citizens were inside having dinner. As a matter of fact, he told himself, a bowl of chili at the Blind Moon might be a good thing.

Soon after he crossed the bridge over the freeway, the city wall loomed ahead; and in its long shadow, dwarfed between two neighboring structures, stood the little building that was the Blind Moon of Los Angeles. Its narrow windows were already casting streaks of light across the darkening pavement as Thomas tied his horse to the post out front.

He pushed open the swinging door and crossed directly to the bar. "A pitcher of draft beer, please, and a bowl of chili," he said to the girl who was washing glasses.

"Coming right up, sport," she said. "Where you sitting?"

"Uh, back there," Thomas pointed to a table against the wall, then crossed to it and sat down. On the wall across from him was the photograph of Negri and Jean. They're both dead now, he thought. In less than a week that picture has become very old.

"Cheer up, pal," the barmaid said, walking up to his table. "Your beer and chili have arrived."

I suppose that's as good an excuse as any for cheering up, he thought. "Thank you."

He gulped the beer, holding his breath, until his throat stung, and then set the glass down and let the alcohol relax him. God, I'm tired, he thought. When do they call time-out for rest around here?

He refilled his glass—awkwardly, for he used his left hand. When he'd filled it, someone sat down across from him and held forward an empty glass. "You owe me one," came a hoarse voice.

Thomas looked up, and smiled in recognition, "Uh, Jenkins, right? The scholar from Berkeley."

"That's right," the old man whispered with a jerky nod. "Listen, I've got to leave town."

"Oh? That's not as easy as it used to be, I hear," Thomas remarked as he filled the man's glass. "Why are you leaving? You finish your research?"

"You could say so." Jenkins grinned mirthlessly and reached into an inner pocket of his coat. "You know Spencer, don't you? Of course. I talked his girlfriend into getting me a copy of the key to the city archives."

Thomas looked at him with more respect. "Let nobody deny you're a true scholar, Jenkins," he said. "Did you find this . . ." he racked his memory, ". . . Strogoff letter you wanted?"

The old man looked near to tears. "I did. Here," he said, pulling an envelope out of his coat. "Hold it for me. It's too big for me to . . . it's just too big for me. I've got to get out of the city, and then I'll send you an address to which you can mail it. I'll pay you well for helping me, of course."

Thomas turned it over; a new seal held the flap closed. "You've read it," he said.

"Yes. I wish I hadn't. Don't you read it, please. Just hold it for me.

Will you give me your word that you'll do as I say? I'll pay you five hundred solis for mailing it to me unopened."

Thomas considered it. "Okay," he said finally, "I give you my word." Five hundred solis is five hundred solis, he reflected.

"As an actor and friend of Spencer's?"

"As those things, yes."

Jenkins clasped Thomas' shoulder. "God bless you, boy," he said. "I was afraid I'd have to try and leave the city with it on me; and if they'd found it at the gate, well—" he blinked. "God bless you. I'll dedicate the book to you."

"Thanks." Thomas watched, half mystified and half amused, as the old man stood up, wiped his wet eyes with a coat-tail and scurried toward the front door. Poor old bastard, Thomas thought. All upset over a letter some philosopher wrote ten years ago. And look, he never even touched his beer! Thomas poured it back into the pitcher as the door swung shut after the old scholar.

"Hold it, Jenkins!" came a cry from the street. Thomas was up out of his chair in a second, suddenly alert. Very loud and close, six gunshots rattled the windowpanes. Thomas walked quickly to the kitchen door and pushed through it, hearing the front door slam open as he did. "Nobody move!" someone shouted in the dining room he'd just vacated. "This is the police."

Out the back door, lad, Thomas told himself. He hurried past the sinks, quietly opened the screen door at the rear of the place, and slipped out into the alley. He picked his way quickly and cautiously through the shadows, and when he had slipped by the back ends of two dark buildings, and the city wall was a scant stone's-throw ahead, he turned left again and followed a short, unpaved strip of dirt between two high walls back to the High Street sidewalk. Barely twenty seconds had elapsed since the six shots had been fired.

Thomas peered around the wall, back toward the front door of the Blind Moon. A half-dozen policemen loitered out front, a couple of them crouched over a body that lay motionless in the street. So much for poor old Jenkins, Thomas thought nervously, and the *Collected Letters of J. Heinemann Strogoff.* He noticed that he was still holding the envelope Jenkins had given him, and he shoved it hastily into his back pocket.

After a few minutes three more officers stepped out of the Blind Moon. "Nobody in here's got it," one said.

"It's not on him, either," spoke up one who'd been hunched over the body. "We must have missed it at his place." Lining up in formation, they trotted away south on Spring.

I've got to get back to the theatre, Thomas thought, so I can see what's in this damned letter. Gladhand will probably be interested, whatever it is.

Thomas was prodding his phlegmatic horse down the southward side of the Spring Street bridge when one of the ubiquitous beggars called hoarsely to him, "Rufus!"

Thomas looked at the passersby, thinking that perhaps the beggar knew one of them.

"Rufus, goddamnit!" the beggar said, louder this time.

Thomas reluctantly turned his horse around and halted beside the ragged, slumped figure that had hailed him. This is probably a trap, he thought worriedly; I should move on and get this letter to Gladhand. Then he noticed, in the unsteady light from a street lamp, blood glistening on the beggar's chest.

"You're hurt," he said, dismounting quickly from the horse.

The figure, whose face was shadowed under a wide cardboard hat, nodded matter-of-factly. "That's an accurate statement," the hoarse voice allowed.

I've seen that hat, Thomas realized. It's Ben Corwin's.

"Ben . . . ?" he said, pulling aside the hat; and then he froze. The face under its ragged brim, pale and beaded with sweat, was Spencer's.

Thomas dropped to his knees. "Spence!" he whispered urgently. "What happened? How bad are you hurt? Hang on, I'll get you to the Bellamy—"

"*No.*" Spencer seized Thomas' wrist with a blood-sticky hand. "Listen. Don't talk. I've been waiting here for a half hour, I don't have a lot of time left. The cops are wise to you. They know Rufus Pennick the actor is Thomas the monk. I guess . . . one of those cops last night lived . . . remembered Albers' guess. I don't know." He coughed violently and spat blood onto the sidewalk.

"Jesus, Spencer, let me—"

"Sh. Listen. They've got the Bellamy staked out, north south east and west. Waiting for you. I stole some . . . old things of Corwin's and tried to sneak past them . . . put a sword through me, they did, but I got clear anyhow. Also—finally—Evelyn found out . . . *why* they're looking for you. They know you were sky-fishing last Thursday night, and they suspect that you got, in the haul from the bird-man you caught, an android's memory bank. For some reason everyone wants it very badly."

"What android? I didn't find any—"

"I don't know what android. I can't imagine why they should go to all this trouble." He shuddered. "I don't understand any of it."

"Well, how bad are you hurt? Spence? *Spence?*" Thomas leaned over Spencer's pale face, but could hear no breathing. "Spencer, answer me!"

He put his fingers to the young man's throat, and could detect no pulse. "Oh *no.*" He slumped despairingly against the bars of the bridge-rail, and drove his fist savagely at one of the concrete pillars, which started his hand bleeding again. Tears of impotent, confused rage and grief coursed down his cheeks.

"Here now!" intruded a flat, quacking voice. "What's going on?"

Thomas wearily lifted his head and saw, through the blurring of his tears, the stern face of an android policeman gazing down at him. The creature held a nightstick at the ready, and twitched it at Thomas. "What's going on?" it repeated.

Thomas leaped at the android with a snarl, and his fingers were at the thing's eyes even as the nightstick cracked down across his ribs. The sheer maniacal force of his attack knocked the officer over backwards, and Thomas was on its chest as soon as it hit the pavement. His fingers were locked in its hair, and he pounded the moaning head against the curb again and again and again, until muscle fatigue rendered his arms incapable of continuing, and the thing's head looked like an egg that some over-zealous cook had cracked with sadly excessive force.

Thomas stood up on unsteady legs. A crowd had gathered, he noticed, and now regarded him with an air of fearful, timid approval. Thomas wiped his hands to rid himself of a few clinging shreds of hair, and then ran.

When he stopped, completely winded but exorcised of the berserk fury that had possessed him earlier, he was in front of a box-like old two-storey building; on a lamp-lit sign out front were painted the words ROOMS FOR RENT. There's the hand of Providence at work, he thought as he staggered up the walk and knocked at the front door. After a minute an old woman opened it.

"Yeah?" she growled. "I got a big knife here, so don't try anything."

"All I want . . . is a room," Thomas panted. "How much for a room for the night?"

She looked him up and down through suspicion-narrowed eyes. "Twenty solis."

Thomas pulled out the ten-soli bill Gladhand had given him. "Ten's all I have," he said.

"Ten'll have to do, then," she said grudgingly as she snatched it from his hand. "You get room four. Round back." She made as if to close the door.

"Wait a minute. Isn't there a key?"

"No." The door slammed, and he heard the rattle of a chain being drawn across it.

He shrugged, and went "round back" to find room four. It proved to be a narrow, low-ceilinged cubicle that Thomas suspected had been designed as a closet. It possessed a wide range of disagreeable organic odors, and when he struck a match to the nearly exhausted oil lamp, Thomas saw that some madman had painted the warped walls in patches of bright green and orange. He closed the door and shot the cheap, nailed-on bolt.

The bed was a pile of old curtains, strewn with greasy oyster shells. God help me, Thomas thought—when I hit the skids I don't mess around. If this isn't the absolute pit of creation, I hope I never see what is.

He pulled the crumpled envelope out of his pocket and sat down gingerly on the floor. The seal had broken already, and he lifted the flap and unfolded the ten-year-old letter:

12 January 2179

Lawrence D. Hancock
Major-domo, City of Los Angeles
Dear Mr. Hancock:

I was deeply shocked to hear of the grenade attack Thursday last upon Joseph Fowler Pelias, the mayor of your city. I was, though, sir, even more shocked to see the telecast of the "recovered mayor" delivering a speech from a hospital bed on Saturday morning.

I, Mr. Hancock, am the inventor of the artificial constructs known as "androids," and I have done more work with and upon them, I suppose, than any man. Did you, sir, really expect me—or anyone else who had dealt with them—to fail to recognize this "recovered" Pelias for the construct that it is? Those twitches about the eyes, the difficulty in pronouncing nasals and voiced fricatives, the long pauses between switched ideas—the very *pallor,* mottled around the temples—branded that creature as a newly surfaced *android fake,* not ten hours out of the vat.

I do not know, and will not speculate about, your motives in this matter; whether you have made this gross switch out of concern for your city or for the advancement of your personal career. It doesn't matter: your deed must be undone. Announce that complications developed; pneumonia set in; a stray bit of shrapnel reached the heart; hell, man, tell them assassins climbed in through the hospital window and hid vipers among his blankets; but *get rid of that android.*

You must realize that androids, though they can with the aid of PADMUs think rationally and behave according to pre-set priorities, have no intrinsic moral sense. They cannot distinguish right from wrong, any more than a color-blind man can distinguish red from green. An android's actions will reflect only the morals of the person who prepared its PADMU; and don't assume the creatures can't prepare PADMUs for their fellows.

The use of androids as policemen is dubious; the idea of one holding a high political office is as ridiculous as it is terrifying.

Therefore, Mr. Hancock, I am forced to issue to you a threat: if this false "Pelias" is not officially declared dead, and disposed of, within twenty-four hours of your receipt of this letter, I will share my observations with the press.

Yours for more rational uses of science,

J. Heinemann Strogoff

Hmm, Thomas thought. And Jenkins said Strogoff died a day or so after writing this letter? I think I know why, and by whose order.

So Mayor Pelias has been, for the last ten years, an android. I wonder what the real Pelias was like. Wait a minute—then what was this "stroke" he allegedly suffered a week ago, after Gladhand's bombs blew the floor out of his chambers? Perhaps the android was totally destroyed in the explosion, and this stroke story is a stall to buy time until those androids we saw in the vats reach maturation, and one of them is chosen to serve as a replacement. A replacement of a replacement.

When were Gladhand's bombs detonated? Thursday morning, very early. One ten minutes after the other.

And when, Thomas asked himself excitedly, was I sky-fishing? Late the following night.

And what was it Spencer said the police suspect I found in the bird-man's pouch? An android's memory bank.

Thomas began to perceive, dimly, a pattern.

Let us postulate, he said to himself, that the first bomb damaged the Pelias-android's head, and that technicians immediately went to work repairing the PADMU or whatever. The second bomb, let's say, blew the windows out while the android's head was disassembled like an old alarm clock. What if . . . what if a roving bird-man flew in through the broken window, snatched up the memory bank (doubtless a bright, glittery object) and flew back out into the pre-dawn darkness before anyone could stop it? Let's also say, just to explain as much as possible, that something desperately important was in that memory bank, some vital knowledge. What would the government do?

Why, they'd check the bird-men taken in the city nets the next night, and if the memory bank didn't show up there, they'd find out if anyone was sky-fishing that night. And if they found out someone *was,* they'd lose no time, spare no expense, in tracking that person down . . .

That's it, Thomas thought. That is certainly it. The only problem is that I *didn't* happen to find an android memory bank in the damned creature's pouch. The police, Albers, everybody, have been wasting their time.

Maybe, though, I could bluff them by *pretending* to have found it . . . ?

One thing is certain—I've got to get back to the Bellamy Theatre and get this information to Gladhand.

He left room four after blowing out the lamp, and descended the outside stairs to the ground. The Santa Ana wind was still sighing through the city, and carried now the voice of a woman a street or so away who was singing "Bill Bailey." Thomas made his way to the street and read a signpost at the corner. Frank Court I'm on, he saw, and here's Fourth Street. So they've got the Bellamy staked out, have they? Let's see—I'll go west to Hill Street, north to Beverly, and then see if I can't sneak in from the back somehow.

God, what a weary night it's been, and looks like continuing to be.

When he reached the roof of the four-storey Castello Bank on Beverly Boulevard, Thomas painfully flexed his nine fingers and brushed flakes of rust off on his shirt. Stepping away from the fire escape, he padded across the moonlit roof to the southern side, and looked longingly across a fifteen-foot gap at the Bellamy Theatre, its dark massiveness relieved here and there by the yellow glow of a window. The alley directly below, Thomas saw as he peered down cautiously, was shrouded in total darkness—but he could imagine the android sentries that crouched, watchful and patient, in those deep shadows.

He gently broke off a bit of brick from the bank's roof-wall, and flung it down the alley to his left, in the direction of the theatre's stables. After three seconds it clicked against pavement—and several sets of quick footsteps converged on the spot where it had hit. There were a few muttered words and then silence once again.

Thomas pulled his head back and worried for a while. Maybe, he thought crazily, I could break a lock, descend into this bank and find a rope and a few gallons of gasoline. Then I'd just pour the gasoline down on those blasted cops, fling a match (which I'll also have to find) after the gasoline, and then swing across to the Bellamy roof on the rope.

Sure, he nodded bitterly—and even if you could do all that, the other policemen on guard would know what happened, and would just burst into the theatre and drag you out. No, lad; this calls for something more subtle.

Thomas sat down, resting his back against a ten-foot antenna that dated from the lost days of television. The sky was a glittering, infinite gallery of stars, dominated but not overwhelmed by the crescent moon overhead. To the north, Thomas noticed, the dark ramparts of the storm-clouds had swollen considerably. He raised his maimed hand and was chilled to see how ragged and mutable it looked against the eternal ranks of stars in the cathedral of the sky. I don't want to cover the moon with my hand, he thought—I'm afraid the light would shine through the flesh, as if it were just an accumulation of cobwebs.

Objects were moving, flying, high in the air. The bird-men, the half-wit tax collectors, Thomas realized, winging their way north, back up Laurel Canyon to their nests; carrying in their pouches whatever trash they've found attractive today.

That's the solution, by God, Thomas thought, leaping to his feet. I'll fly across to the Bellamy roof. Put my life in the hands of the god of winds. He set about rocking the tall antenna loose from its moorings, and after a few minutes a bolt snapped and the pole was leaning on him. He tore it free from a section of tarpaper that had been tacked around its base, and then laid it down and began unbuttoning his shirt.

I'll just stretch my shirt over the horizontal cross-prongs on the antenna, and then grip the pole firmly and leap off the wall—the roof of the theatre is one storey below me, and I'll silently glide across onto it. Or else I'll fall, and drink the cold claret of hell tonight with Spencer, Jean, Gardener Jenkins and poor Robert Negri.

When he'd knotted the shirt securely across the metal rods, he strode bravely to the edge of the roof, stepped up onto the coping, raised the antenna over his head—and paused. He thought, What if I fall but don't die? It's only four storeys, after all; I might just wind up in some hideous interrogation chamber with two shattered legs.

With a snarl of impatience and despair, he whirled in a circle on the coping bricks and flung his antenna glider away from him. It crashed into the alley below in the same area his pebble had landed in, and this time the footsteps that went to investigate were not quiet. By God, Thomas thought suddenly, that's a diversion. Now's your chance, lad, if there'll ever be one. Do it quick, without thinking.

He leaped back down onto the bank roof, loped halfway across it, then turned around; he took a deep breath and ran for the edge of the roof, digging in with his toes to muster every possible bit of speed. At the last moment he leaped with one leg, kicked off from the coping with the other, and hurled himself forward through the warm night air.

He hit, with a wrenching jolt, the edge of the Bellamy roof, and managed to crook his skinned fingers over the top before he would have fallen. There was no air in his lungs, and the muscles that could have drawn some in were in shock. Blood poured from Thomas' nose, and ran ticklingly down his neck.

Hop up, lad! screamed the small section of his mind that was still working. Swing up over this parapet before one of those androids glances up! No, he thought. I've done as much as could be expected of anyone. I'll drop, try to land on my head. He tried to release his grip, but his body resisted his decision and clung more tightly.

I guess, he thought, tears mixing with the blood on his face, I guess I can't rest even now. He slowly pulled himself up, swung one leaden leg over the coping, and dropped heavily onto the surface of the Bellamy roof.

"A big antenna with a shirt on it," a voice echoed up from the alley. "Nobody around."

"I don't like it. Trot up that fire escape and take a look at the theatre roof."

"Okay, sir."

Thomas now heard footsteps clanging rapidly up a fire escape. This isn't fair! he thought. I never noticed an alley-side fire escape on this building. He rolled to his feet and limped over to the stairway door.

It was locked. And the banging footsteps were much higher, and mounting fast.

The deck is stacked against me, he thought despairingly. He'll be up over the edge of the roof in eight seconds. I've got to do something decisive, fast.

A wide-mouthed brick chimney poked its yard height out of the roof only a few feet away, and Thomas crossed to it and peered desperately into its inky depths. Then he heard, much clearer now, the android's boots rattling the bolts of the last length of ladder—and Thomas extended his arms in front of himself and dove headfirst into the chimney shaft, trying to slow his fall by pressing his legs outward against the walls.

His arms buckled under him when his fists cracked against a metal plate ten feet below; the whole weight of his body pressed his head into his throbbing shoulder, and his nose-bleed now threatened to choke him.

The echoes of his own bubbling, gasping breath filled the shaft, and he could hear nothing else. The damned android could be playing an accordion up there, he thought, and I couldn't tell. He waited, while his twisted arm grew numb from lack of circulation and blood trickled up into his hair. How truly awful this is, he reflected.

When a good measure of time had passed, and he felt the android must certainly have returned to the alley, Thomas began to think dizzily about getting out of the chimney. No hope of climbing back out, he told himself—my arms are as numb as if they belonged to someone else. All I can move are my legs, and they only have a foot or two of space to twitch in.

Like an electric shock, claustrophobia seized every nerve of him. I can't get out, his mind gibbered, I'll die and rot jammed up in here, *I can't move.* He began screaming and thrashing about as much as he could in the confined space; his head was being twisted even worse as more of his weight shifted onto it, but he wasn't even aware. He was nothing now but a mindless, trapped, screaming animal, absolutely dominated by pure fear.

CHAPTER 10
"With This Memory Bank . . ."

Gladhand was unhappily sipping a glass of port in the greenroom when the screaming abruptly began. They were wild, ragged shrieks that suddenly disrupted the evening calm, and they seemed to come from everywhere at once.

Lambert and Jeff, pale and wild-eyed, leaped out of the chairs they'd been slouched in. "What the hell is *that?*" they both yelled at once.

"I don't know!" shouted Gladhand, dabbing at the port he'd spilled on himself. "Go find out! Hurry!" The two young men ran out of the room as the screaming went on. Several terrified actors and actresses dashed by in the hallway.

Pat ran into the greenroom, her blouse dusted with brown powder and a big fear in her eyes. "Did you hear that?" she yelled.

"Yes," Gladhand said, loudly to be heard over the shrieking.

"Thank God," Pat gasped, and left the room.

Gladhand leaned back in his wheelchair, his hands clenched on the arms, and stared at the cracked ceiling until, an eternal, deafening four minutes later, the hoarse yells ceased. Slow footsteps sounded in the hall a minute or so later and then Jeff and Lambert edged into the greenroom, carrying between them a bleeding, shirtless wretch, shivering and powdered thickly with soot.

"Who is this?" Gladhand demanded.

"Rufus," Lambert answered as he and Jeff laid the twitching body on the couch. "He was jammed upside-down in that little chimney behind the upstairs stove. Had to pull that old blower out of the wall to get him."

"He apparently got hysterical in there," Jeff added.

"Apparently. Rufus? Here, Jeff, give him some port. Lock the door, will you, Lambert?"

Jeff pried open Thomas' jaws and poured a dribble of the fortified wine into his mouth. Thomas swallowed it. "More," he croaked. Jeff obligingly tipped up the bottle and let Thomas drink as much as he cared to. Finally Thomas shivered, opened his eyes, and slowly sat up. His hair was matted with blood, and his face was wet with blood, tears and port. His arms and chest were everywhere cut and scraped, as if he'd fallen from a racing horse.

"Uh, hi," he rasped hoarsely.

"Hi," said Gladhand. "How in the devil's own name did you wind up in the chimney?"

Thomas leaned his head back and sighed. "Spencer's dead," he whispered. Gladhand stiffened. "He apparently," Thomas went on, "caught a sword in the belly. He was far gone when I found him. When he found me. He was waiting by the side of the road to tell me that the police. . . know who I am, and have the theatre staked out."

"I don't get it," Lambert said. "Who are you?"

"Tell you later. Listen, now. Turned out to be true. Cops in the alley. I climbed up on top of the Castello Bank and then jumped across onto the roof here. One of 'em thought he heard something, and climbed up the fire escape to our roof. The stairway door was locked and he was about to step onto the roof, so I dove down the chimney."

Gladhand picked up his own glass from the carpet and held it out for Jeff to refill. "Jeff," he said, "go explain, to the android who will shortly be knocking at our door, that the screams he heard were part of the rehearsal. Uh . . . Celia's grief at Rosalind's exile, tell him."

"I found a letter," Thomas continued wearily, pulling the battered envelope out of his pocket and handling it to the theatre manager. "It was written ten years ago by Strogoff the android-maker, and he says that the assassination attempt of seventy-nine was successful, and that major-domo Hancock replaced the dead, genuine Pelias with an android. So your bombs a week ago only blew up an android copy. Somebody got the real Pelias ten years ago."

Jeff and Lambert looked astonished, but Gladhand only nodded sadly. "A fairly accurate statement," he said.

"And Spencer told me why the police are after me—they think I found an android's memory bank last Friday morning when I was sky-fishing. I didn't, but they think I might have." He sighed. "Now here's my theory: I think your Thursday morning bombs damaged the PADMU of this Pelias android, and a bird-man flew in while technicians were repairing the mayor, and flew away with the memory bank. That's why they say Pelias has had a stroke. Now if there was—and clearly there must have been—something very important in that memory bank, that would explain why the police have been searching for me so desperately."

"There *was* something important in it," Gladhand said. He took a sip of port and went on, "Do you recall McGregor, Jeff?"

"Yeah," Jeff answered. "I haven't seen him around within the last week, though."

"Nor will you ever. I had Spencer kill him at the same time you and Negri were planting the bombs in the mayor's chambers. McGregor was a spy, and managed—by a really respectable program of research and inspired guesswork—to learn quite a bit about the guerrilla side of our operation. He even found out who it is that I plan to appoint as mayor when we overthrow the present government. He got to this android Pelias with all the information before we could stop him, and that's why we had to kill both of them immediately."

"Ah," Thomas nodded. "And that's why they want his memory bank—because it contains the location and strengths of the resistance force."

"That, yes, but the most important thing is the name and location of this proposed successor. The present government would be much safer if that man were dead."

"Oh, come on," Lambert said skeptically; "a lot of people have more-or-less valid claims to the mayor's office, and the city manages to squelch them pretty well. What's so different about this boy of yours?"

Gladhand smiled. " 'My boy,' " he said, "is Mayor Pelias himself. The real one."

"I thought," Jeff said, dizzied by these rapid-fire revelations, "I thought you just got through saying the real Pelias was killed ten years ago."

"No. He was injured by that grenade, quite severely injured, and he was replaced by an android which that treacherous swine Hancock happened to have on hand. As a matter of fact, I think Hancock ordered the grenade attack. But no, Pelias didn't die. He's alive today, and in this city—and Tabasco would give anything to have him killed once and for all."

There came a knock at the greenroom door. "Who is it?" Gladhand barked.

"It's me—Pat."

"Come in," The door opened and Pat strode in. She looked very startled when she saw Thomas on the couch.

"Was that you, in the chimney?" she asked.

He nodded sheepishly. "Yes."

She shook her head wonderingly. "What a voice you've got. And how did you get so messed up?"

"Spencer's dead," Thomas said.

"He is? You look like a cheap crucifix, all bloody and your hair sticking up like that."

Thomas felt nauseated. He turned to Gladhand. "Sir, I was thinking—the police believe I have the Pelias android's memory bank. Maybe we could accomplish something in the way of a bluff? *Pretend* to have it, you know."

"Hmm. It might be a good thing to fall back on," Gladhand admitted, scratching his beard. "Everything's happening so damned fast."

Thomas nodded sympathetically. "What would an android's memory bank look like, anyway? A metal box with wires sticking out all over?"

Gladhand chuckled. "Oh no," he said. "They're much more sophisticated than that. The new ones use a crystal, but ten years ago it would have been a length of wire, about three inches long."

"Good God!" Thomas gasped. "I *did* have it!"

"What?" Gladhand snapped, suddenly alert. "Where is it?"

"I repaired my sandal with it. And then my sandals were given to Ben Corwin. I suppose he's still wearing them."

"We've got to get it and destroy it," Gladhand said. "First thing in the morning, Jeff, you find Corwin, take the wire away from him and melt it immediately. It's soft metal, a match should do the trick."

"Wouldn't it be pretty well wrecked already?" Thomas asked. "Tied in a knot, covered with mud . . ."

The theatre manager shook his bald head. "No. The memories are coded on the very molecules. Melting it is the only way to break it down."

"I've got to go powder my nose," Pat said. "I'll be back in a minute." She walked out of the room.

"Then that's what this week-long 'coma' is," Lambert said. "The absence of that wire."

"Right," Gladhand said. "And even if the android we blew up last week is too messed up to use, they've got several new Peliases brewing, into whose PADMUs they could slip that memory bank. We *can't* let that wire fall into Tabasco's hands. Of course, who'd think of looking for it on the sandal of the most disreputable beggar in the city?"

"That's true," Thomas said. "They aren't likely to look there."

"Nonetheless, I—" Gladhand turned pale. "Jeff! Get Pat! Find her and hold her. Lambert, you too. *Go!*" The two young men leaped out of their chairs for the second time that night and ran out of the room.

"Why?" Thomas asked, suddenly worried. "Is she in any danger?"

"Hah! If I catch her she is! Where's my mind tonight?" Gladhand pounded his forehead. "Why don't I notice things when they happen?"

"What are you talking about?"

Gladhand turned on him. "Have you ever observed Pat sniffling and sneezing and wiping her nose? Right, so have I. Tonight she burst in here, panicked by your screaming, and there was brown powder all over her blouse. She wanted to know if I, too, heard the screaming. Deduction:

the powder was snoose. Who uses snoose? Besides poor Ben Corwin, I mean?"

"Androids," Thomas said reluctantly. "Androids use it."

"Pre-*cisely*. Pat, my boy, is an android—and I should be shot for not figuring it out days ago."

Jeff dashed back into the room, panting. "She's gone, sir. Skooney saw her go out the front door, and Lambert and I looked up and down the street for her—no luck. The androids Rufus said had the place staked out? Not a sign of them. There's nobody around."

"Rufus," Gladhand rasped, "get a shirt. You're all three to go out immediately and find Ben Corwin before Pat and her android brothers do. Go! I'll send some more people out after you to help. It's a warm night, Rufe—forget the shirt."

Lambert and Jeff hoisted Thomas to his feet and the three of them ran down the hall, through the lobby and out into the night.

They paused on the sidewalk: "Corwin likes to sleep in doorways and on benches," Jeff said. "Look in places like that. Ask other derelicts, bribe them, rough them up if you have to, but find out if they know where he is. Split up now; I'll take east. Good luck."

Thomas ran south on the Broadway sidewalk, peering into every doorway he passed and receiving horrified stares from other citizens. He spied two hunched figures in the dimness of a barber shop entryway, and he sprinted up to them.

"Oh Lord," exclaimed one of them, a frail old man with no teeth, "it's the Angel of Death."

"I'll let you live," Thomas panted, "if you tell me where Ben Corwin is."

"He moved by here, headin' south, few hours ago," said the other squatter, a stout woman in a burlap sack.

Thomas pounded onward south, shoving people aside in his haste, until he saw, a block ahead, three androids behaving in the same way. They're on his track, too, he realized; and he admitted to himself now that Gladhand was right—Pat must really be an android. *I'm* the one who should have caught on, he thought bitterly. *I* was in love with her.

He crossed the street and strode on as quickly as he could without drawing the attention of the androids. He was at the Third Street intersection now, and decided to move west. I'll lose the androids that way, he thought, and who knows? this may be the direction Corwin took.

This stretch of Third Street was not as well lit as Broadway, and he had to look carefully into each alley and doorway. He passed a number of rough-looking types, and several times expected trouble; but they all seemed fearful of the wild-eyed, gaunt, blood-spattered creature who paused only long enough to ask them if they'd seen Ben Corwin before disappearing once again into the night.

Twice he had to hide while android police ran past him.

He followed Third to Flower, which he took north. His legs were trembling, his mouth had a dry, brassy taste and his eyes were having difficulty in focusing. I'm not good for much more of this, he thought. If I don't find him soon, somebody's going to have to come find *me*. He didn't want to rest, though; he knew there were things in his mind waiting for his attention, things he didn't want to face.

Just short of the point where Flower dead-ended against First Street, Thomas glanced into a narrow passageway and saw a stocky figure sitting complacently against the wall. "Excuse me," Thomas said hoarsely, shambling up to the man, "do you know where I can find Ben Corwin?"

The old man looked up. "Maybe I do," he said, "and maybe I don't. You aren't the first one to ask me that tonight, neither. A cop was just here."

"Oh yeah?" God, they're quick, Thomas thought.

"Yeah. I told him nothing. They're the abominations of Moloch, them cops. Most sinful things in this whole sinful city. I'll deal with 'em real soon. Would you like a bit of scotch, son? You're not looking real good."

Thomas accepted the proffered bottle gratefully and took a deep sip of the fiery liquor. "I know you," he said as he handed it back. "You're the . . . Lord of Wrath. You gave me scotch to clean my wounds with, a week ago."

"Well, damn my eyes," said the old man wonderingly. "It's the young monk. What have they done to you now?"

"They beat me up and shoved me down a chimney," Thomas told him. "But if I can find Ben Corwin I'll be okay."

"Son," said the Lord of Wrath warmly, "you've come to the right man. I saw Corwin not twenty minutes gone, and he told me he's gonna spend the night on the Malk Cigars billboard on Fremont Avenue. That's two blocks to your left, on First up here. You can't miss it."

Thomas leaned down and shook the old man's hand. "Thank you," he said.

"Anything for a friend," the man answered. "Hey, if you get in any jams—"

"I'll tell them you're a buddy of mine."

"Right."

It was a huge painting, lit now only by the moon, of a dark-haired young man puffing with exaggerated relish on an immense cigar. There was a round hole cut in the man's mouth, and Thomas suspected there had once been a machine behind the billboard to send puffs of smoke out through the hole.

Thomas stared up at the narrow, railed scaffold that ran along the bottom edge of the billboard. Was there anybody up there? Yes, by God, Thomas thought excitedly—if that isn't an arm dangling from the far side, I'll eat my shorts.

After glancing quickly up and down Fremont Avenue to be sure he was not being observed, Thomas ran across the weedy lot to the huge sign's base. One of its old wooden legs had an iron ladder bolted to it, and Thomas swarmed up it energetically, his fatigue temporarily forgotten. The eternal warm wind was cool for him, drying the blood and sweat on his chest and face.

He poked his head over the top of the ladder; at the far end of the scaffold lay a heap of old fabric that would resemble a man only to someone expecting to find a man there. "Ben?" Thomas said, standing up cautiously on the swaying platform. "Hey, Ben, it's me. Rufus, from the theatre." He edged his way over to the sprawled figure, bent down and shook the old man by the shoulder. "Wake up, Ben! I need your sandals."

The old man didn't move, so Thomas carefully rolled him over onto his back. The face was black with dried blood, although the old irregular teeth were bared in a beatific smile.

Oh *no,* thought Thomas with a chill of disappointment, they've beaten me to him. He crouched over the body and pulled the trailing coat away from the dead beggar's legs—and saw the sandals, his own old sandals, still strapped to the bony, discolored feet. He wrenched the left sandal off, and sat back against the sign with a deep sigh of relief when he saw the mud-crusted wire still twisted onto the brittle leather straps. He carefully untwisted it and held it in his palm. A damned little scrap of metal, he thought—barely fit for repairing sandals—but it contains something that powerful men have killed for.

He reached into his pocket for a match, but the pocket was empty. So, he found, were the other three. What do I do now, he thought—eat it? I guess I'll just take it back to Gladhand in my pocket.

He looked again at old Corwin, and noticed now the dark powder that covered his hands and parts of his face. No mystery about what finished him, Thomas thought grimly.

He swung back down the ladder to the ground, strode across the dirt to the pavement and began walking south. He put his hands in his pockets and sauntered along causally, trying now to be inconspicuous.

Three androids were trotting up the sidewalk toward him, their expressionless faces lit at intervals by the streetlamps they passed. Do they know who I am? he wondered, suddenly panicked. My God, I've got the wire in my pocket; the most cursory search will reveal it. Why didn't I just fling it down a sewer when I had the chance? He closed his fist on the wire. If they grab me I'll at least throw it as far as I can, he thought.

He tensed, blinking against the sweat from his forehead, as the three ran the last hundred feet toward him and swiveled their reptilian eyes at him; then they were past, their boots tapping the pavement in unison as they sprinted away to the north.

Weak with relief, Thomas leaned against the nearest wall and allowed himself to breathe deeply. After a moment he took the wire out of his pocket, looked up and down the deserted street, and then wrapped it in an old bubble gum wrapper from the gutter and shoved it into the space between two bricks in the wall, where the loss of a chunk of mortar had left a small but deep hole.

Feeling much freer, he resumed his walk back to the Bellamy, careless now of who might notice him. As he turned left from Fremont onto Second, a two-horse wagon rattled out from under the freeway bridge, and rocked away east on Second after a man in the back flung a bundle of papers onto the far sidewalk. Thomas crossed the street to investigate, and found that it was a wired-together stack of fifty copies of the Saturday morning *L.A. Greeter*.

Thomas thoughtfully untied the baling-wire from around the papers and broke off a three-inch length by bending it rapidly back and forth. He put it in his pocket, took a copy of the paper and resumed his eastward course.

Second Street passed beneath a number of concrete-buttressed bridges between Flower and Broadway, and out of the darkness beneath one of them came a voice.

"Don't jump around, Rufus," it said wearily. "I've got a .357 Magnum aimed at your belly."

Thomas stopped. "You don't have to call me Rufus anymore, Pat," he said.

"I've got used to it," she answered, stepping forward so that her face was dimly dry-brushed in moonlight. "You're heading back toward the Bellamy," she observed. "You've got the wire?"

"Yes," Thomas said. "Are you ready to kill me for it?"

"I'd truly rather not," she said, after a pause. "But yes, I'm ready to do that."

"I seem to remember you saying you loved me. I guess you can't hold an android to a statement like that, though."

She sighed. "There is such a thing as generic loyalty, Rufus. Give me the wire and stop talking."

He took the bit of baling wire out of his pocket and stepped forward. "Hold out your hand," he said. She did, and he slowly twisted the wire around her third finger. "With this memory bank I thee wed."

"Oh for Christ's sake," she snapped, pulling her hand away. Incredibly, there seemed to be tears in her voice. "Don't be species-chauvinistic. You think we're no more capable of feeling emotions than a . . . jack-in-the-box, don't you? Don't move, I'm not kidding about this gun. Listen, the police have had suspicions about Gladhand's troupe for weeks; I was sent to audition so that I could keep an eye on things. I . . . damn it, Rufus, I fell in love with you before Gladhand told me about the underground activities—so *I never reported them.* The police still don't know the Bellamy Theatre is the headquarters of the resistance underground. But then you told me you were this Thomas fugitive, and that was too much. To have kept quiet about that would have been to betray my whole species. And they wouldn't have killed you, anyway—it was essential that they take you alive, so they could find out where you put . . . this." She raised her hand.

"Well," Thomas said, "you've got it now."

"Yes. Goodbye, Rufus. I . . . I'm going to give up police work. I'm just not cut out for it."

"You do all right."

"I don't like the work, though. As soon as I can get out of this city I'm going to go live in Needles."

"Needles? Why Needles?"

"Why not Needles?" She turned away and disappeared silently into the shadows.

A wagon was parked in front of the Bellamy Theatre, and Gladhand, sitting on the driver's bench, made impatient hurry-up gestures when he saw Thomas approaching.

"We're leaving," the theatre manager said. "Pat must have told them about our operations here, so I've moved everybody—"

"She didn't tell them," Thomas interrupted. "I just saw her, and she said she never told them about it—only about me being the celebrated monk. She was in love with me, see."

Gladhand paused. "When did you see her?"

"Not five minutes ago."

Jeff and Lambert came out of the theatre and hopped up onto the wagon. "Hi, Rufus," Lambert said. "You didn't find Corwin, did you?"

"Yes," Thomas said. "I took the wire and hid it, since I didn't have a match. And I took a piece of wire from a bundle of newspapers—" he waved his newspaper, "—and gave it to Pat. She thinks it's the real thing."

They all stared at him for a moment, and then Gladhand laughed softly. "All, it seems, is *not* lost," he said. "They probably won't find out for . . . oh, an hour or so that the wire Pat has is a fake." He turned to Jeff and Lambert. "We've got time to take the heavy stuff after all. Load this cart and the old car out back. Rufus will help. Get moving, now, this can only be a temporary extension."

Thomas followed the two young men downstairs into the theatre basement. "All these crates," Jeff said, pointing to a low wall of wooden boxes. "I think we can each carry one."

Thomas swung one up onto his shoulder and winced at its weight. "What . . . are these?" he gasped.

"Bombs," Jeff told him. "And ammunition for a couple of cannons Gladhand's got hidden somewhere. We took all the guns in the first load, when we evacuated everybody, and we figured we'd have to leave all this behind." He pointed to a length of gray twine that ran from under the crates across the floor and up the stairs. "We were going to blow it all up when we left. It almost made poor old Gladhand cry, to think of losing the Bellamy Theatre."

When they were each hunched under a box they stumbled and cursed their way upstairs, and after twenty minutes and five weary loads they'd filled the wagon.

"Okay," Gladhand said. "I'll move out. You guys fill the car and follow. Are they all going to fit?"

Jeff brushed sweat-damp hair out of his face. "Yeah," he said. "They'll all fit."

"Okay. You know the way—see you in about an hour. Go, horse." He flicked the reins and the wagon lurched into motion.

When they had nearly filled the car and were about to shoulder the final boxes, Thomas went to take a last look at his old couch-bed. "I feel like I've lived here for a long time," he remarked to Lambert. "The first night I—where's that head? The big stone head that used to be on this shelf?"

"Gladhand took it along in the first load," Jeff said, "when we moved everybody out. Come on, now, grab a box and let's get out of here."

They hauled the last crates upstairs, down the hall, out the back door and across the dark courtyard to the car. They dumped them in the trunk and slammed the rusty lid.

"Okay, hop in," Jeff said, closing the driver's door and whistling to the horse. "Wait a minute—what's that?" he pointed ahead.

"It's . . . a TV antenna with a shirt tied onto it," Lambert said.

"Well, get it out of the way." When Lambert had flung the thing aside and got back into the car, Jeff snapped the reins and angled the car out of the alley onto Broadway. Thomas sat back in his seat and closed his eyes, enjoying the cooling flow of air across his face.

When the car slewed messily to a halt, the wheels roaring dully on gravel, Thomas stared curiously at the building they'd arrived at; it was long and low, with the corrugated metal under-roof exposed in patches from which the old decorative shingles had fallen away. Plywood flats were nailed up over every window. A tall metal sign perched precariously on the roof, but it had at one time and another been painted with so many businesses' names that nothing was legible on it.

"What is this attractive place?" Thomas asked.

"It was a pizza parlor not too long ago," Jeff told him. "Gladhand bought it a year ago, apparently, as a hidey-hole."

"Gladhand certainly seems to have money," Thomas observed.

"That's true," Jeff agreed. "He must be independently wealthy—he sure didn't get a lot of money from the Bellamy box-office." He guided the dubious horse around the southern end of the old structure and soon the car was hidden from anyone who might pass by on the road. As he got out of the car Thomas noticed the cart Gladhand had left in parked a dozen feet away.

Gladhand was perched on a chair in the dining hall when they entered. The troupe of actors, about twenty in all, were sprawled about on the tables and benches: most of them were asleep, pillowed on bundles of spare clothing, but a few were sitting up and smoking or talking quietly.

"We could use some help getting this stuff in here," Jeff said.

"Right," the theatre manager said. "Skooney, wake up Terry and Mike."

In a moment they were joined by two big, sleepy young men Thomas had never seen, and with their help the car was unloaded in one trip.

"We'll have a council of war in the morning," Gladhand said when the crates had been stowed with the stacks of others that were already in the kitchen. "You guys have some bourbon—over there—and get some sleep."

"Is there a bathroom?" Thomas asked. "I could do with a shower."

"There's a bathroom, but no tub or shower. See what you can do with some wet paper towels."

Thomas followed Gladhand's pointing finger and found a dark little room with a sink in it. There weren't any paper towels, but there were short curtains in the window, and he tore one of these down, soaked it in cold water and wiped most of the soot and dried blood off himself. He wiped the dust off the mirror while he was at it, but the room was too dim for him to see what he looked like. Probably just as well, he decided.

He shambled back into the dining hall and, after filling a paper cup with bourbon, sat down heavily beside Skooney.

"Hello, Rufus," she said quietly. "I hear you've had a rough day."

He took a long pull at the whiskey. "True," he said. "Rough."

"Why don't you get some sleep?"

A few minutes later he blinked awake, then went to sleep again, reassured to find his bourbon sitting nearby and his weary head resting comfortably in Skooney's lap.

CHAPTER 11
The Last Night of the World

The smell of coffee woke him. It was still dark, but people were padding about and muttering to each other. He looked up and saw that Skooney was still sleeping, so he sat up gently. Streaks of dim gray light were filtering in around the plywood on the windows, and the air carried a damp chill—plainly, he thought, the heat spell is over.

Skooney yawned and rubbed her eyes. "Coffee," she said. "I believe someone has made coffee. Good morning, Rufus." She stood up. "Shall I get you a cup?"

Thomas got to his feet, wincing a little at the aches and stiffnesses in him. "I'll go with you," he said.

They joined the group of people gathered around a huge iron pot, and Lambert ladled coffee into two cups for them. "Trail coffee," he said. "For the theft of which Prometheus was chained to a rock in the Newport Harbor."

It was hot, thick and strong, and had to be drunk black for lack of anything to put in it, so they gingerly carried the cups back to their place by the wall and sat down to drink it slowly. Thomas was shivering, and Skooney borrowed a shirt from someone for him.

Gladhand, propped on his crutches, poled his way to the bar and sat down on one of the stools. "Okay, gang," he said loudly, "settle yourselves somewhere and listen close. Pat Pearl, as you may already know, was a spy, an android." There were a few exclamations of surprise, but most of the actors nodded grimly. Skooney just listened, and Thomas was grateful for that. "I had planned to mount our attack on city hall next Saturday; that's why our opening night was rescheduled to this coming Wednesday. But under these present circumstances, I have moved the date up—our attack will take place tonight, at midnight."

There were raised eyebrows, and a few deep breaths expelled, but no one spoke.

"I have hired," Gladhand went on, "a hundred Riverside mercenaries under Captain Adam Stimpson. They're camped not five miles from here,

291

in the Alhambra hills. They'll dynamite a section of the city wall just north of Whittier Boulevard, and enter the city that way. Our own forces within the city now number about five hundred, and four hundred of these will join Stimpson's army at Whittier and Alameda, and proceed north. The rest of our men will pick up guns and ammunition from a gun-runner near the City College over by Vermont. These will then proceed southeast and attack city hall from the rear while the main force, under Stimpson, attacks from the front. I have," he said with a note of great pride, "four cannons, culverins, two four-pounders and two nine-pounders. Stimpson will have the nines, the rear force the fours."

"All this is happening *tonight?*" Jeff finally said. "I had no idea you had this much organized."

Gladhand smiled. "I've never been one to keep people informed about my activities," he said. "Keep the cards close to the vest, I say. So I want *no one* to leave this building today. Alice is on the roof with a rifle now, to be sure that order is obeyed. If we are harboring any more spies—I don't think we are—they won't be able to pass this information on until it's stale. In the back there," he went on, nodding over everyone's heads, "you'll notice Lambert tacking up papers. These are lists of the various troop assignments; check where you're to go, and who with, sometime this morning. So, until tonight, talk, eat, oil your weapons, and sleep. All the liquor will be locked up at noon, though rum will be available just before the fight for those who want it." He hopped down from the bar-stool and thumped off to the kitchen.

At the bottom of Thomas' cup the coffee was thick as mud, but he drank all of it that could be tapped out. Skooney had set the last half of hers aside.

"Today's . . . Saturday, right?" Thomas asked. She nodded. "A week and two days ago," he went on, "I was pumping a vat of Pinot Noir at the Merignac monastery."

"Pumping a vat?" Skooney echoed.

"Yeah. The grape skins float on the surface in a thick layer, and you have to pump the wine from below over them again and again until it's dark enough. The skins are what give it the red color."

"Oh." She thought about it for a while. "You were a monk?"

"Sort of. An apprentice monk."

"Not a student from Berkeley?"

"No. I made that up."

A muted hissing swept over the building and Thomas realized it was raining. "It's been a hell of a week," he said. "And now rain."

Someone had found the furnace, and after clinking around in its works for ten minutes got it lit and filled it with pulled-down strips of the wall paneling. Thomas stretched out along the wall base and went to sleep again.

Gladhand was thumbing the cork into the bourbon bottle when Thomas shambled up, rubbing his eyes. "Did I wait too long?" Thomas asked.

"Well, yes. It's twelve-oh-one. But go ahead, have a cup for medicinal purposes." Thomas picked up a paper cup and held it out while Gladhand poured whiskey into it. "Sit down, Thomas; there are things to discuss." Gladhand poured himself a cup and sipped it reflectively.

"It's like a chess game," the theatre manager said, half to himself. "You study the situation, the strengths, weaknesses, ignorances; then you construct a plan and begin to put it into effect—but even as you move, the situation changes under your feet. Your opponent can disappear and be replaced. *You* can be replaced. Politics is a very slippery arena."

"Uh, no doubt, sir," Thomas said, mystified by all this.

"Have you looked at the assignment lists yet?"

Thomas shook his head.

"You're to be in the smaller force that attacks from the rear. A man named Naxos Gaudete is leading that group. Spencer was to have been his lieutenant—kind of all-around errand-runner, in other words—and I'm thinking you might do as a replacement."

"What would I have to do? I mean, I don't—"

"Nothing difficult. Just fetch things, carry a few boxes perhaps, relay messages. You won't even be in the actual fighting—wouldn't be anyway, with your trigger finger gone."

"I see. Well, sure; just so Gaudete doesn't expect me to know how to load cannons or anything."

"Splendid. By this time tomorrow, God willing, Joe Pelias—the real one—will be smoking a cigar in the mayor's office."

"Does he know the date's been moved up? Where is he, anyway?"

Gladhand sighed. "You're looking at him," he said softly.

Thomas blinked. "Am I?"

"Yes. Ten years ago, when that grenade blew my legs nearly off, two friends loaded my bleeding wreckage into a baker's cart and drove me deep into the city. I had an ex-wife living down on Central, and she grudgingly nursed me back to health while Hancock's damned android began taking over my . . . job, my life. When I'd healed, as much as I was ever to do, the android was well-entrenched in city hall; so I decided to wait, and organize an underground resistance army that I could use, when the time came, to restore me to the mayor's office. So I grew a beard, shaved my head and had the roots killed, and became Nathan Gladhand, theatre manager."

Thomas shook his head wonderingly. "How long was it before you bought the Bellamy Theatre? You must have worked in cellars and school auditoriums for a while . . ."

"Hell no," Gladhand smiled. "One thing I am not is poor. I had big accounts in a dozen banks between Santa Barbara and Laguna. Under various names, of course, and coded by my thumbprint. This current effort is exhausting my funds, I'll admit, but the money has served its purpose."

"Where'd it all come from? Were you always rich?"

"No. I embezzled the devil out of the city treasury, you see, during my term as mayor. Hah! Ever since my reign the city has been nearly broke, in spite of the taxes. I think Hancock found out about my books-juggling and imaginary committees and all, and paid somebody to throw that grenade at me because of it." Gladhand sipped his whiskey. "Bourbon renewal, I call this," he said, waving his glass. "One sip and the whole neighborhood looks better. Anyway—Hancock was an idealist, you see. Always horrified. Horrified when I had a drink or two in the office, horrified when I gave high-pay posts to pretty but otherwise unqualified young girls; hell, even horrified when I'd hang convicted murderers. So he had me removed from the picture and put an 'infallible' android in my place (he was always at me about how 'morally unfallen' androids were). That was a real laugh. The new Pelias kept the capital punishment and broadened the qualifications for it. And his cops were always gunning down citizens for things like cheating a newspaper machine. Hancock killed himself four years later. Sic semper idealists."

Thomas rolled a mouthful of bourbon on his tongue and said nothing.

"And there'll be a place of honor for you in the new regime, Rufus," Gladhand said. "A nice big office where you can write all the poetry you like. I'll have the government printing office publish your works."

Thomas shook his head. "I can't write poetry anymore."

"Of course you can."

"No," Thomas insisted. "It's gone. I wrote a sonnet—iambic heptameter—this week, and I can see now that it was the last poem I'll ever write. It isn't just that my mind is dry for the moment—I know how that feels, and this isn't it. It's as if . . . as if part of my brain has been amputated."

Gladhand started to speak, and then didn't. "Drink up," he said after a pause. "This business has crippled both of us."

It had stopped raining for the moment, but an icy damp wind whipped at the oilcloth lashed over the two cannons that were being pulled behind the cart Thomas was in. The caravan that rattled swiftly down the three southbound lanes of the Hollywood Freeway carried no running lights, and Thomas, peering back over his shoulder, could only occasionally make out the black bulks of the following troop and ammunition carts.

"Spring Street exit ahead," barked Gaudete, who sat beside Thomas. "Give them two flashes to the right."

Thomas picked up a steaming dark-lantern from the floorboards and, leaning out on the right side of the cart, slid the lantern's iron door open-and-shut, open-and-shut. There was a quick acknowledging flash from the wagon behind, and Thomas set the lantern down.

Gaudete snapped a long lash over the heads of the four horses. His droopy black moustache was matted with scented oil that had run down from his hair during the rain, and he kept sucking at the ends of it. "What's the time?" he snarled.

Thomas glanced at the luminous face of the watch he'd been ordered to hold. "Five to twelve."

"Fine."

Thomas sat back and pulled his corduroy coat tighter about him, and he patted the bulge in his right pocket that was a .45 calibre seven-shot automatic pistol.

The cart bounced up a ramp onto a narrow street paralleling the freeway, and the rearward-facing culverins bobbed their iron barrels up and down under the oilcloths as the rest of the caravan followed.

A deep roar, and another, sounded ahead, and Thomas, straining his ears, caught the distant rattle of gunfire.

"Gladhand's started," Gaudete observed grimly as he snapped his whip again.

They slowed before making the right turn onto Spring Street, so as not to skid across the wet cobblestones. The sound of gunfire was much clearer now, and Thomas pulled the pistol out of his pocket and carried it in his right hand.

After they crossed Temple Street Gaudete ran the horses up the curb on the right, so that the cannons in back faced, across a dark lawn, the tall structure a hundred yards away that was city hall. The six following carts drew up beside them and dozens of men with rifles began hopping out of them and lining up on the sidewalk.

"The fighting's still around front, on the Main Street side," Gaudete said, climbing down to the pavement. "Quick, some of you, get these cannons trained so that they bracket the building."

Thomas climbed down and watched as several men, the backs of their rain-wet sealskin jackets glistening in the lamplight, unchained the cannon carriages and pulled off the covers. Four of them slipped handspikes into iron rings in the carriage trails; they laboriously lifted them and rolled the cannons forward, swung the barrels into the correct positions and carefully lowered the trails to the pavement. "All set, cap'n," gasped one of the men.

"Good. Hop up there, Rufus, and fetch me that big box from under the seat."

Thomas climbed back up into the cart and slid a heavy wooden box over the lip of the seat-rail to hands waiting to receive it. Gaudete supervised the prying-up of the lid and lifted out a four-pound iron ball from which dangled a heavy chain.

"This'll mow their lawn for them," he grinned. The men standing around grinned too, though they didn't understand. "We can shoot from here," Gaudete said. "The curbs will stop the recoil. Just be sure none of you stand behind them. Okay, load!"

Another box was brought forward and ripped open, and a cloth bag full of powder was thrown into the muzzle of each cannon and shoved home with a rammer, followed by a wooden disk rammed in on top.

"Okay, now," Gaudete said, "load this chain shot; one ball in each cannon." The men were lifting Gaudete's unorthodox ammunition—two cannon balls connected by about thirty feet of heavy chain—out of the box when with a blinding, shadow-etching flash of lightning, the rain began again.

"Quick!" Gaudete screeched as the thunder was echoing away. "Cover the touch-holes! Get that shot loaded!"

From the driver's bench Thomas watched the frantic work as sheets of rain thrashed onto the pavement; and then he noticed that the street surface was alive with tiny, wriggling creatures. They were in the cart, too, and he bent down and picked one up. It was a frog. More were falling every second, dropping with the rain to shatter and die on the cobblestones. The street, the sidewalks, the whole landscape, was covered with tiny dying frogs.

The men noticed it, and were uneasy; the two carrying the shot had paused and were blinking up at the sky.

"*Load,* you bastards!" Gaudete howled, waving a pistol, "or I'll see the color of your livers!"

In the next glaring flash of lightning Thomas saw, starkly clear in black and white, the two cannons pointing just to either side of city hall, their rain-glittered muzzles connected by a drooping length of chain. Wedges were now being pounded in under the breeches so that the muzzles were only a little raised from absolute horizontal.

"Okay!" yelled Gaudete. "Twenty of you run to the fighting, trade a few shots, let 'em see you, and then run back here with them chasing you. Halfway across the lawn you drop flat, and we'll touch off both these cannons simultaneously, with the chain stretched between the cannon balls.

That'll cut most of them in half. Then the rest of us will charge in and finish them."

Gaudete designated twenty men and sent them forward through the rain. They skidded and slipped on the new pavement of perishing frogs, and made slow progress.

"Damn, why can't they hurry?" fretted Gaudete, twisting the ends of his moustache. Two more cannon blasts cracked a block or so away and were followed by a fast drum-solo of gunshots.

Thomas sat on the driver's bench of the lead cart, shivering and brushing frogs off his wet clothes. He hefted his pistol nervously. I don't like this, he thought—there's death in the air. It feels like the last night of the world.

"Ha!" Gaudete stiffened and pointed. "I see them!"

Thomas stared into the blackness, but could make out nothing. Then a white whiplash of lightning lit the lawn like a football stadium, and Thomas saw seventeen men running before a tide of pursuing androids.

"Gunners ready?" yelped Gaudete.

"Ready!" called the two gunners, huddled over the breeches to keep their slow-matches lit and the vent primes dry. Frogs bounced unnoticed from their hats and shoulders onto the street.

"They're down! Fire!"

Thomas was standing up on the bench to see better at the moment the gunners touched match to prime. There was a deafening, stomach-shaking roar followed instantly by a high-pitched screech like a million fencing foils whipped through the air, and then the cart beneath his boots was wrenched violently out from under him and flung in broken, spinning pieces for a dozen yards down the street.

He hit the ground hard on his hip, but rolled quickly to his feet, his gun ready. His first thought was that the androids had set up a cannon of their own somewhere north on Spring, and their first shot had struck the cart.

Then he saw the appalling carnage that was sprayed and strewn everywhere; blood was splashed as if from buckets across the nearby building fronts, and bits of men were steaming on the street and sidewalk, mingling now with the frogs that still rained out of the night sky. Nearly half of the eighty men who'd been standing by, ten seconds earlier, were frightfully, messily dead.

The others, mystified as to what weapon had so devastated their companions, and already disturbed by the rain of frogs, ran away north and south on Spring Street, flinging down their rifles.

The androids, completely unharmed, made short work of the seventeen who'd flung themselves flat on the lawn.

I see, Thomas thought. He stood on the fouled pavement, rain running from the sleeves of his dangling arms and from the barrel of the gun that hung in his limp right hand. I see. One cannon went off just a little before the other . . .

And here come the androids.

As the police troops bore rapidly down on him across the lawn, Thomas walked listlessly to the largest section of the wrecked cart and lay down behind it. He patted his pockets: two spare clips. I can, conceivably, get twenty-one of them before they get me. He thumbed off the safety catch and, raising the pistol, got one of the foremost androids in his sights, and fired.

The open windows let in the morning sunlight, a cool breeze, and the sound of shovels grating on cobblestones as Gladhand, still dressed in his old sweater of the night before, was wheeled along the bright-tiled hallway. He looked tired, but joked with the nurses who escorted him, and hefted a paper-wrapped parcel in his lap.

"Here we are," smiled one of the nurses, looking a little haggard herself. "Number twelve."

They steered Gladhand's wheelchair through the doorway into the narrow but cheerfully painted room. Sitting up in the bed by the window was Thomas. His left arm was bandaged and trussed in a sling.

"Have you smoked a cigar in your office yet?" Thomas asked.

"No, but that's on the agenda. How are you?"

"I give up, how am I?"

Gladhand grimaced and wobbled one hand in the air in an it-could-be-worse gesture. "The nerves of your left hand are dead, cut by a sword you apparently parried with the inside of your elbow. The nerves may grow back—I think I read about that happening somewhere—but until they do, your left hand is paralyzed."

Thomas nodded dully. "Well, that's . . ." He could think of no appropriate way to finish the sentence.

"That's the bad news, my boy." Gladhand said. "The good news is this: I have selected you to be the new major-domo of this weary old city of the angels. You can help us prepare for Alvarez. I was going to appoint Gaudete, but he chopped himself in half with that incredibly foolish cannon trick."

"What exactly happened there?"

"Only one of his cannons went off, so instead of sending the chain flying at the androids, it whipped like a rotary weed-cutter and ripped all the men standing nearby to bits."

"I see. Where'd the frogs come from?"

Gladhand chuckled. "Apparently there were tornadoes over the Ravenna swamps when the Santa Ana winds collided with the cold current from up north. The twisters sucked up the frogs—it seems there were an incredible number of them this year—and the storm's wind-currents carried them here. It scared the devil out of the androids." Gladhand searched his pockets fruitlessly for a cigar. "Oh well. I'll send out for some. That was a full-scale retreat that came charging at you—and that's doubtless how you survived; they were more interested in getting the hell away than in killing you, though you did singlehandedly manage to kill ten of them before this sword-cut distracted you. Our guns were pounding them to dust out front, but it was the frogs that broke their spirit. Androids fear what they can't understand."

"Well, that's silly of them," Thomas said dryly. "What have you got there?"

Gladhand happily stripped the strings and paper off the object, and held it up.

It was a head, and after the first few seconds of shock Thomas recognized it. "That's who the stone head in the theatre basement was of," he said.

"Well . . . they're both copies of the same original, let's say. Actually," he said, peering at the thing, "our bombs a week ago don't seem to have done all that much harm; just a crushed-in section here in the back . . . and a few evidences of surgery where they were trying to fix the PADMU. And now he'll never get his memory bank back." Gladhand set the head unceremoniously on the floor.

"Later today I'll show you your office," Gladhand continued. "I'll think you'll be impressed. There's a mahogany desk so big you could sublet half of it as an apartment. It has a well-stocked bar, a walk-in humidor in case you should ever take up smoking, a hand-carved—"

"I get the picture," interrupted Thomas with a smile.

"Yeah, just bide your time here for a few days, and then L.A. will embark on a whole new era, with you and me at the tiller and helm." Gladhand nodded to the nurse, who promptly took hold of the handles of the wheelchair. "I'll see you later," he said. "Right now I have about a million things to do, and the first one is get some cigars. Nurse, if you'll be so good as to propel me out."

"Mr. Gladhand," Thomas said. "You've forgotten your head."

"Oh yes! Thank you. I want to hang it somewhere appropriate; maybe I'll put it on the shoulders of old Johnny Bush-head."

The mayor picked up the head, rewrapped it, and waved as the nurse wheeled him out of the room.

Thomas lay back down in the bed and shut his eyes. Nurses were constantly hurrying by in the hall, asking each other in clipped tones about sulfa drugs, doctors, blood counts and leg splints, but Thomas was soon asleep.

In a dream he stood again on the high Merignac tower, clutching his broken fishing pole, and watched helplessly as the girl-faced bird creature dwindled to a distant speck in the vast sky.

A visitor arrived late in the afternoon. Thomas awoke with a start when she nudged his leg.

"Wha . . . ?" he muttered, blinking. "Oh. Hi, Skooney."

"Hi, Rufus." She sat down on the bed. "I hear you've been getting into trouble again."

"Yeah, that's the facts of the case, all right. This left hand, what's left of it, is paralyzed."

"Gladhand says he doesn't see why that should prevent you from playing Touchstone."

Thomas blinked. "You mean he still intends to do the play?"

"Oh sure. He's planning on making it grander than ever now. Even thinking of blocking off some boulevard and performing it outdoors."

Thomas nodded vaguely, and after a moment pounded his good fist into the mattress. "This is hard to say, Skooney, but . . . I've got to say it. I'm not going to do the play. Wait a minute, let me finish. I'm not taking the major-domo post, either. I'm . . ." He shrugged. "I'm leaving the city."

Skooney bit her lip. "Why?"

He waved his hand uncertainly. "I haven't done well here. No, I haven't. I've lost my hand, my best friend, and the girl I was in love with. The city has a bad taste for me."

Skooney shifted uncomfortably. "I," she began, "I thought maybe you and I had some sort of possibility."

"So did I, Skooney. But I've lost something here."

"You think you'll find it somewhere else."

"No. But I don't want to stay here with its grave. I believe I'll continue my interrupted trip to San Pedro. Sign aboard a tramp steamer, like I intended to from the start."

"What do you know about that kind of life?"

"Nothing. That's what it has going for it."

"Oh. Well," said Skooney, standing up, "that leaves me with nothing to say. Does Gladhand—Pelias—know?"

"No. I only made up my mind a little while ago."

"You want me to tell him?"

"Yeah, why don't—no, I guess I'd better."

Skooney lingered in the doorway. "When are you going to leave?"

"The doctors say they'll release me in two days. That's Tuesday. I guess I'll go then."

"You're . . . absolutely set on doing this?"

Thomas stared down at his bandaged and slung arm. "Yes," he said. When he looked up a moment later, Skooney was gone.

Gladhand visited Thomas three more times, though Skooney stayed away. Tuesday afternoon, when the doctors said he could go, Thomas found Jeff waiting for him in front of the hospital.

"Hi, Jeff," said Thomas, pleased to see someone he knew.

"Afternoon, Rufus. I've got the car parked around the corner. What would you say to a bit of beer at the old Blind Moon?"

Thomas smiled, erasing some of the weary lines around his eyes. "By God, that's the best idea I've heard since the last time we went there. And I'll pay; Gladhand gave me a lot of money this morning."

"I won't argue, then."

The streets were crowded, and it was at least half an hour before they arrived at the Blind Moon. To Thomas' relief, Jeff didn't try to talk him out of leaving the city. Instead, they discussed the relative merits of domestic and imported wines, the dangers inherent in the use of chain-shot, and the rain of frogs whose dried, raisin-like corpses could still be seen strewn like bizarre seeds in the empty lots and back alleys of the city.

They emptied their eighth pitcher of beer and called for a ninth. As a waitress passed through the fast-dimming room lighting the candles, Thomas noticed the ghosts at the other tables. There was Spencer, his red hair hanging down over his eyes, laughing as he told some long, involved joke. Negri sat nearby, pretending not to listen, or at least not to be amused. Gardener Jenkins nodded politely to Thomas as he poured bourbon into his beer glass, and Ben Corwin, standing outside on the pavement, pressed his nose against one of the windowpanes, wondering who'd stand an old man to a drink.

"Let's . . . drink to these ghosts, Jeff," Thomas said, swaying in his chair as he waved his beer glass at them.

"Right," agreed Jeff, topping off both glasses. "Here's to you ghosts!" he said.

"Save us a chair and a glass," Thomas added, and then the two young men drained their glasses in one long, slow draft.

Thomas left Los Angeles early the next morning, by the Harbor Freeway gate. His horse was energetic in the morning chill, and he let it gallop. Thomas wore new boots and a good leather jacket, and a sword on one side of his belt balanced the .45 automatic on the other.

His left hand he kept in his jacket pocket for convenience.

The freeway was uncrowded at this hour—there were only a few milk wagons and private carts for him to pass—and he was slowed only occasionally when he'd have to wait in line to cross one of the narrow bridges that spanned washed-out gaps in the old highroad. By ten o'clock he'd reached the intersection of the 91 Freeway, and here he reined in his horse and paused.

The travelers that passed him may have been puzzled to see the grim-faced young man sitting his horse so motionless by the side of the road; but there couldn't have been many, for after a few minutes he gave a nearly mirthless laugh and, wheeling his horse, galloped away east on the 91 Freeway, away from the sea, toward Needles.

This book was set in Adobe Garamond, using Adobe Pagemaker 7.0.
The book was printed and bound by Sheridan Books of Ann Arbor,
Michigan on acid-free paper.

The New England
Science Fiction Association (NESFA)
and NESFA Press

Recent books from NESFA Press:

Details on these and many more books are online at: www.nesfa.org/press

Books may be ordered by writing   *Coming Soon*: Web Sales.
to: NESFA Press   Fax orders (Visa & MC only):
      PO Box 809   617-776-3243
      Framingham, MA 01701   Send inquiries to sales@nesfa.org.

We accept checks (in US$), Visa, or MasterCard. Add $3 postage and handling for one book, $6 for two or more. ($5/$10 for locations outside the U.S.) Please allow 3-4 weeks for delivery. (Overseas, allow 2 months or more.)

The New England Science Fiction Association:

NESFA is an all-volunteer, non-profit organization of science fiction and fantasy fans. Besides publishing, our activities include running Boskone (New England's oldest SF convention) in February each year, producing a semi-monthly newsletter, holding discussion groups on topics related to the field, and hosting a variety of social events. If you are interested in learning more about us, we'd like to hear from you. We can be contacted at info@nesfa.org or at the address above. Visit our web site at www.nesfa.org.

Editor's Notes & Acknowledgments

This book is the first NESFA Press book produced for Arisia, as well as the first one I have edited. I would like to thank the numerous volunteers from both NESFA and Arisia, without whom this book would not have been possible:

> Ann Broomhead, Elisabeth Carey, Andrew Cowan, Gay Ellen Dennett, Michael Devney, Dale Farmer, George Flynn, Deborah Geisler, David G. Grubbs, Richard Harter, Art Henderson, Joel Herda, Mark Hertel, Charles Hitchcock, Kevin Jackson-Mead, Lenore Jean Jones, Rick Katze, Deborah King, Steven Lee, Paula Lieberman, Benjamin Levy, Tony Lewis, Alice Lewis, Suford Lewis, Claudia Mastroianni, Mark Olson, Priscilla Olson, Sheila Oranch, Joe Rico, Sharon Sbarsky, Deborah Snyder, Elka Tovah Solomon, Carsten Turner, and Tom Whitmore. My apologies to those I've missed.

As a voting member of both Arisia, Inc., and the New England Science Fiction Association, I look forward to future collaborations.

> Lisa Hertel
> Andover, MA
> October 2003